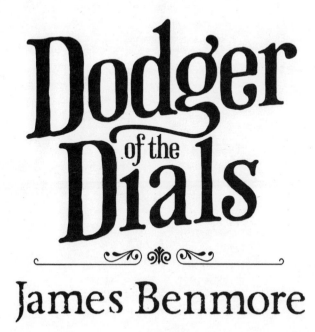

Dodger
of the
Dials

James Benmore

Based on a character created
by Charles Dickens

HERON
BOOKS

First published in Great Britain in 2014 by Heron Books
an imprint of

Quercus Editions Ltd
55 Baker Street
7th Floor, South Block
London W1U 8EW

A CIP catalogue record for this book is available
from the British Library

HB ISBN 9781780874685
TPB ISBN 9781848664104
EBOOK ISBN 9781780874692

10 9 8 7 6 5 4 3 2 1

Printed and bound in Great Britain by Clays Ltd, St Ives plc

Typeset by Ellipsis Digital Limited, Glasgow

To my brothers, Michael and Harry

'Burglary or pocket-picking wanted 'prenticeship. Not so, murder. We are all of us up to that.'

The Night-Inspector from *Our Mutual Friend*

Part One

Chapter 1

The Lady of Stars

*In which the reader discovers me, just two short years since our
last meeting, going about my nightly business*

The whole thing would have gone down very well had it not been
for the bad crow. We was four working the crack on that cloudless
night and if we had all played our parts as given then a good deal
of unpleasantness would have been avoided. But however adept a
burglar might be as he busies himself inside a fine home, he cannot
afford to rely on accomplices what do not know what they're
doing. Now I'm never one for pointing fingers at the less talented,
but young Scratcher, it pains me to record, proved himself to be a
proper liability before the job had even begun.

The first sign of trouble was when we at last reached the small
Kent village, after five hours' travelling, and I heard his quiet sniffle
as our cart trundled on in the darkness. He was trying to hide the
tears from us but to no avail and Tom Skinner, who was always
quick with the *I told you so*, flashed me a hard look.

'This is Whetstone,' I whispered to Georgie Bluchers who was
driving the dairy cart into the village and about to pass by a local
hostelry. He was dressed in a white milking smock so as not to
arouse suspicion but it was gone midnight and there was not a
soul about. 'The crib we want is further along. It's best if we three
foot it over alone and you just trot off and stay hidden.' Tom and
myself had been scouting this location over the past week in a series

of disguises and we knew what was the sharpest cut to approach Whetstone Manor. 'Is your watch wound?' I said to Georgie before we climbed out of the cart. He pulled out his ticker from inside the smock and we compared times. 'Good,' I said when I saw that they was as one. 'Then give us thirty minutes if you don't hear from the crow.' I turned to Tom who was lifting Scratcher down. 'Go over the calls,' I said. 'Once more.'

Tom squawked like a bird twice and I asked Georgie what this meant.

'The policeman is coming,' Georgie replied. 'Time to go.'

'Correct,' I said and then Tom squawked again, only this time it was one long and lazy squawk of a bird cry.

'That means he's gone—'

'Not you,' I interrupted Georgie and turned to little Scratcher. 'You.'

'He's gone to the pub?' Scratcher asked.

'Right!' I nodded in encouragement. 'Which we'll want to know.'

During our secret excursions to this village both Tom and myself had noted that the sole beat constable was inclined to visit the pub after hours for a jar with the landlord. This meant that he would not be coming out again for hours and was unlikely to be patrolling near Whetstone Manor until morning. If this happened tonight then our task would be easier so it was worth the crow informing us. Tom then began squawking in an alarmed manner and there was no doubting what this meant.

'Trouble,' I told them all as I filled up the sack with the necessary tools. In went a knife, a jemmy, two persuaders, a tub of glue, a brush and one loose glove. 'Coming fast. If this happens then Georgie gallops the cart up to the main gate and we'll bundle in and collect Tom on the way back. But if that don't work then it's every man for himself.'

This was the moment when Scratcher could no longer conceal his emotions. Georgie looked most startled to see these open tears as he, like most people familiar with the boy, had always considered him to be a hardened little cove. We had met him two years before when we was trying to escape from some peelers through his house in Bethnal Green rookeries and ever since he had been hanging around our gang trying to ingratiate himself. I had even begun to make an apprentice of him – something many other fledging crims would have considered a great honour. And until this moment he had seemed a worthy student – nimble-fingered and quick with the dash. But now he was acting like we was being most cruel by involving him in our nefarious doing and I sighed at the ingratitude. So this is the thanks I get – I thought as I knelt down to his height – for trying to give an eleven-year-old a decent start in life.

'Now let's have none of this, young shaver,' I whispered with a soft smile. 'It's only nerves on account of it being your first crack. But it's nothing to worry over and we'll be laughing about it afterwards. Ain't that right, Georgie?'

'Course it is,' said Georgie who had become the boy's favourite ever since getting back from the north. He dismounted the cart and came over, took the small black hat from off Scratcher's head and ruffled his dirty hair. 'We'll have a roar later as we split up the money between us. You'll be the flashest lad in London by then and you'll wonder what the fuss was.' But the tears went on spilling.

'What if there's a dog, Dodge?' the boy sobbed a little too loud. 'There's always a dog. Morris Bolter said.'

'Don't you go listening to Morris Bolter,' I replied in a lower whisper. 'That coward ain't ever cracked a crib in his life. There won't be no dog in this house, Scratch. I promise you that.'

I had been informed that Whetstone Manor was without dog by a man what had only ever introduced himself to me as Percival

— a name I have no doubt was made up. This Percival was a gentleman, or so his airs and graces would have us believe, but he had ventured into the London slums two weeks prior for reasons unbecoming. He had already spoken to a prostitute of our mutual acquaintance at the Portland Rooms in Haymarket and told her, at some point in the evening, that he was in the market for a burglar. He wanted a cracksman of higher sort, he had explained, for a delicate job, and not just some lowly area sneak what took careless chances. He wanted someone ingenious in his devices, as brave as he was dextrous and who knew the value of discretion. Now did the fair lady lying in bed beside him know any tradesman like that?

'Percival promised us no dogs and no servants neither,' I reminded Scratcher as I wiped the tears from his eyes with a silk ladies' handkerchief what I kept in my inside coat pocket. 'And it ain't in his interest for us to get caught, is it?' But Scratcher seemed unconvinced and continued to whimper.

'I thought you said this one had steel, Dodge?' Tom snapped from behind me. 'Look at him. I've seen more steel in a chicken-house.' Georgie then tried to defend the boy by saying that every young thief gets the flutters sometimes. 'But do they cry like little girls about it?' returned Tom uncaring. 'He should be ashamed of himself.'

Tom's derision had an effect on Scratcher who then started to look more affronted than afraid which pleased me because anger has always been one of the best ways to motivate a boy. Georgie though, who had not liked the look of Tom Skinner ever since I had introduced them both two months before, put up a protest.

'Watch that mouth, Tom,' he growled 'or whatever you're calling yourself. Scratcher's a good boy and I won't hear otherwise.' Tom asked Georgie what he was going to do about it and I had to shut them both up before the quarelling got worse. Then I turned my attention back to Scratcher.

'When I was your age,' I said in a far friendlier tone than Tom's, 'when I was even younger than you, I used to get pushed into situations far more precarious than this one. Bill Sikes never cared if there was a dog in any of the places he expected me to crawl into, in truth that was one of the reasons he'd shove me through little holes – to find out what was on the other side. I would never treat you in such a disgraceful manner, Scratch, you're a partner and you'll get your fair share when this is done.' Then I dropped my voice into a heavier tone and locked eyes with him. 'But you need to play your part, understand? You get nothing for nothing.'

There was some silent seconds as we all waited in that dark lane for Scratcher to gain mastery of himself. At last he lifted his chin up. 'I just need to get in?' he checked.

'That's all,' I smiled. 'Just get in that house and slide back the bolts for me. I'll do the rest.' Scratcher nodded as I went on. 'You know I'd do it myself if I was your size, Scratch, but it's always easier for a kinchin to gain entry. That's your special talent,' I winked. 'You're so small.'

It appeared that I had won him over and we all began to prepare for the crack. Tom was about to climb the tall tree what provided a clear view of both Whetstone Manor and the village pub where the constable would be and Georgie drove the cart away out of sight. Then Scratcher crumbled again.

'Tom's small,' he said in a cracked voice and I could now see it was never going to happen. 'Not as small as me but enough. I'll play crow instead. I know all the calls and I can climb that tree easy. I'll crack the next place we do, I swear I will, but let me be crow for now.'

Tom, who had a superb crow voice what could carry further than anybody's, just shrugged back at us.

'I ain't fussed either way. Let him be crow if he wants. It's all one.'

So it was agreed that Tom Skinner would enter the house with me instead which, in all truth, was acceptable as I had only wanted Scratcher to come with me for his own education. But Tom was one of the best criminals I had ever worked with and had been my main accomplice for over a year. Getting into this old place would pose no real obstacles for the two of us, so we just watched Scratcher climb the tree to make his nest and, once we was sure he would not fall out, we set off for Whetstone Manor without further delay. Inside that grand Georgian building was a bedroom and inside that bedroom we would find the Lady of Stars. Percival had drawn me a picture and she was so beautiful that I might have even stolen her back for nothing.

Not only had Percival promised us that there would be no servants or dog to worry over we had also been assured that the master of the house was away on parliamentary business for the week. Our careful surveillance over the previous nights had shown this to be true but that did not mean that the place was empty. There would be two people what we knew of in residence, the mistress of the house and one other, and our first job was to ascertain what part of Whetstone Manor they was now occupying. Most of the many windows we saw as we peered through the iron bars of the front gate had their curtains drawn, including the high one on the top floor what belonged to the master bedroom. A long bridle-path circled around to the back of the property and we crept along it, with me carrying the sack, sticking to the shadows all the way.

'Have you seen her, Jack?' Tom whispered as we came to the ivy-covered brick wall what separated the path from the enormous back garden. 'This woman? You must have on one of your lurks?'

'I seen her,' I whispered back as I uncovered the small footholds what I had carved out with a chisel on the night before and hidden over with the ivy. 'She's a heartbreaker.'

I hoisted Tom, who was not much heavier than Scratcher would have been, over the wall first, threw the sack over and then followed using the footholds. I then dropped myself down into a small bush on the other side with a small thump but the walled garden was so deep that we would never have been heard from up at the manor. We crouched down and surveyed what lay between us and the house. I had, in my short career as a burglar, been privileged enough to trespass through a number of impressive gardens but never before had I feasted my eyes on botanical beauty like this. The light of the moon shone down upon an Italian fountain what was surrounded by a vast collection of flower beds the like of which I had never before seen in a private property. Such sights was one of the many pleasures of the profession. We then started to cross the edge of the lawn where it was darkest, passing a pond, the fountain, the small glass fernery and a birdbath until we reached a low hedgerow nearer the back of the house behind which we could spy all the better. Now, a short distance from some stone steps leading up to the patio terrace, I noticed that a white cloth was still covering a wooden table where someone had been picnicking earlier. There was only two chairs and teacups and plates of half-eaten cream cake still left upon the table. This confirmed Percival's prediction that the mistress of the house would have sent any servants away for the week. We looked up to the window on the far left of the upper floor – which we knew was the lady's boudoir – and saw that there was light behind the curtain. Nothing of the sort was detectable from any of the other rooms. I pointed over towards the opposite side of the building where the servants' entrance was.

We darted across the terrace and Tom grabbed a slice of cake as we passed by the table. By the time we had made it down a small staircase what led towards the cellar Tom had taken a big bite and, with a full mouth, offered me the rest. I took the cake, licked away the rest of the cream and tossed the remains aside. Then I reached into my coat pocket and pulled out my trusty lock-picker. This small implement had never let me down before and it did not fail me now. The small lock submitted to its turn but, as predicted, the nuisance door was bolted on the inside.

'It's never easy, is it?' I sighed to Tom who had been untying the sack. We then took out the persuaders – small lead clubs what we hoped not to use but would never leave behind – and the glazer's knife.

'I could climb the guttering,' Tom offered and pointed up to a high window what the waterpipe ran up to. 'Jemmy that open, no problem. I'll find the Lady while you stay here.'

'What you are,' I said as I cleared away the cobwebs covering the large window to the lower scullery and peered inside, 'is a show-off. We'll stick to my plan, thank you very much.'

The scullery was dark but I could make out a clay sink below the inside of the window what would be easy to step down onto. I took the knife to the thin glass and began tracing out a circle wide enough for Tom to squeeze through. As I began circling the glass with a strong cut, over and over, Tom put on the glove from the sack and brushed it with glue. When I was almost done with the cutting Tom's hand was placed against the centre of the glass and soon after it was pulled out and laid down most gentle. The hole was big enough for Tom to then step through with ease, the inside bolts of the servants' door was slid open from inside and I too entered the house.

It was a summer night so we had not brought any dark lanterns with us – they could be cumbersome and might betray our movements – but we needed light now. The air in this kitchen was thick and musty from domestic neglect and we had to stand still while our eyes made sense of the blackness. I could just about see where the large kitchen range was and I tried not to knock over any crockery as I passed the dresser. But as I trod across the sticky floor I felt that there was something peculiar about, black shapes moving on all the furniture and around the walls. Just then – and to my shock – something hit me in the face. I heard a snigger from the other side of the table and realised that Tom had flicked one of the room's many large black beetles at me. 'Behave yourself,' I said as I brushed it away. I was itching from fleas by the time I made it to the far door and was most eager to escape this horrid room. 'This kitchen is a disgrace,' I remarked as my pick worked its magic upon the second lock.

Once out of the kitchen we came to a simple servants' staircase and we crept up it to the main house. In the long hallway of the ground floor we listened out for any noises what would tell us where the occupants was but heard nothing. The mahogany walls was hung with medieval armour and paintings of long-dead aristocratic men and we waited a beat to see if anyone would emerge to challenge us. Then we heard a distant male groan coming from somewhere above and this meant that Tom – who was now holding the sack – could begin filling it with swag downstairs without interruption. Tom opened one door what led to a room full of exciting ornaments and vanished straight into it. Meanwhile it was my part to venture upstairs and snatch back the Lady.

The Lady of Stars was our client's special request and it was all he was really interested in. Anything else what Tom and I might collect from this crack was ours to keep but we was being paid a very generous fee to steal this particular item so I made it my main priority as we would not leave without it. I did not want this Percival person thinking he had hired an amateur.

The broad wooden staircase looked like it was going to be a creaker but it had a thick centre carpet running all the way up and so I ascended as soft as a dormouse. The manor house was large enough for raised voices to carry but I could not be sure behind which door the two occupants could be found. This was the sort of property what would never be unoccupied but tonight at least we was not the only ones who was not supposed to be here.

I knew from Percival where the lady's bedroom was and so I now headed in that direction. I had my persuader gripped tight and was ready for any trouble and I crouched down behind the top banister and listened hard. I then heard some light shuffling coming from down the far end of the landing. It seemed that perhaps the couple was just where I did not want them to be – inside the boudoir – and this could prove a problem. I moved with stealth down towards the noise which, as I grew closer, became the unmistakable sound of love-making. Perfect, I thought, as I tried to hear behind which of the four doors they was engaged. Even if they was in the wrong room there was a chance they would be too distracted by each other to detect my movements.

As I crawled further down the passage I saw that the closest door on the left was ajar and that bright candlelight could be seen flickering through the crack. I inched up to it to see what was happening within and saw a small library room which had a long fainting settee with its back to me. I could see no one at first but I could hear the woman. Somewhere in that room the mistress of Whetstone was having herself a wonderful time and I envied whoever was in there treating her to it. I had to shift my view before I could tell where the noise was coming from but soon spied a silken nightdress lying beside the settee and one bare female foot dangling over the end and twitching in excitement. I then saw her hand lying over the top of the settee and wondered where, given the small size of the furniture, the man was. I could not proceed on my way until his whereabouts was accounted for so I had to risk peeking my head even further inside until I spotted him, still fully dressed and on his knees applying himself for her pleasure alone. I withdrew my head from inside that room and left them both to it.

So my path towards her bedroom was now clear and I grew confident that, if I continued in perfect silence, their night of stolen passion would be undisturbed by my own thieving antics. I crossed over to the golden door handle of her private chamber and it opened onto the fitted carpet with no more noise than a hush. I stepped inside and was gratified to see some already lit candles about so I could begin my search without having to draw the curtains first. The perfumed room was as impressive as all the others I had passed but it was the only one in the manor what felt feminine, with its soft colours and vases full of those garden flowers. I breathed in the room's fragrance and then tiptoed past the four-poster bed and headed towards the curved dressing table what Percival had described to me. It was, as he had said, fully-covered in a muslin cloth and had on top of it an ornate vanity mirror. It was a messy room with discarded clothes tossed all about but everything in it felt refined. The only rough thing I could see was the grubby interloper staring back at me from the mirror.

I picked up one of the candlesticks what was stood beside some sewing materials to help me in my search. I lifted up the sheet what was as fussy as a petticoat and revealed the chest of drawers beneath. I knelt down once the sheet was pulled up and found the little drawer with the miniature golden lock. I then took one of her needles from the sewing kit and in less than five seconds the drawer was open. There I found a blue felt jewellery case with the insignia of Blaze and Sparkle inscribed upon the front and I unclasped it. Inside, and in all her naked splendour, was the Lady of Stars.

Percival had described this glittering necklace as a constellation of jewellery and I could now see why he had become so obsessed with having it. I pulled it out and held it up to the candlelight in admiration. I was tempted now to forget my obligations to him and just keep it myself as it was so rare a find. Either way, I could not dither here for much longer so I placed the necklace into my coat pocket, taking care not to be too rough on the diamonds. Then I closed the case, put it back in the drawer and rearranged the petticoat so I would leave this room as I had found it.

And then, just as I was congratulating myself on another successful grab, the quiet night was interrupted by the sound of the bad crow. It was a high-pitched whine coming from the woods out front, a weak mimic of the sound what Tom had demonstrated to signify that the constable had gone into the pub, and it seemed to last forever. I cringed and knew that it could not help but disturb the amorous activities in the library as it was too peculiar a noise to pass without investigation. I moved fast over to the door and looked out into the hallway to see if I could make it to the staircase before our young lovers had time to react. But before I had even left the room I could hear that the man had already been put off his stroke.

'What in hot hell was that?' he cried in alarm and there was a huff of frustration from the woman.

'You've stopped!' she snapped back at him. 'I said not to!'

The footsteps of the man could be heard stomping over to the far window and, as I approached their half-open door, there was the sound of curtains being drawn.

'There's somebody outside,' the man announced in fright. 'In the trees! Your bloody husband probably.' I was preparing to make a run for it past the door and down the stairs before either of them had time to see me but I stopped when I heard the woman jump to her feet.

'My husband doesn't hide in trees,' she shot back at him. 'He's a knight of the realm.' I could hear her gather her nightdress and make for the door. I darted backwards and back into the boudoir knowing that I had missed my last chance to leave unobserved.

'Well I can see a head moving about outside!' he countered. 'Must be one of his spies!'

I now needed to hide myself before she followed me into her own room as she was bound to do on leaving the library. I made it over to the curtains what was made of three layers of drapes and found that they offered the perfect place to secrete myself behind. Before she had a chance to enter the room after me I was behind them and crouched on the deep sill trying to work out how the noisy the window would be to open.

'Spies!' the woman jeered as I heard her sweep into the room. She was still speaking loud enough for him to hear from the room opposite and I could hear the rustle of the nightdress as she put it on. 'As if he would need spies, you idiot man. He couldn't care two tits for what I get up to!'

I heard her moving over to the little table where I had snatched the necklace from and I readied myself for an outcry once she saw that the necklace was gone. A drawer was pulled, a case was heard opening but no shriek followed.

'You wanted to stop, Humphrey, that's what this is about,' she said instead as if something was in her mouth. 'And I hadn't given you permission yet.' Then I saw the faint light of the candle move through the drapes and realised that she was lighting a cigar for herself. 'You're a waste of blood and organs.'

With that the heavy footsteps of this Humphrey was heard thundering down the corridor and towards this boudoir. 'You insolent bitch,' he declared on entrance. 'You poisonous jade!

Bentley is my oldest friend, God rot you, and he doesn't know *I'm* here.' The woman just laughed back at him.

'He knows about all of you,' she breathed out after what must have been her first drag. The man's voice lowered when he spoke next.

'If that is another of your famous jokes, madam,' he said with a hateful seethe, 'then know that I do not take it in good humour.'

While all this was under discussion I had been busy working out the details of my escape. The sash of the window could be opened with ease and I could see that it would be possible for me to scale down the building to the back garden using the water pipe. All that mattered was that I could get outside before drawing attention to myself. Once I had got hold of the pipe I was confident that I could move faster than they could and be down and off with the necklace before they had even left the room.

'Oh, you think that I've been living as a nun until now, do you?' the woman went on taunting, while I tried to lift the sash. The night was warm and windless so I was not concerned about letting in air and this fiery spat was covering whatever creaks I made. 'While my brute husband sleeps with every whore in Christendom?' There was now almost enough space for me to slip underneath the window and get onto the ledge outside. A couple more inches and I would have my liberty.

'Why your husband should feel the need to sleep with a *single* whore, madam,' boomed Humphrey loud enough for me to risk a greater shove of the window, 'is a great mystery! For he has in his marital bed the biggest harlot of them all!'

Just then the sound of a struggle broke out and the woman began to scream. It seems he had got hold of her now and was manhandling her towards the bed. I could hear her hit him with something and she told him to leave as the light of the cigar was snuffed out. He laughed as something fell over and said that he was done taking orders from her and that it was his turn to receive satisfaction. The sound of this violent outburst was such that I could lift the window to as far as it would go and there was now nothing to obstruct my departure. But something powerful held me there.

It was the thought of Nancy. Many a night, since I had returned from my incarceration in Australia and learnt of her terrible murder, I had suffered dark dreams thinking about what that bastard Sikes had done to her. I had often thought that – had I been there to prevent it – I would have saved her from his butchery in a most dashing fashion. But it's easy to flatter yourself with thoughts like that if history never repeats itself.

'You're hurting me!' the woman cried again in serious distress. The spite in her voice was gone now and I just heard the fear. There was a loud smack and she groaned as her attacker told her he would ruin her looks if she made one more noise. She carried on pleading for help, though, and I wondered who she thought might hear her. She herself had sent the servants away and the only person in this village what might have a chance of coming to her aid was the constable what Scratcher had just announced through his terrible crow was busy getting drunk in a pub. If this Humphrey wanted to overpower her, bash her face in and even kill her, he could do it and leave the house without anybody even knowing he had been there.

With one stroke I pulled back the drapes of the curtains so I could see what was occurring. I stepped back into the room and there was this Humphrey, lying on top of her on the bed and trying to keep one hand over her still screaming mouth while his other hand was unbuttoning his fly. The woman turned her tearful and bashed face to see me and screamed all the louder but he had not noticed

my entrance yet and thought her wailing was still on account of his
own unwelcome advances. So he carried on removing his trousers
while I pulled my persuader out of coat pocket and cleared my
throat.

'Put your drawers back on, Humphrey,' I said and brandished
the club at him. 'And step away from the lady. She ain't interested.'

Humphrey flicked his head toward me and cried out in shock.
Then he jumped up from the bed and staggered back against the
wall which was not a graceful move considering that his trousers
was down by his ankles. His mouth was open but he was struggling
to speak.

'You just thank your lady friend there for her pleasant company,'
I continued staring him down, 'and tell her it's time you was getting
off.' I must have struck quite an aspect, I considered, as I stood by
the open window with a full moon shining in from behind me. For
the sake of the lady I tried to assume as heroic a stance as possible.
I did not move from my position by the window though, as I was
still planning on making my exit through it.

'Another lover?' Humphrey asked the woman at last as he pulled
up his britches. 'Do you have one hidden in every room?' But
despite this, he must have seen that she was just as shocked by my
sudden appearance as he was. Humphrey then turned back to me
and began his pleading. 'You're from Bentley,' he said to me as
he edged his way around the bed towards the foot of it. 'One of
his spies. I knew it, I saw you hiding in the trees. Listen,' he held
his hands out and came forward, 'it was all her. Tell him that. *She*
seduced *me*. I was helpless against her.' Then he gave me a wink.
'And there's a pound note in it if you play the game and forget the
whole thing.'

Just then the woman on the bed sprung up, jumped through the
foot posts between us and made for the chest of drawers where I

had stolen the necklace from. This was unexpected and I worried that she had landed upon my business and was checking to see on her priceless treasure. In my moment of confusion, Humphrey gathered his courage. He charged at me and grabbed me by the chest, sending us both crashing backwards and into the curtains. 'Got you now, spy,' he cried as he tried to grapple me into submission. 'You won't be telling any tales on old Humphrey, on no, sir!'

However, I still had the use of my left arm what held the persuader and so gave him a good cosh around the head. That did the job and he released me, fell to his knees and got tangled up in the drapery. I tried to move from him then but he still grabbed my leg and I turned to see what the woman was doing. She had pulled something out of a different drawer to the one I had been at and was turning back towards us with it. It was a small silver pistol and her hands shook as she pointed the thing.

'You've got one shot, my darling,' Humphrey told her from his position on the floor with his hands still on me. 'Aim steady.' She fired the pistol and I flinched to the side. The shot missed me, flew over Humphrey's head and went straight out of the window. 'Christ Almighty, woman,' he shouted enraged. 'That almost hit me!'

'I was *aiming* for you!' she shrieked and then chucked the empty gun straight at his head. He cursed as it struck him causing him to release me and I made straight for the open door. But Humphrey, to give him due credit, was not letting me escape that easy.

'Get back here, you little bastard!' he roared as I ran out into the corridor. I could hear him forcing himself to his feet and wondered at his resilience. To have taken two strikes to the crown like that and still be prepared to chase me was without question the act of a true sportsman. 'I'll tear your bloody arms off!' he swore as he pursued me across the landing and to the top of the staircase.

I moved fast down the stairs but the place was dark and my footing was not as familiar as his. Just as I reached the bottom steps he made a last ditch tackle and we both crashed down into the hallway together. As this happened there was more crowing sounds from outside. Trouble was coming, no doubt on account of the gunshot, and it looked like I was done for.

Then a sweet female voice called out from another room in the house. It was not the haughty tones of the lady we had left upstairs but that of a low-born angel whispering in agitation.

'Please, sir, the mister is coming!' said the voice from somewhere in the darkness. 'The mister of the house is back early from London, Lord help us. I sees him coming up the lane now, you better scarper for all our sakes!' Humphrey looked up and asked who was there. 'Mary, sir,' the voice replied. 'Mary the maidservant begging your pardon, sir. You better not be found here, sir, you better go!' The sound of Scratcher's crowing was getting louder and more urgent from outside and I could see that this was unsettling Humphrey. 'Let the burglar take the blame,' Mary advised him in a lower voice. 'You should look after yourself, sir, you just go!' Humphrey, who still had me helpless with one knee pressed into my back, twitched his head towards the front windows, then turned back to the nearest open door where this Mary sounded to be.

'Come out here,' he commanded her. 'Show yourself.' But as he stared in that direction he did not hear the quiet footsteps coming from another room to the left of us and nor did he see who approached. It was Tom Skinner, holding a great silver plate above her head, and it came crashing down onto Humphrey's already wounded head. This third strike was too much for him and he doubled over releasing me and I was back on my feet.

I was surprised to see the person behind that girlish voice

suddenly brandishing the crockery in this violent manner. I was so accustomed to seeing her stomping around in trousers and pretending to be one of the boys that even I forgot what she really was.

'Out the front!' I told Tom, once I'd recovered. I could see Georgie through the window, he had driven the cart to the front gate and was working upon the chain with his iron file.

'Hang about,' Tom said in her truer, harder voice. 'I put a big sack of silver down a second ago and now I can't find it.' She laughed at her own stupidity and went off to look.

'There ain't time,' I shouted after her. 'I got what we came for!' Then at the top of the staircase I saw the lady of the house in her torn nightdress and with her tousled hair hanging down over that fresh bruise.

'There's a constable on his way,' she announced in triumph. 'I've just seen him from the library window. He has someone from the pub with him too. You're for it now!'

I opened the door and saw that Georgie had managed to smash open the chain of the gate but had driven the dairy cart away, as two others was indeed running down the lane from the village. The one up front was rattling one of those stupid wooden clackers that London peelers like so much.

'There's three of them,' Humphrey cried up to his mistress while I shouted for Tom to hurry. I was waiting to see if she needed any help before making a dash while Humphrey was getting to his feet again. 'Two men,' he growled, 'and a girl hiding somewhere.' He was clutching his bleeding head and trying to stand and it was clear that he could not tell that Tom was the girl, a butch girl in boys' clothing who could throw her voice better than any. 'It'll be the noose for the lot of them,' he sneered.

Just then Tom reappeared with a sackful of jostling plate and other silverware. 'Thanks for your hospitality,' she said as she passed by and kicked him in the face. He fell backwards and groaned.

We dashed out of the front door then and headed across the lawn towards the gate but was dismayed to see that two villagers was already there.

'Halt!' said the constable in a weak, shaky voice. 'I'm putting you boys under arrest.' It was clear that he did not have it in him to take on two desperate villains and I did not think the publican would be much trouble either. 'Put down the sack, fellas,' he ordered without much conviction. 'You're coming with me to the station.'

'Let's charge them,' I said to Tom as we stopped and eyed them hard. 'And you unload the sack.'

'I just spent fifteen minutes collecting this lot,' she complained.

'The necklace in my pocket is worth five times all that,' I returned. 'Just throw it in the air and let them have it. They won't fight if they can boast that they got the swag back.' Before Tom could argue there was another roar from behind and we turned to see Humphrey stagger out of the front door, his face a red mess. He let out a war cry and ran towards us. We then began running towards the villagers and they in turn charged us. We all collided into each other in the centre of the lawn and Tom's sack of booty went flying into the air.

As expected, the publican was no hero and was more interested in collecting the raining silverware than with taking a chance on fisticuffs. I managed to dodge them all and kept on running but the constable was a tougher cove than I had reckoned on and he pounced on Tom. Once I made it to the gate I turned to see was happening and saw that she was locked in battle with both Humphrey and the policeman and I was considering going back to help her. Then, from Whetstone Manor, the window of the library opened and the lady of the house called out.

'The one with the bloody head!' she yelled. 'He's the leader! The fiend attacked me in my boudoir and was ordering the others about. He's the one to grab!'

'Right you are, milady!' the constable said and let go of Tom Skinner to wrestle with the stunned Humphrey.

'Not me, fool,' he protested, 'she's lying, can't you tell?' But the constable had pulled out his truncheon and gave Humphrey his final whack to the head of the night. He collapsed to the ground again and both the constable and the publican bundled on top of him to the cheering approval of the woman of the house.

Tom made it to the gates with one tureen dish still in her hands and we both looked about for the dairy cart. We turned to see Georgie racing it towards us down the lane with great urgency and he drew the horse up beside us and hollered out for Scratcher. We climbed into the back and I landed on something what crumpled beneath. It was my stovepipe hat what I had left in the cart and I had near ruined the shape of it. We saw Scratcher then, scrambling towards us from the trees, and Tom called for him to hurry up. As she helped him into the back of the cart I padded out the dent on the hat and then took one last look at Whetstone Manor before the horse pulled away. I'll never know if Humphrey saw me in the dark waving my hat back at him as he was being beaten up and arrested. But I like to imagine that he did.

Chapter 2

Sunrise Over Soho

*Returning to London after a hard night's work, the scene moves
from the professional to the domestic*

It was morning by the time our vehicle rolled past the toll gate on
the Old Kent Road and joined the steady stream of traffic back
into the city. By then we was all much more relaxed than we had
been on the journey out and had begun singing some bawdy songs
to pass the time. Scratcher had cheered up a good deal after we had
finished ridiculing him for his poor standard of crowing and he
was now he was enjoying listening to Tom entertain us all with
what had occurred inside the manor.

'They're probably still searching every room in the crib now,'
Georgie laughed as he drove the horse over London Bridge,
'looking for the maidservant. How did you think of that, Skinner?'

'Mary is my given name,' explained Tom as she blew her smoke-
rings out over the Thames. 'And I was all set to enter domestic
service before my family threw me out for thievery. As well as
various other sorts of miscreant behaviour.' Then she leaned back
against the side of the cart and withdrew into herself as we neared
home.

Scratcher still lived with his family in Bethnal Green but he asked
to be dropped off at a spot in Cheapside where some other urchins
was playing in the street. Before he alighted I gave him another quick
lecture concerning the value of a silent tongue. We, for example,

was happy not to tell his pals about his cowardly behaviour on the crack if he too would practice discretion concerning our possession of the Lady of Stars. I then ruffled his dirty mop of hair and told him that we would call round to his home with his share of the bunce after tomorrow's meeting so he was one lucky little lad. 'And you keep safe, y'hear,' I called after him as he went off to play with the other kinchins. 'Don't be getting in no trouble.'

As we approached High Holborn I spied a familiar stallholder further up the thoroughfare who was already setting up for the morning rush of commuters. The lights of the charcoal was already lit in the pots below his table and I saw his son laying out the tin mugs. Georgie announced that he could do with some refreshment after so many hours driving and he veered the cart over towards the stall and called out to the lad for three hot cups.

'You're paying though,' I told him before he could argue. 'Because I won't get much change from this necklace.' But before we could get close to the stall we was surprised to hear the coffee-vendor barking at us to keep moving.

'I knows you lot,' he said and pulled his son back behind the counter. 'You're those villains from Seven Dials and around. Well, I ain't letting you get close enough to pinch another mug.'

'I think you're mistaking us with some others, good sir,' I replied and lifted my hat to him. 'We're respectable paying customers, we are.'

'You're thieves and nothing more,' he shouted back. 'And I've taken my last forged shilling from your little crew. Go bother someone else with your base coin.'

I was outraged by this unprovoked assault upon my company but not as much as Georgie, who reared up the horse to enter into a heated altercation with the man. He cursed him with the sort of colourful language that you did not expect to hear on a public street at that hour in the morning and threatened to get out of the cart for some fisticuffs. I sympathised with the sentiments he was expressing but I still thought it unwise to attract any more attention so I just reached out and touched his coat sleeve.

'Let's just take our business elsewhere then, George,' I said and indicated that he should just move us along. 'It's been a long night.' Georgie agreed but not before throwing the coffee-man a hand gesture what communicated his displeasure in ways what words never could and left him to explain the meaning of it to his son.

'Thieves and nothing more?' Georgie continued to rant after he had driven the cart on towards the vicinity of London where we all lived. 'We're champions of our class, we are. Champions of our class!' Tom nodded in lazy agreement as she spat on her silver tureen and gave it a polish.

'They should be lining the streets for us, Georgie,' I said as he drove the cart down Monmouth Street towards the Dials. The place stank of last night's red wine and of this morning's washed linen and the only souls what was lining the streets for us at this hour was cats and vagrants. 'They should be singing us songs from the windows,' I declared.

The cart drew up outside the pub on the corner of Monmouth and Mercer which is where Tom and I both alighted. We then made arrangements to meet up later in the afternoon as I had my appointment with Percival at five and had no intention of arriving alone. So we tipped hats, bade each other good morning and parted company. Georgie led the cart away up the street towards Covent Garden, Tom took off down St Martin's Lane where she resided with her friend and I headed back towards my new crib in Soho.

I kept one hand in my coat pocket where the necklace was as I crossed through the dangerous maze of alleys and courtyards and smiled at what excitement it was about to stir up when I got home.

Once I reached the end of Crooked Arm Way I stepped into a small courtyard known to locals as Five Fingers Court and looked up to the window of my new lodgings. I noticed the curtains was still drawn as I reached for my keys.

I was vexed to still be behaving like a thief as I crossed the threshold of my own home but I was keen to avoid my landlady who occupied the lodgings below ours. However, as soon as I had shut the front door after me and before I had grabbed hold of the bannister, I heard her thick Irish accent call out from her kitchen.

'Is that a burglar I can hear?' she said and before I had made it halfway up the staircase towards my own rooms she was out into the hallway and stood at the bottom.

'Not at all, Mrs Grogan,' I said as I took off my hat and turned to face her. She was a heavy-set, formidable bruiser with a moustache as thick as that of her late husband. 'It's just Mr Dawkins Esquire back from working the docks.' She gave a small snort to let me know she had no use for my flam.

'Ah, Mr Dawkins? I was not to know. When I hear a pair of male footsteps treading up that staircase, well . . . I suppose it could be just about anyone.'

I let my smile drop to show her I was in no mood for her goadings.

'I'm keen to get to sleep now, Mrs G,' I said cold and turned away from her. 'I've been hard at it.' But she was not to be shaken off.

'Do you have my rent then, Mr Dawkins? Did you earn it last night down these docks of yours?'

'I did as a matter of fact,' I replied with a nod. 'Don't get paid 'til later though. You'll get your money, Mrs Grogan, don't fret on it.'

'All four weeks' worth?' she continued as I made it to the door of my apartment. '*Four weeks!*' I unlocked this other door and turned back to her before entering. 'See that I have everything by tomorrow evening,' she warned me. 'Or my sons are going to come knocking to turf out the pair of you. A thief and a whore I can suffer but I won't keep wastrels.'

I slammed the door shut between us and sighed at how much more disrespect the multitude of London could sling at me in one morning. I hung my hat from a peg on the papered wall and then took off the coat which I folded over my arm. As I did so I heard another, fairer voice calling out my name from within. She sounded surprised to hear me back so early.

'Lily?' I said before I opened the door to our bedroom. 'You alone?'

I'm not sure why I asked that, perhaps it was the landlady's snide insinuations. But as I entered the bedroom Lily was sat up and looking most affronted. She was in her nightdress with her hair dishevelled from sleep.

'Course I'm alone, you cheeky bugger,' she tutted. 'What a thing to ask.' I smiled and threw the coat onto a small upholstered chair what we kept at the foot of the iron bedstead. Then I went over to give her a kiss.

'Only teasing,' I said at last after letting her go. 'Here, guess what I found?' I started taking off my work clothes and sat on the edge of the bed. 'It was just lying there in the street as I passed by minding my own business. I have a feeling you might be interested.'

I heard her jump up over from behind in quick anticipation. I had, in truth, told her all about where I was going and for what purpose on the night before and described the Lady of Stars to her in as much detail as Percival had to me.

'Did you get it?' she asked as she placed her hands on my shoulders. 'Is it here?' I gave a small nod towards the coat as I pulled at my shirt buttons.

'Go and take a peek if you don't believe me.' She got up from the bed and darted over to the chair. 'Not that pocket,' I said as I removed my trousers. 'The other.'

I flung my clothes onto the rug as Lily found the necklace and I then crossed over to open the curtains. She held it up to the morning light and let it dangle between her two hands as she whistled while surveying it. The Lady of Stars seemed even more magical in this humble abode than it had set amid the grandeur of Whetstone Manor.

'We can't keep it,' I reminded her. 'It's just for now.'

'Oh, that right, is it?' she arched an eyebrow. 'You mean you won't let me wear it out to show the neighbours? I was hoping to parade it around the rookeries looking like Marie Antoinette in the hope that someone might stab me to death over it.'

'Turn around,' I said not wishing to encourage any more sarcastic remarks and I inspected how the necklace clasped together. 'Pull your hair up.' She did so and I found the jewellery easier to place around her neck than I had expected it would be. 'There,' I said and kissed her on the nape before reaching for her hand mirror. She took it from me as her hair fell back down onto her shoulders and regarded herself. 'What a beauty,' I said as I watched her. Her manner altered as she looked at her reflection and when she next spoke all the playfulness had gone.

'I'll keep it on this morning though, Jack,' she said. 'Please. Until you go out again.'

I had no intention of refusing her. We kissed again and I said of course as long as it was all she would wear. Soon we was both back on the mattress and as naked as babes save for the necklace still hung around her neck. She stretched her limbs out and began to just enjoy herself as the morning sun rays drifted slow across the room. We stayed like that for some time and she let me love her in the manner in which I had seen the rich people love.

I had first spied Lily Lennox about one year prior to this and from the very first glimpse I could tell that she was going to be the real knock-me-down. She was stood outside the Theatre Royal with two other excellent examples of ill-repute in a very fetching green dress while I was strolling along the opposite pavement with my new silver-tipped cane and heading towards Piccadilly. It had become a habit of mine around that period for my feet to move me towards the brilliant splendour of the Haymarket where all the other fashionable nightbirds of the city would flock. It was a glorious place for a pickpocket to explore as I was forever surrounded by the sons of nobility all promenading with their ladies and acting so careless. I was dressed in my flashest attire in order to blend in with the other dandies and I was at last starting to feel my old buzz coming back. The wounds from Ruby Solomon's bewildering rejection of me had just about begun to heal and I was now in the market for a new fancy woman. I did not want one of those sad, gin-soaked rookery girls what all the other thieves attached themselves to though. No, I wanted a girl worth impressing, someone to steal for who would know the difference between me and every other fellow. And there, stood proud between the two columns of the theatre, was someone who looked like she would be ideal for the role.

She was displaying herself in full view of the passing traffic, mistress of her situation, just gossiping and smiling with her friends. It was as if these wantons was the star attractions of the theatre and the approaching gentleman who would doff their hats and make their advances was just grateful admirers to be tolerated but not indulged. She was, I felt sure, prizing herself high, not wanting to lower her value for the first blunt soldier what would make an offer so early in the evening. They was not the courtesans of the rich but they did look they had the talent to snare a gullible aristocrat if the chance came along. Lily was still laughing at something the girl to her right in the canary dress had said with her hand covering her mouth and she flashed me a look what was both question and invitation at once. I realised that not only had she seen me admiring her but she was waiting for me to make my advance. I decided to dally no longer and, after waiting for a break in the traffic, cut across the road resolved to make good my introduction and seduce her with my honeyed words.

'So how much for a squeeze and a poke then, you gorgeous little tart?'

Lily seemed unfazed by this crude proposition and even a little amused by its forwardness which vexed me much as it was not me what had said it. Because – before I had got close enough to present myself in the fashion of a gentleman and employ the sort of rich language I had found in the more florid poetry of the day – I was beaten to the moment by some corpulent old geriatric. I had not seen him charging down from the other direction of the street but he had managed to swoop in before me and had pitched his woo before I even had time to compare her beauty to a fluttering leaf upon the wind. Lily paid me no regard now as I stood there and waited for this winking, weighty fart-bag to receive his rebuttal and move along.

'If by that, gentle sir, you mean one of those new street games what children play,' she replied in a voice which was like east-end cockney but without all the clatter, 'then I'd prefer to stay here, thank you kindly for asking.' She gave him a little curtsey and I liked her even more now.

'A suck on the pipe then?' he persisted with a wheeze. 'There's a sovereign in it for you if you don't mind taking your time over it. I'm sixty-six, you understand.'

I could see that she was just humouring the old blockage so I stood there leaning on my cane making no attempt to disguise my impatience with him. As I did this her friend in the canary dress approached me to strike up a conversation and I waved her away. I wanted to make it clear that it was Lily I was waiting for.

'I think you've mistaken me for a different sort, sir,' she said in a kind tone. 'A less particular sort.'

'You're a whore, aren't you?' spluttered the old romancer. He cast his eyes about to her companions and then back to Lily. 'You're all harlots. I could have the whole bunch of you if I offered a hundred pounds each.'

'*Are* you offering a hundred pounds each?' asked the canary dress with sudden interest.

'Of course not,' he replied as if she was mad. 'But you would if I did, you stupid horse, so the rest is just haggling. Look here,' he reached into his inside pocket and produced a brown leather wallet and showed it to Lily. 'This is yours if you don't mind working for it.' It was thick enough to be stuffed with notes and Lily cocked her head to the side just an inch as if calculating how much was inside. 'Not all of it obviously,' he made clear. 'But a fair amount.'

'How much is a fair amount?' she then asked and I grew fearful that the fat reprobate was going to win the night after all. But he reacted as though he was being led around in circles by the impossible woman.

'That is the very question I'm trying to ask you!' he huffed in exasperation and stuffed the wallet back into his pocket. Then he swung around to where I was standing and addressed me direct by pointing his own cane at my head. 'Are you the bawd?' he asked. 'You're dressed like a bawd. Try and rattle some sense into your whore, why don't you? I need to be home by ten.' Lily opened her mouth in protest but I was quicker to answer that, yes, these girls did indeed work for me and I stepped over to where he stood before she or her companions could argue otherwise.

'Look here, uncle,' I said as I put my arm around his shoulders as if wanting to speak to him in confidence. I guided him out of view from the main street and under the shadows of the theatre front. 'Peelers are on patrol and you're making a proper fuss.' The old gent grumbled something about how, in his day, you could approach anyone you liked in broad daylight and solicit them without being bothered by the wretched puritans. 'Simpler days, my fine fellow,' I nodded in sympathy, 'I yearn for them also. But if you want to enjoy the exquisite delights of this gay miss,' I pointed the silver tip of my cane over to where Lily was standing with her hands on her hips, a piqued expression upon her face and still flanked by her two friends, 'then it may cost you more than you're prepared to part with.'

'What's so special about her then?' the old gent asked. 'I've already made such an enquiry and am still waiting for her to name the price.'

'To bed a woman like that,' I told him but kept looking at her, 'will cost you far more than you've brought out with you tonight.'

'More?' he exclaimed and pulled away from me. 'God in heaven, you bold chancer, all I want is a quick trembler.'

'The very problem,' I returned and held a finger in the air like some professor about to explain to lesser intellects how the universe works. 'Because if that is all you're after, sir, then that is not what is for sale. Is it ladies?' The girls either side of Lily exchanged a dubious glance as this was exactly the reason that they had set up shop and, as if to prove it, another silver-haired swain was approaching the one in the violet dress from behind and she spun around so he could browse the goods with ease. But Lily held her eyes on mine and kept them steady.

'No,' she smiled. 'There is more for sale than that.'

'Indeed there is,' I grinned and patted the puzzled old cove on the back. 'There is her excellent company for starters, sir. You've never had such stimulating conversation than that which you'll be enjoying with our dear . . .' I gestured for her to enlighten me.

'Lily,' she said and curtsied again.

'The enchanting Lily. Why, she's very knowledgeable about all sorts of interesting subjects, sir. It'll be an education for you I don't doubt.' The gent scrunched his face in displeasure but I ignored him and kept on. 'And that ain't all. For the main course Lily can serve up a wondrous array of delicious delights by way of her many accomplishments. Tell him about your many accomplishments, Lil!'

'Well,' she said and looked away all demure. 'A lady doesn't like to boast.'

'Then let me do it for you, girl,' I said and turned back to the gent. 'Have you ever heard the sound of a nightingale, sir, singing alone on an otherwise soundless evening and thought to yourself that there was an angelic voice, cleansing our souls anew? Because that's what comes to my mind whenever our dear Lily treats us to burst of her lungs. I won't ask her to demonstrate now, sir, else they'll all want her, but ask her to give you a tune when you're alone later on and it'll not disappoint.' The old boy now looked to be in deep discomfort but I would not let him interrupt. 'And should you desire, sir, as I have no doubt you will, to show off your purchase and have our cockney Venus accompany you to some high society ball or other lordly function,' the old man coughed in horror, 'then rest assured that she's a beautiful dancer, sir.' I turned back to Lily who seemed most delighted to have herself spoken about in such terms. 'Ain't that right, Lilybet?'

'And don't forget my pianoforte?' she chipped in as if hurt by the oversight.

'How could I?' I marvelled. 'After all you've told me about your childhood as the daughter of said instrument-maker. Do you know, sir,' I whispered this next part as if it was some cherished secret what I only let out on sufferance, 'that she learnt how to play these delicate tunes by her own ear and not by instruction as others do? That's the depth of talent that you find yourself being offered this evening, sir. That's what you'd really be making a possession of.'

'And what if I don't want all that?' the old boy butted in with a leer. 'What if I just want to head straight for the pudding?!'

'Then what a pudding!' I declared with excitement. 'I was looking forward to bragging about this last thing. Shall you tell him, Lily, or shall I?'

'Oh, let me!' she pleaded with undisguised glee.

'Then be my guest!'

'Sir!' she raised her profile then as if about to be painted. 'It delights me to tell you that I am a whore . . .' she held the pause and glanced my way, '. . . who can speak *seven different languages*!'

I took off my hat and threw my arms in the air in cheer. 'Seven different languages!' I cried for the whole of Haymarket to hear. 'Did you ever hear of such a thing, sir? Of a lady of the night possessing such abilities? Tell him what languages they are, Lily, you brilliant strumpet!'

Lily lifted the fingers of her gloved hands as she ran through them. 'French, Spanish, German . . .'

'German!' I whistled and nudged the punter's elbow. 'Which could come in good and handy should Prince Albert ever come to call!'

'. . . and Portuguese. Those are the only ones I'm fluent in. But I can speak to a fair conversational level in Russian and Italian.' She then held up her seventh finger as if in apology for it. 'The last, sir, is Arabic but I confess I know only a smattering.'

I clapped my hands together and remarked at the many amazing things you can pick up in a brothel if you're quick and eager to learn. But the old gentleman looked as if he was about to topple over at any moment so I brought my proposal to a close. 'So you see, sir,' I explained, keen to impress my point upon him, 'a woman like this is not for the quick jump. You don't take a delectable creature like Miss Lily here up some filthy alley and press her against a garden fence. Oh no, sir, you treat her like a second wife or even indeed a first, if you're not already married. You put her up in some fashionable apartment in a vicinity like – oh, I don't know – Chelsea, and you visit her regular. You grant her an allowance with which she can adorn herself with the most glittering jewels, spray herself with the finest perfumes and entertain you, sir, in the most stimulating lingerie. All of which is for your pleasure sir, and not for hers. You take her out to dine, to dance, to be entertained. You want to be seen with her sir. So answer me this,' I waved my hand with a concluding flourish, 'do you still believe you can pay for all that with the contents of your wallet?'

The old gentleman looked long and hard and with due consideration at Lily who spun on her heels. He then made his one and final offer.

'Two guineas, then,' he grunted. 'For one hour. But you can keep all the nonsense, I only want her to perform one trick.'

Then he named a special request what stopped Lily's spinning fast.

'Charming,' she pouted and crossed her arms. She looked to me. 'Are you really going to let me go under those conditions?' she asked. 'A whore of my standing?'

'No, I will not, Lily, my dear,' I replied and turned on the aged De Sade with venom. 'Run along now, you disgraceful old walrus, before somebody settles you for insulting a lady! You can't expect a respectable harlot to demean herself for just two guineas? What sort of sad and desperate wretch would ever consent to such terms?'

'I would,' piped up the girl in the canary dress. She had been listening to our conversation with interest and, to be fair, two guineas was a decent sum of money for one hour's work. The other prostitute had left with her swain and there was a chance that this one would be left standing if she didn't act. 'I have a room two streets away if you'd like to, handsome,' she said as stepping past Lily and towards the old gent. He looked relieved to have at last encountered someone with a bit of business sense about her and took her arm as she led him off into the night. The evening's performance had been begun and so the Haymarket was now much sparser and Lily and myself was left alone on the pavement.

'And you are?' she enquired. I removed my hat again and bowed deep.

'Jack Dawkins, miss,' I said after I had done so. 'And, if that name sounds somehow familiar, I should also tell you of the monicker I sometimes go by. *The Artful Dodger!*'

'Never heard of you,' she shrugged. 'You in music halls?'

'No, I am not,' I replied as I replaced the hat. 'But I do enjoy a certain celebrity in some localities if you ask the right people. But what is more important is that we are at last undisturbed and I am free to make you my offer.'

'You've just talked me out of two guineas, Mr Dawkins,' she said and threw a glance over her shoulder towards the old gentleman and her friend who was disappearing around the far corner. 'So this offer of yours had better be good. Didn't I just hear you speaking of dining and dancing, jewellery and the like?'

'You did indeed and, should you be so lucky as to become my fancy woman, then I would rule none of that out. But – seeing how we're just getting to know one another – how about we start with some supper and see how we get on? Nearby is a cosy little place I know what serves an eel pie and mash and I haven't eaten all night. Why don't you join me? They do a nice soup as well.'

'Eels?' Lily laughed in ridicule. 'After all that and you just want to buy me a bowl of green for my favours. You've a fine nerve Jack Dawkins, I'll say that for you.'

'An oyster house then,' I said and reached into my pocket. 'And we can visit all the concert rooms and halls afterwards. But, in all truth, Lily, I don't intend to pay for a single farthing of the evening's fun.'

'That right?' she responded. 'Well, if you're think I'm going to pick up the expenses then you've come to the wrong tart. Listen, Mr Dawkins . . .'

'Jack.'

'Jack, then. You might be quite the sensation in your own vicinity but you need to understand something,' she stepped close to me and spoke in a tone of warning, 'I'm a Slade girl.' I shrugged to show her that I did not know or care what that meant. 'And one way or another,' she continued, 'you're paying for a Slade girl.'

'No, I am not, Lily,' I said. Then I produced something what changed her countenance quick. It was the fat brown wallet what belonging to the old gentleman and it was as stuffed as a pigeon. 'But somebody else will be. Now come along,' I offered her my arm. 'Let's you and me go and have ourselves a very pleasant evening, shall we? And you won't have to do a single thing you're not inclined to.'

Lily laughed as I handed her the wallet so she could count the contents. 'You know what, Mr Dawkins?' she said at last as she took my arm after all, 'I think I am in the mood for some of those oysters after all'.

Chapter 3

A Drop of Courage

Showing the criminal life to be a much harder way of life than it might first appear

The early afternoon cry of a rag-and-bone man woke me some hours later on that day when I had returned from Whetstone and I rolled over in my bed to go another round with Lily. She was not there however and I was still too sleepy to realise what that could mean. I closed my eyes again and returned to my dreams and it was some minutes later that I recalled that she still had the Lady of Stars around her neck.

I then pounced out of the bed and I looked around the room most frantic. The necklace was nowhere. Not on the sideboard, not back in my coat pocket, not on the chair. She had taken it.

'Lily!' I screamed as I hopped into some trousers and placed the braces over my shoulders and ran towards the window, hoping that I might still have time to see her making off across the courtyard. But, save for some kinchins what was throwing pennies against a wall, it was empty. I darted out of the room, putting on my coat as I did so and dashed towards the front door calling her name. I passed the other open doors of our apartment as I ran – glancing in quick to see if she was in either the kitchen or the parlour – and was so gripped with the thought of my loss that I did not pay any attention to the small puddles of water what I almost slipped upon in my hurry. So it was not until I was halfway down the staircase and into the bottom part of the house that I at last heard Lily's voice. It came from behind me, she was still in our crib and the relief was overwhelming. The puddles was from the water buckets what she must have brought in up from the pump outside which meant she was bathing herself. My jumpy bones steadied themselves and I went back upstairs before Mrs Grogan could ask us what the racket was.

'Where you off to?' I heard Lily call from the back parlour. I stepped into the room what overlooked the backyard and saw her in the area not visible from the hallway. She was sat in the tin bathtub and there was three empty water buckets by the side of the tub. Her silk robe hanging from a wash-stand and she was scrubbing herself with some fancy bars of soap what I had stolen for her as a recent gift.

'I was looking for you,' I replied as my breathing began to slow again. 'I had a panic.'

'Ah, bless you,' she said and pretended to splash me. 'Thought some robbers had made off with me, did you? You are sweet.'

I nodded to say that this was exactly what I had thought and then there was a second where we just looked at one another. I could see she was working out what had really rattled me but I could not help giving it away first. 'Lily,' I ventured – knowing what offense the question could cause – 'where is the necklace?' Her face darkened as she took this in.

'Did you think I ran off with it?'

'No!' I returned and laughed at the ludicrousness of the idea. 'Of course I never.'

'You thought I'd stolen it from you.'

'Course not! I wouldn't even entertain the idea, Lily. I know you'd never do me a wrong turn.' There was another long pause as she held my eyes and said nothing. I softened my voice and broke the silence. 'Where is it, though?' She sniffed and turned her head towards the window behind her. On the dresser underneath I saw it wrapped within a small hand towel. I crossed over, unwrapped it and saw that she had given the necklace a good wash and was letting it dry in the sun. I took it in my hands and inspected it for damages.

'You've given it a nice clean, Lily,' I said as I held it up to the light. 'Thanks. Percival should be well pleased with—'

The door behind me slammed and I turned to see that the bath was empty and the robe had gone.

For the next hour – and in spite of all my many attempts at appeasement – I could not get a civil word out of the sullen miss. I tried to cheer her up by promising her that I would take her to St Bartholomew's Fair that coming Saturday – a social event I knew she was very keen on – and that I would be happy to pay for everything. But Lily was deep in sulk and so instead I just left her alone and readied myself for the hour when my gang would come to collect me for our appointment with Percival.

After I had washed myself, and used the buckets to throw the dirty water out of the rear window and onto the patch of dry grass below, I started to dress for the meeting. I considered wearing some of my flashest colours in order to impress our paying customer when I strolled into the arranged location but, just before I reached for my bright blue waistcoat, I remembered that Mouse Flynn was coming with us and that an all black outfit would be more appropriate. Mouse had suffered a recent bereavement and was sure to be dressed in full mourning so it was right for me to do likewise. Agnes Dunn, his beloved kept woman, had died in childbirth just two weeks before and Mouse was devastated. It was a very sorrowful event in our local community as Agnes had been popular and I had promised Mouse that, as his top sawyer, I would ensure that his baby would never want for nothing. I had already found a local midwife to take care of the child and had paid for a decent stone to be placed over his mother's grave. I was the treasurer of the local burial club but the few coppers I had been paid from the Flynns was just enough to keep her out of the paupers' end of the graveyard. The stone was my own expense and this outlay was among the many reasons why I was so behind with the rent. But, I told myself as I tied the laces of my black shoes after dressing myself, if you want to run a crew like mine then you have to be forever making them love you. And more important than that, I considered as I walked over to the small parlour mirror and inspected how handsome this black suit was making me look, was that they must want you to love them back. That was the best way to inspire loyalty in a criminal gang, I considered.

Soon the sound of pebbles being thrown against pane was heard at the front of the house and I crossed the apartment to the bedroom. Lily, who was in the kitchen, complained that the queer girl must be here again and that one day she would break that bloody window. Lily did not care for the way Tom would alert me to her presence but then Lily had never liked anything about Tom Skinner. I lifted the bedroom window and stuck my head out to greet the three noble crims what stood in the courtyard below. Tom, who occupied the centre of the yard and was flanked by the other two, lifted her hat and grinned as she rested on her cane while, to her left, Georgie was chomping into an apple. On the right, as I had predicted, was Mouse Flynn, his suit of black contrasting with the loud attire of the other two. I told them I would be down in a second.

'Mouse is out there?' Lily asked in surprise after I had explained the black. 'Not Scratcher?'

'You can't expect a kinchin to come to business meetings like this one, Lily' I told her as I went over to give her a goodbye kiss. 'It'd be irresponsible.' As I went to approach her she looked like she was still going to turn me away instead of kissing me goodbye. 'There is no one I trust more than you, Lil,' I said before giving her a quick embrace.

'Which is not saying much,' she returned but she let me kiss her and I darted out of the door. I was halfway down the staircase before she whistled for me to stop. 'You know, for a pickpocket,' she said as she stood at the top of the stairs with the necklace I had placed in my coat pocket moments before now in her hand, 'you're an easy touch.' I rolled my eyes and stepped back up to take it from her. 'Good thing you can trust me,' she smiled after we kissed again.

By the time I had made it down to the courtyard, having dodged another awkward encounter with Mrs Grogan, Lily had stuck her head out of the bedroom window to talk to the recent widower about his baby, Robin.

'He's better than gold and the image of his mother,' Mouse said back to her as I shut the door after myself and nodded them all hello. Lily gave Mouse her love and said she would be visiting the babe soon before shutting the window without even acknowledging Tom or Georgie. I stepped forward and the whole company turned.

'Very good, troops,' I said, and made a show of inspecting their uniforms and bearing as if I was the officer and this lowly courtyard our barracks. I would not tolerate scruffiness in a member of my gang and was pleased not to find it here. I also noted with approval that all three carried canes what was similar to mine and this was not the first time I had set a trend among them. My silver top was fashioned into the image of a bird with a protruding beak and theirs was all also bearing icons of the natural world. Georgie's top was moulded into the shape of a horse's head, Tom's was that of a cat's paw and Mouse's was of a fox with its toothy mouth open, which was perfect for forcing open stubborn bottles. The silversmith what must have forged these stolen items was quite the artisan but I liked mine best as the bird's beak could be used to hook itself into any door panel what I chose to hit with the cane and prise open a hole for a smaller thief to crawl through.

'I ain't ever seen a smarter bunch of lads,' I remarked as I swivelled the bird's beak up and over so the cane was now held behind my neck as I strutted past them. There was four of us, including Scratcher, what had stolen the necklace and the money would be split equal. Mouse was only coming so that we would look like an organised mob in front of Percival, and he would receive some coins for his trouble.

So I turned about and led my happy band out of Five Fingers and out through the maze of the slums towards the direction of Temple. We was followed for a spell by a young Irish lad of about eleven who skipped behind us asking what we was doing and where we was going. Young boys such as he was often captured by the romance of a gang like ours and this one was making a proper nuisance of himself as he buzzed after, imitating our cocky swagger. It was not until we reached the bottom of Drury Lane that we at last shook him off and then the four of us crossed the thoroughfare of Pickford Street. Knowing what a troublesome gang of villains we must have appeared as we did not even stop for carriages but just let their drivers avoid us instead. Finally we drew near to Temple Bar but it was not to the legal district itself where we was heading. Instead Percival had chosen as our rendezvous a quiet little public-house down a narrow lane nearby called the Drop of Courage. This was the sort of place where the families of the accused might visit before or after taking professional advice, a much lower haunt where solicitors might be found but the criminal element was also not unwelcome. Percival had no doubt selected it as it was a place where his class and our class would not look so suspicious talking to one another.

The sum of money what he had promised to pay us for the safe return of the Lady of Stars was considerable, as much as I had ever been offered during my short career as a burglar-on-demand. I hoped that if this transaction went well then it would prove to be the first of many such engagements as Percival might start recommending me to other wealthy gents what might have similar felonious requests. It would be good, I reflected as the four of us turned into the long sooty lane what led towards the pub, to at last start making some real money from these God-given talents of mine.

We had advanced halfway down the lane before two figures what had been blocking our passage at the end made themselves visible. One of them had been lying in a slump between some empty barrels of ale outside the pub and we had at first taken him for a drunken vagrant. But, as we drew closer, he stood up in a manner of confident sobriety just as another man emerged from around the corner like he had been waiting there. They both held large wooden sticks.

The four of us stopped in our tracks and, without exchanging a word, raised up our canes. We clutched them by the bottom and brandished the heavy silver icons at the other end like the weapons they truly was. Then we stood in such a way that communicated to these two roughs that we was not to be mistaken for their usual prey. We was four while they was just two and our canes had longer reaches than their thick clubs.

Then they did something what was most peculiar for urban robbers. They both reached behind their backs and pulled up matching hats what had been dangling from their necks on string. Then they tugged up what at first looked like black neckerchiefs and with them they masked the lower half of their faces. The hats was three-cornered and belonged to the previous century.

'Good afternoon fellas,' said a voice from behind us. We spun around to see three other coves stood in our wake what was hatted and masked in the same fashion. Two was set further back down the lane and holding clubs just like the first. The fifth was stood much closer to us and was pointing two long-barrelled barkers at me and at Georgie. 'I'm Dick,' his voice was a proud and unmistakeable Irish, 'and these here are my Turpins. And, just so you're in no doubt, be assured that I would not hesitate to shoot.'

Even with his face half-masked, I could tell that he was all of a grin and in love with his own mischief. I considered handing over my purse and telling my gang to do likewise in the hope that they would then be satisfied and move on.

'Lower those smart sticks, so,' this Dick continued. 'And we'll be taking that necklace of yours if you please.'

My three confederates all turned to me in surprise. I could not contain my dismay at his words and, for some moments, I was at a loss as to how to proceed. But I had no intention of handing over my hard-won treasure to this sniggering bandit and so I steeled myself and raised my cane even higher.

'This is Temple Bar, Dick,' I returned and felt my gang all stiffen themselves for battle. 'There are lawyers and peelers all over what'll come running at the first shot so spare us these stand and deliver theatricals. We ain't bumpkins.'

Dick raised his eyebrows. 'You're a brazen one,' he chuckled and cocked the pistols. 'And it'll be over in a heartbeat, I swear it.'

I considered our chances. He could easily shoot me and Georgie with those pistols and his four Turpins, who had been closing in slow from both sides, would make short work of the other two. Georgie turned to me, itching for the word to charge, but I had already begun lowering my cane with one hand while my other reached for my coat pocket.

'That's best,' Dick nodded and I could see the heavy weights of his guns already drooping as my cane slipped down through my hand. 'That's the smartest way. As my dear old mammy used to say it always—'

But we never learnt what Dick's dear old mammy used to say on account of the silver bird at the end of my cane being smashed upwards into his face most sudden. He staggered backwards and fired off one cannon but it hit the brick wall to the left and he almost dropped the other. His then roared and charged but mine all followed my lead and each spun around to face their nearest challengers, going at them with their vicious canes. Weapons clashed all around, the sounds of street war rang out and I concentrated on their leader. I dropped Dick with another sharp punch to his face and he went down onto his back. Georgie ran past us and headed towards those coming in fast from behind but as Dick fell his second weapon fired and the shot hit Georgie's leg. He cried out and staggered in front of them and they both started bashing him with their wooden clubs. I stepped onto Dick's chest and he howled as I went straight over him to help Georgie. They both turned and rushed me and I struck one on the ear with my bird-cane. The other Turpin landed a blow with his club into my side and the force of it took me down.

'That's the one,' I heard Dick shout in a hacking voice. 'He's got the necklace in his pocket. Gettit off him!' I tried to fight as they advanced again but soon they had me helpless against the wall and was searching through my coat pockets.

At the other end of the alley, I could see my other two soldiers locked in battle with their robbers but Tom had already taken a proper beating from hers who, with shameful disregard for her sex, had her on the ground and was punching her. Meanwhile Mouse, who when things turned violent was always tougher than his size and customary mildness would have people believe, had gained victory over his Turpin who had dropped his club and was under serious assault from the fox-cane. But Tom's assailant finished with her, jumped onto the back of Mouse and the two men defeated him.

Dick was up again and using his mask to dab at the blood underneath. He then walked towards where I was being held up just as I was trying to bite at the Turpin whose hands was going through my pockets. Dick flicked his wrist and revealed a sharp silver blade and held it close to my neck. 'Stop struggling,' he hissed as I was punched again in the stomach, 'and let this happen.' I groaned as they started patting my waistcoat hard until they found the necklace.

'This it?' asked the Turpin as he pulled out the Lady of Stars.

'Well, what else would it be?' Dick shot back and then told him to stuff it in his own pocket. Then, with his blade still pressed against my neck, he turned back to me as his four Turpins made to leave. 'I've a mind to kill you anyway,' Dick declared. 'But I wouldn't much care for the mess you'd make. So count yourself as a lucky Jack.' He then put away the knife, gave me one last punch and I fell to the floor in a ball. I could see Georgie clutching his wounded leg and I heard the sounds of the Turpins' wicked laughter as they ran off. I lifted my head and saw that Tom and Mouse was also curled up and beaten at the end of the lane where the pub was. Both their canes had been snapped in half.

Chapter 4

Thieves and Nothing More

A scene which is all dark questions and smoky suspicions

Only once the Turpins had fled out of sight did the good patrons of the Drop of Courage come out to inspect the rumpus. They made a good show of only just now chancing upon the scene and some people ran up to the wailing Georgie to help him. I tried to stand and I had a terrible urge to get myself and the others out of the vicinity fast. Some smart gentlemen, who I guessed would be local lawyers, was telling us that the peelers had been sent for and we could give our descriptions of the robbers to them. A stretcher was coming, they told us, to take Georgie to the nearest infirmary where we should then follow. I caught eyes with Tom who had a fresh bruise on her left cheek but was gathering herself together and I could tell she was of the same mind. We needed to grab Mouse and scud away when I heard a refined voice calling my name.

'Ah, Mr Dawkins, here at last.' I turned to see Percival stepping out of the back entrance of the pub and ignoring all the surrounding chaos. He tapped his fob watch as he moved past the other gentlemen and pulled me away from their hearing. 'The money is close by,' he said as if oblivious to what had been happening out here. 'And can be sent for at once. But first I must of course see the necklace.' My first thought on seeing Percival was, of course, that he must be the villain what had arranged this travesty. This seemed plain as he was the very person what had chosen that unfamiliar tavern as the place of exchange and all this talk about wanting to inspect the necklace must just have been his weak and insulting pantomime designed to throw us off. And so, to show him that I was not so slow as all that, I crossed straight over to him, grabbed him by the coat collar and shoved him against the brick wall so I could charge him with playing us for dupes. I spoke quiet so as not to be overheard by the various onlookers and accused him of hiring these cheaper robbers to ambush us in order to pay less for the necklace. I asked if he thought I was green enough to fall for such a dodge but, in all truth, Percival appeared to be as shocked about the theft as I was and he became most indignant at the accusation.

'I haven't told a soul about our business,' he said as I released him for appearance's sake and he begun straightening his clothes. 'Gentlemen of my standing do not boast of their criminal connections, you'll be amazed to learn. And what's more,' he was whispering in my ear now, 'I would still pay full price for the thing if you can get it back. There! I wouldn't say that if I had plotted against you.' This, I had to admit, was probably true and he wrote down an address at Barnard's Inn to contact him if the necklace was retrieved. 'You've no idea how unhappy I am with you for losing it, Dodger. I'd been assured that you and your collective were careful thieves and now *this*!' He waved his hand over my torn clothing like a disapproving mother. 'Fighting with other robbers in broad daylight,' he shook his head. 'I'm disappointed. Get it back, for God's sake. Because if I haven't told a soul about this meeting,' he said as he looked about for any approaching peelers before making his leave, 'then somebody did.'

He now seemed to regard my gang as though we was just the latest set of unreliable tradesman what was making his upper middle-class life intolerable. I decided to let Percival scarper off then as he would be simple enough to track down if it came out that he was lying and I turned my attention to more pressing matters. I saw Tom and Mouse trying to clear away some interfering gentleman what was trying to get Georgie Bluchers to be stretchered off to a nearby hospital and I knew we had to get away as fast. Georgie – like most people of my class – had a horror of hospitals and he thrashed against those what was trying to take him there. I strutted over into their midst and started telling them all to mind their own business.

'We don't have time for no stretchers,' I announced and gestured for Tom and Mouse to take Georgie by the shoulder. 'This man needs surgery fast. I happen to know of some medical students what live hereabout what'll set his leg right in no time. You kind people just go inside and back to your drinks, he'll be all right with us. Go on,' I shooed them all away as they dithered, 'shove off out of it!'

The grumbling crowd soon dispersed and the four of us made off around the corner and went in search of these students who was not as fictitious as they may have sounded. These young men lodged together near Fetters Lane and they was nice respectable boys from good homes. They was known to me on account of their habit of buying opium from off of my friend Herbie Sweet, who himself purchased the goods from my own stolen supply. So – knowing that these fledging surgeons would be easy to incriminate and intimidate – we reached their home, bashed on their door until they had no choice but to admit us and convinced them that they would help Georgie or face severe consequences. Then, once they had promised to remove the shot and fix up our luckless friend, the remaining three of us scudded off towards Holborn, moving fast through the by-lanes and heading north. We didn't stop until we reached somewhere we knew would be safe and we could discuss this turn of events in private.

★

Barney, the landlord of the Three Cripples pub in Saffron Hill and a man who had once been the closest friend of my old departed teacher, Fagin, unbolted the back entrance of his tavern after I had rapped upon it with my cane using the secret signal, a short but loud series of knocks what only I ever used. An evil chained-up dog with a frothing mouth was barking at us but we ignored him as the door swung open and his master welcomed us in.

'Dodger! How wonderful to see you, my boy!' he beamed as soon as he was sure who it was. 'I was only yesterday saying to old Lively that we never . . .'

But then he registered our bruises, cuts and the bloody fogle what Mouse was holding up to his nose and his countenance soon changed. We must have looked to him, with our achey movements and pained faces, like the very trio his pub was named after and he hurried us into his hostelry as if he expected our attackers to still be in pursuit.

'Who done this to you, boys?' he asked as Tom and myself had helped Mouse limp over the threshold and he had bolted the door behind us. 'Peelers?'

'Some Irishmen,' I told him and he nodded his understanding. 'We're hoping you might help us fathom which ones.'

Mouse, who had taken the worst beating, was ready to collapse in that small back hallway and I asked Barney if we could use his taproom to crash down. Barney told me that there was a card game in progress through there. 'There's a shocking amount of drunk whisky bottles in that little room, Dodge, and someone is always losing, are they not? Might be safer for you to just go through to the bar instead.'

So instead we went to one of the many dark corners of the main saloon which was just as good as being in a private room. The Cripples was a thieves' den after all and it had been almost designed to accommodate clandestine discussions such as the one we was about to have. We sat ourselves around a small table against the far wall of the saloon with boarded partitions what helped to screen us from prying eyes. Barney fetched us a pot of water and some flannels to dab at our cuts as well as three small glasses of whisky each and we sank these drinks without speaking. We lit up some clay pipes, and eyed everyone in the bar through their own clouds of tobacco smoke to see if any was paying us too much mind. There was always plenty of Irish in the Cripples and I wondered if anyone here might know who the Turpins was. The room was already thick with smoke and bustling with the low sort – prigs, fences, swindlers, magsmen, mollies and whores. I knew most in the place – and some raised their glasses to us as they passed by our little hole – but they would have seen from our demeanour that we did not care to be approached. Pickled Liz, a prostitute what lived in a room above and who never left that building, swayed over to us, burped a greeting and asked if we would be interested in her company. Tom told her to clear off and so she turned around and tottered back to the bar a few short feet away. Then Barney asked someone to strike up a melody upon the piano at the further end of the bar and offered one of the ladies a free drink if she would lead the place in a song. In this way our conversation was drowned out by the noise and once I was sure that nobody was eavesdropping I leaned in close to my two companions.

'Now then,' I began, 'what in high heaven was all that about?'

The others shrugged in answer.

'We took a proper battering,' Mouse said at last, 'there's no denying it.'

'Did either of you recognise who those Turpins was?' I said as Barney brought over four pots of beer for us and handed them out.

'Behind the masks? Could they have been the Sikes gang doing voices?'

Tom, with a wet flannel pressed hard against her bruise, shook her head and Mouse said that he doubted it. The Sikes gang was not the sort to hide their faces while fighting, they would have liked us to know it was them.

'*Turpins?*' Barney asked as he pulled up a wooden stool and squeezed his fat self in around the small table. 'What's one of those then?' He had left his daughters to tend bar while he joined our discussion and he looked most bewildered as I told him about the metropolitan highwaymen we had just encountered. After I had recounted the whole tale I asked if he had ever heard of such a gang before and if he could guess at the identity of the jockey-sized leader calling himself Dick.

'If I hear of anyone sporting a smashed mouth what he didn't have yesterday,' Barney offered, 'I'll be sure to tell you. But no, nothing tinkles.'

'London is full of Irishmen,' Tom observed as she drew on her pipe and cast an eye over the comely girl what had entered into the chorus of 'Making Love in The Derry Air'. 'It's needles and haystacks.' Her voice lowered then, readying itself for the dark alleys our conversation was to go down next. 'More to the purpose,' she said after taking another drag on her pipe, 'is how they knew we was coming? And that Dodger had a priceless necklace on him?'

This was indeed the most urgent question of all. As far as I was aware the only people what I had told about the business beforehand was those what would have gained more from a successful delivery than from being in league with the Turpins. Tom, Georgie and Scratcher would receive less money if they had to split its value between five others and Mouse had taken a savage beating. Georgie had been shot in the leg but who knew what sort of deal any one of them could have struck with the rival gang. I viewed them all now with suspicion and – in my foul humour – was happy to let them know it.

'We've lost a small fortune this afternoon, boys,' I said, 'and I mean to get it back. So if either of you two have something to tell me then now is the time. It'll be too late tomorrow.' Mouse looked at me in surprise.

'Are you asking us if we're unsafe, Dodge?' he checked. Tom stared at me as smoke puffed out of her nostrils and I returned her fierce look in answer.

'I suppose I am, Mouse, yeah,' I replied while still eyeing Tom. 'Because it's clear that somebody in our company is not.'

Tom scowled as she pushed back her stool. 'You need correcting for saying that to me,' she pointed as she stood up. 'I don't care if you are top sawyer, you don't call me a splitter and not answer for it. I'm the straightest crook you know!'

'I want answers, Tom,' I told her. 'So sit yourself back down. I'm going to be asking the same questions of Georgie and Scratcher in time but right now I'm asking you. Who did you tell about our meeting with Percival?'

'Not a soul,' she shot back. 'And I should knock you down for even asking.'

'What about your Janet?'

'I never talk to women about work, Jack,' she said as if the question itself was mad. 'We all know they can't be trusted. And besides,' she put some bite into these next words, 'I ain't the one living with a Slade girl, am I?' Mouse and Barney looked at each other in discomfort as I asked her what that was supposed to mean.

'It means,' she continued staring at me as she sat down again, 'that if there is any member of this gang with a fancy woman of dubious virtue then it's our great leader. My Janet knows nothing about how I make my earnings, she just takes money from me and buys herself nice things. Ebony Bet, Georgie's girl, can be trusted not to talk to anyone on the grounds that she don't speak no English anyway. And – Mouse – I don't doubt that your dead Agnes is the very model of discretion. Lily Lennox, however . . .' she snuffed out her tobacco and tapped it into a tin spittoon, 'there's a chit with a history on her. If I was you I'd start asking your questions at home before you cast aspersions over your own gang.'

'You know something, Skinner,' I leaned in closer and hissed at the side of her face what was not purple from the fight, 'if you was a real man you'd have a matching bruise on your other cheek by now.' She cocked her head, daring me to do my worst but I preferred to keep hitting her with words. 'You wouldn't even be in this crew if it weren't for me, you impertinent mare. No other London gang would touch you, so remember who your benefactor is and shut your sharp mouth. I know my own fancy woman and she ain't been near her old bawd since the very day I met her.'

'No need to get all lit up, Dodge,' Barney intervened in his meek manner. 'We're just thinking out loud, right, boys? We're just crossing out names to see who's left.' But now even Mouse Flynn, who I had never known to utter a word of doubt against me, began to question my assurances.

'You didn't tell Lily about the necklace though did you, Dodger?' he asked me. 'Before you'd even stolen it? Did she know about the meeting today?'

'Of course he did!' Tom answered for me. 'He's always trying to impress her and saying too much. I'd wager she even tried it on when he got home this morning. She knows more about this job than you do, Mouse.'

Mouse stared at me and asked if this was true. I took another long drag on my pipe and shrugged. 'So?' I said.

Tom threw her hands into the air as if she was declaring the matter closed and Mouse groaned. Barney coughed and said that he had some barrels what needed attending to and he scuttled away.

'You think Lily has told other crooks about our doings?' I asked them in disbelief. 'Well, that shows how little you know her then. Because she ain't a Slade girl no more, she hates the man. She's a Dawkins girl if anything.'

Tom shook her head and sighed. Her manner now became less aggressive and accusing but this was replaced with a patronising edge I did not much care for either.

'Listen, Dodger,' she said and tried to pat my hand with hers. 'We all know you're safe. You're probably the most honest man I've ever met which, to be fair, ain't saying much. But have a think, why don't you? Trusting your lady friend more than your own gang is the backward way around. Especially *your* lady friend.'

Again I bridled at the way she saw fit to speak of my Lily and was about to take her to task. But I was shocked to see Mouse nodding along with her.

'She makes a fair point Jack, he shrugged. 'I love Lily to bits but you never know with some people, eh?'

Thunderous applause erupted throughout the bar as the song reached its bawdy climax. I glanced over the saloon and bit my tongue in agitation at the unwelcome suggestions my friends was making. The notion that Lily might have betrayed me was one my mind wanted to reject but now that it had been placed in there it was like a flea I could not catch. Tom was right, I should not have been so free with my secrets, but I could not believe for one moment that Lily had any hand in this counter-robbery. Despite this, I wanted to get straight back to my crib so I could assure myself that they was all mistaken and – as the people in the bar began calling out for another tune – I stood up to put my coat back on. I then reached for my hat from off the peg as they both got to their feet also.

'Right then,' I told them in a huff, 'I'm off home. But we shall continue this discussion tomorrow. Until then I expect the both of you to find out all you can about these rude bandits. Nobody steals from me, it ain't the natural way of things.'

Tom kept her eyes fixed on me, her face a question.

'I, meanwhile, shall be making my own enquiries,' I answered her look. 'Lily has had nothing to do with any of this dirty business, of that I'm sure. But if it transpires that she has spoken out of school then I shall soon uncover it.' I spoke then in a darker tone what even I myself did not recognise. 'And I'll settle the matter myself.'

Chapter 5

The End of Summer Fair

In which the days begin to grow darker

'Whatever happened to the fortune-telling pigs?'

It was the following Saturday. Lily and I was walking arm-in-arm past the many vendors of Bartholomew Fair and there was a familiar smell of roast pork about.

'And all the jugglers and the decent harlequins,' she continued. 'This here carnival is a shadow of itself.'

We bumped into another couple what had approached from the opposite direction to watch the well-worn clowns of the season and Lily broke off to make a big fuss about how much she admired the lady's flowery dress. I meanwhile, explored the gentleman's left-side coat pocket while his eyes was on my beautiful escort and, once I had executed the perfect dip, I signified to Lily that we needed to move on now. Once clear I inspected the find and discovered that the cove's pocket contained just enough to buy us a pot of whelks each.

'See what I mean,' she tutted as we paused to eat them by a side attraction of distorted looking-glasses what made people seem either fatter, thinner or more frog-eyed than they really was. 'You used to meet a more affluent set of people around here.'

Lily and I was at last on speaking terms again following the furious row we had had when I had returned to our crib after the Turpin assault. I had been so shaken by the theft of the Lady of

Stars and by what poison my gang had then poured into my ear about her that I was all lit up for a fight by the time I burst back into our apartment. She was sat at our little desk with a pen in her hand and writing a letter and – in my mistrustful frame of mind – I imagined that she must be communicating with her co-conspirators and I bounded straight over and snatched the letter away. It turned out she had been writing to her estranged sister up in the country and she took great offense at my oafish behaviour and some very cruel things was said on both sides. Lily became most enraged at the suggestion that she might have played some part in this plot against us and she pointed out that if she had told other thieves about where we was going and with what then she would hardly still be sitting about waiting for me to come home now, would she? Soon Mrs Grogan began knocking on our door to tell us both to keep the shouting down but even after that it was a few days before relations between us improved.

But now, as the two of us worked the crowd of this once-popular annual event, it seemed as though romance had won through and I was again reassured that my darling girl would never betray me and she, on her part, had forgiven me for suggesting otherwise. But this did not alter the fact that my pecuniary situation was now somewhat straitened and so I too was disappointed by the lack of real money found in the young gent's purse. I had managed to pay Mrs Grogan enough so that she and her sons did not make us homeless but it was a mean time what with all my other expenses. I had begun to resign myself to the unwelcome fact that the Lady of Stars was lost to us as, for all I knew, the Turpins could have returned to Ireland by now. And so, after much time and energy had been wasted upon the matter, I had begun to accept the truth that Percival's generous reward was forever lost to me and that I was better off not dwelling on it further.

'This sounds agreeable,' I said to her once the whelks was finished and we headed towards where some fiddlers was playing. Three of them was sat upon the strongest branch of a tall tree and underneath a rope-dance was in progress. I knew that Lily could never resist such entertainments and I was keen for us to at least have a fun time while we was here. After I had flipped the last stolen shilling to the master-of-the-rope we was admitted into the ring where scores of other merry couples was already whirling about, bouncing, clapping and stamping within the great crush. We joined hands and she began to twirl and I soon noticed that every other male eye in the ring was on her as she danced and I was overcome with love for the girl. The little orchestra above soon reached the end of a lively jig and we all took the moment to catch our breaths before they struck up again. Lily was laughing with all the excitement and I took the opportunity to pull her towards me for a kiss. But, just as the strains of the fiddles resumed and we took each other's hands to spin as a circle of two, her eyes widened as she spotted something behind me. Every couple around began spinning but Lily would not budge, she just took root and continued staring over my shoulder. The joy of the dancing vanished from her face and, as I turned to see what had upset her, I assumed that the young gentleman whose pocket I had picked would be standing behind me ready for a rumpus.

But instead I found my attention pulled towards the shaded part of the tree where two men was eating cold meats from the same small plate and watching us close. One of these coves, who was chewing on some boiled tongue and whispering into the other man's ear, was known to me. His name was Morris Bolter and he was someone what I had very little affection for. He was a restless, friendless person who was forever attaching himself to harder crooks and behaving toward them in a servile manner. He had arrived into London from the country around the same time that I had been transported to Australia although I had only met him upon my return. He had introduced himself by claiming that he had been present at my trial in the Old Bailey, saying that Fagin had sent him along to report on the sentence. He seemed to think that this information would ingratiate himself to me, but I rejected his advances of friendship as he had, to my trained eye, the stuff of the sneak about him. So I took no delight in seeing him here spying on me once more and whispering into the ear of a green-hatted stranger.

However it was this stranger, and not Bolter himself, what had made Lily start. It was clear at a glance that he was of the criminal class — we always know our own — but I could also tell from his rich red coat and stiff black hat that he was prosperous enough to be considered a top sawyer like myself. He was about ten years older than me though and was handsome and held himself well. He at first reminded me of Bill Sikes on account of the sense of threat what accompanied him but I revised that impression because Bill was a man for the shadows, he would never dress with such flamboyance and draw attention to himself like this.

This man saw me looking back as Bolter continued his whisperings and, as he lifted a morsel from the plate and put it into his mouth, I saw him give Lily a small nod of acknowledgement.

I turned back to her and saw the very real alarm in her eyes. 'We should go, Jack,' she said and tried to pull my hands to follow her in the other direction. 'You know who that is?' I stood there, still holding onto her hands in the centre of the dance as other couples spun around us. I then looked back to the men and saw that they had at last turned their attention away from us. Bolter was sniggering about something that this flash cove was saying.

'It's your old bawd,' I said then with certainty. 'Weeping Billy Slade.'

'*Let's go, then!*' she said as she managed to free herself from my grip and stepped away. But I had no intention of being seen running away from a man with as fearsome a reputation as this Slade and so I remained where I was and continued to stare him down. I was about to tell Lily that we should continue to dance and that if Slade wanted to cut in then he would be given a polite refusal. But Lily had already spun around, was shoving her way through the other dancing couples, under the rope and away from the scene. So now I was in the centre of a rope-dance with no partner and I must have looked like a proper fool. I had no choice but to chase after her. By the time I caught up with her she was halfway through the fair and I grabbed her hand before she made for the exit.

'Stop running, Lily,' I told her. 'I don't know what grievances he thinks he still has with you, he'd never hurt you with me about.' Once she was assured that Slade was not in pursuit she calmed herself and put her hand on mine.

'But it's you I'm most worried for, Jack,' she said as if I had failed to comprehend the seriousness of the situation. 'Weeping Billy . . .' she checked again over my shoulder to watch out for him as she spoke, '. . . well, he's what you might call the jealous type.'

Weeping Billy Slade was a name I had heard uttered a lot ever since my return to London and not just from Lily. He was spoken about by my criminal acquaintances as if he was some jungle celebrity – a man-killing tiger best admired from the safety of a high branch. It was said that he had been born in Manchester and as a child had been put to work in the mills there before two of the smaller fingers on his left hand had been nipped off in the spindles. This explained why he was always seen gloved – the short nubs he was left with was disguised with wood what filled out the empty finger-sleeves and helped him to hold a blade steady. Part of the legend what surrounded him was that he had left for London soon afterwards but not before setting fire to the mill what had disfigured him.

He was now famous for running one of West London's most heavy-soldiered gangs what was into every dark activity considered profitable. A large part of his criminal income though was through bawdy work and he operated out of a brothel in Hammersmith called Molly Gay's. This place was notorious for providing its affluent clientele with a higher standard of harlot then they would find in the pubs and back alleys of the rookeries and these fair maidens was known as Slade girls. Lily had been a Slade girl until I had stolen her away and it's never been considered a smart move to steal from a crook bigger than yourself. Lily had spent enough time in his company and she had witnessed many terrible acts of violence what he had meted out to those who crossed him and so if she thought he was worth running away from then perhaps she was right. But later, when we was sat together in a tearoom some distance from the fair, I did my best to convince her that she was fretting for nothing.

'I should think,' I assured her with a mouthful of sponge, 'that if a man like him meant us any harm he'd have done it by now. And if Morris Bolter has told him who I am,' I shrugged with little attempt at self-effacement, 'then he won't be bothering us no further.'

Lily sipped her tea and said nothing.

Chapter 6

The Undertaker's Apprentice

*Wherein I receive a visitor and hear a name
what I do not much care for*

Pebbles tapped against the window pane at Five Fingers Court and I felt Lily's hand stroke the hairs on my chest. 'That queer girl must be here again,' she murmured before rolling onto her side away from my half of the bed. I reached over to the bedside chest and grabbed my pocket watch as I told Lily that she needn't get up. I would take Tom into the kitchen and boil a kettle while she slept on, I promised, and we would be gone before eleven. Tom and I had planned to spend the day scouting the genteel districts for the next set of houses to crack – always a more complicated business than the layman might imagine – and I was expecting her at about half past ten. So I was most surprised to see that the little hand of my ticker had not yet crossed the eight and I concluded that either the dratted thing needed winding or this was not Tom outside in the courtyard after all.

I lifted my head from the pillow, searched for where I had left my underclothes and – once I was halfway decent – crossed to the window. Just as I did so another pebble hit the pane, this one thrown with such force it almost cracked the glass.

'Tell her careful,' scowled Lily from the bed. 'We've got neighbours.'

'It ain't Tom,' I replied as I looked through the curtains and down onto the goblin-faced pelter who was stood in the courtyard grinning up at me. He was wearing the same suit he had on at the fair two days before this and he had a newspaper under his arm. 'It's Morris Bolter.'

I heard Lily's rustle as she sat up in bed behind me and I lifted up the window to ask this country cock why he was disturbing me at so unsociable an hour. Did he not know that most burglars was getting home from work around this time?

'Bolter?' Lily whispered as I popped my head out of the window. 'Don't invite him in.'

'Morning, Morris,' I greeted him with affected conviviality. 'Good job you told me you was down there. I've a full bed pan up here and was just about to empty it out onto that very spot. Would've made a right mess of your nice suit.' Bolter's laugh was short and weak.

'Yer a funny one, Dodger. That's what I likes about yer. Always funny.'

'What can I do you for?'

'It's what I can do *you* for, eh, young squire?' he chuckled and winked, his country accent still rough as ever. 'A friendly call, you might say, but with some business attached. Gonna let me up?'

'No!' Lily hissed from behind.

'What sort of business?' I asked. Bolter squirmed.

'Not the sort I'd like to declare for the whole vicinity to hear,' he said. 'But profitable. Very profitable. I also got some information what I know would be of interest to yer. Something I discovered while flicking through this.' He held up his copy of the *Morning Chronicle*.

'Yeah?' I squinted hard but could not make out the headline from where I was. 'I'm impressed that a rube like you can even read such a fancy paper. They teach letters in the provinces, do they?'

Bolter's smile dropped and he tucked the paper under his arm again. 'I's a charity boy,' he said in a hiss. 'So I'd wager this gives me more education than most around here. And I knows enough to know the name of an old enemy when I chances upon it in print.'

'You'll have to narrow that down,' I said thinking on some of the many rumours I had heard about his work as an informer. 'I hear you've got countless.'

'Not just an enemy of mine,' he smiled again, enjoying knowing something what I did not. 'An enemy of yourn an' all.'

'I'm a well-loved member of the community,' I replied and looked around the courtyard to make sure he was alone. 'I ain't got no enemies. Who you on about?'

'The name I found in this morning's paper,' he said tapping it with his long fingernails, 'is one I hear tell that you have very little love for.' And then he said two words what never failed to capture my attention.

'Come in for some tea, Morris,' I told him before shutting the window. 'I'll be down in one second.' Then I turned around to get dressed and saw Lily's hot stare burning into me. 'Sorry, Lil, but it sounds like he's got some news,' I explained as I hopped into some trousers.

'News about what?' she huffed.

'About Oliver Twist,' I replied as I made for the door.

'Oliver Brownlow,' said Bolter as he handed me the paper, 'is what he goes by nowadays. Take a look for yerself. Front page.'

The kettle was already on the bubble and we was both sat around our small kitchen table as he rubbed his hands with undisguised glee. I had forgotten how big his head was and yet how small his face. I folded out the sheet and read.

The *Morning Chronicle* was a dull paper and the article could not have been drier. It was all about changes what was occurring within the Metropolitan Police Service and my first thought was that Oliver must have become a peeler or something. I did not bother to read the story in detail and only scanned the text searching for his name but could not find it anywhere. I did however come across another familiar name what I did not much care for either. An Inspector Wilfred Bracken of E Division. He was the same officer what I had first encountered on my very first night back in England and who had been making a nuisance of himself ever since with his special brand of civic interference.

'This here Bracken is a holy terror,' I said as I read some lines about he and another high ranking officer called Mills was being tipped for promotion. 'He's forever crashing around the Seven Dials vicinity and harassing my gang as if we was the only villains in London.' I was vexed to be reading about his career achievements in a respectable news organ as, on top of everything else, he was also the very peeler what had arrested my mother some years before. He had told me this himself on our first meeting and boasted that this action had resulted in her death by hanging. 'Why are you showing me this, Morris?' I asked after I had poured us both another cup of coffee. What's it got to do with Oliver? Just point to the important bit so I can get on with my day.'

'You ain't reading it proper,' Bolter grinned and tapped the bottom of the page. 'Look again.'

And then I saw the words, right underneath the main story and printed in little italics.

Reported by Oliver Brownlow.

'Seems that our old friend Oliver has got hisself a profession,' Bolter sneered as he blowed the steam away from his mug. 'Journ'list.'

I said nothing for a short while as I drunk this information in and let it stir about inside. Bolter had been right to assume that this name would prick my interest. Oliver Twist – the sniveling workhouse boy what I had discovered all those years ago starving to death on the streets of London and who I had rescued out of pity – had indeed done well for himself if he was now writing for a reputable paper like the *Chronicle*. I recalled him being about a year younger than myself, making him now only twenty years of age, and I marvelled at what social elevation was possible for young orphans who peach upon their own class and get themselves adopted into a new one.

'Seems he's received a decent education an' all,' I sniffed as I searched the rest of the paper in vain for more information. Then I laughed at the strangeness of the discovery. 'The things that this city can sick up will always be a wonder to me.'

Ever since I had learnt that it was Oliver Twist what had been responsible for the destruction of Fagin, Nancy, Bill and the rest of the Saffron Hill collective I had been making a big noise about how I should like to settle him for their sakes. I had heard that he had been adopted by some rich old cove and that these two had been callous enough to visit Fagin in his Newgate cell on the night before his execution for no other imaginable reason than to gloat. But now that Morris Bolter had brought his name up again I realised that it had been over a year since I had made any concerted effort to track him down and make him sorry him for his crimes. I had been so busy and ambitious in recent times that I was ashamed by this reminder of my negligence upon the matter. I crumpled the paper up in frustration and tossed it back into Bolter's lap.

'Well, I recall why I hate the treacherous snake, Morris,' I said as I got up to search the cupboard to see if we still had any of those fancy biscuits left what I had stolen from that tea-shop. 'But what's your connection with him again?' Bolter sat up straight and smiled that sickening smile of his as I offered him a biscuit to dip in his drink. He had told me of his bad blood with Oliver before and seemed pleased to be given the chance to do so again.

'Why, I knew and hated the boy before any of yers,' he boasted. 'Back in Mudfog, the town where we both come from, we worked as apprentices in the same funeral home for a spell. He was under me and would not do as bid and so I said some nasty stuff about his whore mother – every word of it the truth – and he took it ill.' Bolter bared his yellow teeth and wheezed out laughter. 'Lashes out at me, would you warrant it? Well, I respond in kind and gave him the best thrashing of his young life. Ha Ha, Dodger, I wish yer'd a seen it. Yer'd a been cheering me on as I pounded him. Yer'd a been proud a' me!' He lifted up his free fist in triumph as if he wanted me to admire those spindly-looking arms. Why he thought I would be impressed to hear about him beating up a kinchin at least five years younger than himself was a mystery but I said nothing and let him continue. 'If only I'd a known that fine old Jew what I knows yer were so fond of earlier in life,' he then said in a more solemn manner. 'I'd a told him to tie young Oliver in a sack and chuck him into the Thames before all the trouble had begun. Mark it, Dodger, I hate that lad every bit as much as yer do, maybe more I reckon.' He gave me a long wink as the soggy half of his biscuit dropped into the mug. 'It's what we have in common.'

'Well, as ever, it's a delight seeing you again, Morris,' I said in an effort to hurry him along. I knew that Lily would still be hiding in the bedroom, her ear no doubt pressed against the wall and just willing me to show him the door. I had no desire myself to keep company with this writhing eel for any longer than need be and so I moved the conversation along. 'But, outside, you made some mention of business. You want to work for the Diallers, is that what this is about?'

'No, I do not,' he said as he tried to fish out the dropped biscuit from his cup. 'But I know a man who likes the Diallers to work for him.' It was painful watching him make a mess everywhere so I handed him a teaspoon to make the task simpler. 'D'yer recall seeing me at the fair this Saturday gone, Dodge?' he asked once his task was complete and he had deposited the wet biscuit remains onto the front page of the paper.

'I do,' I replied as I sipped my own coffee.

'Well then, I was most sorry to see yer take off so quick,' he said. 'I was hoping to make an introduction. Recall that man I was stood next to?' I nodded. 'Know who he is?'

'William Slade.'

'S'right,' he grinned. 'Weeping Billy Slade he goes by. I reckon your current fancy-woman woulda told yer all about him. I hear she and he was awful close once upon a time.' He whispered this, no doubt aware that Lily would be eavesdropping. In turn I raised my own voice so she could hear my reply.

'She's mentioned him, yeah,' I said, a picture of unconcern. 'Said she didn't much care for life in his bawdy house. She lives here now and if your Weeping Willy has an objection to it then tell him he can take it up with me. It can be pistols at dawn if fancies it.'

Bolter burst into laughter and told me how funny I was. 'An objection? Course he don't!' He wiped his eyes in mirth and hooted again. 'Billy Slade don't mean yer good lady no harm, Dodge,' he then declared as he slapped me on the knee. 'He's happy for the girl!' He was again speaking loud enough for Lily to hear and proceeded to explain how pleased his friend had been to see her again at the rope-dance. 'I's told him all about who yer are, Dodger, don't fret none. He knows yer a man to be respected, a man what'd make his old favourite good n' happy. Slade's all business and if he had time to go chasing after every harlot what walks out on him then he would not be as rich as he is. And is he rich?' Another wink. 'Oh, yessir! Yes indeed!'

I glanced over to the kitchen door and out in the hallway I was sure I saw the shadow of Lily listening in. I knew what a great relief all this would be to her and – I confess – I was glad to hear it myself.

'It ain't her he's interested in,' Bolter pointed his chewed fingernail at me, 'it's yer. He's heard all about yer activities as a cracksman, Dodge. Yer've a reputation, yer know yer have. And he likes what he's heard so much he's asked me to make yer an offer. An alliance,' Bolter smiled as he put his empty mug down, 'with Weeping Billy Slade. Just think on it, Dodger, yer'll be rich.' He began clapping his hands together like a maniac. 'It's yer lucky day all right!'

'You mean, he wants me to run his gang for him?' I asked uncertain of what was being offered. 'As top sawyer?'

Bolter stopped smiling and shook his head. 'Course not!' he snapped. 'He'd be top sawyer. Yer'd just be working for him, doing what yer do now and paying him half.' It was my turn to laugh.

'Tempting,' I said. 'But I'd much rather keep all my winnings for me. Thank Mr Slade for his interest though.'

'Yer don't unnerstand, Dodge,' Bolter persisted. 'There are benefits to being under his wing. But don't listen to me, come and hear Billy out. He explain things so much better.'

'Jack's got a gang of his own,' came Lily's voice from the doorway. 'He don't work for no others. Be a good dog and tell your master that.' She was standing in the room now in her greenest dress and with a fierce eye trained upon Bolter. He seemed to be most rattled by her aggressive manner and stood up from his stool.

'Oh, and this one speaks for yer, does she?' he asked me while keeping his eye fixed on her. 'Why, if my Charlotte thought to interfere in my business so I'd give her another black eye for her trouble.'

'And if I was your Charlotte, I'd give you two back,' Lily answered. 'Jack, show him downstairs.' Bolter turned to me, dumbfounded.

'Yer ain't gonna let a woman tell yer what to do, are yer?' he said. 'Yer yer own master, Dodge, say it's so.' I drained my mug, placed it on the table and smiled at him.

'Thanks for visiting, Morris,' I said all cheerful as I got up to see him out. 'I appreciate what you've told me about Oliver Twist. I always enjoy hearing about what my childhood chums are getting up to. Now fuck off before I open a window and throw you out. Head first.'

Tom Skinner had never heard of either Oliver Twist or Oliver Brownlow before and she seemed most uninterested in his journalistic career when I mentioned it in the drinking den several hours later. The offer from Billy Slade had made more of an impression upon her however and, like me, she did not trust it much.

'What benefits?' she asked after knocking back her third glass of White Fire gin. 'We ain't making enough as it is without giving half to some chancer from West London. Cheek of him!' She slammed the glass down onto the table and burped.

We had enjoyed a most productive afternoon scouting the suburban areas of London for warehouses to crack and had now retired to this splendid new gin palace in St Giles where we could discuss our findings at leisure. There was a particular well-stocked warehouse we had discovered near Hackney Wick and, after making some discreet enquiries from the porters what worked within, we had hatched a plan to get at the merchandise. Tom reckoned she was adept enough to sneak into the place during working hours and secrete herself behind some stock or up a chimney and stay there undetected until lock up. Then I would drive up with the large cart once it was good and dark, she would open the locks from the inside and, if we was quick, we would soon make off with a fine haul. Mouse would be needed to play crow and the whole venture was sure to be very profitable for all three of us.

'Imagine us,' I said to her, our voices covered by the hissing of the gas lamps, 'going to all that trouble and then handing over half of our findings to someone who ain't helped to lift one rug onto the cart. It's the laziness of it that would irk as much as anything.'

Tom agreed and so we finished our gin and made for the door. Outside we buttoned our coats underneath the fancy parapet as the dark was already starting to draw in. It was early evening but I was keen to get home so we made to say farewell. But, just as we was tipping each other the hat, we heard a deep male voice calling from the other side of the road.

'Mr Dawkins! Miss Skinner!'

We looked over to see the tall silhouette of a man approaching from the other side of the street. In the dark we could make out his deep scarlet coat and a large carriage was tied up behind him which two other men was climbing out of.

'There you both are,' he puffed and rubbed his large gloved hands together in a genial way. 'A little birdie told me you was here. I'm glad I caught you before you left, I do hate wasted journeys.'

As he grew closer I saw from the gaslight of the gin-house that it was the same man from the fair. He was the only one of the three who was smiling. There was something of the circus about him – he was all teeth and bravado like a lion tamer – and I knew that he was setting Tom as much on her guard as he was me. 'My name is William Slade,' he continued as he reached us, 'and I know both of you gents by reputation. It is *Miss* Skinner, isn't it?' he said tipping his hat towards Tom. 'I was told that you sometimes prefer to be called *Mister* and, if so, I'll be happy to oblige in future. How do you do?'

He offered her his hand and, after she had shaken it without much enthusiasm, he then shook mine. I could feel those wooden nubs I had heard about inside the glove. The other two men – both of which was wearing matching red bowlers – began to position themselves either side of us so we could not run off. 'I would like to convey to you my apologies,' Slade continued, 'for sending a certain Morris Bolter to your address this morning. Mr Bolter is a maladroit individual who is apt to give a false impression. I fear that he may have miscommunicated the friendly nature of my invitation.'

I admired his speaking style. His accent had something of the north about it but he knew his way around the dictionary and I made a note to look up the word maladroit at the earliest opportunity.

'And it *is* still an invitation,' he went on. 'In fact, I've come here tonight to impress upon you the agreeable nature of the kindly offered hand.'

'Well there was no harm done, Mr Slade,' I said back. 'And if you want to stop by the Three Cripples one night this week then I'll be glad to stand you a glass of gin. It's in Saffron Hill and we can discuss any business you would care to at length.'

'Better yet,' Slade said as he raised his cane up and tapped it against my right shoulder before I could leave. 'Why not come with me to Hammersmith now. I own a house there, perhaps you've heard of it. It's called Molly Gay's.'

I hesitated and looked to Tom who was having her own path of escape blocked by the red bowler on the left. Slade's grin had widened enough for it to start to look painful.

'It has a very relaxing atmosphere, I think you'll find,' he continued, 'and – while still friendly – this invitation is also insistent.' Tom looked back at me and shrugged. It was clear that this was not an offer we could afford to go on ignoring.

'Please yourself, Mr Slade,' I sighed with much reluctance. 'Let's take a trip west then, shall we?' He looked most pleased and nodded as if he had been expecting no other answer. Then waved his hand towards the carriage as if we had won it in a tombola.

'Very good,' he announced as we was led towards the cab and he opened up the door for us. 'I think you'll find the trip will be to everyone's gratification.'

Tom and myself was then bundled into the vehicle and sat crushed between the two heavy men. Slade meanwhile climbed into the driver's seat, took the reins himself and sped the horses westwards through the city.

Chapter 7

How to Sin

Relating the events surrounding my first formal visit to the
house of Molly Gay

It is often claimed — and always by the sort of authoritative coves what would seem to have conducted the census themselves — that there are as many brothels throughout the city of London as there are public-houses. And considering the sort of rough rookeries what I was most familiar with — Saffron Hill, St Giles, Seven Dials, Whitechapel — I would have thought that this was even a low estimate. Round my way every second abode rented out rooms to pragmatic ladies of industry and their many dependents but a fellow would sometimes have to turn two street corners before finding somewhere decent to drink. But it was also well known that if you moved outward from the heart of the metropolis — and away from London's glittering West End — then houses of ill-repute do become more scattered, rare and mysterious. By the time Slade's carriage had thundered through the main thoroughfare of Kensington and had entered into the streets of Hammersmith, I was already beginning to wonder if any of these more genteel houses we was passing could ever be the lair of such a notorious bawd. With their black cast-iron boundary rails, white-painted frontages and well-kept flower gardens none of them seemed to betray the barest hint of shame.

'Woah there!' we heard Slade cry as the horses reared up in a pretty lane close to the riverside. 'Miss Molly Gay's, gentlemen! House of pleasure!' I was surprised by the boldness of this announcement – he did not seem to care if the whole neighbourhood heard. Although it was dark now we could still see that the house we was being led towards was as modest as every other in the vicinity, with a paved path of little red and black tiles winding through the rose garden and up towards the tall front door. The drawn curtains however was deep crimson and we could hear from within the sounds of sweet female laughter and stringed music. So this, I thought perplexed as I tried to see what was going on inside the lighted front parlour through the crack in the curtains, is the hellish place from where Lily had fled. It looked from the outside to be so much more pleasant than where she had ended up.

The door bore the brass image of a goblin woman's face with the knocker in its mouth to which Slade pointed after rapping on it. 'See that,' he explained to Tom and myself as we waited on the steps behind him, 'it's supposed to be Queen Victoria. Looks nothing like her, does it?'

'I dunno,' said Tom. 'I can see the likeness.'

I was expecting to be received by Molly Gay herself or perhaps by one of the girls what worked there. And, though I had no mind to lie with any others while Lily was my woman, I must confess to feeling some excitement as I heard the chains being unlatched from within. Considering the reputation of this establishment I could only assume that I was about to be presented, as the door swung open most soft, with some of the most heavenly harlots that this great city had to offer. I straightened my hat in anticipation of what delights was about to greet us.

'Yer here, then,' said Morris Bolter as he peered out from the light of the doorway, his scowling face even uglier than the one on the knocker. He was holding an over-filled brandy glass and swirling the liquid as he eyed me with contempt. 'I knew he'd get yer afore long, Dodger,' he sneered as if he had just won some imagined victory over me. 'Hope yer've left the shrew at home and bought some manners with yer this time.'

'Move out of it, Morris,' Slade said as he pushed inside first and made the former charity boy stagger backwards into the hall and spill brandy over his shirt. 'You're not to be answering doors or helping yourself to the drinks cabinet, eh? Gentlemen of quality do not wish to see your ugly person when entering a house of sin. It'd put them off, I should think.' Bolter looked about for something to wipe the brown stain as Slade turned and welcomed us across the threshold. '*Messrs* Dawkins and Skinner are important guests,' he declared in his theatrical way, 'and will be treated accordingly.'

The reception room was warm and wide and its rich-patterned carpet went all the way to and up the staircase. A grandfather clock ticked away against the wall and various instruments of nautical interest hung from the walls. I had burgled many a home as fine and as fashionable as this one but never before had I been invited into one as a guest. The man who followed Tom and myself into the house shut the door behind us before taking our coats and hats. There was a number of hatstands along this hallway and I noticed some more of those curious red bowlers hanging from them. Slade meanwhile continued to bully Morris Bolter for what appeared to be our amusement.

'I don't recall telling you to make yourself comfortable, Morris,' he said as he snatched the brandy glass away from the smaller man. 'You've enough chores to keep you occupied until doomsday, I would've thought. Where is Miss Gay? She should be here to greet our callers.'

'She's upstairs,' Bolter sniffed after producing a handkerchief and rubbing at the spillage. 'Getting painted again. Yer asked me to greet the *gentlemen*, remember?' He glanced over at Tom as he said this and curled his lip. Then he lowered his voice and addressed Slade in a dark manner. 'While yer other men are down at the bottom of the garden,' his smile was cruel as he whispered. 'Seeing to yer guests.'

'Very good,' nodded Slade and then turned to give Tom and myself a small bow. 'I have some quick business I must attend to in the outhouse, gentlemen. Perhaps meanwhile Mr Bolter will show you through to the sitting room,' he pointed towards the shut door behind where the peculiar string music was heard, 'and you will have whatever you desire.' Another toothy grin cracked out across his face. 'We serve all the poisons.'

So that is what a harp sounds like, I thought, as we was led into the plush and smoky sitting room and saw what was making such an agreeable sound. I had often seen such things illustrated in books but until now I had no idea of their tallness and just how marvellous they sounded when played by someone with talent. In the far corner of the well-furnished room was a gifted young lady, dressed only in a loose bedsheet and holding onto the neck of her instrument with one hand while strumming at the strings with the other. She was being ogled by one ancient old gent from the settee opposite who looked old enough to have been born when togas was in fashion. This pug-nosed fellow puffed on his cigar and paid neither Tom nor me any mind as we sat ourselves on nearby chairs. There was also two more half-dressed young ladies draped either side of the old reprobate and one was filling up his flute glass with more champagne.

'We'll have some bubbles an' all please, Morris,' I said to Bolter as he slouched over to the drinks cabinet in his sullen way. 'The best you got.' I pulled over a fancy foot-rest and stretched out on the chair as he popped open another cork and muttered to himself.

He must have been most disgruntled to be serving me after the unpleasantness of our last meeting and was doing little to disguise it. 'Take a sip yourself if you care to,' I went on pretending to ignore his attitude. 'I won't tell no one.'

The door opened behind us and I turned to see what lovely visions was approaching us. But even if I had of been entertaining wicked thoughts about betraying Lily in this den of iniquity – which I swear I never was – then they was soon dashed when I saw what was being offered. It was two girls, both very pretty and smiling all sweet with their powdered faces and little night-dresses on. The eldest of the two came up to where I was sitting and enquired whether or not I wanted company for the night. She could not have been older than twelve.

'No thank you, dear,' I replied in a thin voice. 'You run along and play.'

They turned and left the room again and I looked back to Bolter in disgust. 'Not funny, Morris,' I said. 'They was kinchins.' He sniggered as he poured the champagne glasses to the brim and brought them over.

'They're the newest,' he said as he handed the first glass to Tom. 'And they gotta learn on someone, ain't they? I'd wager yer Lily was about that age when she first went to work here.'

Bolter was sort of creature what was begging to be punched in the face at the best of times and so I was all fixed to stand up and oblige him then and there. The other champagne glass was still in his outstretched hand and he was waiting for me to take it. I just stared back at him and thought on how satisfying it would be to drag him over to the harp and shove him through it like a slicer. Bolter sensed my aggression and altered his tone.

'There's others upstairs, yer know,' he told me with a less steady voice. 'Older ones. Yer can have whatever yer care for, Dodge. It's like the man said – we got all the poisons.'

It was Tom who broke the silence.

'We're thieves, Bolter,' she told him after taking a strong swig of her champagne. 'And we don't pay for nothing. We got women at home what sleep with us for the pleasure of it – something I doubt you could ever boast of. Now give me a refill and run off. We're both sick of the sight of you.'

Bolter scowled back at her and looked ready to retaliate with his own verbal assault but – before we was treated to what no doubt would have been a glorious display of silver-tongued gallantry towards the opposite sex – he was interrupted by the door swinging open again. From the perturbed look on Bolter's face, we was once again in the presence of the master of the house.

'Morris, Morris, Morris,' Slade said with a small chuckle. 'Hospitality just isn't your gift is it, old son? But then I find myself wondering – as I often have before – just what on Earth your true gifts could ever be.' He stepped across the room and waved off Bolter's attempts to defend himself as he took the champagne glass from out of his hand and took a sip. 'Introductions, I suppose,' he then said as he turned and looked towards Tom and myself. 'I never would have known that the striking young man at the dance last week was the famous Artful Dodger if you hadn't been there to enlighten me. But beyond that you're really just a waste of skull and bones.'

Slade winked at me then and – in spite of my wariness of the man – I found myself smiling back at him. There was a natural presence about him in close proximity, a charisma what I had not been ready for. I wanted him to like me even though I had been told many repulsive things about his cruelty by Lily and had just moments before been outraged by the age of the children he set to work. He was an evil bugger, this was plain, but then so was most of the people I had grown up with so I struggled to hold it against him. I envied his clothing, the black waistcoat he had on looked expensive and the shirt was a fine cut while his whiskers was thick but well-barbered. I was even finding the northern accent to be somehow exotic.

'It's a nice crib you got here, Mr Slade,' I said by way of conversation. 'I'll give you that. You must be doing well for yourself.'

'I keep the wolf at bay,' he said and smiled at some men what had entered the room behind him. 'And you can call me Billy if you don't mind me going by Christian names also, Jack,' he nodded and then looked to my lieutenant, 'and Tom. I've heard good things.'

'It's Jack if you like, Billy,' I said. 'But my real friends call me Dodger.' I felt a small wince of guilt as soon as I said that. I was glad that Lily could not see me being so free with her old bawd.

'Dodger, then,' Slade grinned back at me.

Slade then signalled for those girls to take the elderly man upstairs now to where a more comfortable room had been prepared and the harpist was told to stop playing and leave us too. Once these had all left us Slade had his men move the furniture around so we could sit in a circle and discuss our business while Bolter stoked the fire and fetched more drinks. Slade poured the champagne he had taken out into a nearby pot plant and commanded that he wanted the decanter of brandy brought over with some glasses – for him, his two guests but not for Bolter himself. 'I can't bear to see more spillage,' he said rolling his eyes towards us. I noticed that he did not ask us if we cared to switch drinks – it seemed that if Weeping Billy was drinking brandy then we all was.

'Before we get into things I would like to raise a toast,' said Slade once Tom and I was seated on the settee what was still perfumed from the prostitutes. 'To clear up any confusion for one thing.' Bolter had poured out the glasses by now and retreated to the corner of the room while we waited for Slade to raise his glass. 'There was a misunderstanding at the fair I think. When Lily — the girl you were dancing with and who used to reside in this establishment — saw me looking at you both. I fear from the way that she reacted that she must be under the impression that I'm holding some sort of grudge against her for running out as she did. And it is irksome when a whore who owes me her income behaves in such a way, I will confess. But I want to impress upon you, Dodger, that bygones are most certainly bygones where that direction is concerned. I hold no malice against your girl, I even have fond recollections of her time here. She was always too nice for this place anyhow and I was glad to learn from Morris that she now resides with a successful a crim such as I hear you to be. You make a nice couple I think.' His ungloved hand raised the glass up and stared at me with a face I found unreadable. 'To Lily Lennox,' he said, 'a fine escort for a fine thief.'

Tom looked towards me to see whether she should do likewise. I waited a beat, to eye Slade and make him see that I considered his declaration important, before raising mine too.

'To Lily, then,' I said and held his gaze hard, 'and to her continued good health.'

Tom echoed the words and we all drank from our glasses as one. Once this was done Slade seemed to relax and unbuttoned his waistcoat. One of his men produced a silver cigar box and offered one to each of us as Bolter walked over with some matches. Then, once we was comfortable, Slade came at last to the business at hand.

'In the criminal underworld of London today,' he announced as if it was from a speech he had prepared earlier, 'there is no thief more famous than the Artful Dodger, or Dodger of the Dials as he sometimes goes by. Even when still a young lad, I am often told, the Dodger was greatly admired for his dexterity with an open pocket. Is that not right, Morris?'

'So they say,' sniffed Bolter.

'In all honesty,' Slade said with a wink, 'knowing that this very evening I was to meet the legendary thief myself I almost considered leaving my more valued items at home locked up.' He followed this with a mighty laugh. 'And we'll be sure to check the silver on his way out, eh, Morris?'

I shrugged in mock-humility and told them that they was making me blush. But Slade told me to save my false modesty because this was just the beginning of the wonderful things he had heard regarding all things me.

'Because in the last year your reputation as a burglar has eclipsed even that of the late Bill Sikes, bless his departed soul. It's said in some circles that you've turned simple house-breaking into an art form, Dodger. That you move through great homes like a ghost does and empty it of all that is priceless. Even well-to-do gentlemen, so I'm told, have begun approaching you and paying you to steal items on demand and that you charge high figures for performing such services. It's said that what you earn from these activities is beyond that of any other cracksman in the land and that your Diallers,' here he turned his attention away from me and towards Tom, 'are as brilliant as they are loyal. And I hear that a certain Tom Skinner is invaluable to you.'

He turned back to me to see if I would deny anything he had said. I did not.

'What you have heard is accurate, Billy,' I said trying to look unaffected by his tribute. 'You are indeed in the presence of a fantastic pair of thieves.'

Slade chuckled at this and said he was glad to hear it. Then

Slade looked over to Bolter and gave him a small signal that I did not understand. 'Fantastic is right,' he then continued. 'If what I hear about your adventures is true then you're also daring and audacious, ambitious and clever. Qualities I value very highly.'

Behind me I could hear Bolter creeping from one end of the room to the other. I felt a sudden terror that we was being set up for an attack and turned to see what he was up to. He had reached a small office desk and was unlocking one of the drawers with a small key. Was he about to produce a weapon, I panicked, and come at us from behind?

'But let me ask you this,' Slade continued trying to force my attention away from him. 'The one burning question. A question that rather begs itself actually. If the two of you are so very ingenious, if the Diallers are some of the highest earning thieves in the capital, a claim you do not deny, then why, oh why, are you both so very poor?'

I turned back to face Slade as his voice had dropped on that last word. His smile was still fixed onto his face but there was a menace there now, a hard challenge.

'We ain't poor,' I replied while I stared him down. 'And we're getting richer all the time. You'll see.'

'Not what I hear,' said Slade and now all the lightness and humour had vanished from him. 'Not this time. I hear you can't hold on to anything, that's your trouble. I hear that you're London's most admired thieves, yes, but I do not hear that you are its most feared. Not by a long road.'

'Whoever it is what's told you that we ain't feared,' said Tom from beside me, 'they never say such things to our faces. Most peculiar that.'

'Good in a fight, are you, Tom?'

'Very good,' she replied. 'So's Dodge.'

'How many you killed then? Either of you?'

There was a sharp pause. Neither of us said anything in return.

'Come on,' Slade persisted and then looked at me. 'How many people you put in the ground? Or am I to believe that the great Artful Dodger is still, to use the language of the fox-hunter, unblooded?'

Morris Bolter now came around to where he was sitting with what he had fetched from the desk. It was a brown parcel and as his master took it from him I noticed with great unease how much Bolter was enjoying this part of the evening. He knew something I did not and his wicked smile wanted me to know it. Slade began unwrapping the parcel.

'I thought so,' he went on. 'It's another thing people say about you but this time it's never as a compliment. Means you're soft and that if you have something worth taking then why not go ahead and take it. They'll be no recriminations. Dodger hasn't the stomach for it.'

I saw the light of the fire catch upon the diamonds as they spilled out from the parcel and into Slade's clutches. He held the necklace out between his two mismatched hands so there was no mistaking it.

'Or at least that's the word on the street,' Slade smiled as he took in the surprised reactions of his two guests. 'Correct me if I'm wrong.'

'The Lady of Stars!' I cried in outrage.

'So you're the devils what took it!' Tom leapt up from her seat in a second and reached over to grab it back but one of Slade's henchmen was up first and he shoved her back down again with some force.

'Now, now,' Slade said with a stony stare. 'No snatching. Not in this house.'

I looked at the stolen necklace in Slade's hands and wondered at how it could just reappear here like a watch in a magic trick, and suddenly I felt very angry at seeing it again. That object was to have been our fortune, or at least the beginnings of it, and now here was Slade boasting of how he had swiped it from us. In just a few short seconds I had gone right off him.

'I did not steal anything from you, young Thomas,' Slade announced as if offended by the suggestion. 'Nor would I employ any who would, as it's not my way to steal from other thieves. No, I merely heard about your misfortune from someone connected to the Seven Dials community. I was very angered when I heard about the travesty, I don't like to hear of clever thieves being ambushed by dumb ones. It feels unnatural somehow. So I made my own more forceful enquiries about who did take it, enquiries that I'm happy to say where more fruitful than any you may have launched.'

'You're saying that you found them?' I asked not disguising my distrust. 'The Turpins? You tracked them down and got it off them.'

'I did indeed,' Slade said. 'They headed up north as soon as they stole the necklace from you, so my sources told me, and so I had some of my lads pursue them. As you can see the hunt was a success. They hadn't even got that far.'

As I peered closer towards the necklace I noticed that there was something different about it from when it was last in my possession. It was stained around the edges with something dark. Something red.

'I wonder,' Slade said as he folded the necklace back into the brown paper and got to his feet, 'whether you care to meet them for yourselves. These Turpins, the ones we dragged back here.

Two of them are in the outhouse at the far end of the garden, I've just been checking on them a moment ago. Let's reunite you.'

This outhouse was small, made of orange bricks and set deep into the furthest part of the long back-garden, hidden from view by some over-hanging trees. Slade held out a black light as he led us down a path while explaining that he liked to have a place of business what was far away from the bawdy house. 'The cries that come out of this little hideaway,' he said as we came up to the green door and knocked twice, 'would make too strong a contrast with those that come from the main house.'

Some light rain had begun to fall which did nothing to calm my nerves. I was already wary of heading into this low building with Slade and this was made worse when I noticed that there was no decent windows to the place, just air shafts and small gaps in the walls what had iron bars across them and was boarded from the inside. Even though there was now four men escorting us there through the drizzle, including Bolter, I still rebelled when the door was opened from within by another henchman in a red bowler hat.

'We ain't going with you,' I said as I saw that there was a few steps inside what led downwards to a lowered concrete floor. There was candlelight flickering from within and I could hear some muffled groaning and rasps. 'You can't make us. If you don't like it then we can have it out now but Tom and I don't go down without a fight. We'll make an almighty racket that even your neighbours won't ignore.'

Slade paused and looked at me. His eyes then glanced over to Bolter and then back again as if he was considering taking us in by force. Then he spoke to me like a long-suffering parent making bargains with an unreasonable child.

'I'm sorry you don't trust me yet, Dodger,' he sighed. 'The

whole purpose of this exercise is to win that trust and I see I still have a long way to go. Well then. Why don't we let Tom Skinner go home and then you come in without her? That way should you never return from inside – or whatever else is disturbing your imagination – then she can inform any interested parties where you were last seen? It's a shame as I was hoping for her to join us but if it will make you feel more secure . . .'

I looked to Tom who agreed that she would go straight back to the rookeries and alert my whole gang to my current whereabouts. I did not doubt that she would get there safe as she was always most adept at losing shadows and unwelcome escorts.

'If any harm should come to our top sawyer, Mr Slade,' Tom said, who it seems had decided against using Christian names with him, 'then you'll learn just how frightening our mob can be when our backs are up. This place, by way of instance,' she thumbed the bawdy house behind her, 'will become an urgent fire hazard if we don't get Jack back.'

I expected Slade to flinch at this bold threat but instead he just nodded in approval. 'Oh, Tom,' he smirked, 'such flaming passion. I do hope Dodger and I come to some arrangement because you're someone I would very much like to know better. Off you go then.'

With that, Tom tipped her hat and headed back up the garden and around the house while I steeled myself to continue into the outhouse. The biggest henchman entered first, bobbing his head under the low doorway, and then Bolter followed. Slade held out his hand for me to go next. 'Very well, William,' I said as I prepared to enter the dark hovel, 'let's meet the Turpins again.'

Candle lamps was lit all around the walls of the inside of this dark dungeon but it still took me some moments before my eyes could adjust to the place. There was a stench of wood shavings and something else unpleasant and the air was thin. The candles illuminated many sharp metal gardening tools what was hung around the walls and in the centre of the room was two men tied to wooden chairs. These two was the groaners and raspers what I had heard from outside and Slade circled them as the rest of his gang entered the outhouse behind me and shut the door. The bound men had their mouths gagged with these thick foul-looking rags and both of their faces was bleeding and bruised in a way what I could never imagine healing. Some string circled their necks.

'Don't pity them, Dodger,' said Slade in a severe voice. He no doubt saw the look of horror what must have been on my face and stepped towards the small man on the left to reach behind him. 'They're your enemies, don't forget.' Then he pulled up the bent three-cornered hat what had been dangling on the string and placed it upon the man's head. 'This fellow calls himself Dick. But I believe he goes by Fergal when he's not pointing pistols at brother thieves.'

I looked at the little man what had been so brazen on that afternoon in the Temple when his face had been hidden by a mask. Now he looked more beaten than anyone I had ever encountered.

'The other men who robbed you,' Slade sniffed as I stared at the damage what had been done to them, 'are dead. It's no more than they deserve I think you'll agree. These two have taken an almighty punishment but they might still walk out of here alive if you want it. What do you think?'

'His teeth,' I stammered in distaste. 'You've smashed them right in.'

Slade looked surprised at this and turned to the big henchman. 'I don't think we did,' he said in an uncertain way. 'Did we?'

'No, Mr Slade,' the man relied like a sergeant-major. 'His mouth was like that when we found him.'

Then the little man in the chair, this Fergal, jerked towards me and swore something as more blood sprayed from his mouth. His face was so damaged and his breathing so heavy that only the 'fecks' and 'eedjits' was intelligible.

'Ha!' said Slade who seemed to understand every word. 'Fergal here said you did that yourself when he took the necklace from you. Hit him with a stick or something.'

'Oh yeah,' I said, remembering how I had struck him in the mouth with my bird cane. 'So I did.' All of Slade's henchman laughed at this and Slade himself crossed over to me and patted my shoulder.

'So you are worth something in a fight after all,' he said. 'Good for you.' Then he leaned into my ear and spoke in a mocking whisper. 'But even that didn't stop him from taking your necklace now, did it?'

Then he began to unwrap the brown parcel again and held out the Lady of Stars so we could all see it sparkle under the lamplight. Slade's own face was shadowed and when he spoke next it was with a cold, hard edge. 'You're the very worst kind of thief, you know that? The worst kind.'

I could think of nothing to say. I was shocked by this sudden attack against my criminal prowess after all the complimentary things he had been saying about me up in the bawdy house. I was at a loss as to how to retaliate considering how I was all alone in this dismal place and surrounded by only his crew and these two battered Turpins. But when he spoke next I realised that it was not me he was looking at.

'You listening, Irishman?' he spat at the hapless Fergal. 'Crooks like you make me sick. You're barbarians. Jumping out on superior thieves like Mr Dawkins here who is trying to make a craft of the thing and snatching what he's earned like a selfish child. You're just not part of the community, are you?'

'Community?' Fergal exclaimed and laughed back with bitterness. He was forming his words better now but there was still plenty of fire in him. 'What community? He's a thief, I'm a thief! What's it to you?'

As soon as he finished speaking, a fist smashed into the side of his head and the chair toppled to the floor. I winced at the sight of it. I had taken some beatings myself in my time – not least during my spell in that Australian penal colony – but it was clear that that experience was nothing compared to the suffering Fergal had been enduring.

'See what I mean,' Slade sighed at me as his men then went to prop Fergal's chair upright again. 'He just doesn't see it. He doesn't understand how greatly things are changing throughout this city and how his sort of behaviour just won't do anymore.' Slade turned his back on Fergal and gave me his full attention. 'London has altered even within our own lifetimes, Dodger. And there is real potential for people in our line of work to advance ourselves if we get organised.' His men wiped the blood away from the faces of both Turpins as he spoke. 'After all, the police have sorted themselves out, haven't they? Some criminals hate the peelers but I don't. I respect them in all honesty. I'm old enough to remember the old Bow Street Runners and they were a shambles. Different police in different districts, none of them with any clue as to what the others were doing. Nobody paid them any mind and it was chaos out there. Anyone could be a criminal in those days, there was no separating the talented ones – such as us – from the savages – such as Fergal here. It was easy. Not so under the peelers. They're like an army, an urban army, so much more sophisticated and effective. They have these different divisions but they share information, help each other out. You've got your different ranks – with the constables taking orders from the sergeants who take orders from the inspectors and then there are the superintendents at the top. And it all runs so smooth. I mean, look how scared of them we all are. What I'm getting at is, Dodge – why don't we do likewise? Join forces. Work together as one for the benefit of all. That's the thought I'd like you to take away from tonight.'

'You want us to behave like the peelers?' I said and in spite of the miserable environment I could not help but be amused at the thought. 'With me as one of your constables, I suppose? I don't know about that, Billy. I ain't one for taking orders.'

'A constable?' Slade laughed. 'No, I wouldn't insult you with such a lowly station. I brought you here tonight because I thought you'd like to run your own division. The Seven Dials division. Your rank would be more akin to an inspector if anything. You'd be doing everything you do now with your gang, but as part of a wider community of thieves and under my protection. Take this,' he shook the necklace under my nose knowing full well how much I wanted it back. 'You stole it. But someone stole it from you. Then I, the wider community, got it back. If you want to take it away tonight and move it on then I'm happy to let you. But I get half. That's what I mean by community.'

I hesitated before answering but I already knew I would accept that offer. I could not afford to pass up on returning the promised prize to Percival after all, as it would strengthen my reputation as a professional thief, a reputation what had been damaged after the attack of the Turpins. But I hated the idea of giving someone like Slade a share of all my future findings and so was reluctant to enter into a continuing arrangement with him.

'Well that's too bad, Dodger,' Slade replied after I had told him that I was not interested in a long-standing partnership but would be happy to do business with him this one time. He withdrew the hand with the necklace in and his manner became much more threatening. 'Too bad, because you're either agreeing to work under my protection or you're not under my protection at all. That's the way of it. I'd be sensible and choose the former if I were you. The Turpins, for example, are not under my protection and things aren't sweet for them.'

The hint was unsubtle and I could dismiss it no longer. I was on the verge of making a very powerful enemy if I did not make a friend of him first and one look at Fergal's face was enough to convince me I had no other choice. It was clear that Slade saw himself as some sort of high-ranking thief who should be profiting from all the efforts of those below him and that there was serious consequences for those who refused to play along.

'So I'd be head of the Dials division?' I asked trying to make sense of the offer. 'And I'd be paying upwards to you as my superintendent of sorts?'

'Oh no, Dodger,' Slade scoffed. 'I'm more of a commissioner in this scenario. None higher.'

'And I get what in return?'

'You get to be a Slade man, that's what. Meaning that people like him,' Slade pointed at Fergal, 'won't ever make the mistake of crossing you again. Because in doing that they'd be crossing me. If you agree to these terms then the word will soon get out and you'll be treated different, I promise you. Respected more. Like I said back in the house, your gang aren't killers which is why nobody fears you, but that will change if you fly under my wing. Everybody knows what I'm capable of.'

Slade walked over to the bigger Turpin, the one who had been silent all this time, and grabbed his hair.

'And the other benefit is shared information.' He shook this Turpin's head all rough like he expected the neck to snap. Then he held his hand out to Bolter who passed him something as though he had been waiting for the signal. It was a sharp, gleaming blade. 'As with the peelers,' Slade continued as he placed the blade under the man's neck, 'we'll exchange our knowledge between divisions. By way of for instance, this fellow here told us an awful lot earlier on while we were slapping him around. About how his gang knew that your gang possessed that priceless necklace in the first place.' He scraped the man's neck with the blade – light enough not to cut. 'Perhaps you would like to know which of your associates betrayed you, Dodger?' he smirked as he slid the blunt edge across the man's throat and watched him tremble in terror. 'I know.'

'Tell me then,' I asked, disturbed by whatever he might be about to reveal. But I was horrified that he might cut the man's throat in front of my face and just wishing that he would leave him be.

'No, Dodger,' Slade said and at last stepped away from his victim. 'Not while we don't have a deal. But I'll say this, you won't like it much. Your house is in a mess, old son. There is a nasty leak. And leaks need plugging.'

There was no use hiding how unsettled I was by both this comment and by the whole proposal. But I considered what advantages there might be from forging such an alliance and I had to admit it made sense for me. Because Billy had been right earlier when he had said that other criminals did not fear me enough. I was no Bill Sikes and hurting people was not a talent I could boast of possessing. True, I had been in countless street-fights but I was no killer and villains tend to notice weaknesses like that after a time. That's why the Turpins did what they did and why somebody betrayed me. I was not a man with the reputation of doing the things that Slade had built a whole outhouse for and this was why he was richer and more successful. Here I was, for instance, witnessing the torture of men who I had every reason to hate, and there was still something in me that wished that they would be spared and that we could all just come to some sensible arrangement and go home. I was most ashamed of this softness I had when it came to matters of blood and if I was going to better myself, to advance as a modern criminal in the new age, then I needed to inspire the sort of fear that only true men of violence are capable of. That was the only way I would ever find myself living the sort of monied life I had always coveted. I needed to ally myself to someone more dangerous.

'Very well, Billy,' I said after some moments' consideration while the Turpins struggled in their chairs some more. 'I'm in.'

Slade clapped his hands together in satisfaction and chuckled. He turned to Bolter and handed him back the knife.

'It seems that Fergal and his cousin can leave here alive after all,' he instructed as he placed his hand around my shoulder again. 'Because I want them to spread the word about Dodger here. He's ours now. They need to tell people that.' Then he raised his good hand again and offered me the necklace. 'We'll work out our terms back at the main house, Jack,' he said as he guided me towards the door. 'Just you and I. And then, if you find them acceptable, I'll give you the name of the sneaking traitor within your own division.'

His grip tightened as he said this, and he hissed like a snake as we stepped back into the garden.

'And you can tell me just what you intend to do about them.'

Outside, as we walked together back up towards the bawdy house, the rain had started to fall heavy.

Chapter 8

Paul Bradley

I take care of my responsibilities

It must have been over two hours later when the carriage I was riding in made it to Bethnal Green. The address I was heading towards at this early hour was near Bill and Nancy's old crib but I had asked Slade, who was up front and driving the horses, to let me alight along a nearby street where there was no one around to see me get out. I was alone in the cab and full of troubling thoughts about what had passed between him and myself that night and the big promise I had made before leaving. As I travelled through the night I touched the Lady of Stars what was resting in my inside coat pocket and I wondered if I had got it back at too high a price.

'It's a filthy night,' said Slade once I had stepped out onto a dirty puddled pavement and told him I would be fine from here. 'Both for you and for this Paul Bradley.'

I pulled my hat down onto my head as low as it would go and lifted up the collar of my coat. I was protecting myself against the rain as well as trying to conceal my identity from any onlookers. But I had to raise my voice when I called up to where Slade sat to be heard over the downpour.

'You said you'd have the necessary tools?' I said and held out my hand.

Slade nodded under his own wide-brimmed hat and reached over to an open bag what was beside him. Then he leaned down and offered it to me so I could take whatever I needed from within. There was a strong jemmy among a number of other house-cracking tools and I took that and placed it into a small brown bag of my own.

'Is that all?' asked Slade with the bag still open. 'Could be cleaner to cut through glass. Speeds the job up.' I looked up at his face what was hidden under the shadow of his hat and noticed how different his manner now was compared to the geniality of earlier. I paused as I considered what he was implying. 'If you're not up to it,' he continued, noticing my hesitation, 'then I'll give the job to one of my men. Just say.'

'No,' I replied and snatched a glass-cutting knife from the bag. 'Leave it to me. As you said earlier, it's my leak and my problem to see to. You go.'

I put the two items into my bag and pulled on the rope tight as Slade said goodnight and drove the horses away. At once I darted into a nearby alley to lose myself in the warrens of this area and I began to approach the house I needed by quiet stealth.

On the day on which my gang and I had walked towards the Drop of Courage pub for our meeting with Percival we had been followed by a young Irish boy from Soho to Temple who, at the time, I had just thought was a scruffy admirer. I had tonight discovered however that he was a relative of Fergal's and had signalled to the rest of the Turpins when we was coming and by which cut. This was the lad that had told them about the Lady of Stars in the first place. Slade had got the truth from his tortured Turpin that this lad had been told all about the burglary in Kent, the necklace and the meeting-place by someone connected to my own gang.

Ever heard of Paul Bradley, Dodger? Slade had said after I had agreed to work under him. *Because that's the name of your betrayer.*

I came to the tall thin house at the end of the street what I knew was where this Paul Bradley lived with three large families. It backed on to an alley and had sturdy guttering what I was sure I could climb up if I was quick. I only needed to get up the water-pipe to the first floor window ledge and a simple jemmy would grant me entrance. The rotten weather was my friend on this night; it was unlikely I would be seen or heard as I scrambled up the pipe and so I hooked the bag onto my belt and crossed over to the house, letting the dark night and the rushing rain conceal my movements.

Treachery such as his cannot go unpunished, I heard Slade's words as I climbed up the side of the house, *it sets a bad example. You've responsibilities now to your community.*

The window opened with a hard shove of the jemmy and I lowered myself into the landing of this mean little place. Almost everyone who lived here was either a thief, a prostitute or the child of such and they would know me at a glance. But once the window was shut behind me, I was sure that I could get to where my quarry slept before any confrontation. I knew this house, I had been here before except on that previous occasion I had exited through the window on the floor above. I recalled that this had been the room what I now wanted and so I crept upwards towards it. There was few burglars in the capital more adept at this sort of thing than I and so I was soon inside the bedroom and looking down the two lines of beds in which the children of this house was all sleeping.

I tiptoed past each bed looking at the faces of the slumbering children as I searched for the one what had betrayed me. And then, right at the far end of the room, I found little Paul Bradley lying asleep face down on his threadbare pillow and under two moth-eaten blankets. He was a restless sleeper and the skin around his neck was red raw from the violence of his own fingernails. I could now see, what with the rough sleeping material and the many insects buzzing about his bed, how he had come by his nickname. I looked about the room to ensure that none of the other kinchins had woken to see me and, once certain that they had not, I crouched beside this boy and prodded him.

'Scratcher,' I whispered soft. 'Wake up, Scratcher. It me, the Artful. I've got a secret.'

The boy did not stir.

'Scratcher,' I continued and poked him some more. 'Wake yourself. It's good news.' At this his eyes opened and he turned to see me. Then his face lit up with delight.

'Dodge,' he said and I raised my finger up to my lips. 'What you after?'

I had not seen Scratcher much since he had made such a bad crow of himself out in Kent and I knew that he was disappointed that I had since been ignoring him. But now, as he saw me appear at the foot of his bed like an out-of-season St Nick, he reacted like I was a dream answered.

'We're going on an adventure, Scratch,' I said as I picked up a small pair of shoes what rested under the bed and threw them down next to him. 'Right this minute. Best get dressed and come with me before anyone wakes.'

'Another crack?'

'A big one,' I nodded. 'Lots of money to be made. To make up for your terrible performance last time I'm giving you another chance. You game?'

Scratcher was up in an instant and getting himself changed.

'You won't regret it, Dodger,' he whispered as he did so. 'I'll do better this time. You'll see.'

'I've no doubt you will, Scratch,' I said as I opened the window out of which I knew from previous experience formed an escape route onto the neighbouring rooftops. But there was a long drop down if you did not make the jump. 'You'll be fine.'

He took my hand and stared up into my face. I felt his small cold fingers within my own and I was overcome with shame about what I was set to do.

'Don't look so fretful, Dodge,' he said as I lifted him onto the ledge of the window. 'I won't let you down this time, I promise.'

Then he jumped onto the far roof and bounded off ahead of me.

I crawled out of the house, onto the wooden ledge and I shut the window after. And, as I looked back through the dirty glass and into the family home what I had just snatched him from, just one thought occurred. That I had never, in all my days as a thief, taken anything as unforgivable as this.

Chapter 9

A Slade Man

*Showing the many advantages and disadvantages of being an
active member of a wider community*

'It's a new dawn, boys,' I declared with great ceremony to an
assortment of my finest criminal associates from around the Seven
Dials vicinity. 'From here on in – if you make the sensible decision
to stick by me as your top sawyer – you shall never know poverty
again!!'

A big cheer went up around the Three Cripples taproom as
Georgie Bluchers lifted his frothing jug of ale and chinked it
against Herbie Sharp's glass and Mick Skittles whooped in delight.
Barney had just done the rounds with another tray of drinks in
this secure and private location where a dozen thieves had been
summoned to sit around three wooden tables while I spelt out the
new arrangements for them. I was drinking from my own pewter
pot what had the image of a bird scratched on it, the one what
Barney hung above the bar and served to me alone, while the
others smoked on their clay pipes and listened. The mood – save
for one or two stony faces what refused to join in with the party
atmosphere – was high and the excitement palpable. Georgie in
particular was in a merry humour on account of the large payment
I had just presented him with for driving the cart on the night of
the Whetstone Manor crack. He was counting through the notes
with his still-bandaged leg propped up on another chair and was as

happy as I had seen him in weeks. The sum was only half of what he had been promised for the job but I had said that I would explain why this was in due course. But, considering that until now he had only been paid with a gunshot wound to the leg for his troubles, he did not complain much. Georgie was always a half-jug-full sort of cove.

Tom Skinner, however, was one of the few scowlers in the room and the money that she had been given for her part in that robbery did not seem to improve her disposition one ounce. She, of course, already knew that the reason the payment from Percival was much lighter than agreed upon was because the rest had been given to the man from Hammersmith and this was something she seemed to consider an unwelcome turn of events. She sat with her arms crossed and fixed me with a hard stare as I told the rest of them to settle down so I could explain.

'So, as you can all see, some of the people in this room have benefitted from a cash boon this morning. Myself, Tom and Georgie have all at last been paid out for a job we done over a month ago and one what gave us a good deal of trouble. Mouse has also been paid a fee by way of thank you for taking the knocks with us when we was pounced upon by those bandits.' I gave Herbie Sharp a reproving glance as I spoke. 'Had others been there to help us do battle with the enemy then they would have a share in the bounty also. But you get nothing for nothing in my gang. Understand?'

Herbie Sharp, who had been very much enjoying the revelry until now, looked a little put out by this as he had never been asked to come with us on the job and so probably felt it was an unfair rebuke. But he still raised his glass in salute to those of us what was now holding paper money.

'You worked hard for that reward, lads,' he toasted us. 'Good health to you.'

'Cheers, Herb!' beamed Georgie at him after he had put his notes into his wallet and tucked it away. 'And don't forget little Scratcher. He was part of the job an' all.' Georgie then turned to me and asked whether Scratcher had been given his share yet. 'Because I'd a loved to see his face when he hears that it all came off after all. I know he was a bad crow, Dodge, but you got him his due anyway. It's only fair.'

'Don't you worry about Scratcher,' I said in a steady voice what I sometimes used when playing cards. 'He's been paid out already.'

'That right, is it?' asked the thief we called Chickenstalker from the back of the room. 'P'raps that explains where he's gone to then?'

'Gone to?' asked Mouse Flynn. 'What d'you mean?'

'I spoke to Ma Bradley. She reckons he ain't been seen in days. Thinks he's been taken away by fairies or suchlike.' There was a ripple of laughter around the small room at Scratcher's mother, who was known as a drunken liability what seemed to be modelling her maternal skills upon that woman from the Gin Lane etching. The gathered company was in general agreement that Scratcher had in most likelihood run off from his large family of layabout sots as soon as he could afford to and few of them could blame him.

'He's on a spree, I should think,' concluded Georgie after wiping his mouth from the ale. 'Scratcher'll turn up when the money runs dry. It never lasts as long as you might hope.'

'It will now, Georgie,' I said keen to move the subject on from the missing boy. 'Because from here on the sort of money you've been paid today will be coming in regular. That's because of a deal I've struck that is in the greater interest of everyone here. Or at least those of you what are happy to play the game.'

I had every eye upon me now, even Barney's, and they all

twitched to hear more. I had made a grand show of paying Tom, Georgie and Mouse in front of the others so they could all see how prosperous they could become under my continued leadership and all I had to do now was to deliver the caveat.

'Who here,' I asked as I stood against a table and addressed them like they was members of an exclusive gentlemen's club, 'has heard of a man called William Slade? Or Weeping Billy as he sometimes goes by?'

This question, of course, was of the rhetorical sort. They all had heard the stories about going on the thieve in the patches of London what was considered to be his hunting ground. Violent reprisals had been meted out to criminals what ignored such boundaries and nobody wanted to cross Slade if they did not have to.

'Well, what have you heard?' I asked again.

'I hear his gang numbers three times the amount of ours, Jack,' cautioned Mouse, who seemed to have misunderstood my intention. 'He makes 'em all wear matching red hats so you know who you're dealing with. They're more like an army than a regular street mob. We'd be mad to challenge them.'

'We ain't going to war against Billy Slade, are we?' asked Herbie Sharp in horror. 'Say that ain't so, Dodger. We'd be fools to try.'

'He's to be avoided,' agreed Mick Skittles with a sniff. 'On account of the severe way he treats his enemies. He's a terror by all accounts.'

'A terror he may be,' interjected the Chickenstalker. 'But he lives like a king over in Hammersmith, so I hear. He's got bawdy house what caters to the richer set and makes him a fortune. And every girl in it is his to handle however he pleases.'

'I've heard all about that place,' nodded Georgie who was getting most excited at the mention of Molly Gay's. He was looking back at the Stalker and becoming all the more animated as he spoke.

'They're the best whores money can buy so I'm told. Lily Lennox used to work there and she's one what I'd . . .' Then he pulled up sharp and looked back to me as the room fell silent. 'She's one what's better off out of the awful place, eh, Dodger?'

'It's true, my fine coveys,' I carried on choosing to ignore Georgie and sticking to my point. 'Tom and myself went to visit that very brothel the other night at Billy Slade's invitation. We was treated as esteemed guests and had a most pleasant evening.' The others all turned to Tom as I spoke for confirmation but she just sat there with her miserable face on and saying nothing. 'And Slade did indeed strike me as prosperous, I will admit,' I continued before she could finish the story for me. 'Although I would not say that his gang appeared to be more fearsome than ours. If it came down to it, I'd be happy to place a wager on any man here over those tall feathers what work for Slade.'

This aroused more cheering among those what was susceptible to flattery but there was still much disquiet in the room. It appeared that Slade's reputation as a violent criminal was even greater than I had realised. He had risen to prominence during the years when I had been away in Australia which explained why I had been less aware of his legend than these others was. But I could tell by the general reaction of these Diallers that I had been underestimating his influence and this strengthened my conviction that the decision to ally myself with him was a wise one.

'No one here has any reason to fear Billy Slade,' I continued. 'In truth, it was he what returned the stolen necklace into the hands of her rightful owners.' I hesitated and realised I needed to unpick that last statement. 'Or rather returned it to me. This he did as a mark of respect to a crook about who he has heard impressive things. Someone whose reputation is as great as his own.' There was a short pause as every face there stared back at me as if expecting this announcement to be followed with their own name. 'Again, that's me.'

'So that's why the payment was light then?' Georgie understood at last. 'I'm surprised that Slade didn't sell it on and keep the money for himself.'

'You ain't listening then, are you?' I snapped. 'He could have done that but instead chose to return it. Out of respect. Got it now? He's frightened of me.'

'Frightened?' someone scoffed.

'Of you?' laughed another.

'Do us another turn, Dodge.'

'Why else?' I asked, offended by their incredulity. 'He'd much rather have me as a partner than as a rival and to that end he's made a friendly gesture which I have accepted in good grace. Myself and Billy Slade are now in league together. Put that in your pipes.'

That shut them up. There was an impressed murmur throughout the whole taproom but the first person to question the claim was the last I would have expected. Still stood in front the door what led into the saloon bar, with the empty tray hanging down from his left hand, was the meek landlord of the Cripples and he seemed most unsettled by the news.

'What d'you mean by *in league*, Dodger?' asked Barney. 'Meaning you're equal partners?'

'Of a sort, yeah,' I answered although I knew that the exact nature of the arrangement was going to sound shakier than that. 'We'll be working together, hand in glove, as part of the same operation.' This was when Tom uncrossed her arms and leaned forward, her manner all confrontation.

'Working together?' she spat out. 'Does that mean that we carry on with our usual doings and he just takes half the earnings for nothing? Because that's my understanding of this grand deal you've done for us, Dodger. We'll be stripping that warehouse in Hackney, as planned, but only now your new mate gets his share. And for what? Not because he's scared of you but because it's the other way around.' This explosion of disgust was echoed around the room.

'That true?' cried Herbie, outraged by the idea. 'Half of everything? Why would we agree to that?'

'Oh, I get it,' said the Chickenstalker with a sorry shake of his head. 'We're paying him protection. Jack here,' he flicked his hand towards me, 'is trying to dress it up as a good thing, but we're under Slade's thumb or else.' More consternation broke out after this and I found myself despairing at how small-minded and afraid they was all being. I decided to persuade them by using the same language by which Slade had convinced me.

'London has altered much within our own lifetime, boys,' I began trying to recall his exact words as I spoke over the hubbub. 'And there's a real opportunity for the likes of us to advance ourselves if we care to. You know, like the peelers have done.'

'The *peelers*?' asked Harry Wick, as if he had misheard.

'That's right. I mean to say, if you think about it, they've been doing all right, haven't they?'

'Have you run soft?'

'No. Listen. Some people hate the peelers. But not me. I respect them if anyth—'

'Respect 'em?' laughed Mick Skittles. 'You hate the blue lobsters, Jack. You're always running 'em down.'

'True. I do hate them. But look at the way they've organis—'

'The Artful'll be in uniform in a minute,' jeered the Chickenstalker for the benefit of the rest. 'You watch. Just like his brother.' This was a reference to Horrie Belltower, my mother's other son, what had been a disgrace to his people and joined the police force.

A roar of laughter went up around many of the boys and I burned at the injustice of the remark. But there was some gathered what did not find the notion of me praising the police to be at all droll and at the back of the room I saw Ned Nails and Joe McAllister heading for the door what the landlord was still blocking. Ned signalled for Barney to move aside but before they could depart I stopped everyone in the room dead with one very simple action. I picked up my own personal pewter pot, what I had rested on the table behind me, and then slung it with some force straight at the head of the Chickenstalker. It landed with a heavy crack and he jerked back in surprise and let loose an agonised cry. A sudden hush fell upon the room and they all stopped what they was doing and stared. Chickenstalker then leaned forward and blood began dripping out of his nose onto the unshaved wooden floor as he cursed my name.

'Half-brother!' I shouted at him in genuine rage. 'And if you ever insinuate that I'm not safe again, I will end you, Stalker. Understand?' I then turned to the rest and made things even more clear. 'Or someone else will.'

The room was mine once more. The shock of the attack took grip and they all exchanged looks as if unsure what to do about it. They had never before seen me lash out at one of my own – I had a reputation for being very indulgent of my gang's high spirits before this. But it seemed now as though everyone present was regarding me through new eyes and I felt a rush of raw pleasure at it. The only voice heard was that of Barney. 'I think you boys had better sit down again, eh?' he said to Ned and Joe, who was still standing by the door waiting to leave. So Slade had been right, I thought, as I watched these two brawny men take their seats once more and give me their utmost attention. Our people only ever really respect fear.

'Wipe your nose,' I said to the Chickenstalker, putting steel into my voice as I pulled out my own handkerchief and handed it to him. 'You're getting blood all over Barney's floor, you maladroit individual.' I then returned my attention to the rest of them, my blood still high from the thrill. 'Now then,' I said as I saw Mouse's face looking at me as if he had never seen me before. 'Where was I?'

The rest of the meeting was a much smoother affair and I found it a lot easier to achieve clarity of expression when the entire congregation was half-expecting me to throw something else at their heads at any given moment. I was able to explain to them in simple terms the benefits to us joining forces with Slade and before long they all started seeing things my way.

'So it'll work like this,' I said after ordering another round of drinks from Barney which I declared would be on me. 'You just carry on doing what you're doing now. Pocket-picking, house-cracking, stealing horses, running women. However you want to make your living is still up to you. But things will be more efficient from here on. Billy has connections and influence what he's happy to share with me and I'm going to pass these down to you. By way of for instance, if you're a dipper and you want to work a particular patch then you don't want lesser talents scaring off the big game. Billy will see to it that any inferior thieves are kept away from whatever railway station or other public place you go finding in. Either by command or by force and this'll make the whole venture a lot more profitable for you. And for those of you what run bawdy houses –' here I acknowledged Big Hubbard, the only brothel-keeper in the room and someone what I knew was having a hard time in recent months – 'then Slade is happy to send some fresh girls over to yours. He has them shipped in from France, Belgium, Denmark – all over Europe. So that should bring the custom back again.' Big Hubbard seemed pleased by this news and there was many other nods of approval once they started realising how much they stood to earn now that I had been given Slade's blessing. But the question of who was now top sawyer still bothered them.

'So we're paying up to Slade?' asked Herbie. He was shuffling a deck of cards in his restless hands as he often did when troubled. 'We don't have to wear those bloody hats an' all, do we?'

'No,' I replied. 'Because you're my men, not his. You're paying up to me, I'm paying up to Slade. That's the way things'll go.' Once this was good and clear I told them that business was concluded and we all headed out into the main bar. Nobody spoke to the Chickenstalker as they all shuffled out of the room, he was still in disgrace. But before I made it through the door myself I felt a hand reach out and touch my sleeve. It was Mouse, and he said he wanted a quiet word.

'Thanks for the bustle, Jack,' he said once we was out of earshot of the rest. 'It's come at the right time, I've been having it hard of late.'

'I know that,' I said recalling how much he worried about his poor motherless newborn. 'I hope baby Robin is finding that midwife I got for him up to snuff. We'll get him another if not. As I said, you'll be earning more as a pickpocket than ever now. He won't want for nothing.'

'Well, that's what I wanted to speak on,' he said once we was alone in the taproom. 'I want to get out of the dipping game. It don't make me as much without Agnes to distract and I can't see the use in these new advantages if I still have to pay half to someone else. No, don't get me wrong . . .' he continued before I had a chance to promise him that he'd be richer not poorer under the new arrangement, 'I appreciate what you're doing. But I saw how much money Tom and Georgie got for the job out in Kent. And I was hoping you could get me into house-cracking too.'

'You sure, Mouse? It's a riskier art.'

'Not if you're only doing it once a fortnight, it's not. I have to work the crowds every day of the week to earn what you boys do in one evening. All I'm saying is – if any more big cracks come up then you might think about involving me. I'd appreciate it. For baby Robin's sake.'

I smiled and placed my arm around his shoulder before leading him out of the room and back to where the others was striking up a song.

'I'll bear it in mind,' I said to him as we walked through the bar together. 'Now that we're a bigger gang your son'll have the best of everything. It'll be the genteel life for that lucky little bugger. Everything's going to be just rosy.'

'Thanks, Dodge,' Mouse smiled as Georgie placed another pot of ale into his hands and the rest of the boys reached the first rousing chorus. 'You're a good man.'

A china plate missed the side of my head and shattered into the kitchen wall behind me. It was the third I had dodged since getting home and I had to keep moving if I was to avoid the next one.

'You're a rotten bastard, Jack Dawkins,' Lily yelled, ignoring my pleas to just calm down a bit and think of the earthenware. 'And a bloody fool. I told you to steer clear of him, didn't I? I told you he was a wrong 'un.'

'This is expensive crockery you're throwing, Lil,' I reasoned with her as I held out my hands in a gesture of peace. 'And I found it in a lovely home. Show it some proper respect now, eh?' The last plate in her hands span through the air and smashed into a picture-frame just to the left of me as I dashed into the next room.

'I had a whore of a time trying to free myself from Slade,' she raged as she pursued me into the bedroom. 'Do you know how much it took to walk away from him? And now you've gone and put us straight back in his clutches!'

I had been darting all around our little dwelling and avoiding her missiles ever since she had got back from her trip away and I was starting to find it all most wearisome. I knew that she was displeased with me – I had expected that when I had returned in the early hours of the morning after striking the deal in Hammersmith and told her what I had done – but I was sorry to see that she was still being volatile about it days later. She had not had the chance to vent at me at the time as we had urgent matters to attend to first and I had hoped that the storm would have passed by the time she returned from her excursion. But it seemed that the tempest was still inside her and so I grabbed the blanket, pulled it up to my nose and used it as shield until she was done expressing herself through destruction.

'Let's just settle down so we can have a civilised conversation about this, eh, my light?' I asked, as soon as I thought it was safe. 'After all, you needn't get involved at all. It's my business this, not yours.'

'Then how come I've just spent two days travelling to Rochester and back?' she railed against me now that her hands was empty and her urge to throw things looked to be reaching its end. 'To see my pinch-faced, uppity sister. I hate going to her for help, Jack. She'll take any chance to look down on me, the snooty cow.'

Lily and her sister was not much alike. Lydia Wadey was the wife of a provincial schoolmaster and, although I was not likely to be formally introduced to either her or her impoverished husband any time soon, I knew that the relationship between the two sisters was not what you would call cordial. Lily was a fallen woman and therefore a disgrace to her whole family, and this Lydia had said some very severe things to her upon that subject over the years. Lily had been trying to mend relations with Lydia for some time but I knew it would have been hard for her to go and seek out her disapproval once more and, in spite of the cost to the crockery, my gratitude to her for this was deep.

'You did it though, Lily?' I asked as I lowered the blanket down. 'You got them to take in Scratcher? Because, if so, you've gone and saved his life.'

She breathed out hard and her whole self looked more at ease at the words. There was still a fierceness in her but when she next spoke it was with an air of pride at a job well done.

'They took him in, yeah,' Lily nodded. She then crossed over to the wooden rocking chair what was covered in clothes, pushed them onto the floor and then sat down with an exhausted bump. 'Lydia might be all fire and brimstone when it comes to me but she'd not turn away a homeless wastrel when presented with one. I imagine she took a lot of satisfaction in showing me just what a good Christian she is for the hundredth time.' Lily rolled her eyes and then her left hand went up to her brow like it was thumping at her from within. I moved around the bed and came over to where she sat, careful not to aggravate her again, and I knelt down in front of the rocking chair.

'You've done that boy a good turn, Lily,' I said as I took her hand. '*You're* the Christian, I don't care what your sister says.' She gave me a small smile and squeezed my hand back. I raised hers to my lips and kissed it, glad that we was sharing a tender moment together after the chaos of two days before.

It had been a most distressing scene on that rainy night on which I had stolen a boy of not-yet-twelve from his family home and taken him back to my own crib like he was a sackful of burgled booty. Lily had woken to see me standing at the foot of our bed with a drenched and shivering Scratcher and, once I had told her of the drastic action I had taken, she beheld me like I was some cruel goblin in a fairy story who went about stealing boys for my own amusement. But whatever the horror she may have felt when I started with the explanations, it was little when compared to that of poor Scratcher. Until then he had thought he was still going on another thrilling midnight adventure with his old friend the Artful and so had no suspicion of what was really happening until I spelt it out for him in front of Lily. He then burst into tears and wailed that he had not betrayed me to the Turpins and that he never would and please, Jack, don't kill me, I'll be good, tell him, Lily, please, please, please. All of that.

Anyway, I was quick to explain that I had no intention of killing him and that I had snatched him away from his home for the exact opposite intention. I told him to quieten down, as I did not want our landlady to hear all this fuss, and I took them both into the kitchen while I boiled a kettle and I tried to make them see how things stood. Billy Slade, I said as we waited for the boil, had discovered through his own investigations that the Turpins had been told about our theft of the necklace on that afternoon by a young boy named Paul Bradley, otherwise known as Scratcher. This Scratcher, Slade had revealed, had told about the rendezvous with Percival to a local Irish boy. As far as Slade was concerned, Scratcher was a loose-lipped liability and had no place in the new modern criminal empire what he was trying to build. And it was up to me to make an example of him. If I refused to do this very simple action then somebody else who worked for Slade would see to the matter themselves.

So this was why you need hiding, I said to Scratcher, and that way Slade would assume the deed was done and say no more upon the affair. I then asked Scratcher if he could please stop snivelling as it was giving me a headache and not helping one bit. Lily was livid with me then and went over to cuddle him as he began to explain himself through snot and tears. He admitted that he had spoken of our criminal doings to a young Irish boy of his acquaintance but he had only been trying to boast of his association with me and had not known that this boy was himself connected to a family of robbers. This I was inclined to believe as Scratcher had not appeared to have benefitted from giving away such information if the poverty I had found him in was any indication. But this did not alter the fact that Billy Slade had now declared Scratcher to be an enemy of his burgeoning business empire and so his life was under threat regardless of what I believed. I asked Lily, who had known Slade as well as anyone during her time as one of his girls, whether or not she believed that the threat against Scratcher was real and she blew on her tea and considered it. Yes, she said, as she looked with sympathy upon the boy. We had better get Scratcher to somewhere safe at first light. Somewhere where Slade won't be likely to come across him.

'Your sister,' I asked Lily as she rocked back and forth on the chair after removing her country boots, 'what does she know? You didn't mention Slade's name, did you?' I had fetched us both two glasses of hot whisky and I handed one to her. 'Or mine?'

'Don't you worry,' she said in her most sardonic voice, as she took a sip, 'your secrets are safe. I told Lydia that Scratcher was a poor cockney chimney sweep what had grown too big for the task and that his family had started to brutalise him for his lack of earnings. That was enough for her to take pity on him.'

'Good thinking,' I said, relieved that all was settled. 'How is he though? Happy in himself?'

'Of course not, Jack,' she sighed in exasperation. 'He's wrecked.

He's scared beyond wits, missing his mother, missing London and missing you. I said you'd be up to visit him soon. Don't make a liar out of me.'

'I won't,' I assured her, although I could not imagine when the time would come for me to take a trip to Rochester in the near future. I was a busy professional now with my own criminal division to run and I'd spent enough time worrying about this nasty distraction. But Lily had done well in finding so safe a haven for Scratcher and I had begun giving her feet a good rub while she spoke.

'My sister's husband, this Mr Wadey who teaches in the church school up there, he seems a decent sort for a flat. He's giving Scratcher meals and board as long as he helps with some chores and he's got him a place in his school. So Scratcher might even learn something while he's up there.'

'Yeah,' I said in a loving voice, as she leaned back in the chair and closed her eyes. 'It's all turned out for the best.'

At this Lily's pulled her feet away from my hands. 'The best?' she exclaimed as she rocked herself upright, and I half expected her tender little foot to kick me in the chin. 'Jack, what you've done to us – to me, to Scratcher, to yourself – is the *worst* thing ever. I don't think you understand what a danger Slade is. The things I've seen him do are terrible. He's a monster!'

Her voice was rising now and I could hear the footsteps of Mrs Grogan coming upstairs to our apartment again. We was behind on our rent already and the ogress had been threatening to get violent if we did not pay soon. This commotion of the plate-throwing and the shouting was just giving her another excuse to knock on our door and harass us some more.

'Why, Jack?' Lily asked, ignoring my pleas to keep it down a note. 'When we first met you boasted that you never would serve any other master than yourself. I loved that about you. So why would you agree to work for someone like Billy Slade? Someone who is half the man?' There was a banging on the door just as I had expected. Lily ignored it and kept looking at me. 'This'll be the ruin of us, Jack.'

I got up and went over to the door, glad of the chance to change the subject. I had enough money to pay this rent now, thanks to Percival, so I was unafraid of any confrontation. I asked Mrs Grogan who she was through the door and waited for the familiar aggressive answer. But, I was surprised to hear, that the voice that came back was much softer than I was accustomed to.

'It's Mrs Grogan, Mr Dawkins. Your landlady. I was wondering if either you or Miss Lennox might care for anything from the shops while I'm out? Or if perhaps you had some laundry what needs doing.'

I looked to Lily and saw my amazement reflected back at me. I went to unlock the door and I heard Lily caution me. 'Careful, Jack,' she whispered. 'It might be a Grogan trick.'

But when I opened the door and saw her there, standing at the top of the staircase, she had this nervous smile on and looked keen to please. 'Didn't know you did laundry, Mrs Grogan?' I said.

'Well, I'm happy to for yourself, Mr Dawkins,' she replied. 'With no added charge to your monthly rent. And that's another thing. Pay me whenever you get the money, I'm not fussed.'

'Very good of you, Mrs G,' I said with a bow. 'Most appreciated.'

'I'm glad,' she said and, although I may have imagined it, I thought I saw the smallest dip of a curtsey. 'I know we've had our bust-ups in the past,' she went on, 'but I wanted to clear the air. My boy, Teddy, he who drinks with Salty Moon down the Embankment, well he told me about your change in fortunes. So, as I say, I wanted to promise you and Miss Lennox that you'll be getting no more trouble from this quarter. It was important to my Teddy that I tell you that and you can pass it on to Mr Slade, if you please.'

I thanked Mrs Grogan for her timely grovellings and told her that we would not be requiring her services today but would bear her in mind as a laundress in future. Then, once I had bid her good day and shut the door, I turned back to Lily who was stood astounded in the hallway behind me.

'You was saying?' I grinned.

Chapter 10

New Business

*Containing a good deal of helpful advice for
the would-be cracksman*

The first cold weeks of December was upon us.

'Whenever I see you approaching,' said Weeping Billy Slade
during one of our get-togethers, 'you and your Diallers are often
being trailed by a crew of kinchins dressed just like you. Why is
that?'

We was in the dark mahogany dining room of a tavern where he
often insisted we meet and what overlooked the main thoroughfare
of High Holborn. There was only supposed to be the two of us
in this upstairs restaurant — save for the occasional appearance of
a young maid what was serving us pies and ales — and Slade, as
was his custom, was there before me. He was sat by a tall window
and he had positioned himself so he could see anyone approaching
from my way. This was how he would have spotted the raucous
collection of fledging thieves what nowadays followed in the wake
of the Dawkins gang whenever we was seen in public. Slade would
have also seen us pass by the other side of the street to the coffee-
stall holder, the one who had refused to serve us on that morning
when we had returned from our Kentish burgling excursion. Only
now, just five short months later, the vendor would send his son
scurrying across the busy road to us with a tray of full and steaming
mugs without expecting one farthing in return. Across the way I

saw the vendor nodding at me and so I picked up one of the tin mugs, raised it in the air in acknowledgement, took a quick swig, burped and then threw the rest of the black liquid out into the street and into the path of an approaching dray horse. The rest of the Diallers cackled and did the same with their drinks. Then we placed the empty mugs back onto the son's tray, told him to stay out of trouble and walked on without one more glance in his father's direction. It felt good to be respected at last.

'Can I help it,' I answered Slade once I had washed down a mouthful of beef and pastry with the ale, 'if children love me?'

During these regular meetings of our two criminal gangs, Georgie, Tom and the others would all remain downstairs to eat with his red-bowlered men while I would be invited up to dine with the top man. This was so that the two of us could discuss whatever important matters needed attending to in private. However, this upstairs room seemed to have very large mice and I could often hear the occasional small bump from behind the panelled walls. I recognised such noises from the Three Cripples tap room what was full of hidden compartments and peep-holes behind which Fagin used to secrete himself so he could spy upon those who thought themselves unobserved. I had no doubt that this pub was also furnished with unseen nooks behind the panelling and I considered telling Slade not to waste his time with such tricks. He made a good job of feigning ignorance whenever I asked him if he could hear something strange from behind the walls but it was clear he knew we was not alone. However, there was nothing about this conversation what would not incriminate the both of us and so I decided to ignore the human woodworm and just carried on enjoying my lunch.

'I've known some burglars in my time, Dodger,' Slade said once the maid had shut the door behind us, 'but none as reliable as you and your boys. You're the best house-breakers in London.'

'Thank you very much, Billy,' I said, as I gave the pie another liberal splash of vinegar, 'I'll pass the compliment along to the others.'

'It's rare to find such craft these days,' he went on while mopping up the gravy on his own plate with a bread roll, 'the rest are just smash-and-grab merchants from what I can see.'

'Amateurs,' I agreed after I had shovelled another forkful of mashed potato into my mouth. 'Giving the rest of us a bad name.'

'And what astounds me the most,' he continued after we had chinked tankards and drunk to our own health, 'is that I hear that you never take a barker with you on a crack. And that you forbid any of your gang to do the same. Isn't that risky?' I dabbed my lips with a napkin before replying.

'A good burglar has no call to use a pistol and the only risk lies in taking one,' I explained. 'A solid persuader is what you need if you run into bother and so I insist all my boys carry coshes. But barkers are dangerous because if one goes off unexpected and shoots a person dead then you could get the drop if arrested. They'll hang a killer before a burglar, everyone knows that.'

'Can't argue with your logic,' admitted Slade. He laid down his cutlery and waited for me to finish eating before bringing the conversation around to new business. In recent weeks my gang of crooks – the Seven Dials division as Slade called us – had been good earners and I had no doubt that he must have been impressed by the fruits of our labour. The warehouse crack in Hackney had proven to be even more profitable than Tom and I had hoped for and this had been the start of what was still an encouraging run of felonious prosperity. Slade had since given us a good deal of information about wealthy and vulnerable homes throughout the capital and this had made the whole enterprise of being a burglar so much simpler. Such jobs had proven worthwhile for everyone involved and even after we had given Slade his share for moving the goods along we was still well in coin. The benefits of being under the care of a parent criminal such as Billy Slade had manifested itself in other ways too and several Diallers had remarked to me that they was finding the criminal life much more agreeable nowadays.

'So I've got another job for you, Dodger,' he said, and leaned in closer. 'But this one is more delicate than most. It comes to me from someone high.'

'Now there you surprise me, Billy,' I said as I licked my knife clean and laid it down, 'when we first met you said there was none higher.'

'There's isn't,' he replied sounding defensive. 'At least nobody in the criminal world is higher. But the person I'm talking about would not consider himself a criminal in the usual sense. That's why he comes to me to execute certain tasks on his behalf.'

'We're talking about a gentleman,' I guessed. 'Like my Percival?'

'Not unlike your Mr Percival I suppose, only this man – who it would be wildly indiscreet of me to name – sends a good many jobs my way and pays me handsomely for them. He's very keen to distance himself from the lower elements and he engages me to arrange things to his satisfaction. He's made me very rich over the years and I do hate letting him down. That's why I only let my best people attend to his business.'

'And now he wants a burglar,' I nodded in understanding. 'To crack a crib and steal something special for him. Well, you've come to the right man.'

'I was hoping so,' Slade smiled. 'And you're right, of course, he wants a particular item taken which I know is the sort of task you specialise in. It's a safety deposit box. Metal. Black and battered but with silver lining around the edges. About the size of a large jewellery case.'

'I know the type,' I nodded. 'One of them portable ones.'

'Indeed. And this one is unremarkable in most ways, so I'm given to understand. But it'll be the only one in the place so you'll know it when you see it.'

'What's inside?'

'That is information that my client wishes to keep secret. Even from you.'

'But you know?'

'Oh, yes.' He leaned back in his chair and he tapped the tabletop with his gloved hand in an idle way. I could hear the quiet knock of wood on wood. 'I've spent a good deal of time forging a trust between him and me. It was a trust that was hard earned so I wouldn't betray it now. But don't take it personally, Dodger,' he winked. 'I haven't told him your name either. I keep all the secrets.'

Now this irked me somewhat. I did not like not knowing key things about delicate jobs but I could, in truth, understand the need for discretion. This client of his must have been influential enough to be worth blackmailing, someone from a higher class – perhaps even aristocracy. I was itching to know the name and I was sure I would discover it in time.

'Be like that then,' I said instead. 'So tell me more about this crib? Who am I stealing from?'

'Mr Anthony Rylance,' I announced to my three closest associates some hours later. 'A sophisticated man of letters!'

It was night-time now and I had gathered Tom, Mouse and Georgie together in a house in the Dials where I could explain to them the nature of the job we was to undertake. The house belonged to Georgie, or at least he had somehow taken possession of it, and we would not be disturbed.

'Is he a greengrocer?' asked Georgie after a long blink. The rest of us looked at him as he sat on his armchair and it was some seconds before I landed on his confusion.

'Letters, Georgie,' I explained. 'Not lettuce.'

'So he's a scribbler,' Georgie nodded his understanding. 'Has he written anything I might have read?'

'I very much doubt it,' I answered knowing that he could barely spell his own name. 'Rylance is a young man and new to the inking game. He lives in a small apartment by Hungerford Stairs and is employed as a court reporter by day. He takes this metal safety box that we're after to and from his work. He never lets it out of his sight.'

'What's the big performance then?' Mouse interrupted. 'Can't we just pinch it from him while he's out?'

'It's too cumbersome. He'd know we was taking it.'

'So what if he does?' asked Georgie. 'We can just jump out on him on his way to work – masks on – and grab the thing by force.' He rubbed his hands together as if nobody before had ever thought of anything so ingenious. 'Easy money!'

I recalled then why I only ever used Georgie to drive the carts.

'If it was that simple,' I replied and struggled to disguise my impatience, 'then Slade could pay any old ruffian a pittance for the trouble. But instead he came to us. So, as must be obvious, there is a bit more to it.'

'Slade don't want it to look like a robbery,' guessed Tom. I pointed at her and nodded. 'That's why it can't be done in daylight.'

'Right and wrong,' I answered. 'He does want it to look like a robbery but he don't want it to look like it's the metal box we're there to rob. He wants us to break in and strip the whole place clean. So it will just appear as though the box was just one of many things we stole. So that when this Rylance reports its loss to the peelers they won't place any importance on it. They'll just think that we chanced upon a metal case – not knowing what it contained – and added it to the booty. So that's the dodge we're there to perform. Steal the case but don't make it look like we came to steal the case.'

'It must have something very special in it for all this fuss,' Mouse put in. 'Ain't anyone else curious about it?'

'I'm mad with curiosity,' I admitted. 'And I'll try and crack the case to see what is inside before we hand it back to Slade. But even if it's the crown jewels in there we're still delivering it as planned.'

'Answer me this, though,' Tom said. 'How we going to steal it if this Rylance person is as good as sitting on top of it all night?'

'I'm glad you asked,' I replied. 'Because that's the easy bit. Anthony Rylance has been invited to some high-class Christmas event on the nineteenth of December and it's evening wear. So that night we know the metal box will be left unattended. He can't take it with him to some fancy occasion so he'll leave it in the apartment. It might be inside a safe but we've cracked safes before.'

'The nineteenth? Ain't that this Friday?' Mouse said, and looked to Georgie for confirmation. But there was no calendars or newspapers in Georgie's crib so he had to rely on me telling him that he was right. 'How do you know what he's doing then?'

'Billy told me,' I said. 'And I would guess that he was told by the man what hired him. For all I know this person is the one what invited Rylance out for the night to make our task possible.'

We had three nights until the nineteenth and a good deal to do before then. We spent the rest of the evening in plot and discussed who would be playing what roles this time.

'And as ever, boys,' I said as a matter of habit once I had gone over everything else twice, 'no barkers.'

When planning to burgle a property it is within the interest of the professional thief to familiarise him or herself with the address as much as possible beforehand. Often, whenever we was working in one of the capital's more fashionable districts, we would spend weeks monitoring the comings and goings of the residents and their servants, watching to see how often a policeman might pass by on his beat, trying to ingratiate ourselves with the domestics and even penetrating the house in advance in the guise of a calling tradesman. Hungerford Stairs, however, was not a fashionable district and it was clear that this Anthony Rylance was not earning much as a court reporter if this was where he dwelt. The Stairs led to the bottom of the river and there was ramshackle tenements about, although many of these was occupied by ambitious young reporters what wished to be walking distance from Fleet Street. It was a poor vicinity but populated more by flats than criminals so it would be difficult to loiter about without arousing suspicion in the neighbours.

Georgie and I travelled down to the Embankment on the following day with a cart full of seasonal fruit. This was a decent ruse because people are used to having unfamiliar vendors appearing in the days before Christmas, their country carts overflowing with holly, ivy and rich plums for puddings. We arrived at sunrise and positioned ourselves across the way from the building where Rylance lodged and we sold our wares while waiting for him to leave for work. At half eight a man with red curly hair appeared from out of the front door of the large house clutching in his hand a black metal case with solid-looking silver clasps on it. He also had a satchel hanging from his other shoulder and he looked to be running late. This I knew from Slade's description was our Mr Rylance and he rushed past our cart, refusing to buy an offered punnet of berries, before turning up Villiers Street and heading towards the Strand. Once he was well clear I gathered up a big bunch of different winter plants and set off towards the row of houses where he lived, careful not to be so obvious that I was interested in just one address. Rylance rented a small above-floor apartment in the centre of a row of houses and, as I knocked on every door leading up to it, I could tell that the neighbourhood was too well populated for us to occupy a nearby room and break in that way. Instead I worked my way along, earning myself a few shillings from the holly as I went, until I knocked upon the door where Rylance had darted out of. I could hear some dogs barking from within and the door was opened by a young woman with a baby in her arms.

'Morning, Madam,' I said and raised the brown flat cap I was wearing to greet her, 'care for some mistletoe for kissing under?'

'You're a forward one,' she replied, 'I've an husband you know.'

'I seen him,' I said with a wink. 'Was he the radish roof what just pushed past me in his hurry? Looks like he won't be back for a good spell! Leaving us at our leisure.' The woman pretended to be scandalised.

'My husband works nights in the blacking factory, you saucy chancer,' she declared with delight, 'and he could be home at any moment!'

'I see,' I gave a wolfish grin, 'which explains why that fellow was in a hurry.'

'Get out of it!' she hooted. 'That was just nice Mr Rylance what rooms upstairs. He ain't the sort and my Bob knows it.'

'Well, what a nice treat for your Bob when he comes home then,' I raised my bunch of mistletoe, 'to see a sprig of this hanging from his ceiling and his beautiful wife waiting under it for him. Here, let me in and I'll do the hanging myself.'

This woman and her numerous offspring lived in the cramped and damp downstairs apartment of the house. It was very helpful for me to be granted admittance inside as it gave me the chance to understand the layout of the abode above and, as I stood on a chair and tacked the sprig of holly into the wooden rafters of the main room, I tried to imagine what the upper rooms would be like from the walls and partitions of this dwelling.

'Your Bob works nights then, does he?' I said, as if in casual conversation. I was very keen to discover whether this woman would be likely to hear my burglar's footsteps above while she slept down here alone. 'I do hope your man with the red head doesn't keep him awake when he returns from work. There is nothing worse than a noisy neighbour when you're trying to bed down.'

'Mr Rylance is as quiet as a pot plant,' said the woman. 'He's a bachelor and a timid one at that.'

'Bachelor, eh?' I said and cast my eyes about for a bunch of keys. 'Trouble with bachelors is, they get good women like you doing their laundry for them and suchlike. I bet he treats you worse than his own mother.'

One of the reasons why I had wanted to get inside this woman's home was that I hoped that she would have been given a spare key for Rylance should he ever lose his own. This was one of the tricks of the trade and I had stolen many such spare keys on other cracks and nobody had ever noticed until it was too late. It was interesting how unguarded people was with their neighbours' possessions.

'Oh dear me, no,' replied the woman, much to my disappointment. 'Mr Rylance don't get involved with me and I don't get involved with him. I never know what's going on up there and I don't much wish to.'

I tugged at the sprigs to ensure they would not drop. She was going to be no use to me as far as gaining admittance was concerned but I still had some questions for her before I left.

'I'm still surprised your Bob gets any sleep,' I remarked before stepping down from her wooden chair. 'What with them noisy canines I can hear out there.'

The unsettling sound of an unseen pack of dogs had been on my mind ever since she had opened the door and I could not leave the place without asking after them.

'The bullies?' the woman scoffed as I climbed down from the chair. 'There's no harm in them. They may sound a bit fearsome but they're as gentle as lambs.'

'Bull terriers?' I exclaimed as if nothing could have pleased me more. 'Out in your backyard?'

'Four of them,' she nodded with pride.

'Mind if I take a look?' I asked as I went through to the back room of her home before she could stop me. 'An old friend of mine used to keep a bull terrier, you know,' I said ignoring her protestations. 'Bullseye his name was. That was the name of the dog, not the friend. Let me see them, I've a great affection for the breed.'

'But that's the bedroom,' the woman complained as I continued invading her home and crossed through to the window. 'Get out of there.' This room was even damper than the rest as the whole back of the building was built close to the riverbed. I peered through the window to the backyard and there they all were – and a set of animals less like lambs I had never seen. I recalled how much I have hated the vicious creatures with their stupid egg-heads and triangular eyes. All of Fagin's boys had been terrified of Bill's dog and here was four of the brutish things about to make life difficult for me. I did manage to get a good look out at this backyard though and saw how it was separated from the Thames by a tall brick wall.

'My Bob'll be home any second,' the woman warned me as the child in her arms woke up and began to cry, 'and he won't take kind to finding you in there. He'll get the wrong idea.'

'Or the right one,' I said as I flashed her another dirty smile before coming out of that bedroom again. 'I should be getting off then,' I smiled as if there was no harm in it. 'Good day to you, Madam.' I walked towards the door of her crib to see myself out as I wanted to linger in the hallway for a spell to poke about the staircase what led up to Rylance's lodgings. But before I had my hand on the doorknob she asked me if I had forgotten something.

'Shouldn't I be paying you?' she said, and I turned to see her standing in the centre of the room with the babe in one arm and a little girl tugging at her dress. 'For this?' Her eyes raised upwards to the mistletoe above. I crossed over to where she stood, took her face in my hand and, in front of all of her kinchins, gave her a sweet kiss upon the lips.

'You just did,' I said, before bidding them all farewell.

Much later, Tom and Mouse returned to the vicinity by way of the water. They was dressed as mudlarks – river scavengers who survive by drifting along the banks and living off whatever washes up – and in this disguise they was able to investigate the house from the waterside. Many houses along Embankment seemed like they was going to sink into the muddy water at any time. Tom discovered that the one in which Rylance lived could be approached by boat in the dark and it would be possible to climb the tall back walls of the yard and get to the house from that way.

'It looks to me,' Mouse told us when we met at Georgie's hours later and I noticed that he had brought a big brown sack along with him, 'that we could not come at the house from the street entrance as it was too busy even at night. So the best solution is to approach from the river.' I was impressed with how well Mouse was taking to the burglary game. He was already sounding like a seasoned cracker.

'So we're taking our chances with these dogs,' I agreed. 'A pity. They're a nasty pack if their barks is anything to go by.'

'Don't you worry about the bullies,' Mouse told us. 'I've already dealt with them earlier this afternoon.' He lifted up the sack and placed it on the oak table. I thought how heavy it looked and then I noticed the stain print it made on the wood. It was a deep damp red.

Chapter 11

Inky Fingers

Details of what really happened on the night of the big crack

Our little boat banked against the sodden houses well after ten at night. Georgie had been pulling the oars while Mouse held the rudder lines and I reached out with the boathook to draw us in. The river was choppy and fought against us so our landing onto this muddy patch of earth was not what you would call majestic. But it did not look as though anybody was around to pay us much mind, so Mouse and myself took our small sacks out of the boat and Georgie rowed it away. This boat was a perfect vessel to approach but it would be hopeless as a means of getting away so he was under instruction to return to his cart and wait up Villiers Lane for us.

Tom Skinner, meanwhile, had positioned herself on top of the roof of the houses what faced the front of Rylance's lodgings so she could play crow from there. About an hour earlier she had informed us that his crib was in darkness and that the candlelight what flickered from the study window whenever the young scribe was at home was snuffed out. We had waited for as long as we could for darkness to descend even further but there was a chance that the timid Rylance could return from his evening well before midnight so we could not delay further.

We scuttled along towards the tall brick wall what we needed to climb to get into the backyard I had seen from his neighbours' bedroom. We hooked our sacks to our belts and helped each other to the top of the tall yard wall. As this was Mouse's first burglary I had been practising with him how to overcome an obstruction such as this one all day, using the many walls of the rookeries. That had proven to be time well spent as any fool can get over your average garden fence but it took real skill to do what we was doing and scale a wall built high enough not to be scaled. I had shown him several tricks as to how two friends can help each other over an even taller and less accommodating barrier than this one by acting as one. As was typical of him, he had proven a quick learner and we soon reached the top of the wall. Over the way we saw the back of the house we was heading towards. Between us and the windows to the Rylance apartment all we had to do was lower ourselves down to this long brick wall which would lead us to the room we needed. But as Tom's etchings had predicted, the drop to the courtyard between was a considerable one and in the darkness down there I could just about see the kennels.

Without a word Mouse pulled open the cord of his sack. We would have to move with feline grace as we crossed the wall but should these brutish animals below wake up then the six juicy steaks what he had got from Smithfield market should keep them both quiet and occupied. My own bag was full of safe-cracking tools and so I was the first to lower myself down and scurry over the courtyard wall to the other side. This wall was not wide but I was soon across and I climbed downwards onto the ledge below. Mouse followed after me and we could both hear the snores and sleep-growls of the dogs in the yard below as we crossed over them to the house we needed.

I edged along towards the first window and peered inside. The curtains was half-drawn, revealing this to be the bedroom. I had brought along a jemmy to force this open but I was pleased to find that it was already unlocked. All it took was one small shove and the window surrendered itself. It was a piece of very good and unexpected luck.

The bedroom was dark as I stepped in and onto the creaking bed underneath before helping Mouse to enter after me. He emptied his sack of steaks and laid them on the windowsill should we still need them for the dogs. We planned to leave by the front door but these slabs of meat could still prove useful. I, meanwhile, reached into my coat pocket and produced the box of matches and I lit a candle what was stood on the bedside chest. This illuminated a room of such meanness and austerity that it would have not looked out of place in a monastery. There was few items of furniture, a poster of a cross on the wall with a Bible inscription below declaring I AM THE RESURRECTION AND THE LIFE. A small sloping desk at the foot of the bed was covered in sheets of paper and there was some books about but it was hard to see anything of value. I walked over to this desk, hoping we would be lucky enough to find the metal box underneath, but instead all I saw was a copy of the *Morning Chronicle* spread out on top. Mouse opened the chest of drawers to hunt for anything worth taking but all he found was some folded clothes, underwear and some lurid drawings. Not only was the box not present but it was hard to see what else we was supposed to steal. Slade had wanted us to strip the place clean so it would not appear as though the safety deposit box was targeted, but if this bedroom was anything to go by there was little else to strip. So we crept over to the door and opened it into the main room. This room was dark too and I set straight about looking for a safe or some such thing. Mouse carried on trying to fill his sack with worthwhile objects but – again – the pickings was lean. Mouse grabbed at whatever portable items he could but these was of a very mundane variety – crockery, cutlery, a kettle and some odd pieces of porcelain. There was plenty of bookcases and some rum curiosities dotted about but nothing what would wet the lips of any self-respecting pawnbroker. It was not a tidy place either and we was going to have a hard job making it appear as though we had cracked this crib at all. When Anthony Rylance returns, I thought as I left Mouse to it and sneaked over to the other door, he might not notice we had even been here until daybreak.

The little desk we had passed in the bedroom was too small for a busy writer to work on so I was hoping this final room would be his study. I inched it open, taking care not to make any noises what might wake the children what I knew slept underneath. This small room was even blacker than the bedroom as the curtains was drawn tight but I still held my candlestick. I could just make out a big dark shape underneath the window and I could already see that this was a larger desk so I began to move towards it. Then I heard something crumple underfoot. I bent down with the candle so I could investigate what I was treading on and I saw that the floor was covered in pieces of ink-splattered paper. I wondered why such sheets would be strewn around the place and wondered if Rylance really was that messy. This was the first moment when the thought entered my head that this place may have been burgled already that night.

Then I saw the black metal box with silver linings and the question was put beyond all doubt. It was the very one I had spotted Rylance scurrying away with on the previous morning and now it was there beside those papers, lying on its side as if it had been tossed there. It was already smashed open and, as I crouched down to inspect it, I saw that it was empty.

I reached down to feel if anything had rolled out but all I could touch was those inky sheets, and around then my candle was snuffed out. The room was now in almost complete darkness and so I crossed over to the window so I could let in some moonlight.

But, as I reached the corner of the desk and was about to lean over the chair to pull at the curtains, I realised there was something in my way. I staggered and my hands fell onto some obstruction what was in the chair. To my sudden horror I saw that there was a man sitting there, his head slumped onto the desk and more black liquid – like that what I had just touched on the paper – was spreading out across it. I do not remember crying out in fright but I must have done, as Mouse called through from the other room.

'Dodger!' I heard him hiss. 'What's up?'

I just stood and looked at the figure for a moment and half-expected him to turn his head towards me and ask what I thought I was doing in his study. But the man was a dead weight and I saw that his crown had been bashed in from behind. A weapon lay beside him on the desk. It was a pistol and it too was covered in what I now realised was not ink at all. At last I gathered enough wits to pull back the curtains and let in enough light to reveal the redness of the liquid and of the curls on the man's head.

'Jack!' Mouse said again from behind the door. 'Trouble coming. Let's dash!'

But I continued to stare at this bloody mess what had been made of Anthony Rylance. I picked up the barker what must have been used as a bludgeon and – in my shock – I tried to work out how it had got in there. The sound of a crow was heard from outside the front of the house.

'Can't you hear her?' Mouse demanded as he opened the door to the study as he came in to get me. 'Tom is frantic and downstairs—'

Then he stopped still and looked at me standing over the body of this murdered man with a bloody pistol in my hand.

'Jack?' he gasped as he looked from the corpse to me. 'You didn't do that, did you?'

But there was no time to correct this astounding error as the sounds of heavy footsteps charging up the stairs from the street entrance was heard. Mouse dropped his sack in alarm as the sounds of heavy banging came from the apartment door. From behind some hard men's voices was calling out to be granted entrance.

'Mr Rylance, sir! It's the police. Open the door or we shall force it!'

But before we even had a chance to collect our thoughts and work out by which exit it would be best to escape, we could already hear that the door was being forced open. Mouse panicked and dashed out of the study again as if he wanted to make for the bedroom into which we had entered. But I could hear that the door was already being forced and it crashed open before he had even left the study. I then heard the sounds of a struggle as these new intruders scrambled towards Mouse and he cried out. Although I could not see what was happening, I recognised the sounds of police brutality when I heard them. I knew that my only chance of getting away was to leave through the window of this room, which meant stepping onto the desk and over the corpse of the dead man. I pulled the curtains away and cracked the window open and I was halfway through it as the first peeler entered the study.

'Murder!' the peeler shouted the instant he saw the body I was leaving behind me. 'There's been a killing and one of them is making off! Grab him!'

I had already crawled outwards though and was back onto the ledge, but by now the four bull-terriers below had all been woken by the racket.

They was barking up at me and scratching at the walls in their fury. I did not let this stop me from moving, though, and I kept a steady footing as I edged my way along to the courtyard wall. As I did so I passed the window through which we entered and saw Mouse getting beaten by several wooden truncheons through the door. Another peeler appeared between him and myself and charged towards me.

I hurried my passage towards the wall knowing that if I could cross this yard quick enough then freedom would await me the other side. Hiding from the peelers would be possible on the riverbank as the darkness would confound them more than it ever would me. But then my foot trod on something what had not been on the ledge earlier. It was one of the slabs of steak what Mouse had brought along to feed the dogs with and it caused me to slip. The bull terriers below became hysterical with excitement as I almost dropped down towards where they was kept but I managed to grab hold of some guttering first, denying them even more meat. This though gave the peelers the chance to catch up with me and soon two of them was leaning out of the window and grabbing on to me. The barks of the dogs was rabid now as they had already destroyed the first steak but even those savage creatures could not have treated me with the viciousness I then received from those what was dragging me back through the window. As soon as I was forced down onto the floor of the apartment the four public servants all drew their truncheons and began setting about me with a fierceness what I had never before experienced by men in uniform. The brutes seemed to be enjoying themselves a good deal as they battered into Mouse and myself and there was even more howling from then than there was from the dogs outside. It was a long time before any of these peelers grew tired of arresting us.

Chapter 12

The Blue Lobsters

In which I am trapped within the enemy lair

The four peelers what had invaded the home of Anthony Rylance had themselves a police van already waiting outside for us in the street and some manacles to place over our hands. I struggled against these rusty bindings as I was forced down the staircase what led away from the scene but they was fastened so tight that they began to cut my wrists. As I was pushed down to the landing of the house I saw the woman to whom I sold the mistletoe stood in her doorway. She must have been waiting to get a glimpse of the robbers and she gasped in recognition as I passed. She began telling the arresting sergeant all about my visit on the previous day and that she had not trusted me one ounce even then.

'Then you had a lucky escape, madam,' the sergeant told her as his constables forced me out and into the street. 'For this one is a violent killer and has given your neighbour up there a proper bludgeoning.'

I denied this and told the two peelers what was bundling me into the back of their vehicle that Anthony Rylance was given his bludgeoning before I had even arrived. But they was not interested in my protestations and they raised their truncheons to tell me to shut it until we reached the nearest police station. I was sat in the back of the van and as the police horses led us away I looked over to Mouse. Even he looked like he did not believe me.

When we arrived at the nearest police station there was some confusion as the Night Inspector there did not seem to recognise the three arresting officers – the fourth had been left to mind the body – and he seemed most surprised to see them in his vicinity.

'We've come from a different division,' the sergeant explained and pointed at some numbers on his uniform. 'As you can see. My name is Sergeant Dickinson and my constables and I have apprehended these two villains in the very act of murder at an address near Embankment. The body is still there and I suggest you send some of the police from this station to attend to the scene directly.'

'I see,' said the Night Inspector, who lay down some novel he was holding and regarded the unfamiliar peelers as though they was nuisances what was distracting him from a much more diverting narrative. 'And what are you calling yourselves then, eh?' he asked us.

'We're the Innocent brothers,' I declared. 'And we ain't done nothing to nobody.'

I was hoping that Mouse and I could be able to evade having our identities revealed for long enough that if a chance for us to foot it out of here came along we could take it and not be tracked so easy. But, just before the Night Inspector was about to enter us in his ledger under Unknown, one of the arresting constables piped up.

'Sergeant Dickinson,' he said and pointed towards me. 'That one there is familiar to me, sir.'

'Oh, is he now?'

'Yes, sir,' said the constable who I did not recognise at all. 'I've known him from when I was under Inspector Bracken.'

My spirits sank as I heard this. Bracken was always bursting into the Three Cripples whenever he wanted to bully some criminals and loved to harass me in particular. If this constable had served under him then he was sure to know me.

'I believe his name is Dodger, sir,' his voice was flat. 'Or something like that.'

'Dodger is not his given name, I take it, constable?' asked the sergeant. 'What's the surname then?' The constable shrugged and so the sergeant asked the Night Inspector if he had ever heard of me.

He just sighed as if he thought this was going to be a long night. 'I've known scores of criminals called Dodger,' he remarked. 'It's a common nickname around these parts.'

The arresting sergeant looked annoyed and turned to the constable. 'Well, you better send for Inspector Bracken then,' he ordered him. 'For the identification.'

'At this time of night?' yawned the Night Inspector, who did not seem to much care what my name might be. 'Why not just lock them up for now, eh? They're not going anywhere and I'd sooner let the day police worry about them. You'll find a free cell down the end of that corridor and on the right.'

Once the locks on this cell door was turned and Mouse and I was alone, he spoke for the first time since our arrest.

'What happened, Dodge?' he whispered in a frantic way. 'What was you doing with that man?' He was looking at me as if I was a total stranger to him and I was stunned about what must be going through his mind.

'You don't think I killed him, do you?' I asked in amazement. 'He was like that when I found him.' My childhood friend blinked back at me. 'Don't be silly, Mouse, it's me. I ain't a killer. Besides, his head was cracked with a barker which you know I never carry. Have a think!'

'Right,' he said in a voice what did not sound certain. 'Of course you never. I don't know why I thought . . . it's just . . .'

'Just what? How could you even entertain the thought?'

'Dunno. It's the way you've been acting lately. Chucking things at people's heads and being more boisterous and quarrelsome than is normal. I thought you was trying to become more violent. Y'know, like Billy Slade is. I thought Slade had asked you to do it.'

This remark managed to shock me more than anything else I had experienced that night. But rather than take him to task for his moral misconceptions about me, I instead knelt down and started giving him some advice.

'They might think they know who I am, right, but it don't follow that they've placed you. So give them a false name because if there is a chance to escape then we need to take it. Things look bad and I've a feeling they'll get worse soon enough.'

Some hours before daybreak I was proven right. We heard the locks of this holding cell turn from the other side and I heard the voice of Sergeant Dickinson talking to someone.

'So if we're right about his identity,' I heard him tell this person as the bolts was slid, 'then your constable is the one to tell us. I'm glad we sent for you, Inspector.'

The droning voice what replied was a familiar one.

'I shall be able to tell you myself,' I heard it say, 'he's not a person you forget in a hurry.'

The door opened and in Bracken walked with his tombstone face and bird-shit pallor. He looked at me as though he held me in similar high regard and spoke to Dickinson who followed him in behind.

'You are correct,' Bracken said with his fixed eyes on mine as I was sat on a wooden chair. 'It's Dawkins. The same man who showed me a pardon he had received two years ago telling me that he was a reformed character. This turn of events is unsurprising.'

'I'm not guilty, Inspector,' I said knowing that it was useless to go on pretending I was someone else any longer, 'the dead man was there already. I was just burgling the place. I'm an innocent man.'

A third policeman walked into the cell as I said that and tutted my given name as though in a disappointed manner.

'John Dawkins,' said Horrie Belltower with a sad and insincere shake of the head. 'Come to this. What would our dear mother say if she could see you now?'

'It ain't how it looks, Horrie,' I pleaded with him. 'I ain't the killing kind. You should know, we're brothers after all.'

'Half-brothers,' he returned without a smile. Then he looked over at Mouse and pointed at him with his truncheon. 'This one's name is Mouse Flynn. And he's always been a troublemaker an' all.' Mouse groaned in the chair next to me and I told Horrie he was a disgrace to the family.

'Splendid,' Dickinson remarked and clapped his hands together. 'That's all we needed confirmed. Now, we've inconvenienced you and your constable for long enough, Inspector, so I shall let you both get back to your own division. Me and my constables can see to things from here. He'll get his comeuppance, don't you worry about that.'

But Bracken did not move. 'S Division, I see?' the old Inspector said slow.

'That's right, sir,' the younger man replied and again pointed to his numbers. 'That would be the Hampstead station.'

'But you're not in Hampstead now?'

'No, sir,' Dickinson replied. 'We were sent to the Embankment following an anonymous message received by our commanding officer.'

'An anonymous message?'

'Indeed, sir,' the sergeant nodded and gave a small chuckle. 'Don't know who sent it but then that's the anonymous for you.

Heh.' Then he stopped laughing under Bracken's stony gaze. 'Tragically, we were not in time to save the life of Mr Rylance,' he continued in an altered tone.

Bracken turned back to me and sniffed. 'You did however manage to apprehend one of this city's most notorious criminals. Be sure to congratulate your commanding officer for me.' I was getting the impression that Bracken was a little jealous that he had not been the one to fix the cuffs on me.

Sergeant Dickinson then followed Bracken out of the room and Constable Belltower made to follow. 'Hold up!' I shouted before Horrie could shut the cell door after himself. 'What's going to happen to us?'

'You'll be put before the judge, John,' said Horrie with a heavy sigh, 'and God help the pair of you then. You know what the punishment for murder is.'

'But ain't we entitled to a lawyer or something?'

Horrie seemed to think about this then as though nobody had ever troubled him with that question before.

'In all truth, John,' he smiled as if amused by his own ignorance, 'I have no blooming idea. Sleep well.' The door swung shut and the locks was turned.

We was kept in that cell until the courts was ready for us and we had little communication with the outside world save for some visits from a lawyer who Barney had sent down on our behalf. All other visitors was banned but Horrie popped his head into the cell on the morning of our trial so he could show us something. It was a cutting from a halfpenny broadside what was circulating the city and would have been found pinned upon the walls of pubs and coffee-houses for all Londoners to enjoy. It went like this: –

Fair people all, do steel your hearts, to hear of horrid violence
Of that which fell upon the crown of honest fellow Rylance.
Alone he sat, while hard at work, of danger unaware,
But to his home like rats did creep a vile and wicked pair.

Two burglars came, with hearts of black, they stole into his house,
The first was Dawkins, first name Jack, the second went by Mouse.
These two thieves of much ill-fame (for their names they are notorious),
Behind poor Rylance sneaking came, to commit a crime injurious.

A deadly blow! An armed attack! The reporter he was done for,
And now with blood upon their hands they tried to make a run for –
Liberty! And so they fled, to the window for release,
But who should burst into the room but some swift-footed police!

And so to trial these wretches go and justice has one hope,
That the judge of the Old Bailey will give these boys the rope!

Horrie seemed to find the verse very amusing but, seeing as he was not a strong reader, he got one of the other constables to read it out to us. I was glad when he at last buggered off home.

The judge was a shrinking walnut of a man and I had a suspicion that I had seen him somewhere before. He took a hostile attitude towards Mouse and myself from the start and became most impatient with my fellow defendant when he told the court what his name was. Mouse was not a nickname but the only one my friend had ever known and he had never seen a birth certificate what might prove otherwise. When asked if it was his mother what had named him after a tiny rodent, Mouse just shrugged and replied that he had never even met the woman so he couldn't be sure. This did nothing to endear us to the jury what already considered us close to vermin and our solicitor – a cove named Jacob Slaithwaite – became even more pessimistic about our chances than he had been already.

This Slaithwaite was the same ancient and gin-sodden man of the law what had defended Fagin against charges of being a fence and a kidsman eight years prior. Neither of those crimes was punishable by death so he had very much excelled himself in getting the old Jew the drop for it regardless. But, to his credit, Jacob had also represented me after I had been taken into custody following the Evershed affair two years before and had been successful in securing my freedom on that occasion. He also possessed the admirable virtue of hating the new police as much as any criminal, which I hoped would prove beneficial in this situation. I had a deep distrust for most other solicitors as there was many a dark tale about back-handed lawyers what worked against their clients for profit. Jacob, at least, was one of us.

The high-walled but sweaty room was full of spectators eager to see how the much-publicised Dawkins and Flynn trial would unfold. In particular, the press bench was crammed with noisy scribblers, none of which seemed sympathetic to our plight. Some of them called out for the judge to give us the rope before the trial had even begun. Of course Anthony Rylance had himself been a court reporter so I suppose that we could not have expected much even-handed coverage from that quarter.

The first person to give testimony was the arresting sergeant and he explained to the court how he had been sent to check upon the safety of Anthony Rylance. His superior officer, so he claimed, had received an anonymous message saying that the man was in deadly danger that very night and so he ordered Sergeant Dickinson to gather some constables together and proceed to the address forthwith. He then told how he and his men had forced their way into the property and discovered Mouse and myself still there with the fresh corpse of the murdered man. There was two pistols on the scene – the one what I had used to smash in the victim's head and another found on the floor of the front room what Mouse must have dropped.

'Untrue!' I cried, enraged by his words. 'We never carry barkers, you can ask anyone! They was there before we arrived.' The judge banged his gavel at this outburst and told me to quieten myself, and I then turned on Slaithwaite to ask why he was not making these sort of objections on my behalf. He advised that it would be better for us to just appear as docile as possible but as he spoke I could smell the alcohol on his breath.

Next to take the stand was the senior peeler who explained how this anonymous message he had received had arrived at his station via electronic telegraph. It warned that the life of Anthony Rylance was in urgent danger. This officer – who was called Detective Superintendent Mills – was convinced of its veracity and so despatched his minions with due haste. The court treated this Mills with a lot more respect than they did us and he was dressed to intimidate in his full uniform of high rank. He looked a lot like Bracken, it occurred to me as I watched him swear upon the Bible, with his beardless mutton-chops and tall, looming stature and I wondered if the Metropolitan Police grew these people like trees.

'From where was the telegraph sent?' Mills was then asked. But it was not our lawyer who asked the question – he had long since dozed off – and nor was it from the judge. No, the question instead came from the press bench and I had to crane my head around to see who had spoken. 'You must know that at least, Detective Superintendent?' the questioner continued.

DS Mills looked perturbed, as if he was being accosted by a drunkard on the street, and he looked to the judge to see if he should answer. The judge rebuked the caller but then mentioned that it was a fair enough question and expressed surprise that the defence had not asked it.

'The telegraph came – oddly enough – from here, your honour,' Mills then explained. 'From the Old Bailey itself. We have endeavoured to discover who sent it but until now have had no luck. I can produce the document if the court requires it?'

'That won't be necessary,' said the judge and his pug-nosed face squinted with displeasure towards the press bench. 'Now if the *Morning Chronicle* has no further question . . . ?'

'Did the witness have any prior knowledge of the victim, your honour?' the voice called out again. 'Was Mr Rylance known to the police?' I looked again at the huddle of journalists now shoving each other in irritation but I was unsure as to which of them was addressing the court in so abrasive a manner. 'And if not – why did the Detective Superintendent not consider the message a hoax?'

'I had never heard the name Anthony Rylance before,' Mills responded in an indignant manner. 'I took the message seriously because it was a death threat and I am a public servant. And considering what my officers discovered upon arrival at the stated address, it is a good job that I did not think it a hoax.'

The judge, meanwhile, had become enraged and was banging his gavel like a demented blacksmith. He called for order from the press and once the court had settled down he thanked Mills for his trouble and declared that there would be no further questions. Mills nodded and left the courtroom.

The testimony of Mouse and myself was of course met with nothing but derision and disbelief from everyone present which was ironic as I was – for once in my life – telling a courtroom the truth. There was no use denying burglary but it was a hanging for murder what we was trying to avoid and so we confessed to our crimes and no more. I left out the part about how we was put up to the job by someone else as I knew it would not have helped our cause much and I had the criminal code to think of. But this meant that I had no good reason to be creeping around the property of a man who no doubt seemed to be more impoverished than myself and when I told them that I had come to steal a metal deposit box – what I claimed to have seen him carrying on the streets and just assumed contained something worth having – I was asked why no such box was there in the apartment.

'Yes, it was,' I protested. 'I saw it there when I entered the room and it was already emptied.' The prosecutor announced that the police inventory had not catalogued such an item and he put it to me that I was making the thing up. My true intention for entering the Rylance home that night – he put it to me – was murder. Cold, premeditated murder. And all this talk of mystery boxes was simply a desperate lie to escape the noose.

Soon became time for the jury to retire. They was back within ten minutes.

When I heard the head juror declare us both guilty I was overcome with a vivid sensation. It was as though rays of sunlight had just burst through the tall windows of this courthouse and the room had reddened. Something invisible struck me behind the legs and I collapsed onto the floor. I was lifted up again by a pair of gaolers so I could stand for the sentence while beside me Mouse had begun to shake. The judge then announced that we was a wicked pair of criminals and that, considering that it was impossible to tell which of us had committed the foul deed, he would be sentencing us as one. He made much of the fact that I had been transported once before by the Crown and that I should never have been allowed back to contaminate this fair country. He put on his black cap and cleared his throat.

We was to be taken from that place and led through the underground tunnel what connected the Old Bailey to Newgate Prison. There we would be kept until the hour of execution which would take place in two weeks' time.

As he spoke I looked up to the galleries above to see if any of my familiars had come to support me in this dark and heavy hour. The only face what I recognised was that of Lily Lennox. She was crying for me without reserve and I wanted to shout up to her and tell her to dry her eyes as it would be all right. But I could not imagine what on earth I could base such an assertion on.

Beside Lily was another woman who I did not recognise. She had in her hands a small baby and when Mouse looked up towards this child he shouted out the name of his infant son in despair. But the gaolers soon had hold of us and they began leading our resistant selves out of the courtroom.

'This *still* ain't the shop for justice!' I cried in outrage before they could force me from the court. 'You're the murderers, not us!'

But the whole place had now erupted into noise and clamour as I was pulled from the scene. The only sound I kept hearing though, as we was led downwards through the Bailey and towards the dim lights of the Newgate tunnel, was the persistent cries of little Robin Flynn – who had that day been sentenced to grow up an orphan like his father.

Part Two

Chapter 13

The Black Stage

*A most dismal Christmas Eve over which the noose hangs
like poisoned mistletoe*

'*Hats Off!*'

The voice was low and theatrical and it cried out from somewhere deeper within the crowd. I could not see from my low position to who this voice belonged but it impressed me as rich and familiar, like my father's would have been had I ever known the man.

'*Hats off for the condemned!*'

It was the hangman's voice, I guessed as I forced my way through the thick crowd towards where I knew the scaffold to be, but nobody was paying it much mind and I did not see any of the gentlemen nor ladies remove their headwear as a mark of respect for those about to be executed. Instead they continued with their jostling for a better position, drunken squabbling and gallows humour – nothing makes Londoners more excitable than a bloody good hanging. Thousands of them was gathered together in this tight space outside of the prison but I needed to forge forwards if I was to reach the affluent hundreds, the ones what had bought tickets for the front spots.

'*Behold the Black Stage!*' cried the voice again and I realised that it was not the hangman – he had still not appeared and this voice was coming from somewhere else. It seemed to come from the other ticket-holders, those who occupied seats at the overlooking windows and balconies and whose pockets remained out of reach. Yet the pickings was still rich the closer to the scaffold you got and so my friends and I continued forwards. *'The Cross-Beam!'* continued the voice, although we was all too diminutive to see much among the hot crush of adults what surrounded us. *'The Rope!'*

The tone of the voice was peculiar and it was hard to tell whether it was gloating, as countless others had come here to do, or whether it was issuing a dread warning. But, as our small gang of three weaved our way to the uppermost part of this wedge of space between St Sepulchre's Church and the doors of Newgate, I was struck by the odd sensation that it seemed to be addressing me alone. We soon reached the front of the spectators, having travelled further in than we had meant to, and the three lines ahead of us began to part. For the first time in my life saw the horrible sight what others had come here to relish in.

'All the hideous apparatus of Death!'

The makeshift platform stood proud outside the Debtors' Door, its carpentry neat and exact. It was much blander than I had been expecting but it also looked like an empty stage waiting for actors to bring it alive and the three patient nooses dangled from the scaffold. All what separated it from the baying crowd was a low wooden fence and, should any high-spirited wag wish to cross that barrier, jump onto the unguarded platform and play with the ropes for our entertainment, then there would be nothing stopping him. But nobody dared to. They just remained at a safe distance and continued calling for the real performance to hurry up and start.

A small hand tapped me on the sleeve. I did not look down but instead kept on staring up at the gibbets as I dropped my own hand down to meet it. A heavy pocket watch was passed between us and I could hear the ticks as I placed it within my coat with the rest of the booty. Mouse had done well on this, his first big outing. He was still only eight then meaning that I must have been around eleven, and that watch had been his third good find since we had entered the crowd. I had explained to him the importance of passing any valuables along to me once the pockets was picked so that if he got grabbed then the beaks could not touch him. Some boys was reluctant to do this but not Mouse. He knew he could trust me to keep his things safe.

'They're coming, Dodger!' said the boy to my right. 'They're bringing them up! It's begun!' I flashed Jem White one of my sternest looks because he was supposed to be concentrating on the thieve and not enjoying the spectacle and, what was furthermore, I did not appreciate him using my name in public hearing.

'You trying to get us to twist an' all?' I hissed in a low whisper but he looked back to me like I was the one who was being a fool.

'Stealing ain't capital, Jack,' he said, as if he could not have cared less who overheard him. 'They won't hang either of us for that.'

I was about to scold him for setting a bad example in front of the younger boy but it was too late as he was right, the show had begun. The immense crowd launched into a mighty roar and swelled forward as the first turnkey appeared at the open door and led in the rest of the procession. He was followed by three hobbling figures, all hooded in what appeared to be brown potato sacks with rope cords around their necks, two other gaolers and – bringing up the rear and earning the greatest cheer of all – the current hangman of the Stone Jug. Around us feet began stamping and chants of *Jack Ketch, Jack Ketch, Jack Ketch* rang out. Ketch has been dead for two hundred years but such was the notoriety of Newgate's most celebrated executioner that his name has since been thrust upon anyone what has ever succeeded him. This Ketch, with the aid of the gaolers, was securing the nooses nice and tight around the necks of the three condemned

– one woman and two men. The man in the centre was thin and would have been tall if not so hunched.

'They're shivering,' said Jem with some contempt. 'You'd think they'd show a bit more steel than that.' I turn to ask Jem if he thought he'd be putting on a better display come the day of his own appearance on the black stage but I was interrupted by another tug from Mouse's hand. He had another trinket for me to take.

The executioner told us to remove our hats and this time the command was answered. I took off my own silk topper and, as I did so, I sensed that the hunched man had turned his face towards me.

'Can they see out of those masks?' I asked nobody in particular and a smart gentleman beside me scoffed at my question. Then the Ketch asked the three condemned – in a voice what carried for all our benefits – if they would now like to confess to their sins for which they was about to receive this final earthly punishment. If they did so, he told them, they might be spared further torments in the world beyond this and so it was worth a go. None responded to this entreaty save for the hunched man in the centre. He was shaking something violent now and raised his masked head up.

'Strike you all dead!' was his muffled cry. 'What right have you to butcher me?'

I looked back to Jem to see if he considered that to be a stronger performance. But Jem had vanished into the crowd and I could hear that Mouse had begun to sob. I took his little hand again but this time to comfort him. I told him that he should trust me. That all was going to be just rosy.

The Ketch then pulled his lever and we heard the thud of the trap. Before I had time to turn away I saw all three figures drop and dangle like puppets and the sight was a horror to me. I turned down to see to Mouse but he had already turned hysterical. The crowd roared louder than ever now but it did not sound like the cry of triumph I had expected, more like sudden outrage. It was as though this triple hanging was the last thing anyone here had expected to see.

'Don't look, Mouse,' I bent down and whispered into the ear of my young apprentice. 'Don't look and it can't hurt you.'

But the crowd grew bold once more and soon they was stamping again and cheering for the executioner to take a bow. I closed my eyes and soon the only sound I could hear was a thousand voices of the city all paying their noisy tribute.

'*Jack Ketch! Jack Ketch! Jack Ketch!*'

I must have been making a proper fuss during my first night's sleep in the condemned cell as a pair of rough hands shook me awake and someone told me to hold my tongue. I opened my eyes and strained to make sense of my dark surroundings and of the person what was leaning over me and speaking in an old and unkind voice. I was lying on a thin mattress on the stone bench what passed for a prison bed and I was clutching at some sweaty rag of a blanket. There was a fireplace what someone had lit and this was supplying the principal source of light. There was also one small window high up on the wall behind me but it was dark outside so it was from the fire's crackle that I saw the side of the man's face. He was grey and wrinkled and he looked to be fixing on breaking my neck if I did not calm myself first.

'Enough Jack Ketching, you young wretch!' He spoke like he had not taken a drop of anything in weeks. 'We don't need reminding of Ketch, we'll meet him soon enough.'

I looked about the rest of the cell and saw that it was large enough for two more of these stone beds. Mouse was sitting on one and staring up at the barred window. He did not seem to be paying any attention to this old cove what was rasping in my face about someone called Old Edwards.

'Old Edwards don't wish to be sharing his cell with none others on his final nights alive,' continued this man. 'Old Edwards will bloody throttle you if you don't pipe down.' Mouse then turned his head towards me and nodded to see me awake.

'He's been carrying on like that for the past hour now,' he said, as if he was already bored of the performance. 'Took me an age to fall in that Old Edwards was himself.'

'One more murder won't matter much to Old Edwards now!' continued Old Edwards and he spat upon the ground. I now recalled seeing our aged cellmate when we was first tossed into this shared accommodation by the turnkeys but I had been in a state of high emotion at the time and had not introduced myself in a formal manner. And so it therefore followed that this old sod was under the false impression that he was the dominant prisoner in this little room and in this misconception he needed correcting. I took a moment to wipe the sweat from off my brow with the sheet and I then forced myself up to meet my confused aggressor face to face.

'If Old Edwards knows what's good for him,' I said locking eyes and pointing over to the unoccupied bench, 'he'll go back to his own side before Young Dawkins here knocks the last remaining tooth out of his head.' The old man looked surprised by this sudden flash of fire and he inched backwards at it. His long grey hair flopped down over the sides of his head like a pair of dog ears and he gave me a low growl to show me he was unafraid. But, like any dog, he seemed to recognise a fiercer animal when he saw one and so before long he picked himself and crossed back to his own bed.

'Just keep your peace then,' he muttered as he went. 'That goes for the pair of you.'

Once this matter was settled, I sat myself upright and took an appraisal our situation. Unlike Mouse and myself Old Edwards was wearing brown and shapeless prison clothes while we was still dressed in the suits what Jacob had provided us with before our trial. Mine was by now much crinkled and covered in sweat but I still felt an odd pride in being better dressed than most prisoners would be. I scratched behind my neck and stared into the fire. My head ached from the thinness of the pillow so I felt no urge to lay back down again. Then, seeing how nobody else was going to say anything, I decided to instigate some conversation.

'This place stinks of vinegar,' I observed, and I gave the older man a look like I suspected it was emanating from him. 'And piss,' I added.

'It's for the lice,' said Old Edwards like he resented my implication. 'Lice spread typhus so the gaolers scrub it into the walls to kill them off.' I got the sense that he enjoyed knowing more about this dungeon than I did. 'The vinegar I mean,' he added. 'The piss smell is from the bucket.'

He had a small lisp what I imagined might be the result of his split lip and I wondered if the turnkeys had given it to him. I gave him a short nod to acknowledge thanks for the information and another silence passed. But then I was up from my bed, clapped my hands together and crossed over to the fire to warm them.

'You know what this place could use, eh, Mouse?' I said as I crouched over the licking flames and tried to affect a more agreeable manner. 'Some festive decorations. It's Christmas Eve today in case you've forgotten. But you wouldn't know it looking around this miserable hole, eh? They ain't made much of an effort for us, have they? It's all cobwebs.' I blew at one such web what hung from the side of the grate and then I pointed at the place on the wall where a Sheriff's notice was hanging. 'I would like to see a nice holly wreath covering that, wouldn't you? Or perhaps a picture of some robins in the snow. That'd be cheering. Also, how about some chestnuts to warm over this here fire?' I added, and looked over to Old Edwards. 'Who do we see about all that then?'

The old man hesitated before answering. He looked unsure as to whether I was jesting with him or not. 'Ask the turnkeys,' he suggested at last. 'They'd give you something in exchange for your suit there. They paid me two pennies for my clothes and they weren't as smart as the ones you two boys have on.'

'And what d'you want tuppence for in this horrible place?' asked Mouse in sudden irritation. 'You're set for the noose same as us, ain't you?'

Old Edwards became despondent at this mention of his imminent fate and he looked down to his shoes. 'Gave the pennies to my daughter when she came,' he rasped, 'if you must know.' Mouse's demeanour altered at the words. He pulled himself forward to perch on the end of his bed.

'You can do that, can you?' he asked our cellmate with keen interest. 'Give money to visitors.' He looked over to me after Old Edwards had nodded. 'I'm selling my suit then,' he declared. 'And giving the money to Robin when his midwife visits. She's bound to come.'

I experienced a sharp stab of guilt on hearing that. I had been bragging to Mouse not so very long ago about how together we would see to it that his son would never want for nothing. And now here he was excited at the prospect of bequeathing the boy with two measly pennies before he departed the earth. I had proven to be a rotten top sawyer to him and his next of kin and, what was furthermore, I was at a loss to imagine who might come to visit me what would be worth giving such coins to. My mother had been hanged herself some years before and, considering that

Kat Dawkins was never the sentimental sort anyhow, I very much doubted that she would have come to visit me in prison even if she was still alive. Would Lily come? I hoped so. But my sort of person does not set foot into Newgate if he or she does not need to. I have known plenty of good friends what may have occupied this very cell over the years and, to my great shame, I had not visited one of them.

I felt that despair was then about to overcome me and I slumped down onto the stone bench in silence. I wanted to cry but fought hard not to. I would not lose mastery of myself in front of Mouse and this other person.

'Well then,' I sniffed, after what felt like an hour of all three of us just staring into the fire had passed, 'if the turnkeys want my clothes off me then they'll have to make a more generous offer than that.'

Mouse seemed surprised to hear me resume the conversation after so long a pause. But I stood up and occupied the centre of the cell so he could see that the same old Jack Dawkins was in here with him and that our terrible circumstances had not damaged my spirits just yet.

'No, sir, I shan't be selling my portable property for pennies and neither, Mouse Flynn, should you be. We're celebrated murderers, we are.'

I looked to Old Edwards to see if he was impressed by the announcement but his eyes did not leave the flames.

'That's right, Edwards,' I continued regardless. 'You're in the company of famous men. You should see some of the publicity what we've been getting over the past few days. Our suits would be worth a fortune to Madame Tussaud's if only she could get her greedy paws on them. I daresay that the enterprising madam is working hard on our waxworks already, eh, Mouse?' I grinned at him then and he just stared back at me like I had run mad. At last he managed a weak smile in return. I pointed to him for the benefit of Old Edwards.

'That there is the notorious Mouse Flynn,' I said by way of introduction, 'and my name is Jack Dawkins, better known as the Artful Dodger. Don't pretend you ain't heard of me, you'll just embarrass yourself.'

'He ain't listening to you, Jack,' said Mouse as the old boy ignored us. But there was something about his tone what suggested that what he was really telling me was that he wasn't listening either.

'He doesn't have to,' I crossed the cell and sat myself down next to Mouse on his bed, 'but you do. Because there is something very important I need to explain to you, Mouse.' He looked back and I could see tiredness and defeat on his face. While I had been having nightmares he had been weeping to himself about our plight – that was obvious from looking into his eyes. 'Because you are going to see your little boy again. And I don't mean when his midwife visits. I mean, out there,' I indicated the small barred window. 'On the other side of those walls.'

'We're sentenced to death, Jack,' he replied with a crack in his voice. 'A reprieve ain't likely. Jacob said so.' I put my arms around his shoulders to show him what good company he was still in.

'I ain't talking about a reprieve, am I? Jacob is right, nobody with any power is interested in helping us. There ain't a soul in this world what would stick their necks out to save ours. No, we have to look out for ourselves if we're to live to see old age.'

Mouse blinked. His mouth opened but to no purpose.

'Because I've got no intention of getting hanged in two Mondays' time,' I told him. 'It's a barbarism no decent Englishman should be prepared to suffer and old Jack Ketch will just have lump it. I had already made up my mind to take flight before the judge had finished speaking and you, my boy, are coming with me. By the time the gaolers comes to collect us, we shall be long gone from Newgate, from London even. We'll be on the continent, I imagine, sipping wine and learning the local language with your baby Robin playing at our feet.'

'Escape?' he said at last. 'But how?'

Now there he had me.

'Well, I ain't worked that out yet, Mouse. I've only been in here ten minutes, give us a chance. But stop looking so gloomy, eh? It's going to be just rosy.'

'You always say things are going to be rosy, Dodger,' he said at last. 'That's all you ever say and they never are.'

This sullen response took me back a bit. I felt it was thin gratitude for the deliverance that I was offering him. From the other bed came an awful groan though as the old man heaved himself into life again.

'Escape?' he wheezed. 'From the Stone Jug? Old Edwards calls you a fool.'

'I don't recall inviting Old Edwards along,' I replied, 'so tell him to mind his own business.'

'It can't be done,' he continued, 'and you'll be killed trying.'

'Killed, you reckon?' I replied, employing all my powers of parody. 'How awful. Well, if my life's in danger I don't think I'll bother.' I turned to Mouse and rolled my eyes, hoping he would give a smile. He said nothing.

'You can mock,' Edwards persisted, 'but there are worse fates than a dignified hanging.'

'I doubt that.'

'I had a friend once,' he persisted as he reached for a bent poker to touch the fire, 'what was here twenty year ago. Sentenced to drop. But on the Sunday night before his execution he breaks free from his cell and somehow gets into the south quadrangle just outside here. Tries scaling a drainpipe but, just as he reaches the roof, falls and breaks both his legs. A very long drop, this one. Surgeon dresses his wounds and he's carried to the gallows anyhow. Blood gushes from both of his damaged limbs as he thrashes under the noose. They say the first four lines of spectators was all sprayed crimson. No dignity to it.'

'I don't wish to offend you, Edwards,' I said once he had finished with his delightful tale, 'but your friend sounds like a proper clown. Countless people have escaped from this prison over the years. I've met several of them down the Three Cripples, among other places.'

'You've met several liars then.'

'Your trouble is that you're lazy,' I told him. 'And you lack my ambition.' I turned from the old man and back to Mouse. 'Let's not listen to him. He's nothing but doom. We'll escape out of here through hard work and daring. Just like Jack Sheppard did.'

With that Old Edwards gave another moan and dropped down onto his bed. 'Not another one on about Sheppard!' he said. 'That was a hundred year ago.'

Jack Sheppard was a highwayman from the previous century. He must have been a hopeless crook – as evidenced by the way he was forever getting himself captured – but his fame rested instead on his skills as an escapologist. He had broken out of prison four times and two of those occasions was from Newgate. I had read about his exploits many times and, for all I knew, I was now occupying the same cell where Sheppard had managed to first unfetter himself. He had not escaped through the window – as even without the iron bars it was the size and depth of a small bread oven – but had continued his campaign of liberation by instead climbing up the chimney and somehow gaining access to the room above. I jumped up from the bed again and strode back to the grate for examination.

'Don't you put out that fire!' warned Old Edwards once he saw what I was trying to do. I wanted to better inspect how large a space there was for a person to crawl inside and in doing so was using a small brass fire shovel what rested beside the wall to bat the flames down some. The old man jumped up from his bed and came running over to me with his fists ready, 'I said, don't touch that fire!' I was back up again before he reached me and I managed to fend him off with a light shove. But although the man stopped in his tracks he kept on glaring at me and adopted a fighting stance that seemed practised but also unsteady.

'That fire stays ablaze!' he continued shouting. 'It's all we got left in this world. Just some warmth and light before our final hour. Don't you put it out or you'll put out the last thing we have!'

'I ain't going to put it out,' I answered back. 'Or if I do I'll get it relit again. But I need to see if I can squeeze up this passage.'

'You can't, so leave it alone!'

'I can! It's what Sheppard did. He went up the chimney, smashed his way into the grate in the room above, broke through three other doors and made his way up to the high wall. Then he tied some blankets together and hooked one end over a chimney before lowering himself down onto the opposite roof. He achieved all that unaided. But there could be three of us if you could just stop being so difficult and start helping out. We could be out of here in a third of the time.' The old man hesitated and behind him I could feel Mouse leaning in closer. 'A bit of solidarity is what we need. Are our interests not all the same? One last fire? Not if we work together there won't be.'

Mouse got up from his bed and came towards us. 'You reckon

that's true, Dodger?' he said as he began looking into the fireplace. 'You think there's a chance?'

'We have to try,' I replied.

By now Old Edwards' blood had cooled and he had unclenched his fists. But instead of responding to my call to arms, it seemed as though the fight was leaving him and he returned to his bench while Mouse took the fire shovel from me and bent over the flames.

'Edwards is old,' he said with a weary sigh. 'Too old for escapes. And besides, you don't understand. It don't matter what Sheppard did or did not do. This ain't even the same prison.'

'This is Newgate, innit?' I said, as I joined Mouse by the fireplace. He had by now almost extinguished the fire and was waiting for the smoke to settle so we could investigate within.

'It's Newgate, yeah, but it's altered. Most of it has been rebuilt over the years.' The smoke was now beaten down so I stuck my head into the fireplace and looked upwards. It was very hard to see. 'The outside walls are taller now,' Edwards went on. 'Harder to climb down from. And it's near windowless.' I climbed into the small fireplace as far as I could go and started to try and explore where it would take me. The space was cramped and pitch dark. 'Most of the rooms beyond the fireplace would be occupied,' I heard Old Edwards droning on. 'So why you think you won't be spotted trying to move through them is a mystery.' I carried on and raised myself up as far as I could go. And then I felt the iron bars stretching across above me. Three thick rods all blocking my way. I looked beyond them to survey whether it would be possible to continue upwards if I could just remove them somehow. It looked unlikely.

'Now be a good lad,' said Edwards as I at last crawled out and back into the cell, admitting defeat. I did not need Mouse to tell me that my face had turned black, I could feel the soot caking my cheeks. 'And get that fire lit again. Before we all freeze to death first.'

Hours later, when no light was coming in through the window anymore, Mouse and myself huddled around the dying embers of the fire. We had our blankets over our shoulders and whispered to one another as Old Edwards snored from his bed.

'Tomorrow,' I said to Mouse, who was rubbing his hands over the last of the warmth, 'I'm going to ask the guards for some stationery. Some paper and a pen. They'll give it to me if I tell them I want to confess on it.' Mouse looked up from the flames.

'Confess?' he spoke as if he had been waiting for me to say that. 'So you did kill that man?'

'No!' I replied, once more affronted as to how he could believe that. 'I've nothing to confess to,' I hissed. 'At least to no murders.' He looked disappointed as if he had been hoping that I would say otherwise. It occurred to me that if I did own up to the crime then Mouse would be spared the noose. Perhaps that was why he had taken a sulky attitude when I was telling him about my hopes for escape earlier. He must have been praying that my plans to arrange his stay of execution would be simpler and more selfless. 'Confessions are for the repentant,' I put him right. 'And I ain't the type.'

'Then what do you want the paper for?' he asked. 'It's too late now to start your memoirs.'

'I want to write down everything what really happened in Rylance's room,' I replied. 'The way I found the body, the description of how he had been struck, the manner in which the metal box was already opened. And I want to send it to Billy Slade.'

'Send it? Will they allow letters?'

'Probably not, but I shall smuggle it out somehow. We'll slip it to the first person who comes to visit either of us. Perhaps Billy will even visit himself if we're lucky.' I edged forward to Mouse, in part to get closer to the fire but also so that he could hear my whispers better. 'Everybody thinks we're murderers, right, because that's how it looked. And that's how it was made to look. Even you thought I had killed Rylance at first, Mouse, and you was only in the other room. So imagine how it appears to the rest of society. The police, the courts, the newspaper men. They think we're guilty because they have no reason not to. It's been made easy for them to think the worst.'

Mouse sighed. This was something we had already discussed many times in our police cell before the trial. 'Someone got in there first and done him in,' he said as a statement of fact, 'and we was sent there to take the blame for it.'

'Right,' I nodded. 'You have to admit, it's a clever ruse if you do want to kill a person. Nobody believes the burglar, ours is not a trade to inspire that sort of sympathy.'

'And so it follows that the real killer is whoever got Billy Slade to hire us,' Mouse said, repeating words I had already said to him on the previous days. 'And so Slade must know who the real killer is.'

'Perhaps he does, perhaps he don't,' I shrugged. 'Perhaps he knew that the job was suspicious before sending us in there and did not much care. Or perhaps he – like everyone else in the country – just assumes that we did it.'

'Why would he think that? He knows we're just cracksmen.'

'Yeah, but it looks like something went wrong, don't it? That's what they'll all be thinking, see. Not just the flats but the whole of the London underworld. They'll think that we broke in there and surprised Rylance. A fight happened and we ended up killing him. Why would they think it's any more complicated than that? Only

Tom and Georgie know for sure that we did not have barkers on us and what can they say? Anyone they tell will just think it's criminal solidarity speaking. As for Slade, well he may well suspect we was set up or he might just think we're a pair of incompetents. I need to put him right.'

The fire was out. I got to my feet and took my blanket back to my bed.

'But what'll Slade do about it?' asked Mouse as he did the same. 'He won't come to our aid.'

'No, but he'll know not to trust this mystery man of his again and he could make him pay. And word will get around the community, Mouse. Meaning that your baby Robin might not grow up thinking his father was a killer.'

The sudden mention of his son silenced him. He lay down and covered himself in the blanket as I did likewise. I realised then that I had been speaking in such a way what suggested that I did not think we would dodge the gallows after all. I whispered over to him some final words before we both attempted sleep.

'We will escape from here, Mouse. I promise you that. You just stick with me and things will be rosy.' I lay down, shut my eyes and congratulated myself on managing to keep such an optimistic outlook in spite of the many adversities what I was undergoing. It is important to maintain a strength of mind during such testing times, I thought.

Before long I could feel dreams descending upon me again, the stamping of feet, the jeers of the crowd and that hated name being chanted over and over again.

Chapter 14

The Long and Forceful Punishment

Wherein I familiarise myself with life in a medieval dungeon

They had already lain out the coffin for Old Edwards when we entered the chapel. The nine of us what was sentenced to death over the coming weeks had to shuffle past it and two other wooden boxes, our movements restricted by the heavy fetters what had been placed around our arms and legs. We was ordered to seat ourselves in the condemned pew what was reserved for us alone while the rest of the chapel was already packed with unchained bodies waiting for the sermon to start. As I passed by the many rows I saw some of the long-serving convicts and tried to catch an eye. But they all looked away from us, most of them at the floor, and none made a sound.

It was Boxing Day but also the morning before Execution Monday and so this sermon was for the benefit of those due for the scaffold tomorrow. These three coffins was the very ones what they would be buried in afterwards and their soon-to-be occupants – Edwards and two other unfortunates – was all directed to sit at the end of the pew closest to them. In this way the Newgate Ordinary could address most of his sermon in their direction so that the rest of the congregation could be in no doubt as to who the stars of tomorrow's show was to be. It was a large enough chapel and it needed to be, as not only did the entire prison attend these weekly services, but it was also stuffed full with local residents what had paid the keepers of the gaol for admittance. These Sunday gawpers did not mind being heard whispering about us and many of them began eating once the sermon had begun. Elsewhere in the chapel I saw the female convicts who was kept on the far side from the men. The turnkeys made a big effort to separate us from them and I was chastised for even glancing in their direction. The only woman I was permitted to look upon was a trembling leaf named Alice who was sat on our pew near us. She was due to swing on the following Monday.

'It is only repentance that can save your eternal souls now,' droned the puffed-up old prune from high up on his pulpit. 'Only God's forgiveness can protect you from fiery damnation. This the Bible makes abundantly clear.'

This cove was an Ordinary in every sense. A squat, unremarkable man with nothing of the performer about him. If I was in his place and playing to a packed house like this one I would try and put some showmanship into it. I'd be pointing my finger up to the heavens and going on about fallen angels while all the time throwing my voice so even the Old Bailey ladies at the back could hear. There wouldn't be a dry eye in the place once I was done with them. But this grey cove had the peculiar talent of making even Fire and Brimstone sound as dull as a legal document.

'If, however, He should choose not to answer your prayers,' continued this master of ceremonies, 'then Hell awaits you. Such it is writ in the Bible and so there we have it.'

I was sat next to Mouse at the furthest end of the pew and I glanced along the length of it to see Old Edwards at his end, head bowed and hands clenched in furious and desperate prayer. Alice, meanwhile, was inconsolable, and she could be heard babbling about how she had never meant her baby any harm and it had only been an accident. Soon every other convict along this pew was praying too, including – I was amazed to notice – Mouse. I had never had him down as the religious sort and so his behaviour was a bafflement to me. But, I thought as he muttered away next to me, thoughts of imminent death was often apt to do funny things to a person.

I, however, just sat on that cold wooden bench and stared back at the Ordinary with as much defiance as I could muster. Prayer was not an indulgence what held any interest for me and the reasons for this was twofold. In the first instance, I was not guilty of killing Anthony Rylance and so I felt that I had nothing to ask forgiveness for anyway. I was an innocent man – that is if you're prepared to overlook my many pilferings – and so to the Lord's warm bosom I was assuredly bound. I was sure that He would agree that the injustices done against me was far greater than any of the small misdemeanours I may have committed in my time and so I did not feel as though this business of eternal damnation was my concern, in all honesty. Let these seven real murderers what Mouse and I was being made to share a pew with cower behind prayer if they cared to but my mind was busy plotting. Because, in the second instance, prayer was an activity required only by those what was resigned to their fate and I had no intention of still being here by the time they had a coffin ready for me. I was not set to swing until the Monday after next and this gave me plenty of time to make my lucky.

'Death is not the End,' the Ordinary went on, 'for any of us. It is only to be feared by those with hands incarnadine.'

'Hands in where?' I turned to Mouse and whispered.

But it was Alice who answered, coming out of her penitent position to do so. 'Hands incarnadine,' she whispered before returning to her prayers. 'It means us.'

Nobody had come to visit me so far. Visitors was permitted on

Christmas Day and Mouse had been seen by the midwife woman who was now taking care of his son without payment. He had promised to get some money for her to continue to look after little Robin and he was still planning on selling his suit for this purpose. But the turnkeys had announced with undisguised pleasure that no one had called to offer their season's greetings for the poor Artful and this I found to be very hurtful. My disappointment in Lily Lennox was deep as, although it had been a comfort to see her weeping for me from the galleries of the Old Bailey, she had been unable to visit my police cell before the trial and now it was starting to look like she was not coming to Newgate either. I could understand why none of my Diallers was paying me a visit – once a thief is sentenced to death he is already dead, that is how other thieves view it, and I was nobody's top sawyer now. But Lily had been sharing my bed for over a year now and I would have expected more love and loyalty from her than this. But now that my fortunes had fallen and I was captured by the state it looked as though she had disappeared from my side. My heart burned at the abandonment.

Once the Boxing Day service was over we was all led out of the chapel and back to the Felon's Press Yard to take some exercise with the long-serving convicts. Old Edwards, Alice and the others who was swinging tomorrow was all returned to their cells to contemplate their sins while the rest of us was unshackled for the walk. We then joined the group of thirty other convicts in the high-walled hexagon yard and proceeded to tramp around in a slow and shuffling circle while the turnkeys looked on to make sure that none of us spoke to one another. I was desperate to engage anybody in conversation but whenever I tried to speak to any of the old lags I was told to shut up by a turnkey. The long-servers looked reluctant to respond anyhow and they seemed to be trying to avoid me and Mouse. Perhaps they thought that death sentences was catching.

And so instead I had to carry on with that dull rotation for another hour, wondering for what purpose the gaolers felt I should have for exercise if I was due for the drop. However, the benefit of these press yard walks for me was that I got the chance to make a study of Newgate, its layout and workings. I was very practised in the art of breaking into locked places and, it occurred to me as I searched for potential weak spots in the prison walls, that breaking out of a locked place was not so very different. I had still not quite devised how exactly escape was to be achieved but I had no doubt that a solution would present itself if I paid attention.

Soon the long-servers was led back to their cells and we condemned was taken to our quad where we could spend the rest of the morning at our leisure. There had been no snow over the last few days – which was unusual for Christmas – but now a heavy frost covered the cobbled floor and we was given thick coats to warm ourselves as we stayed in that communal space to share cigars, drink and converse with one another. The silent treatment, I was then informed, was just for the long-serving convicts who was expected to be reformed while in here and the authorities thought it best for them to have as little contact as possible with bad influences. But this hope of reformation did of course not apply for us who was set for the noose and so once we condemned men was alone things became much more convivial.

'I don't care for the cats much,' I said by way of an opener once I had taken a strong swig from a bottle of whisky what belonged to another convict. 'Sinister looking things.' This convict squinted at me in confusion as he took back the bottle he had won at gambling the previous week. The Newgate turnkeys was well known to run a decent trade in getting prisoners such treats to play with.

'Cats?' said the whisky owner in an Irish accent once he had wiped his lips with the back of his hand. 'I ain't seen no cats.'

'You ain't looking then,' I replied and told him that I had marked six cats in the press yard, two in the chapel and that there was four in this very quad looking down on us right now. This convict, whose name was Meehan, cast his eyes around the quadrangle walls for any feline observers but did not spot them.

'If there was any cats about,' he grizzled, 'I'd smell 'em. I can't abide the creatures.'

'He means them stone cats,' said Mouse, as the whisky was passed to him. 'Up there.' He pointed to the first of the many discreet little statues what was poking its head over the top of the quad's one door where the turnkey was standing. Then he showed them where the other three was, high up on the other walls of the quad, the same colour as the brick work and as ugly as gargoyles.

'It's Whittington's cat,' the turnkey informed us with a chuckle. 'Keeping watch over the human mice.'

I had marked the stone cats because I was making a thorough note of everything I might be able to use to help me scale the walls should I be able to gain entry to this courtyard after dark. The task looked difficult, however I did notice some large windows high up on the building side of the courtyard. These was barred like the rest and it struck me that they was much larger than any cell windows I had seen elsewhere in the prison. I asked this Meehan if that part of Newgate – what was the floor above the condemned cells – was where they kept the debtors.

'Debtors are on the north side,' Meehan told me after a loud sneeze. 'Up there is where they keep the women. Now who's for skittles? I need to win some more whisky.'

Much to my surprise the next hour was almost pleasant and that, even with the terrible fate what hung over our heads, we six men still managed to distract ourselves with gaming, bawdy humour and some well-earned profane language. All the convicts had something to bet with – be it clothes, drink, actual coinage or, in one case a fob watch what I very much desired on account of there being no other clocks inside our cell. The turnkeys then produced a set of nine-pins and some balls for us to entertain ourselves with until lunchtime and beyond.

'So you're going to hang an' all, eh?' said Meehan just as I tossed my first ball. 'And whose fault is that?' I struck the wall beyond, missing every skittle.

'Did you ask me that to put me off my stroke, Meehan?' I asked as he pulled a sly face. 'I shall have to watch out for you.'

'I only meant,' he smiled as he picked up his own ball, 'who was the judge what done for you? Mine was called Venmore-Rowland and he was a hard-hearted man indeed.'

'Judge Aylesbury,' Mouse answered as Meehan knocked down six pins with ease. 'That was the name of ours.'

'I know of him,' said the one who had bet the fob watch as the skittles was replaced. 'He sentenced my brother to death for killing a policeman.'

'Your brother killed a peeler?' Mouse asked in genuine shock. Nobody liked the blue lobsters but you would have to be a mad dog to think you could get away with something like that. 'He must have been longing for the noose, your brother.'

'Yeah, well, he claimed he was innocent,' replied this convict whose name was Tanner. 'But don't they all?'

'We *are* innocent men,' I informed them all. 'We just fell in with a bad crowd.'

'Unlucky for you then,' said Tanner as took his throw and struck a seven. We all whistled in appreciation at his skills and then it was the turn of Mouse. Mouse's ball, like mine, missed every pin. 'And your luck ain't changing much,' Tanner grinned as he told us to remove our smart shoes which we had put up.

As the skittling continued Mouse and I continued to lose our jackets, waistcoats and cufflinks until at last we had to remove our trousers and place them on top of the ever-growing pile of prizes. The other convicts seemed very amused to see us shivering in the cold as the games continued and there was lots of jokes about how at this rate we would be leaving this Earth with less than we came in with.

'As for me, I am *not* an innocent man,' said Tanner as he inspected the quality of our belts, 'I've killed several people and I bet I'm one of the few in here what'll admit to it.'

By now everything worth having was on the pile and it was a large haul. The worth of it would not have got you much on the outside but in Newgate there was buying power in these possessions. When my turn came next I threw a floorer without any real effort. Tanner congratulated me on my first lucky throw but Meehan was a little sharper. He had just bet a purseful of shillings what his wife had given him on her last visit and I could tell he had now realised they was not as safe as he had thought. When Mouse threw next it was another easy strike. Within two rounds we was both dressed once more and the whole pile was ours.

'Swindlers!' Meehan spat to the floor as I counted the coins in his wife's purse. 'They should be hanging you for bad sportsmanship as much as anything.' This would be the last of life's many defeats for these men and few took it with good humour. Tanner, though, was not as bothered about losing the fob watch I had wanted so much.

'I'm happy to be rid of that anyhow,' he said with a shrug. 'It's got a loud tick on it and I don't care to be reminded of the passing seconds.' He then wished me luck with shutting the contraption up.

Mouse and I counted out the value of our winnings and I hoped that the turnkeys would soon start showing some interest in us now we was Newgate rich. This was the main reason I had wanted to win the game – so that I could start paying for privileges from the guards what might be useful to us in escaping. They did not disappoint.

'That's a good score, son,' the fatter of the two turnkeys beamed. 'What do you plan on spending it on, I'm wondering? We can get you smokes, drinks, whatever. You've only got a short time left to decide.' He was rocking on the balls of his feet with glee but just then he was interrupted by a shrill voice what provided another suggestion.

'What handsome boys!' It was a woman's voice calling down from the large windows above. 'The ones with all the nice things!' I looked up to see the top half of a red-headed woman with dishevelled hair and who appeared to be in a state of undress. She had lifted up the glass on her side of the window and her left hand was around one of the thick iron bars what she stroked in a manner most suggestive. Beside her was another woman who was just as unkempt but younger and black-skinned.

'They'll want to share all his winnings with us I 'spect,' this other woman added. 'They'll want to give 'em all to us in return for our unending love!' The red-haired woman laughed at her friend and there was much leering from all the convicts who was gathering under the window to hoot back at them. The turnkeys meanwhile shut the door to the quad behind them and the fatter one crossed over so he could tell them to quieten.

'Behave yourself, Sessina!' he shouted up in a tone less commanding than the one he used on the male convicts. 'That's not the way now. If the governor sees you flaunting yourselves so brazen there'll be trouble.'

'And not just for us, eh, Max?' the red-haired woman shot back and blew him a kiss. Then she indicated Mouse and myself. 'Be a good boy and tell those handsome brutes down there that they knows where to find us. We ain't going nowhere.'

'Even if they will be,' sniggered the black girl and they both shrieked with laughter as the glass window fell down between us with the force of a guillotine.

Turnkey Max then made a convincing performance of shouting up at them in rebuke. 'We'll have none of that now, ladies!' he declared loud enough for the whole of Newgate to hear. 'A little more decorum from the women prisoners, if you please! What would Mrs Fry think if she could hear you now, eh?' But, once this admirable display of censoriousness was over he placed his arms over the shoulders of Mouse and myself and walked us over to the other side of the quad for a whisper. With one arm around my shoulder and an eye on Mrs Meehan's coin purse he got straight down to business. 'The flame hair is called Sessina Ballard,' he informed me with a music-hall wink. 'And she don't disappoint. The other's name is Black Meg and she's available too if you prefer the type. But whatever it is either of you are after just give the word because there is all sorts up there.'

'And you're the man to arrange the visit up there, are you?' I enquired with interest. I had been wanting to strike up an acquaintance with a gaoler what was of a corruptible bent and it looked like this here Max was my man.

'Or bring them down to your cell if you'd rather,' he offered. 'I wouldn't recommend it though, their quarters is more comfortable than yours.'

'And who gets the coins? Them or you?'

'Some of those women would entertain you for nothing,' he told me, 'if they thought you'd get them with child. Female prisoners get treated like queens if they can plead the belly so they're very welcoming of male seed.' He was relaxing now and seemed less concerned by who might overhear. Some of the other convicts had wandered over to hear our chatter also. 'But it could cause a lot of fuss and enquiry so you still need to pay. Some for them, some for me and a lot for Rum Mort for allowing it to go on. But you've just won enough on skittles to keep all of us happy, ain't you?' He patted me on the back and reminded me that there was not much else for me to spend it on in these remaining days.

'Rum Who?'

Tanner had walked up close to us now to join in the conversation. 'I can see you've never been to the Stone Jug before, Dawkins,' he said. During the skittle match both he and Meehan had been comparing notes from their previous – less fatal – experiences in Newgate Prison.

'Newgate is a web, lad,' Meehan put in. 'And at its centre there sits a dirty great spider what goes by Rum Mort. Nothing much happens within these walls without the Rum feeling a twitch upon the thread. The rest of us is just flies.'

'So who is he?' I persisted. 'The governor of the prison?'

'In all but name, yeah,' Max sniffed. 'The Rum Mort governs all from a solitary cell and woe betide any man what crosses old Rum. But don't you concern yourself, lucky Jack, you won't even meet the fiend. You just pay me what you've won there and I'll distribute to the interested parties. Come now, what's it to be? We've got old or young up there, meek or wild, ebony or ivory. It's your last ride so feel free to be particular.'

I was far less interested in taking advantage of his offer than I was in learning more about this Rum Mort person who wielded so much influence. It was clear that the turnkey was referring to a top prisoner and so this was someone what I very much wanted to speak to. I was familiar with such dominant figures from my time in the Australia penal colony as there had been a convict there who had intimidated even the soldiers and that man ruled like a king. Gaolers may come and go but such prisoners are a constant, growing in size and power over the years until the gaol is theirs.

'I will not be requiring any female company just yet, thanks for offering,' I said to Max with a wave of the hand. 'In truth, I would be much more grateful to be granted audience with this Rum Mort you speak of. There'll be something in it for you if you can arrange things accordingly?'

'Well the Rum Mort don't wish to see you,' was his curt reply. 'Or any of the other prisoners.'

'What about Sessina Ballard?' interrupted Meehan.

'What about her?' sniffed Max.

'When I was in Newgate last year I was told that you turnkeys took her to visit the Rum's cell regular. The rest of us never even laid eyes on the man but we all knew that if you wanted to speak to Rum then you went through Sessina.' He turned to me and added, 'not that any of us ever dared.'

Turnkey Max then confirmed that there was indeed an intimacy between the mysterious Rum Mort and the red-headed woman and that, since we was all so curious, he would tell us a story about it.

'There was a terrible business on account of Sessina about a year gone,' he confided. 'Which'll help you understand why the Rum Mort needs avoiding. It's an incident that still gives me the chills whenever I'm in the press yard.' He looked over to the shut door of this quad then to ensure that none of his superiors was about to walk in before continuing. 'There was a prisoner here then, a Frenchman. I had taken this Frenchman to spend an hour in the company of Sessina but he had failed to heed my warnings about not abusing her. By the time he was done she had been treated most cruelly and there was bruises all over her body. Well, Rum Mort hears of it and ain't happy none whatsoever.' His voice grew even quieter then and the few of us standing close by had to lean in to hear. 'Any of you lot ever heard of *Peine forte et dure*?' We all exchanged blank looks. 'It's French,' he added in case we was wondering. 'Well,' he continued, 'it's the name for a form of torture used in Newgate back in medieval days and it's how the press yard got its name. It involved tying a prisoner down with cord and stretching them along the yard floor. Then they would place a wooden plank across his chest and, one by one, add metal weights. A horrible business what no man could endure. They outlawed the practice centuries ago and it's not been used since. Except by the Rum Mort.'

The other turnkey had walked over from guarding the door now to join the conversation. 'It was me what unlocked the door to the Frenchman's cell on that morning,' he said. 'It was the day after he had battered Sessina and the man had vanished in the night. None of his cellmates would tell me how he had escaped, they all claimed he must have got out while they was sleeping. An alarm was raised but it did not take long to locate him. We found him in a right mess, lying naked on the cobbles of the press yard underneath a plank of wood and thirteen heavy bricks crushing him down. Imagine it!'

Max then changed back to his earlier jocular manner and he began poking me in the stomach. 'So don't you even think about getting involved with the Rum Mort, young Dawkins. Because there are even worse fates than that of being hanged inside this prison.'

I had to admit that as I thought about what that Frenchman had suffered through, as one brick after another was placed on top of him until his whole chest had collapsed, I did start to wonder if this Rum Mort cove was better off avoided. But if he could have arranged all that in less than a day then it followed that he also had the power to get somebody onto the other side of those high walls. So I still needed to speak to him one way or another.

'All right Max,' I said as he began trying to get me to part with my recent winnings again, 'I'm convinced. I am keen on an hour of female passion after all.'

'There's a good convict,' he cheered before touching his nose in conspiracy. 'You just leave the particulars to old Maxie here and I'll see to it you have whoever you fancy. Got any ideas?'

'I do, yes,' I said and reached into my pocket to pull out the coins for him to see again. 'Now that you mention it, I've always had a weakness for red hair.'

Max raised his bushy eyebrows and began to caution me not to make the same mistake that the Frenchman had. But before he had finished, the door to the quadrangle was opened from the inside and both turnkeys altered their manner, stood back and stiffened. However, it was not a prison superior what entered the quad but another turnkey who announced that visiting hours was now upon us.

'Four for this lot,' he announced and then looked to Mouse. 'Someone's brung your baby to see you.' Mouse looked happy for the first time since our arrest and I patted him on the back. 'And your mother's returned,' the turnkey said to another young convict. Then he checked the notepad in his hand. 'We've also got Mrs Meehan and a Mrs Jack Dawkins.'

It took me a beat to make sense of that comment.

'*Mrs* Jack Dawkins?' I asked. 'You sure?'

This amused the others. 'Now, it'd be a right old comedy if she were here for me now, wouldn't it?' Turnkey Max roared to the amusement of all. 'Have you forgotten your own wife already?'

'A Mrs Dawkins has come to see me?' I checked with the new turnkey while ignoring the laughter. 'She's here in the prison at this very moment?'

'In all her glory,' he leered. 'And I don't blame you for looking happy about it neither. She's a proper picture.'

'That right?' asked Max. 'Then I wish she really was here to see me then!'

More lewd remarks followed but I paid none of them any mind as inside me every organ was flipping over each other with joy. It had to be Lily, it could be no other. She must have come with some ring on her finger or a forged marriage certificate and they could no longer refuse her the visit.

'You're a lucky cove, you are,' continued the turnkey as myself and the other three visited men followed him out of the courtyard and into the corridor. 'Well, for a man condemned to death that is.'

Chapter 15

Mrs Dawkins

Wherein my spirits are much lifted by a vision most fair

Before escorting us to the visiting chambers, Turnkey Max took Mouse and myself back to our cell after I had given him the bottle of whisky as a gratuity. I wanted to show the guards that I was someone worth doing favours for so he then allowed us to spend time at a basin to make ourselves presentable for our guests. After some washing I asked Mouse how I looked and he smiled and assured me that I looked even handsomer than I had at my own wedding. Mouse himself seemed keen to clean up for the young woman what had brought his baby and I realised for the first time that she was more to him than just the carer of his child. Then we was both taken to the place where our visitors was waiting for us.

The very thought of Lily's appearance in this horrible place was having a miraculous effect upon me. She had renewed my sense of hope and doubled my resolve to escape by coming here. As I entered the arched cell, what used to be a stable and was now one of the visiting chambers, I could feel my feet quicken to meet her. The convicts was separated from the free people by a metal grille at their end and the first person I saw was Mouse's girl – the one from the trial with his baby in her arms. He ran towards the grille, they both touched fingers, and it looked to be a most tender scene. However, there was no sign of Lily Lennox.

I looked through to the visitors' side to see where she could be hiding but all I saw was one long bench where a lone woman was sat with her face down. She was playing with some child's toy in her lap but although I could not get a good view of her I could see that she was too short to be my Lily. She wore a respectable blue dress and bonnet, her hair was all yellow curls and furthermore, she was heavy with child. I looked along the rest of the passage for my fancy woman but the only other people I could spot was talking to prisoners in neighbouring cells and so I whistled over for one of the turnkeys to tell me where she had got to. As I did this the pregnant lady raised her head, saw me and her face lit up with joyous recognition.

'Husband!' she cried as she attempted to lift her heavy self up from that wooden bench. 'My darling Jack,' she went on. 'I thought they'd never let me see you, I've been waiting here so long!'

Needless to say I was much surprised by this sudden outburst of love from a total stranger. However, I kept enough wits not to show it to anyone and watched as the same turnkey what had come to inform me of this visitor walked over to the bench to help the lady up to her feet. He had been right to describe her as a picture, she was indeed very beautiful, and I was certain that I would have remembered had I ever met the girl before, let alone married her and got her into that delicate condition. As she grew closer to me I took in the scent of her rose-tinted perfume what even this musty and straw-strewn old cell could not hide.

'Here he is, Mrs Dawkins,' the turnkey said once they had reached the metal grille. 'I told you we haven't hanged him already.' He gave a fond chuckle and it seemed as though he was most taken with her. 'He's been asking after you all Christmas. Ain't that right, Mr Dawkins, sir?'

'Jack!' sighed the apparent mother of my unborn before I could answer. Her gloved hand reached up and our tips touched through the barrier. 'My love,' she continued. 'I've tried ever so hard to see you. I've been praying for your salvation day and night.'

'He's lucky to have a loving wife like you, Mrs Dawkins,' said the turnkey with a nod. 'Very lucky! I should be so fortunate to have so fine-looking a lady what with me being a lonely bachelor such as I am.'

I was most affronted by this cheeky chancer trying to press his advantage with my soon-to-be widow while I was still stood there before them. I was about to take him to task for his inappropriate conduct before remembering that I had no clue who she was anyway and so he was welcome to her.

'Well, what are you waiting for?' he rapped the grille with his baton. 'Ain't you going to greet your poor spouse?'

I studied the face of this young lady and I could not place her. I was still trying to get over the stab I felt on realising that Lily was not coming after all and so I had not given myself a moment to imagine who it might be. And yet as I looked at her the more she began to strike me as someone I knew. Her eyes was lowered in a demure fashion but when they looked up to meet mine I saw a sudden fire in them that the turnkey did not. It was the look of an instant but it revealed all.

'Hello, my dear,' I greeted her and I could not suppress smiling at her disguise. I could not imagine how much discomfort poor Tom Skinner must be in, wearing that frock and wig, but I was stunned at how well she had managed to alter herself. 'It's so lovely to see you again, my turtledove.'

Another secret glance from her told me not to push my luck. I knew how much Tom hated to dress herself in anything feminine and so all this must have been a great indignity for her. So I could not help but feel very touched that she had put herself through such an unpleasant ordeal just to see me and my gratitude for this was deep. Soon the turnkey announced that he would leave us alone so we could say our last farewells and she was quick to resume her part as the unassuming Mrs Dawkins.

'Wait!' she cried and touched his shoulder before he could walk off. 'You can't let me see my husband for the last time like this! Not when we can't even hold one another as man and wife!' The turnkey stopped in his tracks and turned back to Tom and his expression became less genial.

'I think I can, Mrs Dawkins,' he admonished her. 'We can't have married couples fondling one another in full view of everyone else. It wouldn't be decent.'

'Sir,' she pleaded with a tilt of the head, 'I want only for the father of my unborn child to lay his hands down here.' Her free hand lowered and she touched her swollen belly. 'So he can feel his child kick one last time.'

'Very well, Mrs Dawkins,' he sighed as he led her over to the small doorway built within the grille and fumbled for whichever key might open it. 'Let's take you and your husband here somewhere more private, shall we?' He threw a less kind glance in my direction. 'For his final kiss.'

We was then led away from the other visitors and towards a smaller hold what was known in Newgate as the Grate. It was called this on account of its large cross-barred window what looked out onto the street outside and from where debtors was sometimes allowed to beg for alms. The interior of the hold was bare save for a short wooden bench and another chair and the turnkey said that we had less than five minutes.

'I won't wander far though, Mrs Dawkins,' he promised and then looked down to the small wooden doll she was carrying about with her. 'Planning on giving him that are you? I'll need to inspect.'

Tom handed him the doll, what was of a frightening figure of a man in black clothes but with red paint on its hands, and I could see that it was very much like those what Dick the Dollman of Clerkenwell was known to manufacture.

'Ugly article,' chuckled the turnkey who was feeling it for sharp edges. He held it up so he could view it next to me. 'Much like its model.'

'Is that meant to be me?' I asked in disgust and looked to Tom. She beamed back as though she expected me to be flattered by the travesty.

'It's a gallows doll,' she said. 'For the crowds on Execution Monday. You're a celebrity.' The turnkey gave the doll a shake but it did not rattle. 'There are some made of Mouse too. Dick the Dollman says he'll have done scores of you both come the day of your hanging.

'Scores, eh?' I replied and I found my revulsion being replaced by queer pride. It was like discovering that someone had built a statue in my honour. 'I've been immortalised,' I said and smiled at it.

'Five minutes, Mrs Dawkins,' said the gaoler. 'No longer.' Then he tipped his grey gaoler's cap to us and shut the door so we could have some matrimonial privacy.

I at once crossed over to the grated window, to see if I could effect my escape through it. There was a small gap in the steel bars for outsiders to slip money through to a begging debtor but I could see it would never grant me my freedom. Tom, meanwhile, had plonked herself down on the bench and kicked off her dainty shoes.

'That disgusting creeper,' she whispered in her truer, less simpering voice, 'took all sorts of liberties with my person. If his hand had touched my rump once more I'd have grabbed it and broken his fingers.' Although we had heard the turn of the bolt, she still had to be careful not to drop her charade too soon. There was a small square gap in the door through which a turnkey could spy on us.

'And you a married woman with a child growing in you,' I tutted with one eye still fixed upon that square as I moved over to her, 'the disgrace of it.' I saw the turnkey's head still hovering around outside and so I continued to play the part of a grateful husband, bent down on my knees in front of her and kissed her on the hand. 'Thank you for coming,' I said and lowered my head down so my ear was pressed against her belly.

'Lay yourself here,' Tom said in her wifely voice and began guiding my head across to the desired spot on her big bump. I had to admire how authentic it appeared and I wondered what she had stuffed in her dress to achieve the look. My ear then fanned over the spot on her belly where she was directing me and I could feel something metal. 'Touch him with your hands,' she said and I lifted my head and felt for where the item was stuck inside her dress. There was a very discreet slit in the bump and I was able to dip into the dress. Within was an iron file small enough not to be noticed by the guards. I hid this up my own sleeve and then Tom leaned forward as if she was going to whisper sweet love-talk into my ear. 'And there is a map of the prison inside the doll,' she said. 'An old lag I know who now lives in Clerkenwell drew it out from memory though. So it might not be as reliable as all that.'

She leant back again and I glanced over towards the square in the door to see that the turnkey was no longer watching us. 'You need some air,' I said, in case he was still out there. 'Let's get you over here to this window, Mrs Dawkins.' My delicate bride got to her feet and I dragged the wooden bench to the far end of the Grate and we sat down together. We could now converse with greater confidence if we kept our voices down and I took Tom's left hand in my right and stroked it most tender. Tom lowered her chin down and whispered in her natural voice.

'I crowed good and hard, Dodge,' she told me. 'But those peelers moved fast. They was into the lane and knocking down the front door of Rylance's house in a blink.'

'Mouse heard you,' I said as I felt for where the doll unscrewed. 'It weren't your fault.'

'Didn't say that it was,' she snorted. Then she dropped her voice so low I had to rest my forehead against hers to listen. 'They moved *really* fast though. Didn't look for no door numbers or nothing. They knew you was in there, Dodge. They expected you.'

'I know,' I nodded and reached into my own pocket. 'At the trial the peelers said they received a telegram from someone telling them that we would be there murdering Rylance. That would have been sent by the real killer, the person whose name Billy Slade wouldn't tell me.'

I produced a folded up piece of paper on which earlier that morning – before we had gone to chapel – I had written down my side of the story for Slade to read. As I had told Mouse, I was unsure what Slade knew about what had happened in that room but I wanted people to read my version of events. I handed it to Tom and told her that I wanted her to deliver it to Slade so that he and the rest of the criminal community would have no doubt. 'He must know the identity of the real murderer,' I explained as I tried to hand it over. 'So he can make him pay. Be sure to make him understand that I'm innocent so he knows not to trust that guilty person again.' Tom batted the paper away and looked at me as though I was soft.

'You think that Billy Slade don't know full well what happened?' she said. 'Jack, Weeping Billy *is* what happened.'

It had, of course, occurred to me too that Slade might have had some knowledge of what his client was intending but it seemed unlikely that he might have orchestrated such events himself. I doubted he would have had the power or the motivation. I held on to the piece of paper for a moment and considered why she might be so much surer of his involvement than I was.

'You think that Slade himself sent that telegram from the Old Bailey?' I checked. 'On his client's behalf?'

Tom shook her bonneted head. 'I don't even think there was a telegram, Jack. I think it was all gammon.'

'There was a telegram all right,' I told her. 'You wasn't at the trial and you didn't hear what I did. The peeler what testified – the one who ordered his men to go to the scene – he was high-ranking, a Detective Superintendent. He said he was responding to this telegram and he offered to show it to the judge and everything. Why would he do that if there wasn't one to show? I'm sorry, girl, but your imagination is getting the better of you again.'

'I was at the trial if you must know,' Tom replied in her cold voice. 'Dressed up like this so nobody would recognise me. I was stood about three spaces down from Lily Lennox in the galleries and I saw all. I saw a lot more than you did from the sound of things.'

'Oh yeah? Like what?'

'Judge Aylesbury,' she replied. 'The short pug-nosed old man in his silly wig. Didn't he look familiar to you?'

As she said that I recalled thinking that the old man's face did tinkle a bit but, at the time, I could not place him. But, hearing that Tom had recognised him also, I searched my memories again. And then – in an instant – I fell upon where I had crossed paths with him before and the surprise of it slapped me awake. He had looked so different without his wig on, sipping champagne and leering at a half-naked harpist.

'Molly Gay's,' I said then and it felt as if I had known all along. 'He was the old man on the settee when we first arrived. The one who Slade sent upstairs with two girls.' Tom nodded while I chastised myself for not recognising him sooner. 'Which means . . .'

'. . . Which means that Slade has power over him,' Tom finished the sickening thought for me. 'Maybe he's blackmailing him or perhaps he just pays him in whores. But it's no coincidence that he was overseeing your trial, Jack, that I promise you.'

I sat there and thought about Billy Slade for a few seconds. I had never doubted that Slade was a villain out for his own interests but I found it hard to believe he would go out of his way to trap a fellow thief, a brother starling. I looked down at the wooden image of my doomed self what I still held in my hands and tried to make sense of his actions. 'Where is the profit,' I asked myself aloud, 'in seeing me dead? I was his top earner.'

'The day after you was arrested,' Tom answered, 'Slade appeared in the Three Cripples with a mob of those red-hatted boys he surrounds himself with. He came to speak to all of the Diallers present and ordered us to repeat his words to those associates of yours who wasn't there. He told how you had killed Scratcher for betraying you and now you had gone and killed this Anthony Rylance person. He predicted – and was since proven right – that the judge would make you swing for the Rylance murder. As you can imagine, most of the Diallers turned against you when they heard about what you done to poor Scratcher. He was a very popular lad, you know. Many of the boys was disgusted by it.'

'But I didn't kill neither of them!' I protested not caring if the turnkey was lingering outside the doorway. 'Scratcher is alive and well and living in Rochester!' Tom looked surprised to hear that. Once again, I was stunned by what some of my closest friends was prepared to believe about me. 'I hid him away so Slade wouldn't kill him.'

'Well, either way,' she shrugged as if it did not really matter, 'Billy Slade has taken control of the Diallers. He's our top sawyer now.' I almost broke the gallows doll in two when I heard that. So that was Slade's interest from the start – he wanted to steal my entire gang by seeing that I got pinched. There was many evil acts a criminal could carry out but betraying your own kind was the lowest. And after all his talk of community! Tom could see how angry the revelation was making me and she leaped at the chance to make me feel even worse. 'I tried telling you, Dodger,' she said, which, in fairness, was true. 'You was the one what wanted to be a Slade man, remember.'

I let out some well-chosen curse words then and again the turnkey came to the door window to see what was wrong. So I collected myself in case this visit was brought to an early end and went back to whispering so he would move along.

'You was right then,' I admitted with bitterness. 'And so was Lily. You both warned me against him and I wouldn't listen.'

'I may have been wrong about her though, Jack,' Tom said in a begrudging tone. 'About Lily. I'll give you that much. Because she's one of the few what doesn't think you're a killer.'

'That's because she was the one who helped me hide Scratcher from Billy Slade,' I told her.

'I see,' Tom said and added, 'so I may have had her character all wrong then. She won't have a word said against you.'

'You've seen her?' I asked.

'I went straight to your crib on the night you was taken and told her what had happened.'

'How did she seem when she heard?'

'She weren't happy.'

'What sort of not happy?'

'How many sorts of not happy are there?'

'Lots of sorts as it happens, Tom,' I snapped. 'I'm discovering new ones every minute.'

Tom made herself comfortable on that bench by spreading her legs apart in an unfeminine fashion. She could only play the part of a woman for so long, it seemed. 'Well, there was tears if that's what you're asking me,' she shrugged as if the subject was already boring her.

'Then why hasn't she visited me?'

'She tried when you was in the police cell before the trial. But those peelers was guarding you close and they don't welcome visitors here much neither. That's why I've had to get all tarted up.' She waved her hands over her dress and make up. 'I feel like a clown.'

'Is she still at our crib?'

'No,' Tom hesitated before telling me this next thing. 'One of Billy Slade's first commands once he had declared himself top sawyer of our gang was that he wanted your fancy woman brought before him. But by the time the red hats got to Five Fingers Court she had fled. She ain't been seen since.'

Again, I felt the anger filling me up as I realised how I had allowed Slade to snatch my life like away this. My love was in danger, my gang had turned their backs on me and history would think me a killer if I couldn't break out of here in time to set things right. I was innocent of murdering Anthony Rylance but – given the chance – I was more than ready to kill Slade should I ever meet the man again. I was about to start giving Tom a series of instructions about how she should set about protecting Lily against Slade and also avenging myself and Mouse but just then the lock in the door began to turn. Tom was back up into her feminine pose before the door had begun opening.

'Time's up, Mrs Dawkins,' said the turnkey as he entered the Grate. 'I hope you've said goodbye as that is the last time I'll allow this intimacy before he hangs.' I was frustrated by his appearance as there was still so much to discuss. But I crossed over to my false wife for a last embrace. 'That's enough of that,' he said, and placed his baton in between us.

I wanted to thank Tom for all she had done today. Not only had she provided me with useful items to escape with but she had shown great loyalty while others had not. Mouse and myself had a true friend in her but it was now impossible now for me to speak free.

'Thank you for coming to see me . . . darling . . .'

'Mary,' she prompted.

'Mary. Give my love to the family and in particular little Lillian.'

'If I see her I shall,' she said and curtsied both to me and to the turnkey before another came to lead her away.

'Don't feel too glum, sir,' the turnkey sighed in a rare moment of sympathy as we watched her disappear up the corridor and out of the prison. 'Gallows dolls never do capture a person's handsome side.' I looked down again to the toy – what had been designed to look like me with blood on my hands – and I decided that I did not much care for it after all. In truth, I wondered if I had ever before seen anything so hideous in my entire life.

Chapter 16

Gallows Dolls

In which the dials of the Newgate clocks tick louder
by the minute

The bells of St Sepulchre's, the neighbouring parish church, tolled at dawn on the next day to wake the condemned. They need not have bothered. None of us in that little cell had slept well through the night and morning light had crept through the bars of our window and illuminated an awful stillness.

My thoughts was now even more disturbed by what I had learnt from Tom Skinner's visit – about the treachery what Slade seemed to have played against me – and all I wanted to do was talk it out it with Mouse so we could plan our revenge on top of our escape. But Mouse and I had not spoken much to one another since we had returned from our visit and this was out of respect to Old Edwards. He had spent his last night alive down on his knees in prayer.

A clergyman was admitted into our cell to administer consolation to Old Edwards soon after the toll and he spoke with him about matters spiritual while ignoring myself and Mouse. It would be our turn to receive such attention on the following Monday and so for now we was to just watch in silence as our cellmate was asked if he was ready to issue a full confession for his crimes once upon the scaffold and in full hearing of the crowd. The old man said that he would do this without hesitation, that he would be glad to do it, and he thanked the prison officials for giving him the chance. I had never asked Old Edwards for what crime he was set to hang but I could tell from his attitude that, unlike us, he was guilty of it.

Then two turnkeys fettered the arms and legs of the prisoner and, without another word, they placed a bag over his head and led him from the cell for the last time. Mouse and myself was left alone then but still we did not speak. He sat on his stone bed and I sat on mine and it must have been a full minute before I heard his quiet sobbing.

'Come now,' I whispered as I got up from my mattress and crossed over to sit beside him. 'Don't despair. He was ready to go. You heard him say so. Be brave, Mouse, that won't be us.' I placed my arm around him and he leant into my shoulder so he could cry some more. He was starting to quiet himself when we heard a distant roar from the far side of the prison. The crowd was cheering and there was no doubt as to what about. Then the bells of the church chimed once more.

I did not remove my arm from around him as I knew he was not done and sure enough the tears resumed. I kept telling him that it was going to be all right. That our fates would be different to that of Old Edwards and that he should not lose hope. We shall get out of here, I whispered into his ear as his body juddered and rocked, you and me. As I said all that, I knew that it was as much for my own benefit as for his. Witnessing Old Edwards being taken away to the gallows had been terrifying and my own spirit had been very much shaken by the sight.

'This shouldn't be happening, Jack,' Mouse said after some moments silence. 'We don't deserve to be killed.'

'Nobody deserves to,' I replied. 'Not even Old Edwards, regardless of whatever he done. It's a barbarism, plain and simple.'

Then Mouse dropped his face into his hands and as he did so he muttered something. I just about heard the words but was so amazed by the poison in them that I asked him to repeat what he had said, but louder. He hesitated at first but then he lifted his face up again and turned it towards mine.

'I said,' his eyes was still wet from the tears but they was raging too, 'that this is all your doing!'

The words whipped me and I shoved his small body away from mine so we could have it out. The cheek of him, I thought, as he continued staring at me like he had never done before. Here I was trying to be all paternal to the lad and he goes and he repays me with this wicked accusation.

'My doing?' I shouted back at him. I was livid and had to stop myself from battering him, from taking all my own pent-up anger out on the one person I could reach. 'I never asked you to become a burglar, you know. I never put no gun to your head and forced you into Rylance's home. Recall, you asked to come out on a crack. You're your own master, Mouse, don't go thinking otherwise!'

'You always say things'll be rosy!' he returned then with some force. 'And they never are!' He wiped his eyes. 'I don't know why I've ever paid you any heed.'

'Now you listen here, you young—'

'No, you listen!' he shouted. 'You treat crime like it's a game, Dodger. You always have, it's how you get the rest of us to go on along with you. But this ain't a game, is it? Death is coming for us this time next week and you're still fool enough to think you can escape it! You're still acting like it's a bit of fun for us all. But this is the end, this is! You told me – you *promised* me – that if I stuck with you as my top sawyer then my son would grow up into a gentleman. You said he'd have a better life than the one we had, that he would be spared all of our hardships. But what chance does Robin have of that now, eh? He'll just grow into a street rat like we was. And the rats are doomed from the start.'

'We ain't doomed, Mouse,' I said. 'Stop saying that. And your little Robin has got every chance of growing up as fine a gentle—'

'How? With his criminal father hanged for murder? His future's already writ!' Then he dropped his head down again and moaned into his palms. I could think of no response to this and I have to confess that his assault had struck me hard. He was right, this was not a game and the noose would claim us if we continued to do nothing. I could feel that my own skin had become gooseflesh from even contemplating the idea that our attempts at escape would not be triumphant and I knew that I had been avoiding such dark thoughts for this very reason. But one of us had to stay strong, I reminded myself. One of us had to see the way out.

'Prisons do rum things to a person,' I said at last, and walked over to my stone bench again. 'And it seems as though you, Mouse, are becoming a pessimist under Newgate's influence.' I lifted the straw mattress and showed him the metal file what Tom had given me and the map of the prison what was hidden inside the doll. 'And pessimism is a very unappealing quality in a person if you don't mind my saying.'

'You're not going to start on about getting out again, are you?' His whole frame slumped and he stared up at me like I was the one what was going mad. 'There is no escape from Newgate. It's an impossibility.'

I sat on my mattress again and the two of us stared at each other. Then – just before the creep of doubt and despair what had taken grip of him found its way over to my side of the cell – I rolled out the little map of Newgate's three quadrangles and the best suggested routes of escape. 'Mouse Flynn,' I said in a much quieter tone as I made a study of it, 'let's hope you're wrong for both our sakes, eh?'

★

Prison routine was just the same on Execution Monday as it was on every other day for those of us who remained. When we was taken to the courtyard with the other condemned men – the place where we had played skittles the day before – nobody mentioned that three of our number had been hanged on that very morning. We all pretended to be oblivious to it as the turnkeys handed us a pack of cards. But conversation between us was much slower than it had been on Boxing Day and the mood was sombre.

We was being watched over by five turnkeys – two more than had been present on the previous day – as well as those strange stone cats on the walls. The other convicts had between them enough currency to try and win back their possessions from yesterday and so play commenced. I had something on my mind though and was keen to raise it.

'Anyone of you lot ever heard of a cove called Weeping Billy Slade?' I asked once a game of Slow Sevens was in progress. 'He's from Hammersmith way.' Meehan said that he recognised the name but could not place from where and most of the others shook their heads. Only Tanner had something interesting to tell me.

'Is he a tall fella from the north with a deformed hand?' he asked as he lay the first seven of the game. 'Runs a bawdy house for rich people?' I nodded and asked how he had met Slade. 'I haven't,' Tanner answered 'but my brother used to work for him.'

'Is that the same brother who killed the peeler?' I asked, trying not to look too interested. I had a terrible hand but Mouse had just given me a secret signal that he was holding the cherished diamond seven. Tanner nodded and I asked what his brother's job for Slade was.

'Well, he did all sorts for him but a lot of the time he just strutted around in a red bowler hat, trying to looking hard. Slade was obsessed with his people wearing those hats, or so Will told me.'

The side of Meehan's mouth twitched as I lay a meaningless six of spades. This meant that he had the matching seven. 'Will thought that Slade was a prince though, for all his curious ways.'

'How did your brother come to murder that peeler then?' I asked after I picked up a diamond five so that the rest would think I was chasing the suit, leaving Mouse free to play as he pleased. We had already won this game which was a shame because the stakes was still low. 'Was he drunk?'

'Nothing like that,' Tanner replied as Mouse laid his winning card early so that nobody would suspect him of being clever. There was plenty of money among these convicts from yesterday's visits to be placed down yet. 'Will was cracking a warehouse when this peeler caught him in the act,' said Tanner as the other cards was revealed and Mouse was given his meagre winnings. 'A fight must have broken out and Will clubbed his head in with a pistol. Perhaps he *was* drunk, now that you say it. It was unlike Will to be so stupid.'

'But he claimed he was innocent, you said?' I said as I took the deck and began shuffling. 'What was his defence?'

Tanner laughed. 'He said that he had found the peeler like that. That someone must have killed him just minutes before and scarpered. A terrible story, Judge Aylesbury didn't believe him for a second.'

I looked over to Mouse as the cards was dealt out for the new game. I had told him about Slade's crooked relations with Aylesbury earlier but we both managed not to betray the hot emotions what hearing such a story had caused. Yes, it looked as though Slade had ensnared other unsuspecting criminals – such as this Will Tanner and perhaps many more – with similar traps to the one we ourselves had been caught in. But we had gambling to do and so our faces remained blank.

There are, I must confess, few card games over which I am not a master — be it by either fair means or foul. As we sat there on the cold cobbles of the courtyard we played through many rounds of French Whist, Old Spades, Young Maid, The Silent Knave, Dead Canary, Irish Dead Canary, Egyptian Snap, Fast Whist, Kiss the Queen and Natterjack. Some of these amusements I had even invented myself and Mouse and I only lost the ones what we chose to. As we played, I continued to question Tanner about Weeping Billy Slade but he did not seem to think that the man from Hammersmith was in anyway responsible for his Will's downfall and was quicker to believe that his brother really was a murderer. That was the trouble with being a criminal, not even your own kin believe you when you are innocent.

Mouse and myself had not spoken much since our argument earlier that morning but the storm had passed and we was again working together as one. I would never apologise to him for being a bad influence what was forever leading him into trouble and he would never apologise to me for saying that I was a bad influence who was forever leading him into trouble. We did not need to say such things — we was like brothers and our mutual forgiveness was assumed.

After some hours of relentless play, Mouse and I soon won all there was to win from our luckless adversaries and so the gaming reached its conclusion. The other convicts did not take their losses in a spirit of good sportsmanship however, and when we collected the coins, trinkets or articles of clothing what they had gambled, there was a strong sense of hostility towards us. But I had not wanted to strip doomed men of their final earthly possessions just for the fun of it. I had wanted to accumulate this comparative wealth for the purpose of paying my way out of this prison if I could. I was hoping that I might be able to make Turnkey Max

– who had seemed so corruptible on the previous day – into my well-paid and attentive butler. I was hoping I might have enough money now to arrange for him to leave certain doors unlocked or to just turn a blind eye to any escape dash what might take place while he was on duty. Or perhaps – I hoped as I strolled over to where he was standing in his grey guard's uniform – he could introduce me to this mysterious Rum Mort who was said to wield so much power and he could be convinced to help me over the wall. But, as soon as I reached the courtyard door what Max was guarding, I discovered that his attitude towards me had shifted since yesterday.

'I cannot help you with that, Mr Dawkins,' Max sniffed after I had said the name Rum Mort again. He was not looking me in the eyes but fixing them ahead like a royal guard. 'None of the gaolers here can.'

'I'm prepared to pay, Turnkey,' I persisted and showed him the purse of coins in my hand what was among the prizes what I had just won from Meehan. 'You name your price and I shall try to meet it.'

'If you was to offer me all the treasures of Croesus, I would not help you, sir. Run along and play with your friends, there's a good prisoner.'

I was most taken aback by this sudden obstruction in a man what had been selling whisky bottles on the day before and offering to play the bawd. I demanded to know the meaning of his change in character.

'I had you down as a capitalist, Max. Ain't my money as good as the next man's?'

He shifted his head an inch toward me then and his voice became a threat. 'No, your money ain't, *sir*. I'm sorry if I gave you a false impression upon our first meeting but there will be no trade between you and me of any description. That is my last word upon the matter.'

I then asked the two other turnkeys what was standing either side of him what they thought was up with their pal. But before either of them could answer we was interrupted by a voice from above.

'Handsome!' It was the red-headed Sessina Ballard again calling down from the open window of the female quarters. 'You with all the money. The rich one!' She was alone this time and was speaking only to me. 'What might your name be, I wonder?' she asked. I crossed over to the centre of the courtyard to reply to her but as I did so Turnkey Max darted past me and pointed his stick up at her.

'It ain't your concern what his name is, Sessina!' he shouted back. 'He ain't coming to see you. Just shut that window or I'll come up there and make you sorry for it.'

Sessina carried on as if he was not even down there. 'Jack Dawkins, yes?' she said to me. 'The famous Artful Dodger what we've heard so much about. That you, is it?'

I pushed past Max and replied loud enough for anyone to hear what might be listening in also. I was hoping that she was making these enquiries on behalf of someone else. 'That's me, all right,' I called back. 'Jack Dawkins of the Seven Dials! And if you're as cosy with this Rum Mort fellow as I hear you are then tell him that I'm interested in meet—'

But I was interrupted in the flow of my offer by the sudden swing of a truncheon. Turnkey Max struck me in the belly good and hard and the shock of it was crippling. I folded onto the floor while all the other convicts stood up from their games and cried outrage at the violence meted out to one of their own. But the other turnkeys all turned on the convicts and threatened them with the same, and in this way revolution was averted.

'Get Dawkins here back to his cell,' Max ordered his men. Then he leaned down to address me on the cobbles. 'I was told you was trouble, Dawkins, and it seems that you are. You need special watching, you do. From now on you'll take your meals in your cell, no more gambling and a ban on all visitors.'

'No visitors?' I complained as I was pulled up by the two other turnkeys. 'Even my wife?'

'She'll be turned away,' said Max with a dead expression as one of his men began dragging me out of the courtyard. 'You need to learn good behaviour.'

Before I vanished through the iron door and away from Mouse and the others, I glanced up at the window where Sessina had been. The glass was shut now and she was gone.

Back in my cell, I was at a loss to understand what had just happened. Confining me there was a heavy-handed punishment considering I had not done much and I wondered if I had misread Turnkey Max, who just the day before had seemed a much more agreeable cove. The only explanation I could imagine for this sudden over-reaction from the guards was that they had been warned against me – Max had just confirmed as much himself. I wondered who could have said that I was trouble though. Perhaps the prison authorities had identified me as one what was more likely to break free from these walls than most and so was now tightening their locks. Or perhaps Max had been told to guard me close from someone else, someone outside of the prison. Well, one thing was for certain, if these guards thought these extra measures would hold me down then they was much mistaken. Because, as the lady out there had said, I was the famous Artful Dodger. And I had, by this time, already decided how I was going to get out of here.

★

The plan what I had devised for breaking out of Newgate was very much modelled on what I knew of Jack Sheppard's own simple but successful break for liberty. But there was a number of obstructions and unknown elements what I needed to deal with before Mouse and I could make our lucky. For one thing, the locks on our cell door was covered with iron plates which would need removing before we could pick them. But a bigger problem was the two iron bolts what the turnkeys slid over the outside of the doors before they locked us in for the night. Furthermore, I did not know if a night watchman was positioned on the other side of our cell door, guarding the dark and subterranean corridors after lights out. And so that night, the night after I had been dragged from the courtyard, I decided to find out. I waited until after the church bells had chimed midnight and then I tiptoed over to the door of the cell and began calling out in a desperate voice.

'Treasure!' I shouted just loud enough to be heard by any turnkey what might be on the other side. Nobody answered back and so I raised my voice some more. 'I know where there's a fortune hidden. Jewels and plenty of 'em. Diamonds, rubies, emeralds, a real hoard. Let me tell you where it is, turnkey, and you can have half and give the rest to my widow. How about it?'

There was an answer but it was not from a gaoler. Meehan was in a cell two doors down from my own and his reply was fast and hissing.

'Keep it down, Dodger,' I heard him say. 'Tell me and I'll tell my wife. We can use it to pay for both our freedoms. Don't tell no turnkeys, they're all thieves!' His voice was then joined by a chorus of others from behind locked doors, all offering their services upon the matter, but no gaoler came running to silence them or to ask for more information. From behind me, Mouse asked what I was on about.

'I just wanted to see if we was guarded by more than just locks and bolts at this hour,' I explained. I waited a few more minutes for the neighbouring prisoners to settle down. 'We ain't,' I observed.

'As soon as we're beyond that door, Mouse,' I said to him an hour later as we both lay on our beds in darkness, 'it's about speed and nerve. Because once those bolts are out of the way we need to move through the prison fast.' I could hear the rain falling down through the small barred window and I longed to be outside in it, free and clean. 'This old prison is all shadows,' I continued, 'and shadows'll be our friends as we hide from the guards and dash through it. We'll be heading towards the roof and, if this map Tom got us is any worth at all, I think I know how to get us there.'

'And then you want us to jump down onto the neighbouring houses?' Mouse asked again, although I had been over my plan with him a few times. I rolled onto my side so I could reassure him.

'Mouse, plenty of people have done it before. We'll need to use bed sheets like they did to lower ourselves down the side of the wall before jumping and it'll be very dangerous. But when anyone has ever escaped from Newgate, this is how they did it, including Jack Sheppard. It'll be easier than it sounds.'

Mouse was quiet then and the only sound what could be heard was the loud irregular ticking of that faulty fob watch. 'Perhaps Old Edwards was right, Jack,' he muttered at last.

'About what?'

'About there being less dignified deaths than a hanging. At least if I go by the rope I'll get to confess to my sins before I'm taken.'

'You ain't got no sins!' I snapped at him. 'We're innocent men, remember, so stop talking like we ain't. Nobody ever *wants* to jump across a five-floor drop, Mouse, and if we was just lifers then I'd live here forever rather than risk it. But listen,' I was sitting up now and trying to catch his eye as he looked away, 'if anyone can make that jump, it's us. We're condemned men which means we're more inclined to try than other prisoners and we're also gifted burglars. Look at how we broke into Anthony Rylance's lodgings. I mean, all right, the whole thing was a disaster once we was inside but the crack itself was perfection. We walked across that high brick wall as steady as tight-rope walkers. We'll win, Mouse. We've got the will and we've got the skills.'

I could see in his eyes now that I had roused him into action once more. He looked over to the doorway again and when he spoke it was as if he had never faltered for a second.

'The trick is to remove those outside bolts somehow without anyone hearing,' he said, articulating the problem. 'Even if the turnkeys aren't in the corridor that don't mean that they won't hear us from above. But once they're slid across the rest should be easy.'

'I know,' I said, and crossed back over to the door. 'If this was a house-crack we'd get someone on the other side to do that for us.'

Then Mouse looked up at me and I could tell a decent thought had struck him. 'What was that thing what Fagin said about bolts?' he asked me, and started clicking his fingers as he tried to remember. 'When Bill visited that time. "*The secret to a bolt, my dears,*" he said . . .' Mouse stopped as he tried to recall the next bit. But I knew what he meant and I finished the sentence for him.

'. . . *is that they are always more than just the bolt!*'

Chapter 17

Goodbye to Newgate

*Demonstrating just how easy it is to get over
these medieval walls*

When Turnkey Max unlocked our doors on the following morning I greeted him throwing a few choice swear words at him before he had even stepped into the cell. I had a strong suspicion that he was keeping me under close protection on command and I doubted it was given to him by the prison governor. 'How much is Weeping Billy paying you, Max?' I sneered as he made a quick search of our cell while another turnkey took Mouse to the shared hall for breakfast. I would again be expected to spend the day in my cell alone and I could think of no one who would benefit from this unfair situation more than Slade. 'Because it's the Devil's money and you should be ashamed of yourself!' Max looked straight at me as he handed our soil pans to another turnkey to remove.

'I've met plenty of devils, Dawkins,' he answered, and his hand reached for the cell door. 'And, believe me, there are far bigger ones in here than out there.' He slammed the cell door between us and I heard him whistle as went away.

I had not heard the bolts slide over on the other side of the door, however. The only time they was employed was at night because that's when they was needed most. But they was uncalled for during the day because once you broke out into the corridor beyond then your only possible route would be up through the winding staircase and this would lead you straight into the path of those keeping watch in the courtyard. Which meant that these bolts was vulnerable by day and that was the time to tamper with them.

The bolt is just one part of what makes a bolt, Fagin had explained to Bill Sikes within our hearing many years before. Burglar Bill had come to Saffron Hill to ask the old Jew for some advice about a delicate jewellery shop he wanted to crack. The outer doors of this shop was bolted together with two strong padlocks what fastened onto a thick iron bar what ran the length of the wide door. It was all very well for Bill to destroy those with his strong bolt cutter but this would make him very conspicuous. Cut bolts would be visible from the busy road should anybody pass by while he was still within and so he could not risk destroying them. But Fagin had the solution. He vanished into one of his upstairs rooms where he hoarded things and returned with two padlocks. Fagin then turned them upside down and the bolts of the padlock slid out. *Bolts is only bolts when they're screwed, my dear,* he explained. *Otherwise they're just iron rods protecting nothing at all.* So Bill could cut the padlocks off and then get an accomplice to hook these two replicas to the door once he was inside. To a passing observer all would appear normal.

'From what I can see, all the bolt sliders in this building have six small screws,' Mouse said to me when he returned later. 'And I met someone today what can get us all we need.'

'The Rum Mort?' I was sat cross-legged in the centre of the cell and had started to play shove-ha'penny against the wall while I listened.

'No,' Mouse said, 'Nobody's mentioned him to me all day. It was a lifer in the press yard. A cove called Hannigan.'

'I thought the lifers and the condemned was not allowed to converse,' I asked as another shiny coin bounced off the wall.

'Security around us ain't as tight as it was while you was out there, Dodge,' Mouse observed. 'It's as though you was the one they was only ever really guarding.' This troubled the both of us and Mouse leaned forward and spoke even quieter as if he thought even the lice in this prison could be informing against us. 'I know you think that Slade has been paying these turnkeys to lock you up all day, Dodge,' he whispered. 'But that don't make no sense to my mind.'

'That's because you think that Slade don't have the reach to bribe so many guards,' I said as I flicked the final coin so hard it bounced off the wall and back into my lap. 'And perhaps he don't. But remember that he has this mystery client, Mouse. The one he works for above all others and who must have wanted Rylance killed. Whoever that is, he must have the power to control what goes on in this prison. That's the person trying to stop me from getting out.' Mouse shook his head.

'Then why ain't I locked up in here with you?' he asked then. 'I'm convicted of the same crime, ain't I? It'd be just as dangerous for Rylance's real killers if I got out but the turnkeys don't seem as fussed about keeping me on a short chain. No, it's something else, Dodge,' he pointed at me. 'It's something about you and you alone.'

I had been jingling all those coins together in my hands but stopped as he said that. 'Something about me alone?' I muttered as I looked over to the empty bed where Old Edwards had been. 'What could I have ever done to deserve more confinement than you?'

Mouse shrugged and said that he was not certain but he had got the idea that I was being kept away from other prisoners for a particular reason. 'Perhaps you're too cocksure for them, Jack,' he suggested, and there was a sharpness to his voice what I was unused to hearing. 'Too flash for someone facing the noose, that is. They might worry that you're as clever as you seem to think you are.' I looked over at him then to see if he was trying to mock me but he was quick to return the subject along to what this lifer had told him in the press yard. 'So Hannigan reckons he can get us anything we want,' he went on, 'for a price. So I told him what we're after and he says he'll have it by Thursday. He's a good fella, that Hannigan.' Mouse was good at making new friends, it was one of his many talents.

I then gathered up the coins and flipped two over to him 'Those are for him then,' I said as he caught them, '*after* he has delivered the goods. Tell him not to spend it all in one place.' I then made a tiny tower from the rest of the coins and put them next to Mouse's bed. 'The rest you can give to that woman what's been looking after your Robin when she next visits.'

'Cheers, Dodge,' he said as he scooped them into his hands. 'She'll appreciate that.'

'Don't mention it,' I said, 'we innocent men need to stick together.'

Thursday came and, as he had promised, Hannigan managed to slip a little bag to Mouse as they walked around in that press yard without the turnkeys spotting the pass. Mouse smuggled it back to our cell and we emptied it out on a mattress to inspect. There was a small tub of glue, a little brush, some screws and a screwdriver. We already had three bed sheets in this cell – including those what Old Edwards had been sleeping under, what had not been removed for laundry – and I just had to hope that these would carry our weight.

'What if they snap, Dodge?' Mouse asked me again and not for the first time as I got up to extinguish the candlelight on what I hoped would be our final full night here.

'Then we drop to our deaths,' I said as I snuffed it out and the room was cloaked in darkness. 'So let's just hope that they don't.'

Part of the reason why Jack Sheppard had been so famous for his escapism was because he had bid goodbye to Newgate twice. On his third incarceration however, he had failed to break free and they hanged him at last. His problem was that he was never smart enough to know when he had won. After getting out from prison, he would continue to loiter around London getting into more trouble until he was recaptured and there is only so many times that you can push your luck. This was the thought what crossed my mind as the bells of St Sepulchre's announced it was morning again, and Mouse and I readied ourselves for the day. Once gone from this vinegary-smelling cell, I told myself, I was gone for good. I would never risk recapture and the hangman would never have the pleasure of my neck.

I had my ear pressed to the cell door and heard the turnkeys chattering as they came down the winding staircase. I checked that the Sheriff's notice was still hanging from the wall and would not drop off once they was in here and reveal the missing brickwork where Hannigan's bag was stuffed. All looked as it should and so I returned to my bed as they unlocked the cell and tried to look as belligerent as possible so they would expect nothing was out of the ordinary.

'Why don't you spend your money on drink like the rest do, Dawkins?' Max asked after he had performed a rough search of the cell and found some of my winnings under the mattress. 'No point hoarding things where you're going.' I warned him to keep his pilfering hands from off of my property. I wanted him to think that he had found the only things worth looking for in this cell and it seemed as though I had been successful. They led Mouse away then but before they locked me in I asked Turnkey Max if he had forgotten something.

'They want washing, I think you'll find,' I said, and pointed to the soil pans. 'And see that they're clean this time.' The other turnkey rolled his eyes but collected the smelly items for removal. 'You should be able to eat off them,' I added.

'Anything else, *your Majesty*?' Max said once he was outside again and his hand was on the door.

'That'll be all, my good man,' I replied but he had already slammed it shut.

The second I was alone I crossed over to the door and listened for the inevitable turns of the locks. As ever, I did not hear any bolts sliding. Then, once I was sure that the guards had left the corridor I gathered the bag from its hiding place in the wall and took out the file what Tom had given me and set about working on the iron panels what covered the locks. These was screwed in but the turnkey what had taken the soil pan would be gone for twenty or thirty minutes.

I was able to pull the panels off even faster than I had hoped and, once they was laid aside, I inspected the locks. These was stiff but they could not resist the pick and I was pleased at the ease with which I was out and into the empty corridor.

According to the noisy fob watch, the turnkey returned with my breakfast and a clean soil pan in less than half an hour. But by that time I was sat back upon my bench in the same position as I had been when he last saw me. As far as he must have been aware, I had not moved an inch.

That evening, at around ten o'clock, the turnkeys came around again for their final check on the condemned cells before dawn. Mouse and myself glanced at one another in suspense as we listened for the night bolts to slide over. Each made a faint noise as the turnkey slid one after the other but there was nothing else to suggest that anything irregular had occurred. The bolt had not clattered to the ground, the glue had held and the severed screw heads was still in place. Mouse smiled at me as we heard the turnkey walk away.

We then spent some time tying the three bed sheets together and pulling at them to see if they was up to the task. Then, once the parish church chimed one, we readied ourselves to leave. The iron panels what covered the locks, and that I had removed earlier, was now just stuck in place with glue. I prised them off with the file and again I took the picks to them. I had been practising this action throughout the day and could now perform it with a flick of the wrist.

The door now needed to open with as little sound as possible. I had stuck the bolt sliders back in place with a generous amount of glue so that the turnkeys would not think them tampered with. We counted to three before shoving and then we both pushed hard at the door with our elbows in one solid thump. There was a bang, not too loud but loud enough, and the door had shifted outward. We halted then to hear if any turnkeys was coming to investigate the noise but none did. The other prisoners in the neighbouring cells was heard stirring though and I had to hiss at them before silence fell.

In the darkness I could see that the door had not opened enough, the well-glued bolts was resisting too much. But I could tell that one more hard push would do the job. I indicated to Mouse to put some real power into his next shove and we went at the door again.

This time a horrible clatter as the top two of the glued bolt-holds gave way and clattered to the floor. The bottom bolt was still stuck in place though and I told Mouse to shove again, hard and immediate. The sound it made was not loud but it was strange enough to betray us. Any nightwatchman what was stationed at the top of the winding staircase could not help but be alerted to it. So we banged our third and final assault upon the door and this remaining bolt at last fell too. Our door swung open.

With my metal file in my hand I darted out into the pitch black corridor ignoring the disturbed cries from the cells around. I reached the bottom of the staircase down which any investigating turnkey would come and crouched in the shadows beside it. The metal file was held up in my fist and I prepared myself to strike anyone what might come down to challenge us. Just then I saw a light at the top of this staircase what could only be from a guard's lamp.

'What happening?' came the voice of a guard. 'Who's down there?'

It was not a young man and I could see from the lamplight that he was hesitant to come down. He was no doubt wondering if there was a desperate convict down here what would be prepared to kill him. So, for that matter, was I. The file was a sharp weapon and could even do fatal damage if it needed to. I considered then – as I held my breath and listened to hear if this old boy had the steel in him to descend – if I had it in me to take a life tonight. Society had locked me up for two murders I was innocent of. Would a real murder be the thing what was needed to secure my freedom? I had never wanted to be a killer but I feared this turnkey was going to give me no choice.

'Who goes there?' he demanded again but it was a weaker call and I could hear that he would be easy to overpower. He had more to lose from any confrontation than I did and if I was in his place then I should be the frightened one. My whole self was wound to spring if he was foolish enough to be a hero but I just wished he would be sensible and move off so we could pass up this staircase unhindered. But he stayed there, with the reflected light of the lamp still shaking against the stone wall.

At last the lamplight began to retreat away from the staircase. He had made the right choice not to come down here alone but instead to go and fetch help. As I heard his hurried footsteps heading off in the other direction I breathed out and loosened my grip upon the now wet file. I then used my shirt sleeve to wipe away the sweat from my palms and brow. He would never know how close he came to me giving him a deadly blow and, I suppose, neither would I.

I turned to look for Mouse and found that he was already at my shoulder in this dark corner. It was clear that he had been watching me with my arm raised to strike, and there was a look of horror upon his face. He had the sheets looped around his neck and waist and was holding the tub of glue. I grabbed him by the shoulder and motioned for him to follow me up the winding staircase.

Once I reached the top step, I peered out to see if there was anyone waiting, but no one was around. The narrow corridors of the prison would have been impossible to run through had it not been for the lit lamps on the walls every nine feet and so we scurried off, sticking to sides of the wall, swift and silent. We was heading for the north quad, where the debtors was kept. Further along, I peered around a corner and saw that the next run was clear also. Our purpose was to make it out into the courtyard where we had played cards and skittles and then climb those walls to reach the rooftop. We was not far from that courtyard and I still had the small pick in my pocket, but as we was nearing its door we heard approaching footsteps and knew we would not have time before being discovered. So I pulled Mouse back in the other direction until I found a low wooden door what was set into the wall. We crouched into it and made balls of ourselves as the runners came round the corner, as if we was in prayer. I heard the same voice from the staircase then but now that turnkey was all of a puff and talking to the others. They spoke in rapid tones and I could tell that the new guard was younger than the older man.

'We should go to the firearms closet first, sir,' one of them said as I saw the wobbling lights of their three lanterns approach. 'For rifles.' I was certain that these lights would reveal Mouse and myself as we huddled into this doorway and then I panicked as it occurred to me that this here door was the firearm closet itself. I shuffled further into this deep space as they drew closer and waited to be exposed but by some miracle they raced past the door without even a glance our way. We waited for them to turn the next corner which would lead them to our cell before we crept out again and continued to the courtyard.

We was turned around a few more times as we negotiated our way through the ancient, haphazard building but we at last came to the door we needed. I fiddled with the pick until the lock turned. Then once inside the courtyard we could see things much better as the moonlight shone down from above. We did not have long until the alarm bells was rung throughout the prison and the place would then be swarming with guards from all areas. But I used the pick to lock the door behind us and Mouse stuck his finger into the tub of glue and applied it to the lock. These walls of the yard was high walls but we was burglars and we knew how to scale them as there was ledges and footholds as well as a drainpipe that would aid our ascent. We crossed over to the corner what looked less exposed than the rest and I hoisted Mouse upwards to the first window ledge. He then grabbed onto the iron bars of the window and ascended further using the drainpipe. By the time he was up at a window of the second floor he was able to tie the bed sheet onto a bar and dangle it down for me. We continued upwards like this, using the sheets where we needed to but also grabbing onto helpful protrusions like those stone cats. As we reached the third floor we heard a tremendous cry from inside the prison. Then the sound of a bell and guards calling out, 'Hark! Prisoners out of cells! Prisoners out of cells!'

There is nothing like a strong whiff of panic to spur you upwards. We was both climbing much quicker now and was soon up to the fourth and final set of barred windows. The courtyard door with the glued lock rattled and frustrated shouts was heard from behind it. But Mouse and myself was sure-footed and fast and we soon reached the revolving iron spikes at the top. Just as the door far below us was bashed open I grabbed an iron spike, let go of the piping and climbed over the edge like a circus performer. Mouse did likewise further along the wall and if we fell now, then we would have done the hangman's job for him.

'They're up at the roof!' shrieked a voice from below. 'Fire at them!'

Below us, rifles was heard being cocked. I made it over the spikes and heaved myself over this final ledge. Just as I did so a shot rang out and hit the spike I had just climbed over. I rolled onto the rooftop as I heard another shot ring out. Mouse was not yet over the ledge and I heard him scream as the shot missed him by a small margin. I grabbed his arms and pulled him over the spikes to safety. We was both now on the rooftop and unhurt, but we was not free yet.

Knowing our pursuers would soon be up here, we moved as fast as we could across the long and difficult roof of Newgate. The building was made up of three parts and we had just climbed up to the centre tower. However, we had to scale another tower before we reached the side of the prison what we needed to lower ourselves to the safety of the houses across the way. I could already hear the noises of the guards coming behind but the trick to keeping ahead of a chase is to just want your freedom more than they want to catch you.

So, after more climbing and dashing, I reached the edge of the prison before Mouse and was running so hard that I almost plummeted straight over the side. But I stopped myself in time and looked down to the cobbled lane below and was struck by fright. The drop was far more horrible than I had anticipated.

'It's too low down, Jack!' Mouse cried as he drew up next to me and saw the distance to those rooftops we needed to jump to. 'We'll break our legs!'

'You can do it, Mouse,' I assured him, although the gap between the prison and those houses was much more intimidating now we was up here. 'Just remember what I told you. Lower yourself down to a ledge – then jump.' I started tying one end of the bed sheet around a chimney and told Mouse that I would go first and show him how it was done. The turnkeys was still far enough off if we hurried. 'I'll go first and show you,' I said. 'Once I'm across I'll be able to catch you. Don't worry.'

Just then I heard a whistle and a shout from the far end of the roof.

'They're coming,' Mouse panicked and he spun round to see the small dark figures of two turnkeys heading towards us. A third turnkey was further back and rattling a wooden clacker in the air. 'Let's do it then. Let's jump.'

'Very well,' I said and I perched myself over the side of the wall to drop down to the lower ledge.

Something went pop. It was a quiet sound and seemed harmless enough and I turned to Mouse to ask if he had heard it too. He was facing the oncoming guards and his head cracked backwards. He staggered and then disappeared over the wall. A cheer went up from the guard with the rifle.

The shock of it threw off my footing and I called out his name as he vanished from sight. Then I too fell, following him straight down towards the lane.

'Both of them!' exclaimed a guard as I tumbled and crashed straight into the side of the Newgate wall below the roof. 'Superb shot!'

I still had hold of those bed sheets and that was the only thing what saved me. The other end was tied secure to the chimney and I clutched on to that rope. I did not see Mouse's body hit the lane below but I will remember the awful sound he made – and the sudden silence afterwards – for the rest of my days.

'Shot!' cheered a turnkey above my head as the first footsteps reached the side of the roof. 'By God, that'll be an unholy mess to clean up,' I heard him say then as he looked down to where my friend had fallen. 'Where's the other one?'

My cries was desperate then as I dangled there beneath them. The sheets was stretching fast and I had moments before they snapped. 'Here!' I shouted terrified that they could not see me in the dark. 'Pull me back up! I'm begging you!'

'There he is,' said one of the turnkeys. I could hear him scuttling over to the chimney and I felt his hand land on the sheet above me. 'Still clinging on. What should we do?'

'Pull him up of course,' said the wheezing voice of the guard with the clacker.

I was struggling to keep hold of that sheet and I had never been so scared in my life. Then I heard one of the guards – the one what had been carrying the rifle – stop the first from reaching down to grab me.

'Hold about,' he said. 'Why should we? Why don't we just untie the sheet and let him plummet like the other one. He's due to hang anyway and the little sod has caused us all sorts of grief tonight!'

'*No!*' I screamed up at them. '*Please help me! Please!*'

'He makes a point, Baines,' the first voice then said. 'There's only three of us here. Who'd know?'

'*Please don't let me die! Please don't let me die!*'

'What sort of men are you?' wheezed a chastising voice from above. 'That you would let a man drop who screams for his life? We're his gaolers not his judges or executioners. Grab him quick or I'll report the pair of you.'

Three sets of hands reached down then and took hold of me. Soon they had hauled me back onto the safety of the roof. I lay there underneath them then, panting hard and with my eyes still shut. I heard the noble Baines – he what had just argued for my life – tell me to open them. As I did so, I saw his kindly face and I recognised the voice. He was the old guard what had stood at the top of the stone steps and who I had contemplated dealing a fatal blow to.

'You, my boy,' he said, as I looked back at him with more guilt inside me than I had ever felt before, 'just had a very lucky escape.'

Chapter 18

'Oh! God Forgive This Wretched Man'

In which I receive another visitor

After that night, the turnkeys never allowed me out of fetters again. I was manacled by the hands and feet and taken back to my cell, the door of which was soon repaired and even strengthened with bolts and chains so heavy I would never be able to work through them, regardless of how many more files, picks or lucky chances I might be handed. Turnkey Baines guarded me in my cell until after this job was done and we did not exchange a word about the death of Mouse Flynn. Instead, my eyes just avoided the vacant and unlit side of the room where his bed still was and I kept them fixed upon the fire's crackle. One of my oldest friends had just fallen to his death beside me and I doubted if they had even finished washing the blood from the cobbles of Ave Maria Lane yet. The numb sensation I now had in part made me wonder if my own end had come early, as it felt as though some of my own life had dropped away with Mouse.

Once the thick iron door had clanged shut between us, and I heard the many slides, clicks, jangles and clunks of the locking process, there was nothing to stop me from sinking down and into despair. I lay on my mattress and felt the last of my optimism leak away. Over the last week I had fought to convince Mouse that our liberty was assured and I saw now that I had been lying to myself as much as to him. But now he was dead there was no one left to lie to. I was to die on the morning after tomorrow and nothing now would prevent it. The turnkeys had performed a thorough search of the cell and had confiscated everything I had to trade with. The chances of any of my Diallers arranging another visit was too small to count on, while every obstacle stacked against me seemed too great. I was defeated.

Mouse haunted my thoughts. He had wanted a more dignified death than the one he had received last night, one where he could confess his sins beforehand. With my false promises I had denied him even that comfort. *This is your doing,* I kept hearing his sharp words come at me from his dark half of the room. *You always say things'll be rosy! And they never are!*

So – in the long and lonely hours what followed his death – I began confronting the truth about myself. I had blood on my hands after all. I may not have killed a young boy as I had led the London underworld to believe – and nor was I guilty of the crime for which I was set to hang – but Mouse's fatal fall was indeed my doing. I had been a bad influence on him since our very first meeting and had led him to that rooftop – and in more ways than one. And the shame of it was a torture to me.

One mercy was that the gaolers had confiscated that cheap faded fob with its hateful ticking. I understood now why Tanner had been so relieved to lose it at cards. With it gone the only method I had of marking the passage of time was the steady chimes from the church upon every hour. I dreaded every strike of the bell.

At length the short winter light turned to darkness and I grew still as the room turned to black. I was sat on my bed in a hunched position and I still stared at the fireplace, one of the few sources of light save for some candles. I tried to just sit in silence and let my mind deaden itself. So I do not know what time of the night it was when I heard the rattle of the keys outside my cell. In my weak-minded state I almost wondered if more time had passed than I had counted – a whole day perhaps – and, as the locks was heard turning and the chains unfastened, I thought with a jolt that this was it – that the door was now opening for the last time and they had come to take me to the scaffold. I rose to my feet and stared at the candlestick I saw being held by the stout figure of Turnkey Baines. I heard him speak in a soft voice, but he was not addressing me.

'Here he is, sir. Jack Dawkins. As requested.'

Somebody was standing behind the turnkey although the candlelight did not reveal his face. I blinked to get a better look but all I could make out was his tall silhouette.

'How odd,' I heard the voice say as they both looked in on me. 'That he should occupy this cell.' He wore a stiff top hat and I could tell, even in this dimness, that his thick grey coat cost decent money. He did not move as the turnkey stepped into the cell to approach me but continued watching from out there in the corridor. He seemed to be wary to cross the threshold.

'Odd, sir?' said Baines as he stoked the fire to create some more warmth for my guest. 'How so?'

'I've visited this cell before,' said the man whose voice was becoming more familiar by the word. 'At least I think it was this cell. The prison walls smelt of vinegar then too.' He began turning his head about to inspect the whole condemned area as if this business of which cell he had already been to was of the uppermost importance. 'It was some years ago. I was just a small boy.'

Baines had now come over to me and was checking that my manacles was good and secure so I still could not even get a good look at the man as he stepped into the room. He approached the bed where Mouse had slept.

'A small boy, sir?' asked Turnkey Baines as he produced another chain from out of his pocket and attached it onto my wrist fetters. 'We ain't accustomed to let small boys visit the condemned in their cells here at Newgate. A close relative, was he?'

'Lord, no,' said the stranger as he took out a handkerchief and brushed the bed before sitting on it. 'It was a man who I doubt I had even known longer than a few weeks.' Baines chained the other end of this new short fetter to a hook on the wall as the man sat down. 'But I don't think a single night has gone by when I haven't dreamt about that visit.'

I said nothing as the two men continued to talk around me like I was just some dummy in a waxworks museum. I remained on my bed and looked closer at the young man as Baines began to light the lamps around the room. It was still too dim to see but as the light grew brighter I began to get a better view of him. He seemed to have with him a notepad and pencil and he placed these on the bed beside him.

'I return every night to this cell,' he said and I was unsure if the young man were addressing me or the turnkey. 'And I'm always haunted by how terrified the man looked. He wasn't such a bad person, I think. Or perhaps he was, I've never known for certain. But I don't think that he deserved to die like that.'

The turnkey had lit the final lamp and the room was as bright as it was ever going to get. He crossed over to me and shook his head as if disappointed.

'Well, this one here is a right young villain, sir,' he sighed. 'The Artful Dodger the newspapers call him. But then you must know that,' he gave the man a quick chuckle, 'you've been covering the story in your own fine newspaper, I imagine!'

'I have indeed.'

'So,' Baines wheezed, 'just to remind you that I shall be out in the corridor at all times. He can't get too close and if he does just shout, I'll be forced to come in and give him a hearty whack with this.' He touched his truncheon which was still hung on his belt and looked down at me. 'I won't want to,' he sighed. 'But, as we discovered last night, Mr Dawkins here can be a right handful.' Then he turned to my visitor once more before leaving through the door. 'Don't let him give you anything, sir, and do not give anything to him. He'll be thoroughly searched after you've gone so we'll know if you do.' He nodded then at both us, wished us a pleasant interview and then swung the cell door shut.

Once alone with just the man, a silence passed between us. I looked at him hard but he was sat in the dark spot between two lamps and his topper shaded his eyes. After a moment he removed the hat and placed it on the bed beside him. Then he came closer, sitting himself on the edge of the bed and this was when I got my first clear view of his sharp and handsome face.

'Tell me, Dodger,' he said in his voice of refined gentility. 'Do you remember me?'

Recognition struck.

'My eyes!' I said, unable to suppress my astonishment. 'It's you!'

His smile was wistful and he nodded. 'Yes, Dodger. I have often wondered whatever became of you and, I daresay, you have been wondering about me. I was never more stunned than when I heard of your arrest for the murder of Anthony Rylance but I suppose it was fate that our paths should one day cross—'

'*You're the cove from the trial!*'

The man stopped what he was saying and blinked. 'I see,' he said.

'You was there in the press bench, sir, and you called out in my defence when the peelers was testifying against me.' I corrected myself. 'Against *us*. All the other reporters had made up their minds against us, sir, but you was one what took our part. What paper was it you said you wrote for?'

'The *Morning Chronicle*,' the young man replied.

'Well, you've come to the right place for a story,' I spoke with great urgency. I was sitting up straight for the first time since Mouse's death, relit with hope. 'Because what I have to tell you of my wrongful incarceration damns the British legal system and will shock your readers very much, sir, if they have any sensitivities at all.' My excitement was hard to contain and I was filled with gratitude to the young man for visiting me. I still had no clue as to what he had come here for but this was a chance to tell the true story of my arrest to a sympathetic stranger. Had I not been chained to the wall I would have gone straight over and given him a good hug. 'What is your name, sir, if you don't mind my asking?'

'Brownlow,' he said.

'Well, if you're here to write a story, Mr Brownlow, then you may want to take a look at those what run this prison, an' all. My friend Mouse died yesterday on the roof, shot to death by the cruel Newgate guards. And he was – like my good self – an innocent man.'

I continued to babble away at him about how I was a man wronged but he held up his white-gloved hand for me to stop speaking. Then, once I was silent, he shifted on the bench and perched himself at the end so I could see his face even better now. Then he spoke in a soft, delicate tone as if he were a doctor breaking bad news.

'My name is Oliver Brownlow,' he said. 'Formerly Oliver Twist.'

I looked back at him and said nothing. Then I must have cocked my head as if asking him if he would be so kind as to repeat that.

'Oliver Twist,' he said, 'is the name I first came to this city under.

I was starving and homeless and no doubt I would have died on the streets if nobody had taken pity. You were the first Londoner I ever met, Jack. You took me to a place with shelter, food and warmth. And for that I should always be eternally grateful to you. Regardless of what followed.'

I was stupefied by the revelation of his identity, and more silent moments passed. His account of our first meeting was strange and unfamiliar to me, as though he was relating a story what bore no relation to the encounter between us as I recalled it.

'Regardless of what followed, eh?' I said, repeating his words. Then I cocked my head to the other side. 'What did follow then?' He sighed and shook his head.

'Pickpocketing,' he told me. 'Burglary. The attempted corruption of a child. The successful corruption of countless other children. And finally, murder.'

'Murder?' I asked as I took all that in.

'Yes. Of poor fallen Nancy.'

I jumped up from my bed and darted towards him. I had every intention of getting my hands around his throat to choke the very life out of him. If the authorities really did have to hang me for someone's murder then it might as well be for this smug little shit. But the chain the turnkey had fastened to the wall yanked my arms back and I could not get to him. I was like a dog chained to a fence and Twist jerked backwards and out of my reach.

'You've got a fine nerve, Twist,' I raged at him, 'coming here and bringing up Nancy's murder!' I tugged at the chain in the hope that it would break free from the stone wall. 'When you're the boy what was responsible for it!'

Twist looked most shocked by this statement and from outside the cell Turnkey Baines shouted in. 'What's going on in there?' he called. 'Mr Brownlow, sir?'

'It's quite all right, Gaoler!' Oliver replied, although his eyes never left mine as I stood before him still swearing all my curses. 'Don't come in! Mr Dawkins is still restrained and I'm quite safe, thank you!' He spoke with some command but there was a note to his voice what told me how unsettled he was. He may have asked the turnkey to chain me up like this – or perhaps the turnkey had insisted – but it did not look like he had expected this reaction.

'There's a murderer in this cell, Twist!' I spat at him as he sat where my dead friend once had, 'only it ain't the one in fetters. You're the bastard what killed my family and it's you what should be facing the noose, not me!'

'Killed your family?' Oliver responded in disgust. 'What do you mean?'

'By blowing on us! By talking out of school and betraying your own class! You're the lowest sort there is, Twist, and if there's a hell you'll be further down in it than me!'

'You consider me responsible for Nancy's death?' he asked in what looked like genuine confusion. 'Why on Earth?'

'Everyone was nice and comfortable until you came along! We was a happy family what never had a cross word with one another. Then you appeared, pouring your poison into everyone's minds, pitching crim against crim. Worst piece of work I ever done was take you home to meet my sweet Fagin. I should've just left you there on that street to starve!'

A laugh from him then but it was mirthless and sharp, expressing his disbelief. It seemed that he had been expecting our reunion to be somehow warmer than this. 'Dodger,' he said after he had collected himself. 'There was one man responsible for the death of that woman. And his name was Bill Sikes.'

That, of course, was true. But if Twist thought he had won

me over by uttering this cold statement of fact then he was much mistaken.

'Bill killed Nancy on account of you,' I charged him with. 'So her murder is your doing. Then he got hounded to death for it, so that's on you too. And also the destruction of his dog Bullseye what had never hurt a fly.' Oliver opened his mouth to respond but my blood was up and I rode roughshod over him. 'But the worst of it, Twist,' I seethed, 'is what you done to dear old Fagin. After the kindnesses he showed to you – welcoming you into our little den, cooking you bacon fresh from the market, telling you jokes, teaching you tricks – and you repay him by splitting on him to the first rich gentleman you come across. You sentenced that man to his doom just so you could climb up a class.'

I was pacing the short space of the cell now as far as the chain would allow and I was all sneer. He just sat there and took it.

'Yeah, I heard you got yourself adopted by a rich man. Well, that's very cosy for you, I must say. But what about all the bodies what had to fall first? What about the honest cockneys what got strung up for you to flounce off and do the genteel? You sicken me, Twist, you always have! You visited Fagin in Newgate on the night before his hanging, eh? What was that about then? To gloat? By God, I've known some wicked buggers in my time but never one as black as you.'

I stopped my pacing then and breathed out strong. All of a sudden I felt much better than I had in weeks. I sat down again, lighter for the outburst.

'You wasn't even any good at picking pockets,' I remarked as a final kick.

Oliver did not respond for a time and it was clear that my words had landed hard. At last he raised one of his white-gloved hands up to his mouth and let out a little cough. Then he pulled off both of his gloves and placed them aside.

'When my now adopted father and I visited Fagin on that night all those years ago,' he began at last in a quiet manner, 'it was not to gloat. Nor am I here to do that now. Quite the opposite. Whatever else you might think of me, Jack Dawkins, believe that.' I held his gaze and said nothing. 'In fact, the reason for my visit to this cell all those nights ago was to ask your friend for information pertaining to my true identity. And in spite of the mad and frenzied state in which we found him, I am glad to say that Fagin was able to provide us with it. I come to you tonight for similar reasons. I see that you, as he was, are in the grip of a mania that I can only imagine and do not envy you for. But I also find that you are at least lucid and so perhaps there is a chance that we can converse sensibly once you have calmed yourself.' He picked up his notepad and poised the pencil over it as if waiting to write my words down.

'You want information?' I replied. 'Pertaining to your true identity? Well, I'm sorry, Mr Twist, but you've come to the wrong cell. It's not my intention to do you any favours. I don't care who you think you are, you'll always be a shivering street-turd to me.'

He sighed as if he were in the presence of a belligerent child. 'I know my own identity now, thank you, Dodger. I seek information from you regarding a quite different matter.' I did not respond to that. I wanted to hear him speak. 'Now listen,' he said. 'We don't have much time together and I'm keen to press on. But I'm sorry you feel such animosity towards me. I did not expect to be greeted by you with open arms – even if they weren't manacled. But I did not imagine that you bore me as much ill will as this. In my defence I only say that I do indeed feel great guilt about my part in Nancy's demise. She was one of the bravest women I have ever known and it was in her efforts to save me that she fell foul of the savage monster who killed her. As for the monster himself,' Oliver bore his back up straighter as he spoke of Bill Sikes, 'I am glad that he died. He alone among your community deserved to.'

This was where Oliver scored his first point. I too was glad that Bill was dead, so here was something what we agreed upon. But I did not want Oliver to see that he had echoed my own feelings however – I was too keen to show some of that criminal solidarity what he lacked so much – and so I just stared back at him as he continued to counter.

'With regards to Fagin, my feelings are more complicated. He did, as you rightly say, invite me into his home and show me kindnesses without which I may have perished. He also tried to corrupt me into turning into a pickpocket. He wanted to transform me into someone like you and that is not a service for which I could ever thank him.'

A return parry. It seems the boy did still have some fight in him after all. I recalled now that he was never one to be bullied and he had stood up to Charley Bates and myself on a number of occasions when we had tried to dominate him. I braced myself for more of a bout than I had given him credit for and I went in for another swing.

'Turn you into me? Don't flatter yourself, Twist. You think that Fagin expected that a flat like you could have such potential as that. He was never fool enough.'

Oliver picked up his pencil again and began scratching onto the notepad. 'A quote from the man in the condemned cell,' he said while looking down at it.

That was a mean uppercut and it caught me off guard. But I was soon back on balance to deliver my graceful rejoinder.

'Why don't you fuck off out of it, you pox-ridden prick,' I

returned. Oliver stopped his scribbling and looked up to me. 'There. Put that on tomorrow's front page.'

He shifted in his seat. The defiance was leaving him now as fast as it had come and his face resumed its former softness.

'You don't care for me very much, do you, Dodger?'

'Getting that impression, are you?'

'Well, you can continue to hate me. It's not for me to tell you how to spend your final days. But it took a great effort to convince the prison authorities to grant me an audience. You're a hard man to see. Other journalists of my acquaintance tried to secure an interview with you earlier in the week and were turned away. They wanted to bring in illustrators with them to draw a sketch of you to use in publications. You're considered quite the commodity in Fleet Street.'

'Is that why you brought the pencil then, is it?' I said and pointed to it. 'To draw my portrait for the day of my hanging? Do me a favour and capture my handsome side.'

'I was only admitted entrance because my father – Mr Brownlow – used his influence again with the governor here. He thinks that I want to see you – a man condemned to death – so I can write an article for the *Morning Chronicle* about capital punishment. They do not suspect my real motive.'

'And what might that be, I wonder?'

'I want to discover who really committed the murder that you have been found guilty of. I don't believe that it you did it for one second.'

Well, that shut me up. I drew closer to him again but this time it was not with the intention of doing him harm. It was so that I could get a closer look of his face to see if he were in jest.

'If you're mocking me, Oliver,' I then said in an even heavier tone than before, 'then that would be your cruellest act yet.'

'I am serious,' he replied without a beat. He knew he had my full attention now and he laid down his pencil for a moment. 'In fact, I am probably one of the only people in this city that believes you to be entirely innocent.' His gaze was steady as he spoke. 'And I mean to prove it.'

He stood up then and walked over towards the fire. I said nothing as I watched him pick up the brass poker and he gave the coals a quick stoke as I decided it would be better to let him go on speaking. Could this boy here, who I had hated so much, really be the one to clear my name? Could he even save me from the gallows? As he poked at the fireplace some plaster fell down from up in the chimney and into the grate.

'This place is far too old,' he complained as he stood up again and brushed the coal specks from off his rich grey coat. 'They should tear it down before it collapses and kills every soul inside.' He crossed over back to his seat then, folded his fingers into each other and resumed talking. He must have been waiting for me to cool down so we could talk in a more civilised manner.

'You know, the last thing I heard about you was that you were transported to Australia for pickpocketing. That was over eight years ago now and, honestly, I never expected to see you again. I did not imagine that you would ever return to England, I'm not even sure how you were allowed to. But I've often thought about you, Dodger. I suppose you're the sort of person who is difficult to forget. I was quite astounded when I heard that you were one of the two men who had been arrested for Antony Rylance's murder. You and Mouse Flynn of course, who I remember also.'

'You're sat on Mouse's bed now,' I told him and he looked unsettled by the information. He got up, apologised and shifted himself down to its foot as if out of respect for my friend's ghost.

He then told me that he had heard about Mouse's fatal plummet already and he was quick to offer his condolences.

'I know how it feels to lose a friend,' he said. 'It is like the death of a brother for those of us who don't have brothers. I myself am grieving for a very close friend whose ashes I collected from the crematorium just yesterday. He was murdered quite recently.'

'Murdered?' I asked, and wondered if he was talking about who I thought he was.

'My friend's name was Anthony Rylance,' he confirmed. 'So you see my true interest in your case.'

Another moment passed before I responded. I just could not help marvelling at how small this city of ours sometimes was. 'Anthony Rylance?' I said at last, 'The man who I am set to swing for, was friends with you, Oliver Twist?' Oliver nodded. 'Well, that's a coincidence, I must say.'

'Indeed,' was his weary reply. 'My life teems with them.'

'You was both journalists,' I said, guessing at the connection. 'Is that how you knew him?'

'No, my history with Anthony goes much further back,' he explained. 'We attended school together – Dotheboy's, one of the oldest in England. I was sent there by my father soon after his adoption of me. I struggled to make friends at first because of the rough country accent that I still had then and, of course, my awkward parentage. And I sometimes find it difficult to trust offers of friendship.' He threw me a rotten glance then as if that were somehow my fault. 'Anthony was different though. He was an open-hearted lad and we shared similar interests.'

He then went on to tell me that he and his friend Anthony had both wanted to get into journalism as a profession and that together they had left university early to this end.

'I felt keenly,' he went on, 'that somebody should expose the

sorts of social injustices that I had endured as a child. I thought that
– through journalism – I would be able to defend and champion
the poor man, and so I was able to get a job as a reporter on the
Morning Chronicle. Anthony has not been so successful, however,
and he's still yet to make his mark in the profess—' Oliver stopped
then and he corrected himself with a wince. 'I mean to say,' he
spoke with a sadness what I recognised, 'that he never made his
mark in the profession.'

I could tell then that the pain he felt for his dead friend matched
mine for Mouse. And, in a very small way, my attitude towards
him shifted.

'Among the reasons that I superseded my friend in our chosen
career,' Oliver continued after a short exhale, 'was that I am a hard
worker. I investigate my stories during the day and type them up
in the *Chronicle's* office at night. I hardly ever go home except to
sleep and I keep irregular hours. Anthony, God rest him, was, until
recently, apt to be lazy in his work and I think that he resented my
success for a time. But curiously, in the last few months of his life
he became uncharacteristically industrious. He was working on a
story – some tasty piece of scandal, was how he described it to me.
And I could tell that this story was occupying all of his time and
energy even though he refused to tell me what it was about no
matter how much I enquired.'

'Why not?' I asked. 'I thought you and he was such close pals.'

'We were,' Oliver said. 'But we were also rivals in career
advancement and I fear that he was worried I might beat him to
the story if he disclosed the nature of it. I did learn a few facts from
him though. For one thing,' Oliver's eyes darted over to the shut
cell door and then back to mine, 'I know he was looking into the
activities of a very powerful and dangerous individual.'

Oliver gathered his pad and pencil then and walked over to the cell door. It looked as though he was trying to tell if the turnkey were listening in on our chat and he tested the handle to be sure that it was shut tight. Then he crossed over to my bed and sat down next to me, which considering that only moments before I had tried to attack him, was a surprising move. He was now well within my range but I did nothing but lean in to hear what he was about to say. Whatever it was, it was for my ears alone.

'Anthony said that the person he was investigating,' he whispered, 'was in the *Metropolitan Police Service*.' Oliver leaned back then and waited for my reaction. I shrugged.

'And?' I asked.

'Well, doesn't that unsettle you?'

'Not as much as you might think,' I replied. 'Look, Twist, that sort of thing might be news to the *Chronicle* reader but I'm from the rookeries. Round my way it's common knowledge that the peelers are among the biggest crooks going.'

'But I didn't get the impression that he was just investigating drunken constables, Dodger. Or some thuggish or bribable sergeant. No, Anthony was talking about someone much higher up. He intimated that he had uncovered a wide-ranging criminal conspiracy that led to a senior officer who was – from what I could gather – running a large portion of London's underworld.'

I laughed in his face. 'You're wasted in newspapers, Twist,' I told him. 'You should be writing fairy stories with that imagination.'

'You don't think it likely? That a senior policeman could be in charge of criminals? You've never heard of anything of the sort?'

'I've heard of police informers,' I replied. 'But that ain't the same thing because other criminals don't tolerate it. But if you mean to tell me that some peeler is running a gang of crooks, like a top sawyer would, then I can tell you it ain't possible, no. I'd have heard about it.' Oliver nodded for a moment before going on.

'But what if,' he put it to me, 'the criminal gang didn't know that they were controlled by such a person?' What if another criminal acted as the agent between the underworld and their true master? Keeping the policeman's identity a secret. Is that plausible?'

I considered that for some seconds. And then I had to shut my eyes as dull realisation broke in upon me. I thought about the mysterious man whose name Billy Slade was protecting and who had arranged for me to enter the home of Anthony Rylance. I had been impressed by how successful Slade had been at arranging for those peelers to appear at just the right time and arrest me. I had just assumed that he was manipulating them or paying them off. It had never occurred to me that the police might instead be controlling him.

'Yeah,' I said, fighting a sickening sensation. 'That could be happening.'

All my of anger and hatred for Slade, what had been replaced with guilt after the death of Mouse Flynn, was quick to coarse through me again. If Oliver's suspicions was right then my old gang was now working for the Metropolitan Police Service without even realising it and I was the one what had let the wolf in through the door.

'Your face has turned ashen, Dodger,' Oliver said as I raised my hand up to cover it. 'Even more so than before. You have something to tell me? You know the agent?'

'I might do,' I replied. 'You finish telling me about Anthony. He was killed because he found out about such a thing? Is that what you think?'

'Yes, I do,' Oliver replied. 'He wouldn't reveal any of the names of the people involved but he did tell me that his investigations had begun after being approached in secret by a police constable. It was this constable who informed Anthony about a highly corrupt superior officer and said that a number of other policemen knew about the man's villainy. The constable insisted on anonymity and I was told hardly anything else other than the name that Anthony himself had given to the story. He referred to the article he was writing cryptically as *Dark Satanic* and he kept his documents safe inside a little metal deposit box which he never let out of his sight.'

'A metal deposit box,' I repeated. 'Was it black with silver lining?'

'Yes,' he nodded. 'Just like the one you described finding to the court. The one that was missing from the police inventory.'

'Bastards!' I exclaimed aloud then as I realised what wicked games had been played against me. Oliver jumped and told me to quieten myself. 'Double-dealing buggers!' I cried, ignoring him. 'It's as I've always said, Twist! The biggest criminals are in uniform!'

Again, Turnkey Baines called through from the corridor outside and Oliver got up and crossed over to the door to assure him that all was fine, despite the noise. By the time he returned to the opposite bed again I was still fuming but I was ready to listen to more. My eyes was fixed on the stone floor as Oliver continued.

'When I heard that Anthony had been murdered,' he said as he sat down, 'I knew that this powerful policeman must have got to him. I still had no idea which officer it might be and, when your name was released as the culprit, I assumed that you and Flynn had been hired by him to kill poor Anthony. I have to admit, Dodger, that I went to your trial hoping that you would both be given death.'

I looked up at him with bitterness. 'Well, you got your wish then,' I said.

'But it was at the trial that I realised that you were, in fact, innocent. I believed your testimony while the rest of the press bench just scoffed at it. And I believed you because I knew something that they did not. I knew how much Anthony loved poetry.' Oliver smiled then as if at a private joke. 'And I suddenly realised what *Dark Satanic* meant. Or rather who.'

He picked up his pad again and scribbled something onto it. Then he held it up for me to see and I peered in closer so I could read it by the light of the fire.

It read, DETECTIVE SUPERINTENDENT MILLS.

'The peeler who testified against me,' I replied, not caring to keep my voice down. 'The one who claimed to have received a telegram. That is who Slade is working for.' Oliver may have had his reasons for not wanting his name overheard but I was happy for the turnkey outside to hear who was responsible for all this.

'That's him,' Oliver confirmed in a quieter voice. 'Or rather Dark Satanic Mills.'

'Is that his name then?' I asked in confusion. 'He had some queer parents if so.'

'Dark Satanic Mills is from "Jerusalem",' said Oliver still smiling.

'Oh, yeah?' I replied. 'Well, he didn't look Jewish to me.' Oliver suppressed a bigger smile.

'"Jerusalem" is a poem by William Blake,' he explained as if talking to an ignorant peasant. 'Of a very religious nature. It gets recited in churches a lot which you'd know if you ever set foot in one.' He was starting to get a bit cheeky and I was about to take him to task for mocking a man condemned to death. But Oliver was already busy clearing his throat. '"And was Jerusalem builded here,"' he said with a look of concentration on his face, '"among these dark Satanic Mills?"' He then gave a small chuckle. 'Clever Anthony,' he muttered as he began writing again, 'it's a play on DS Mills.'

'Listen, Twist,' I interrupted, hoping that me still calling him by his poorhouse name would annoy him. 'I don't have time to sit here all night appreciating poetry with you. I'm a busy man with places to be.'

'So that was how I knew that Mills was our man,' Oliver continued over me. 'Well, that and his ridiculous testimony which – apart from me – nobody thought to question.'

'That's because the judge was in on the plot,' I said causing him to raise his eyebrows in surprise. 'That much I do know.'

'And you know a good deal more, I imagine?' said Oliver and again his pencil poised over the pad. 'Which is why I'm here. Well, I think it's time for our interview to begin, Dodger. First question. Who do you think is Mills' agent in the underworld?'

'His name is William Slade,' I replied without hesitation. 'And he goes by Weeping Billy.'

For the next few minutes I spoke fast, telling Oliver Twist all what I knew about this whole dark business. Oliver had never heard of Slade before but he was very interested to learn that a High Court judge was seen in Slade's brothel and had overseen my trial, weighing things against me. But it was when I mentioned what Tanner had told me in the press yard – about how his brother, another Slade man, was charged with murdering a policeman in circumstances similar to my own arrest – that Oliver saw a connection with his own investigations.

'There is only one policeman who that can be,' he said and tapped his pencil onto the pad as if it were helping him think quicker, 'Constable Wingham. Anthony himself covered the Wingham trial in great detail. It was weeks before Anthony's murder and the official story seemed so sound. He was killed by a burglar, case closed. But it makes perfect sense now that I think about it. Wingham must be the policeman that came to Anthony with the story about Mills and then Mills must have found out and had him killed. And again, as with you, Slade arranged for one of his own men to take the blame. So there is a discernible pattern.' He was almost bouncing on top of Mouse's old bed now which I felt was in very poor taste. 'What a tremendous lead!'

'I'm glad you're enjoying yourself, Twist,' I said, glaring at him hard, 'but it doesn't alter my situation one bit, does it? I'm going to hang the day after tomorrow for something I never done. How does any of this do me good?'

Oliver checked his enthusiasm and then spoke with more gravity. 'Dodger, nothing would give me greater satisfaction than to save your life, believe me!' he said, holding my eye. 'Perhaps then you will see that I am not, and have never been, your enemy. But you have to understand,' his mood dropped again and I caught a rare glimpse of shame from the boy, 'that I can't do anything with this information until I know who to trust with it.'

I was back on my feet again and so wild that I did not care if the turnkey should come and bring our interview to an early close. 'Then what use are you to me, Twist?' I demanded as I lifted up my chains and rattled them in his face. 'What use have you ever been?'

'I'm sorry, Jack,' he said, sounding it at last, 'but I have my own life to think about. Mills has people killed who he thinks are out to expose him. Anthony and this Constable Wingham, it now seems. I need to tread carefully.'

'Oh, I understand!' I shouted back at him. 'You mean to tiptoe about and take your sweet time with it all. Meanwhile, it's curtains for poor Dawkins here! But you ain't bothered! Your class never care about what happens to the likes of me.' I looked him straight in the eyes for this next thing, knowing it would cut deep. 'You might not think yourself my enemy, Twist,' I said. 'But you've never been my friend.'

I could see that Oliver was bothered by this. Here, after all, was someone what had just told me that he had become a journalist to help defend the poor man. Well, who was the poor man if not me?

'If I can move fast enough to prevent your hanging then I will,' he promised me in a tone what sounded sincere, 'but it's not my fault that your execution is so soon. I came in here knowing one half of the puzzle – Detective Mills – and you have given me the other half – William Slade. So I have enough to work with to build a case – more than Anthony ever did. But I need to approach someone in the police force who I know is not in league with Mills and I have no way of knowing who to trust. You just said yourself that the police were all crooks. In which case, who do I go to with any of this?'

'Wilfred Bracken,' I said without missing a beat. 'He's an inspector what is stationed in the Holborn division. Go to him.'

'I've heard the name,' Oliver said as he wrote it down. 'You think he's a good man?'

'No, he's a cruel, flint-hearted terror,' I declared with some authority as he underlined the words. 'Among other things he's responsible for arresting my mother for a crime what she then hanged for. He's forever pushing his miserable face into my business and stomping around the rookeries like he owns the place.' I sighed then, hating to admit this next thing. 'But if there is one peeler out there what is not a criminal then it's him. I've known plenty of crooks what've tried to bribe him out of arresting them but he never bites. Like I say, he's a joyless sod.'

'Thank you, Dodger,' Oliver said as he put the pad away, 'that's another excellent tip. This inspector may help to clear your name.'

'Well, don't mention that part to him or he might not bother,' I said and just then we heard the sound of the cell door being opened again. Oliver spoke quick before Turnkey Baines could enter the room.

'This was worthwhile,' he said in a hurried whisper, 'and if I can work fast enough and gather more evidence to present to this Bracken then I can perhaps save you from the noose.'

We both turned to see the light from the candlestick held by the turnkey shine through into the room.

'I hope you've found the interview to your satisfaction, Mr Brownlow, sir!' Baines said once the door was opened wide. 'You had longer than agreed upon on account of how it may be the last proper conversation your young subject will ever have. But the big hand is reaching the small hand and it's about to strike midnight, would you believe? It's chapel tomorrow and this fellow must be up early to hear the condemned service. So I'll walk you out.'

Oliver got to his feet but he kept his face fixed upon mine and not on the turnkey's. 'They don't usually allow visitors on Sunday but I'll try to arrange to see you tomorrow too. I will also attempt to see the authorities and get them to postpone your hanging if it can be done. But, Dodger . . .' he came towards me now against the turnkey's wishes, 'I won't make promises I can't keep and I think you know that. So let us part on good terms.' His hand was outstretched. 'If I cannot save you I can at least clear your name posthumously and that I will promise.'

'A fat lot of value a clear name is when you're buried in the earth,' I replied and I almost considered refusing his hand. I had been so angry with the boy for such a long time that it felt unnatural for us to part on friendly terms. But he had come here to see me in my lowest hour and was prepared to take my side which few others would. So, after some hesitation, I decided to take his hand after all and I thanked him for coming.

'I do care about what happens to you, Dodger,' he said before turning away. 'I never wanted to see either you or Fagin end up like this.' Then he turned away and headed out of the cell.

'Oliver?' I said once he was out in the corridor. He turned to hear what I had to say, but it was too late. Turnkey Baines had swung the iron door shut and I was again in darkness. Seconds later, as Baines had said they would, the St Sepulchre bells began chiming for midnight.

Chapter 19

The Many Ghosts of Newgate

*Including a summons to meet the most dangerous
criminal in London*

'It is only repentance that can save your eternal soul now.'

Two coffins was displayed in the chapel for those what was due to hang on the very next morning. There was supposed to be three but the one meant for Mouse was already under the ground.

'And only God's forgiveness can protect you from fiery damnation.'

I had been made to sit at the end of the condemned pew on this Sunday so the whole congregation could tell at a glance which one was the famous killer of Anthony Rylance. The Ordinary was delivering the very same words he had for Old Edwards just seven days before. I wondered if he ever changed them at all.

'If, however, He should choose not to answer your prayers then Hell awaits you.'

I looked at the nearest coffin, the one what I had been told was meant for me. It was too small for the job and I wanted to tell someone. You can't bury me in that.

'Death is not the end. For any of us.'

Beside me sat the woman called Alice Burgess who was also set to swing tomorrow. She was bent over in prayer as was everyone else on the condemned pew.

'It is only to be feared by those with hands incarnadine.'

Soon, and for the first time in my life, I was praying along with the rest of them.

If my midnight reunion with Oliver Twist had taught me anything it was that sometimes a boy born poor can rise up and join the rich world if only luck and hard pushing would conspire together. So it was not true – as Mouse had claimed just days before – that the future of a slum baby, such as his son, was already writ. Robin Flynn, an infant who I felt even more responsibility to now that he had lost both parents, would not have to travel the same road as his father and his uncle Jack had done – things could be different for him. Oliver had proved that such an orphan might not one day find himself meeting the same end as we had. This was the one thing I kept telling myself on the final day before my execution date. That one of the few things left worth praying for was the continued innocence of Robin Flynn.

As I stumbled through the prison – both my arms and my legs was still fettered and I was being led by the guards – I thought of nothing save for Robin and what his future might hold. I had always imagined that Mouse and myself would grow into old men together, both of us made fat and rich on the winnings we had acquired in our leaner, hungrier days. I had told Mouse, on numerous occasions, that his boy Robin would grow up benefitting from our labours and would not want for nothing. But the miserable truth struck as the turnkeys stopped me tripping as we passed the courtyard where Mouse and I had climbed the walls during our failed escape. Robin was much better off without me as his top sawyer. I was a bad influence on all who I met and so his upbringing was more secure without me around to corrupt it. My frame of mind was as dark as it had ever been then and I reflected on whether I did, in truth, deserve to die.

'You deserve to die!' a rough voice cried out from behind me.

The condemned prisoners had been walking in a line – with me at the front – as the turnkeys escorted us back to our cells. But now there was a sound of a struggle and I turned back to see Murdo Meehan – one of those prisoners what I had stripped of his possessions at gambling – and he had broken away from his guard and was running for it. I thought, at first, that he was making an admirable, if unlikely, dash for his own freedom. But this was not the case, I realised, when he came running in my direction with his teeth bared and his manacled arms outstretched.

'You deserve to die, Dawkins!' he said as he made it past the turnkeys and collided into me. His legs was not chained like mine and his hands was around my neck as I was pushed backwards against the wall. 'Mouse Flynn would still be alive if it weren't for you! You deserve to be hanged!' I struggled against him as he tried to spit in my face but I was unprepared for the assault and it was left to Turnkey Max to get him off me.

'Restrain that man,' Max told two other guards as they grabbed Meehan and pulled him away. 'And take him back to his cell first. I'll remain with Dawkins until he's locked up.'

I looked on in confusion as Meehan was forced down the stone staircase towards the condemned cells and the rest of the prisoners was marched past. They all gave me evil looks as I waited with Max until last.

'I didn't know,' was all I could think to say, 'that they all liked Mouse so much.'

'They didn't,' Max said as the last convict disappeared down the steps and we waited to be told that it was clear for us to follow. 'They just bloody hate you. And Meehan there,' he pointed after my attacker with his truncheon, 'has good reason to. Know why?' I shook my head. 'Every Monday morning we hang three condemned prisoners in public viewing if there are three to hang. But no more than three. Any more than that – some feel – would be obscene.'

'Obscene?' I replied in a dry voice. I had not drunk any water for hours and my throat hurt after having had Meehan's hands around it. 'Just one is a grotesque. But why . . .' but then it dawned. Mouse was dead. So there was a space on the gallows.

'Right,' Max nodded. 'Your little antics the other night have shaved a week off that man's life. He wasn't due to swing until next week.'

'But that can't be fair,' I said, horrified at the injustice. 'Shouldn't a lawyer be stopping it or something?'

'Oh, yeah, he's notified a solicitor,' replied the turnkey. Underneath his moustache there was a small smile what he did not even attempt to hide. 'Who will receive the letter early some time tomorrow. There's a reason why we hang people early Monday mornings, Dawkins,' he winked. 'All the meddlers are not at work until the deed has been done.'

Then he grabbed me by the arm and began tugging me back to my cell and I knew that here – as if I needed it – was one more thing to feel rotten about before they killed me.

For the next hour or so I was locked up and alone and the only sound I could hear was that of Meehan swearing all manner of vicious curses at me from over in his cell. I did not shout back – indeed I did nothing but count the chimes from the church bells outside – but I cannot pretend that hearing his abuses did much to improve my black mood. Then, at some point in the late afternoon, the door to my cell opened once more.

'Gentleman to see you,' grunted the turnkey. 'On the Sabbath as well. Must have paid a pretty penny.'

'Oliver Twist?' I asked, sitting up with a sudden alertness what I thought had died in me. I could feel my beaten spirit being recalled to life by the very thought that my long-lost childhood acquaintance had returned with good news. I was in the rum position of feeling nothing but fond thoughts towards this boy who I had, until last night, detested.

But as soon as I was led into that arched visiting chamber and I saw the lone figure waiting for me behind the grille I knew that it was a not a friendly visit. The man stood there with one hand in the pocket of a thick and flashy pea-green coat and he wore a matching hat and a red waistcoat. I tried to break away from the turnkey – as Meehan had broken away from his – so I could run down the length of the chamber and try to smash through the grille to get at him. But my manacled legs prevented me and the turnkey kept good hold of my fetters as he led towards me the fiend.

'Oh dear, Jack Dawkins,' smirked Weeping Billy Slade as the turnkey drew me near. 'How sad to see you appearing so wretched less than a day before they hang you. It's a tragic scene this but, I must admit, not an entirely unexpected one. You always were the hangable sort.'

'I know what you are, Slade!' I roared at him through the grille. 'You're a thief-taker! You're in league with the police and setting up hard-working boys such as myself. I'd spit at you if I weren't so bleeding parched!'

I shouted the words loud enough so that anyone close could hear the damning accusation but considering there was only a handful of turnkeys within earshot, most of them on his side of the barrier, I may as well have been talking to the bricks. Slade knew it and shrugged at the man what was now preparing to lock me in the cell with him.

'Would you warrant it, Gaoler?' he sighed with his good hand holding onto a bar. 'He's berating me for being a decent citizen and informing the police about his criminal activities. As if that were something to be ashamed of. What a warped system of values this sorry creature has. No wonder it should have come to this.' But I had no intention of letting him get away with that flam so easy.

'You arranged for an innocent man to take the drop for Constable Wingham!' I shouted for the guards to hear and he flinched in surprise. 'Just as you set me up over the killing of Rylance. So spare us this "good citizen" act, Slade, because you're the worst there is!'

I saw some of the turnkeys exchange glances then but Slade had regained his composure and was sighing at me. 'What sad fictions a desperate and worn-out mind will come up with. I pity you, Jack Dawkins, I honestly do.'

The turnkeys then left me in that chamber with my enemy which was all right with me as I had some more forthright language what I intended to direct his way.

'When the rookery boys learn what your true business is, Slade – and they'll learn soon enough – you're going to lose more than your other fingers. Gangs like mine, and like yourn an' all, don't care for those what deal with the police, and their punishments is worse than those of a court. I'd rather face the noose than what you'll suffer through when it all comes out. You won't be all smirks then.' Slade did not seem at all unsettled by this however.

'Your gang is my gang now.' He was leaning into the bars close and whispering. 'But you're right, they can't abide collaborators. So it's just as well nobody is going to live long enough to tell them, eh?' His wolf grin spread.

'The truth gets around,' I replied with a snarl. 'I've been telling everyone who'll listen about how a peeler has made a bitch out of you. Even after I'm dead those words will travel.'

The grin vanished and his voice was all threat. 'Well, that's why I'm here, isn't it?' he said. 'Or did you think I came all the way down to Newgate just to gloat like some clumsy villain in a stage melodrama? No, Jack Dawkins, I came to find out what you know and it seems to be quite a lot. Whatever rumours you may have overheard about the unfortunate demise of Constable Wingham I cannot guess at. But that's not important, as you're to die tomorrow. What is of uppermost importance, however, is who you yourself have been peaching to? That is what I came to learn.'

We locked eyes then and I said nothing. I would never reveal what allies I might have on the outside and he must have known that. But he pulled a questioning face for a moment and I flashed him some defiance before his sly smile returned.

'And I already know the answer!' he announced with glee. 'Two names. Mrs Mary Dawkins and Mr Oliver Brownlow. Written above mine in the guest ledger over there. Now who on Earth are those people, I wonder?'

I cursed him again and he laughed at me. 'Distant relatives,' was my weak reply. 'And they don't know nothing about nothing.'

'Your dead mother was called Kat,' he spoke as though he was thinking his way through some child's riddle just for fun. 'So Mrs Dawkins is not her. More likely it was either one of your two fancy women disguising herself as your wife. If it was Lily Lennox then there is no problem – she's been dealt with. And if it was the strange one – the chit in trousers – then that will be dealt with too. I've dispensed with much tougher characters then that unnatural tart in the past.'

My hands was on the grille and I rattled it hard. I swore so much at him that a turnkey had to come over and threaten me with a truncheon if I did not settle myself. But I was distraught to hear that Tom Skinner's life was now in forfeit and even more distressed about Lily. What did *she's been dealt with* mean?

Slade bit his lip and looked away from me until the turnkey left us alone again.

'It's this Oliver Brownlow character who troubles me more,' he then continued, thinking aloud. 'He came here late last night, so the ledger says, outside of visiting hours. Now, I know every name in the criminal world and I don't know that one. Which means he isn't from the criminal world.' His eyes flicked back to mine then. 'Who is he, then, Jack Dawkins,' he demanded, 'and what is his interest in you?'

'If you've hurt Lily,' I warned him, jabbing my finger into the metal what separated me from his face, 'I'll—'

'You'll do nothing,' he said sharp. 'You're beaten, come to peace with it.' Then something appeared to happen to his face. The smirks and grin fell away and I saw him, mask off. He came even closer then so he could hiss at me. 'Don't you know why I hate you so much?' he asked. 'Why I befriended you just so I could one day orchestrate your ruin? Because when DS Mills asked me to provide a burglar to take the blame for the murder of that journalist I could have picked any cracksman, he wouldn't have minded which. But I wanted it to be you. It had to be you.'

'Why?' I asked in genuine bewilderment. 'We was in business together. I was making you big money.'

'You stole from me, Dodger,' he replied in a flat voice. 'And nobody steals from Billy Slade.'

At first I was at a loss to imagine what he thought I might have pinched. During the months of our business arrangement I had – on occasion – handed over less than half of my gang's real earnings to keep the difference for myself. But that was not a hanging offence. His disfigured hand was now out of his pocket and he was pointing it in my face.

'The whore was mine,' he said and there was pain in his voice.

'She was a Slade girl and one I valued highly. And then, one night, she just steps out to work at the Haymarket and never returns. Just vanishes into thin air and when I at last discover where she has ended up I am told that she is living with some flash chancer called Jack Dawkins.' His nose was pressed against the grille and his eyes was fixed on mine. I got the sudden sensation that it was he and not myself what most wanted to tear down the barrier between us.

'Is that it, Slade?' I cried out in disgust at him. 'All this fuss over romantic rivalry? You've gone and arranged my arrest and execution just because I ran off with your woman? That's the most pathetic thing I've ever heard. You should be ashamed of yourself!' Slade backed away again and I saw the small marks of the grille still printed there on his nose. 'Grow up, Billy,' I continued. 'I mean, couldn't you have just moved on to someone else like every other broken-heart in the world? That's what I did when my first love left me for another. I just stepped out and met someone prettier. I didn't go around dreaming up dark plots like a mad person!'

It was Slade's turn to rattle the grille. 'Well, you picked a dangerous substitute, eh?' he spat, and I took a step back. He no longer seemed to care what the turnkeys might overhear. 'Because Slade girls come with a price. A price both you and she are now paying!'

'What have you done with her?' I cried out. His voice returned to a whisper and he contained himself once more.

'I investigated,' he announced. 'Discovered where she had run off to after your arrest. To some ungodly place in the country, it turns out. Rochester! Some of my men have just returned from there with her in the carriage and they found something else while up there. That little boy you said you'd done away with – Scratcher you called him – alive and well and attending some Ragged School.

I knew you hadn't killed him, you don't have the heart for it.' He spoke like he thought me pitiful.

'I've heart enough to kill you, Slade,' I shouted back at him. 'I'd ring your neck like a chicken.' The nearest turnkey looked over and told me to quieten down. 'I'll feed you to the dogs!' I continued. Slade's response was loud enough only for my ear as the turnkey's came closer.

'Lily's in my outhouse now, Dodger,' he taunted. 'The one I took you to, remember? Where I kept those suffering Turpins? I'll decide what's to become of the cheating whore when I get home. After I've discovered who this Mr Brownlow is, of course.'

I became most hysterical and I tried to grab at him through the grille. Then a turnkey hit me in the back of the legs and I crumpled to the floor in agony.

'It appears that Mr Dawkins here has become quite emotional,' I heard Slade say above me to the turnkeys. 'And can we blame him with what he's to face tomorrow morning? Best to take him back to his cell, I think, gentlemen, so he can prepare himself for the big event. He'll make a handsome corpse, we'll give him that.'

After I was taken back to my cell, my neighbour, Murdo Meehan, was quick to resume his campaign of abuse against me from his. But I shouted out – in a voice much fiercer than his – that I would bust into his cell and finish him even earlier if he did not knock it off fast. Meehan went quiet then and I did not hear another peep out of him.

Billy Slade's visit, as ironic as it might seem, had been just the tonic. Because before he had come and taunted me with his success I had been all out of fight and had even started to prepare myself for death. But now, all fired up after hearing what he planned to do to my friends and loved ones, I was back to my old self and determined to break out of this prison once more. I had people on the outside – Lily Lennox, Tom Skinner, Scratcher and now, in a bizarre turn of events, Oliver Twist – who all needed me to make my lucky so I could prevent them from suffering at Slade's mismatched hands. I was spitting mad and my mind scrambled to find some answer to my plight.

My leg fetters had been removed by now but my wrists was still chained. I had pleaded with the turnkey to take these off also but he told me that he was under orders to keep me manacled on account of my previous escape attempt. So I soon found myself pacing the cell, kicking at the walls and screaming out for someone to help me. After about an hour of this, I collapsed onto the stone floor and stared up at the cobwebs what covered the ceiling. Sunday evening was on the turn and, for me, the last of the sand was about to pass through the hourglass. I could think of no solution to how I would achieve my liberty save for making a run for it on the gallows itself. Perhaps, my brain buzzed, I could make use of the clergyman what would come tomorrow morning to administer consolation as he had to Old Edwards. I could steal something from him, an item from his pockets, and pick my locks with it while I was walked to the scaffold and then make a desperate dash. Or, what would be more effective, I could find something what could be fashioned into a weapon – a piece of glass for instance – and hold it to the clergyman's throat. Then the gaolers would be forced to show me to the exit or else.

None of these ideas – or any of the others what I was toying with as the cell grew darker – struck me as much use beyond fantasy. So, even after this renewed burst of hope and mental vigour I had been experiencing, my spirits still soon sank again as night fell. My thoughts then was all of a turmoil as to what was going to happen tomorrow and I now just wished that someone could be here to comfort me. I wished that Lily was there to put her arms around me, as she had whenever I returned from a hard crack, and then kiss me. But she was in the clutches of Billy Slade and had been taken back to that house of torture at the bottom of his garden. Would he kill her? Torture her? And what had he done to poor Scratcher? I was stricken with remorse that there was nothing I could do to save either.

The church bells struck midnight and so this was now the last morning I would ever see. I counted each chime as it struck and when the twelfth was sounded, I rolled over onto my knees. I knew, as I began to pray again, that my only hope for vengeance lay in Twist. Just because he was unable to save my life did not mean that he could not triumph over Slade and Mills after I was dead. But it would not be long before Slade learnt who Oliver Brownlow was – his crony Morris Bolter knew and would tell him if asked. So Twist would need to be very nimble if he were to triumph over those villains. At that point my faith in that poorhouse boy I had found lying in the street was the only thing keeping me from despair.

I was never a religious man and neither earlier in the chapel or now had it been God who I had prayed to. Everything I had ever been told about Him suggested that He would have had very little sympathy for my situation and so, instead, I had found myself praying to the many ghosts of Newgate. I reasoned that ghosts was something what Newgate would be full of and so I prayed to all the luckless thieves what had occupied the condemned cells before me. They would listen to me if no one else would.

And then, from the darkest part of the room, I heard a voice, kind, rich and familiar.

You didn't listen, my dear, it said in gentle chastisement. *You didn't heed my warning.*

Oliver had said that this cell was the very one where Fagin had spent his final nights alive. And it seemed that my heated imagination had summoned him now. I blinked and saw his twinkling self, sitting on the edge of my bed and shaking his head in sorrow. He raised his finger in the air, like a disapproving schoolmaster, and he counted the three words.

Don't. Get. Caught.

More of that plaster fell from inside the chimney. I wondered if Twist was right about how Newgate was starting to crumble. It had been sat here, in the middle of London, since the Middle Ages and could not last another hundred years. In my dark mood I wished that the whole place would fall about me now crushing all occupants, including myself. If I were going to die, it might as well be dramatic.

Even more plaster fell, this time causing a burst of heavy dust to blow into the tiny cell. Then some brickwork followed. I looked towards the fireplace and wondered if my prayers had been answered. The old prison was giving in at last.

A horrendous noise now as I heard something formidable thunder down the length of the chimney. I found myself retreating to the far side of the cell to avoid its impact and when the rubble landed it filled the cell with such a cloud I thought I would choke to death then and there. I coughed, shielded my eyes and waved at the dust and I almost began shouting for the turnkey to get me out of here. It was then that I heard voices. Women's voices.

'That's enough, Meg!' I heard the first voice say. 'Too much noise!'

'It won't squeeze through,' said the second.

'Force it!' said a third voice. 'Force it through!'

I made my way back to the chimney as the dust began to settle and I crouched by the mouth of it. There was now a large pile of bricks what had extinguished any fire and was blocking me from peering inside. I did not care to stick my head in anyway as more brickwork was raining down although now the downpour seemed less accidental. I coughed again and threw my voice up the chimney.

'Who's up there?' I demanded. 'You trying to kill me?'

The first voice answered. 'Jack Dawkins.' It was not a question. 'Start clearing the grate of all that brick. We're sending something down.'

I pulled the two old candlesticks nearer so I could see better and did as she bid me. Before long the rubble was all removed and I called back up again to say I was ready to receive whatever. Then another load of brick fell just as I was leaning in and I had to move quick from risk of having my head smashed in.

'You stupid horse!' the first voice cursed. 'If you kill him, you'll pay dear!'

'I had to, Sessina,' Meg replied. 'There's room to push it through now.'

Once this new cloud of dust was waved away I called up to ask them what was occurring. There was a long pause. I grew so impatient to know that I decided to risk a peek inside. With the candle in one hand I leaned into the chimney piece and looked upwards. Through those three iron bars I saw some movement. Something was coming down at a slow pace but I could not fathom as to what. I withdrew my head again and waited to see. Finally my delivery appeared. A bundle wrapped in brown paper had lowered itself into view. It was attached to a piece of string.

'Got it yet, Dawkins?' asked the voice I now knew belonged to that red-haired convict, Sessina Ballard, what I had seen in the courtyard window. 'Hurry and untie, we have other, things to lower.'

I took the bundle and released it from the string. The wrapping turned out to be one of those religious tracts what the Ordinary was forever handing out in chapel that had Bible passages printed on. John 11.25 — I AM THE RESURRECTION AND THE LIFE. I pulled the tract away in a hurry to reveal my gift. It was a long metal saw with the sharpest teeth I had seen on such a tool. Wrapped around this was a blue slip of Newgate paper with the Whittington cat insignia on it. Underneath that a rough hand had scrawled a message. I rolled out the paper as the string ascended back up the chimney and read the legend.

You have been granted an audience with the Rum Mort!

Chapter 20

The Rum Mort Revealed

Wherein I am surprised

The metal saw was indeed excellent but it needed some hard work behind it if it was going to do much damage to those bars above. Considering the confined space and the awkwardness of the angle in which I was working, as well as how every so often more plaster and brick would fall down and miss my head by inches, it was almost an hour before I managed to make a decent groove into one of them. It had already done a fine job of freeing me from the chains – and my renewed freedom of movement as well as this exciting turn of events was spurring me on – but the task was an arduous one. At last the saw made purchase of the middle bar but the teeth was starting to rub themselves flat. Soon though a second bundle was lowered down on that piece of string. As I untied that one I was reminded of what I had been told on that first day in the courtyard. *Newgate is a web, and at its centre there sits a dirty great spider.* It seemed as though the Rum Mort meant to pull me to its centre.

Another large chunk of brick grazed past my head and I cursed up to them that the work was hard enough without having to dodge this rubble. Sessina apologised and I heard her tell the others that they was supposed to be pulling the bricks inward. It sounded like there was a whole gang of females up there and as time passed more light shone down from the widening shaft above, making things easier for me. The new bundle contained a thick file and, because it was smaller than the saw, it was easier to work on the cut already made by the larger tool. It took an age before I started to feel real progress upon the bar but on I went. After all, I had no other real plans for the evening.

I knew that I only needed to remove two of the bars and then I could use the third as a step upwards. But the passage above me was small and sooty and I did not relish the idea of getting stuck up there where I could choke to death. At length, I cut through the end of the first bar and, after several strong tugs, I had it pulled down flat. As I worked on the next, I felt something soft lower itself down onto my head. They had now sent down a rope of knotted bed sheets what they intended to pull me up with.

As I had hoped, the third bar proved a valuable aid once the first two was away and I forced myself up into the chimney. It was possible to imagine that a child or a dwarf could ascend this passage with ease but, for a full grown man such as myself, the climb was agonising. I had never been pressed so tight and, as I clung onto the rope, the convicts above helped to pull me upwards. To die trapped in this airless tomb would be a far more horrible death than the quick drop what I had been promised in the morning but the voices of the women above, what I now counted as at least five, was a great encouragement. I could tell that there was a mighty effort being performed by the friendly whores, thieves and murderesses on the other end of the sheets, but I wondered how high I needed to go.

It looked to me as though the chimney flue bended away before I would reach the next fireplace but, as my hand reached up to the part of the wall where the women had been chiselling away, I discovered that I had no need to climb up that far anyway. I just needed to get up high enough to be level with the floor above, where the women had made their hole in the wall. Many hands grabbed mine as I felt where the shaft was and I was helped upwards as my body scraped against the insides of the chimney.

'Come on, love,' I heard this Meg say as the sounds of the women's straining grew louder. 'You can do it, almost there.' I got the queer sense, as my head at last made it up to the break in their wall and I saw the dirty and wild faces of the women pulling me through into their tiny space, that I was being born again and that this grubby quintet was my dubious midwives. Sessina Ballard was dripping with sweat as she chiselled away at the space around me – it was still far too tight to pull me through but my arms was into their room and I could at least breathe free again.

Finally, there was a large enough break for me to force myself into that cell by kicking at the wall of the chimney behind and the women all grabbed at me and urged me to keep pushing. My shirt was now well torn and there was grazes along my body from the scrape but, after more effort was applied from all concerned, I at last made it through into that well-lit room. I flopped onto the ground in exhaustion and the women all let go of the sheets and stood around me congratulating themselves upon a very difficult delivery. I, meanwhile, was seized by a series of hacking coughs and Black Meg, who had been stood by Sessina at the window on that day when I had first seen them, brought me over a pot of water what they had ready. Once I had drank it down I was able to contain myself and get a good look around at the odd environment where I now found myself. It was a large cell with four beds and there was far more bedding and furniture than in the one I had just left. These five women all looked down on me as I handed Meg back the pot and exhaled.

'Good evening, ladies,' I said after I had at last wiped my mouth and was breathing normal again. 'And to what do I owe this unexpected pleasure?'

Sessina looked down on me with her hands on her hips and with curiosity in her eye. She pointed at a stone bench and told me to sit there while I recovered. 'That's just the start of tonight's exertions,' she said once I had done so. 'It's almost one now and we're already running late. Eliza,' she turned one of them, 'fetch the Mort. Alice was out of her hold an hour ago and it's only this young dandy what's been keeping us all waiting.'

This Eliza did something even more astonishing then. She opened the unlocked door and walked out into the corridor without even checking to see whether there might be any guards on patrol on the other side.

'We've got the run of the whole quarters tonight,' Sessina whispered. 'It ain't so much a prison as a nice ladies' dormitory up here.' I was about to ask how this was possible when a puffed-out and perspiring woman sat on the opposite bed pointed at me with disapproval.

'He ain't supposed to be up here though,' she scowled, her face all perspiration. '*The special boy!* Rum has gone too far and now there's a bloody great hole in the wall. They'll be a whore of a time for those what remain.'

Sessina paced the cell and bit on her fingernails. 'Rum'll fix it,' she muttered. 'The Rum fixes everything.'

'Special?' I asked then. 'Why am I special?' They all turned to me in surprise. 'Don't misunderstand me, girls. I'm happy you're taking me on . . . well, whatever all this turns out to be. But what is it?'

All four of the remaining convicts stopped what they was doing and looked at me stunned. Black Meg was the first to speak.

'Don't he know?' she said to Sessina. 'I thought he knew.'

'So did I,' Sessina replied, and kept her eyes on me. Then the big woman piped up.

'He don't know,' she tittered and some other women began giggling too. 'No one's told him.' A shriek of laughter then. 'No one's told him who he is!' Sessina told this woman to be quiet and approached the bench where I was sitting.

'You're Jack Dawkins, yeah?' she said as if she thought I had lost all memory during the ordeal of the chimney. 'From Seven Dials?'

'That's me,' I replied. 'The Artful Dodger. What of it?'

'Thank gawd for that,' breathed out Meg. 'I thought we'd pulled up the wrong boy.'

Sessina's eyes didn't leave mine. 'Well then,' she said, as if that settled it. 'You're special then, aren't you? To the Rum Mort, I mean.'

I looked again at every face in this lamplit room and nodded. 'I see,' I said at last. 'He's heard of me. Respects me. Is that it?'

An explosion of laughter then from all around the cell. The fat woman, in particular, was beside herself with mirth. 'Sessina!' She kept chuckling as she gripped the arm of the smaller woman what had sat beside her and pinched hard. '*He really don't know!*' The smaller woman was biting her lip with excitement and her short legs had begun kicking out over the side of the bed like an infant's. Even Sessina, who until now had seemed the most serious, was trying not to laugh.

'Do you know what Rum Mort means, Dawkins?' she asked. 'It's old Newgate cant,' she explained, 'for great lady. The Rum Mort is a woman.' There was another amused snort from the opposite bench. 'And she's about to step through that there door so you might want to make yourself look presentable.'

'They're here!' said Meg, who had moved over to the door to keep watch. 'Hurry up with those sheets, Bertha,' she said to the fat one. There was a flurry of activity from all about as footsteps was heard approaching the cell and Sessina stood to receive the Rum Mort.

Three women then entered the room. The first was Eliza holding a candlestick and she made way for the second. This was young Alice Burgess, the murderess from the condemned pew who was set to hang beside me tomorrow. From the dust and soot what she was covered in, along with the dumbstruck expression fixed upon her face, I guessed that she too had only heard of this escape plan tonight. She then made way for the third woman who stepped in and shut the door behind her. She looked me up and down and shook her head in disgust at my ripped clothing and blackened skin.

'Well, well. You could have made an effort for your dear old mum, Jacky,' said Kat Dawkins with a tut, as I stared back at her in amazement. 'You could use a bloody good wash. Now come over here and give me a nice big kiss, eh?'

I was more shocked by this appearance than by anything else in my entire life which, considering some of the dramas I've lived through, is saying something. It took me several moments before I could make sense of the vision. One of the many ghosts of Newgate had just manifested herself before me and was spitting into the palms of her hands.

'Not gonna say thank you, then?' she said as she crossed over to me rubbing them together, and a mean smile appeared. She then started trying to wash the soot away from my cheeks. 'Thin gratitude, that's what it is,' she said as I resisted her attempts to scrub my skin clean. 'But that's boys for you, I s'pose. They never appreciate all we mothers do, eh?' She then placed her hands on my shoulders and gave me a kiss on the forehead. 'I shoulda had girls,' she added. 'Girls got gratitude.'

I could still summon no response. I had spent the last two

years thinking that this woman was dead but now here she was, standing right in front of me with her old expression of deep disdain stuck upon her face. Her curly hair now had white streaks running through it and she appeared a bit taller on account of these big boots she was wearing. I wondered if this here was a ghost or a doppelganger the like of which you read about in the gothic novels. But when I looked into her eyes I noticed they was still odd-coloured. One blue, one green. It was my mother all right, and there was no use denying it further.

'I was told you was dead,' I spoke in a voice what may have had more outrage in it than I had intended. 'Hanged by the neck I was told.'

'And I was told you was in Australia,' she replied flat. 'Yet here we both stand.'

I felt a smile crack across my face then and it might have been one of pride. I had never enjoyed a close relationship with my mother – indeed the complete opposite was true – but finding her here alive in Newgate Prison, and controlling all what went on around her, did something very powerful to me. I had to fight an urge to embrace her which I knew she would hate for me to do.

'Got back two years ago,' I said instead, overcome by a terrible need to impress her. 'I was given a full pardon by the Governor of New South Wales, see. I made a fortune as a sheep farmer, the pardon said, and did all right for myself.'

'That right?' An ironic sniff. 'Well, Jacky, I'm glad to see you've stayed out of trouble since.'

More laughter then from the other women but my mother broke away from me to flash them a hard look and the cackling stopped dead. 'I hope you've finished tying them sheets, you fat old wart,' she sneered before spitting onto the ground. 'Or I'll shove you over the wall without the benefit of one. And that'd be a fast plummet indeed.'

Bertha was all contrition. 'Sorry, Rum,' she said and went straight on with her work as my mother turned back to me and winked.

'My first night back in England,' I said, now that my thoughts had been given a chance to straighten themselves, 'I met the man what arrested you. Inspector Bracken. He told me you was dead.'

'That's your excuse for never coming to visit me, is it?'

'Well, why would he say that? Why let me go on thinking it?'

'How should I know?' she scowled as if she had in a moment lost all in interest in the topic, 'I ain't his wife. You can ask him yourself if it bothers you so much. Now stop bothering me with your questions when there's work wants doing. We need to chuck a sack over your head.'

She spun around and started giving out orders to the other women. I stood on my spot and watched her just like I had done when a kinchin, feeling as scorched by her turned back as I had then. Maternal affection was never something I could read in her, Fagin turned out to be more of a loving presence than she ever was. But tonight she had just fished me out of my death dungeon before my hanging and told these others I was special. So my emotions now was all of a confusion. Sessina Ballard came over and placed a hand on my shoulder. In her other hand was what looked to be a thick potato sack of the same sort they throw over the condemned heads on hanging day.

'Put this on,' she said. 'To cover your ugly phiz.'

'You ain't putting that over my head,' I said and batted the thing away. 'Where we going anyway?'

'Towards the debtors' quarters,' said Sessina, and she tried again to place the brown bag over me.

'That's where the gallows is!' I protested, grabbing it from her in defiance. 'Forget it. I ain't going near the rope with that rotten thing over me.'

'What do you think we're going to do, you stupid boy,' Kat called over from where she was wiping Alice's face. 'Hang you early? Do as you're told.'

But I tossed the hood aside and told her no. Then my mother, who had been addressing Alice in a far softer manner, snapped her head around to face me.

'Very well,' she jeered. 'You can crawl back down into your hole if you're going to be like that. And tomorrow morning, when they force another bag over you, don't pretend your mother never tried to help.'

'Why've I got to wear it?' I returned, feeling most petulant.

'Because I've got influence, Jacky, as you can see,' she stepped back towards me. 'I've helped women convicts out of here before – over the walls and, in some cases, straight through the gates. But they was ones what nobody would miss, their names just scratched out of the Newgate register and never again spoken of. You and her,' she thumbed towards Alice, 'are a good deal hotter. The whole of London will notice when you two ain't on the scaffold tomorrow and that they won't like one bit. This needs more care.'

'The turnkeys won't be happy,' Sessina confirmed. 'Even Max is keen to see you swing and he's the most corruptible. When he discovered that you and the Rum was related – after that time when I first saw you in that courtyard – he made a big show of getting you locked away so you wouldn't use the connection yourself. But the Rum's done a good job since of showing them that she don't care if you live or die.' My mother raised her chin at this and kept on staring. 'So this'll all come as a great surprise when they open your cell tomorrow. Put the hood on,' Sessina handed me the sacking again, 'to hide who you are.'

My mother, meanwhile, had already turned back to the trembling Alice and was placing a sack over her head too. 'Shh, shh,' I heard her say, 'all will be well soon. I've even brought my son, Jack, along to take care of you. That's why he's here.'

'All right then,' I said and picked up the sack again. 'Whatever you want, Rum.' It felt less ridiculous calling her that then it would be to call her mother.

'Hear that, sweet one?' she said in a soothing tone to Alice. 'He's a good boy really. When he's not running off to live with strange Jewish men.' She threw me a stinking look and I was reminded of how long the woman could hold a grudge. Alice began to calm herself then and the rest of the women gathered up the various tools what they had been using into a workman's bag and made to leave.

'It's time,' my mother said once the last candlestick but one was extinguished. 'We must away.' The big woman led the way out carrying a dark lantern like what we burglars use to light the paths at our feet. 'We'll lock this door afterwards so they don't see the damage until morning. It'll be too late by then and if they still have to hang something they can find a dog or a tramp.'

Sessina picked up a cleft stick with the remaining lit candle in it and said she would follow last as the rest of us left the room. The corridor of the female quarters was as dark and daunting as those what I had run through just nights before, with a series of dim lamps hanging along the medieval walls. Meg took Alice by the hand as Sessina locked the door after us.

'Hood!' my mother hissed at me then. 'How many times you need telling, Jacky?' I decided then that I would wear the headwear of the condemned after all, and so placed it over my head as bid.

'Ain't you cut out any eyeholes into this?' I complained as I adjusted the sacking. One of the women was helping me to get comfortable within it and her hand took mine. I was surprised when I heard my mother speak to me and realised that it would be she what would be guiding my steps through Newgate.

'I'll be your eyes,' she whispered as she began to lead me through the passages like a kinchin. 'And try not to trip, eh, dear?'

Newgate had many different corners and I guessed that the Rum Mort had more power over some parts of this prison than she did over others. It seemed as though the guards in the female quarters had been paid to look the other way but once we had travelled beyond that vicinity the women became much more careful. The only time when I could remove the sack was whenever we reached another spiral staircase and either went up or down it.

'If a guard stops us,' my mother whispered to Meg as we edged our way down one such staircase, 'you have the knife.'

'Yes, Rum,' Meg replied, and I saw the sharp blade in her hand before we reached the bottom and the rough material was placed over my head again.

We turned down several passages, pausing whenever we seemed to come to a doorway. The sounds of muffled filing and chain-rattling was then heard as the women broke through whatever barred our way. Then, just as one such obstruction had been removed, I felt the sudden grip of my mother's hand dig into mine and I was pushed against a wall as another hand raised up to my mouth to silence me. I saw through the potato sack material that the few lights we was carrying was being put out fast and all went black. Our entire party shuffled back and then, from somewhere deeper in the prison, I heard the sounds of footsteps coming closer.

It was hard to tell what was occurring but I imagined that the approaching guard was on the other side of this door. My mother

– in a very faint voice – spoke one word as the footsteps drew near. 'Meg,' she said to the knife-holder. But her tone was saying *be ready*.

I heard the footsteps come to a halt and I stopped breathing under that hood. None of the others made a sound either and I just waited to hear what would happen. But, to everyone's relief, the footsteps continued onwards and our hiding place was not revealed. Once all was silent again, I was pulled through that doorway and we kept moving.

Getting across the prison continued to be a proper confusion. The journey was stumbling and awkward but we was soon going down more steps than up. I kept in line and watched my footing while all the time experiencing a distinct unease about these shameful turn of events. I was glad to be out of my cell – there was no doubting that – and I was buzzing to find that the chance of freedom was with me once more. However, none of this was how I had envisioned my glorious escape. Ever since I had been cast into this Newgate I had imagined that my eventual breaking out would be a direct result of my own cunning and agency so there was a spoilt, ungrateful part of me what was somehow embarrassed about all this. The attempts what I myself had made to free myself from captivity had proven disastrous and now I was undergoing the humiliation of having my mother come back from the dead just so she could lead me to safety. It was an undignified exit from Newgate for a criminal of my standing and I imagined that the ghost of Jack Sheppard was peering at me from the shadows and chuckling over it. His own legendary escapes had not required any maternal intervention, that was for sure.

'This is the door we're after,' the Rum Mort whispered as we all bumped to a halt and she released my hand. 'The locks is heavy so wait while we bust it open. Take them sacks off, if you're all of a sweat.'

Once I had removed my hood I saw that we was now in the narrowest corridor yet. It was said that the rooms of Newgate get smaller as you are led towards the scaffold gate and so I reasoned that the noose must dangle close by. The women had set to work on a small but heavy-bolted iron door at the end of this thin corridor and I kept hold of Alice's small hand what was now damp with fear.

As I watched my mother, who was calling Fat Bertha a cack-handed cow for her failure to file through a bolt with any speed, I recalled the sharp agony I had felt when first told of her execution. I had been surprised then by how much the news of her death had shaken me considering what a poor relationship we had always had. She had always acted around me as if I were nothing more than a growth what had been put inside her against her will which, for all I knew, may well have been the case. But now here she was arranging all this so that I – and this Alice person – could escape the gallows. I did not know what to make of her.

'Lazy Jack!' she said as the filing came to an abrupt halt, 'get over here and do this for us, eh? It's disgraceful, watching your mother labour while you just stand there pulling faces.'

I crossed over to where she stood, took the file from her and, without a word, finished the job. Soon the final padlock was destroyed and the door was forced open revealing a narrow staircase what led down into blackness.

'This takes us underneath the kitchens,' said the Rum Mort. 'To an under-cellar full of the worst food. It's gonna stink but get used to it because it'll smell rosy against what follows.'

My mother snatched the tallest candle from Sessina and gave it to me. 'Jacky is going first. That's why we brung him. To be our canary.' I took the cleft stick and decided that I was done with feeling awkward around her.

'Allow me to lead the way, ladies,' I said and winked at the younger women, 'but follow my light close. I don't want none of you getting lost now.' Meg and Eliza both smiled at me and I turned and went through the door, holding the candle low. This illuminated just enough to see the first few stone steps leading downwards and a rope bannister running down the length of the wall. I used this to steady myself as I took careful steps down into the cellar. The place stank of rotten meat and the air was thin and musty and I was unprepared for how cold it would be. Halfway down I came to a lamp in the wall from which I was able to light the candle and the others began to follow me down. 'What's down here?' I asked as I reached the bottom of the steps and looked about. 'You been digging a tunnel?'

'We ain't dug nothing,' my mother said after I had lit some more lamps and revealed a cramped room full of wooden boxes, sacks of potatoes and oats. 'London done the digging for us.'

As soon as there was enough light to see better the women put down whatever they was carrying and Sessina, Meg and Eliza all started removing their prison clothes until they was down to their underthings. The others walked over to a big stack of boxes in the centre of the room and peered at them to ensure they was the right ones. 'These are full of dead prisoners' things,' sniffed my mother. 'Clothes and such. Get them shifted.' I helped them move the heavy boxes aside and, underneath, a bolted-over trapdoor was revealed. Two of the women unbolted the doors to this trap and pulled it back. Far down below I could just about hear the rush of a stream.

'The old Fleet River,' explained the Rum Mort as if she had uncovered a stash of gold. 'Still alive and flowing underneath the city. And it's gonna wash you all to freedom.'

I leaned over the trap and peered down into the depths of this hole. I couldn't even see the water it was so far down but the stench coming up from down there was pure evil.

'Wash us?' I laughed in disbelief. 'That's a sewer.'

'It ain't a sewer,' she replied, 'It's an underground river.' Then she leaned over the hole and I saw her react to the same stink that I had. 'An underground river flowing with shit,' she added.

'It could be bubonic, Rum,' Meg said, once she had got into her trousers and was placing a second pair of socks over the ones she had on. 'We could catch the plague and bring it back up to the surface with us.'

'If you would like to stay here, Megan, my lovely, then you are welcome to. But you asked me to get you out of Newgate and I'm obliging, ain't I? Jack and Alice here are going to hang tomorrow so they're both better off taking their chances down in the stink, in my humble view.' She sniffed as Sessina began tying some string around the bottom of her trousers so they was tight against the boots. I was then handed some string of my own and advised to do likewise. Meanwhile, Bertha had pulled away the shutters from the dark lantern so it shone from every side, and was tying the end of the bed sheets to it.

'The gaolers must know about this trapdoor,' I said as I tried to work out how far down the water was. It sounded a fair drop.

'They do,' my mother said. 'They throw rotten food down there and more besides, I'd wager.'

'So why ain't it guarded?'

'Because it's suicide to go down there,' piped up Bertha, who was not changing her clothes. 'You're mad to do it, you'll die in the filth.'

Sessina Ballard was busy now tying the trousers tight around

Alice's ankles and did not respond. Kat Dawkins though offered a retort by way of smacking Bertha around the back of her head.

'How many have tried and lived then?' Bertha continued, after rubbing the back of her neck. 'None. Your bones'll get flushed out into the Thames at Blackfriars Bridge after a time. You'll be gnawed at by giant black rats the size of pigs.'

'No, we won't,' I replied, getting everyone's attention once more. 'I've known toshers who have been down worse holes than this one, in search of treasure in the sewers. I ain't concerned about going down there,' I looked to the Rum Mort, 'provided I can get back up again. Because we can't stay down there forever.'

'Deep breaths and you'll all come up smiling,' was all my mother had to say on the subject and so I was glad that Sessina was on hand to explain things better.

'A couple of year ago,' she told us, 'the old river blew itself up. You recall the Great Shit Explosion of Forty-Six?'

I nodded, the explosion was hard to forget. The bang was said to have been made by trapped gases down there what had created enough pressure to burst in spectacular fashion. You couldn't even pass by Farringdon, there was so much sewage in the street. When the filth of the Fleet shot through into the Thames it caused a boat to ram into Blackfriars Bridge.

'One of those cracks appeared in a basement in Old Seacoal Lane,' continued Sessina. 'Which is where we're heading. Right, Rum?'

My mother nodded. 'An enterprising woman of my acquaintance lives in that house and is going to fish you all out again. What time is it now?'

'Five to two,' said Meg after looking at her pocket watch. 'They're expecting us to leave when the church bells chime twice. We shouldn't wait much longer.'

My mother then pulled out a coin-purse from her left dress pocket and tossed it to Sessina. 'Here you go, girls,' she said as it was caught. 'Freedom's on me.'

Sessina tied the purse to her belt and the rest of the escapees continued to dress themselves in dead men's clothing. Some mismatched gloves was produced from a box in the cellar and I took some for myself. Then we waited for the right moment to climb down into the Fleet as Eliza and Meg lowered the lantern down into the hole. Before leaving though I found myself itching to share some moments with my mother, the Rum Mort. I had last seen her when she had dragged me from the Three Cripples taproom seven years prior to this and so I was still just astounded to find her here alive. I wanted to speak to her some more to try and make sense of the vision. But conversation between us had never flowed easy and I wondered how to start.

'Should I tell Horrie?' I asked her as an opener, knowing that my half-brother was always more her favourite than I ever was. 'That you're still alive?'

'Horrie already knows,' she replied to my surprise. 'Has done for years. He visited me here some years back to boast of his disgrace.'

'Did he?' I asked in disgust at the thought that Horrie had never seen fit to tell me of our mother's survival himself. 'What disgrace was that?'

'He came in his uniform,' she spat on the floor and shook her head at the memory. 'As soon as the peelers turned him into one of them he marched straight down here to tell about it as though he thought I should have been proud or something. She watched over the women as they worked, and spoke cold. 'He ain't a son of mine no more.'

'I still am though, ain't I?' I said to her in a quiet voice. 'I mean, I must be.' She turned to face me then. 'You're helping me escape and I never even asked you to. So you must still think of me as a mother should.' In the lamplight I saw her blue and green eyes blink like they she had only just noticed that I was there.

'Course you're my son,' she answered after a silent second. 'And the prison guards know it. I can't let them what think they run this place get away with hanging my boy, can I? I got standards to maintain.' Then another silence descended and we both went back to watching Sessina hook the other end of the bed sheet to the trapdoor.

'Why don't you come with us?' I said then, as the rest readied themselves to go down. 'It don't make sense for you to just help others to their liberty. You should be freeing yourself.'

She looked at me with bewilderment in her face. 'I'm the Rum Mort, Jacky,' she said. 'Don't you understand? I'm a queen in here.' Then she nodded at the open trap. 'Out there,' I thought I heard a drip of regret in her voice, 'I'm just a madwoman.'

'It's time,' said Meg and closed the face of the pocket watch. 'They'll be waiting.'

'Very well,' said my mother and she crossed over to the trap. 'Now get down into that river, Jacky, before I push you into it.'

I peered again down into the hole and saw that the lamp now lit up the Fleet much better. The water was moving fast.

'That's the rain doing that,' said Meg. 'It'll be treacherous.'

There was some slimy iron steps in the brick wall what led downwards but I doubted if these had been used much in recent centuries. I prepared myself for the descent.

'When down there you need to untie the lamp so the others can use the sheet as a rope,' ordered the Rum Mort. 'Then you wait until all have followed, holding the lamp for 'em, and you proceed from behind. You're looking out for them, they ain't looking out for you. So don't slip.'

'Whatever you say, Rum,' I said and took a strong breath in before climbing down.

The iron steps was slippery but I was quick to get down them and soon I was above the watercourse. I could see that, although disgusting, the water was not so deep and as I dropped myself into its stream it only came up to my knees. The rush of it, though, almost knocked me over, but I grabbed onto a scum-covered iron loop before stumbling. The noise of the tunnel was a shock and I could hear but not see rats all about.

'I'm down,' I shouted up as I took in my first full gulp of the rancid air. My whole self shook with revulsion. 'Hurry!'

Sessina came down after me before I had even untied the sheets. When she joined me in the stream she pulled out a candle and cleft stick what she had in her belt and lit it from my lamp.

'Tell the others to bear left,' she shouted and I noticed that here the river split into two passages. 'Follow my light.' She then headed off downstream but her movements was slow. Water poured in from these round side-channels and I knew that this was rain making our task all the harder.

Meg was next. She took out a handkerchief and held it up to her face before following Sessina's light. Young Alice followed but she took such a long time getting down the steps that I wondered if she would ever make it. She seemed too petrified to let go of the iron bars and I shouted up at her to jump. Instead, she slipped and screamed but I was quick enough to catch her with one arm before she crashed down into the water. She then waited for Eliza, the last of the escapers, and once down she and Alice headed off together. Then I saw that the knotted sheet was being pulled back up again. I looked up to the trapdoor above my head and tried to see my mother looking down. There was a faint flickering above and I could just about make out her silhouette as the last of the sheets was pulled in.

'Mother?' I shouted up before left to I follow the others. 'Thank you for this! You done me a right good tur—'

But before I could finish expressing these words of filial gratitude the trap door was slammed shut and that was end of that sweet moment. So instead I just turned and headed off to where I had been directed, moving as fast as I could through this vile and forgotten tunnel.

Part Three

Chapter 21

Under The Fleet and Above

Word of my miraculous escape reaches some ears before others

If you were to visit Newgate Prison on a clear day and follow the path from there down to the Old Bailey road, as if heading towards Blackfriars, before turning left into Old Seacoal Lane, then you would find it an unchallenging stroll. It is a short distance and you could run there before the long hand on your pocket watch had even performed a single revolution. If you were to attempt the same distance underground however, and was knee deep in rushing shit, as I was doing on that first week of 1848, then you would find the experience to be that much more of an ordeal, I can promise you.

The passage of the once exposed river was nasty and narrow and, although the stream moved fast, I still had to wade through sewerised water. My senses was under heavy assault but I forced myself onwards through the slimy tunnel breathing only through my nose. There was more of these scummy loops for me to grab hold of as I kept on moving and held the lamp high. Around me was a multitude of vermin, all eyeing me from dark places but, as those toshers had told me, rats would not attack if ignored. I strained to see the lights of the women ahead but the piercing screams of Alice, who was having by far the worst reaction to this hellish environment, told me they was not far in front. The rain above us must have been getting heavier as, before long, more water was rushing in from out of those side channels. This had the effect of bringing the water level up to the waist but also helped me move quicker along. After about five minutes of marching I began to hope that I had already passed under the walls of Newgate and was free of its hold.

When I caught up with the others I saw that relations between Eliza and Alice was not cordial. Eliza was trying to force Alice to get a hold of herself and move quicker. She had an arm around the girl's shoulder and was shouting in her ear but as I came close she let go of Alice who slumped to her knees into the river.

'Hopeless bitch!' Eliza screamed at me over the noise of the water. 'You take her.' She waded off towards a thin shaft of light what was now visible from the top of the tunnel just ahead. Alice was on all fours in the river and her clothes was splattered with crap and so I reached down to lift her up again.

'See that,' I said as I held her shivering body. I was pointing towards the shaft what Eliza was now under. 'That's where we're going. This is over soon. We're going to live, Alice.' She grabbed my shirt with her brown-caked fist and picked herself up. I felt a great responsibility towards this girl what had been set to be my scaffold sister in a few hours' time and, because she was becoming so immovable, I decided that there was one thing for it. 'You carry the lamp,' I said handing it to her, 'and I'll carry you.'

As we approached the place where the light shone down from, I saw Eliza trying to get up some wooden step-ladder what had been lowered down from above, but her passage upwards was obstructed. She was engaged in an altercation with someone up there who I could not see. As I drew near, with Alice in my arms, she turned to me.

'Look! The Rum's boy has got her!' Eliza was heard shouting. 'She ain't abandoned, you stroppy tart. Let me up!' Eliza then forced her way up into the break in the roof. I carried Alice up to the ladder and I saw two heads looking down on us. The first was Sessina's and the other belonged to a stranger who I guessed must be the owner of that house.

'Now *there* is a gentleman,' remarked this woman on seeing me with Alice in my arms.

'Lift her up, Dawkins,' said Sessina. 'We'll take her.' Alice was only little but by now it seemed like she had doubled in weight what with all the sewage she was covered in. I hauled her upwards and told her to reach out for the others and soon the women had got hold of her and dragged her up. Once she was through I cast aside the lamp, took hold of the ladder and ascended into the freedom of that small cellar in Old Seacoal Lane.

'Cast your clothes down into the river,' ordered the lady of the house, whose name I never discovered, once I was fished out of the hole in her floor. I had landed into a room full of women for the second time that night. 'Then get in one of them tubs.'

The four female escapees was all unrigged from their sewer-ruined clothing and was stood in these bathtubs where some other members of the household was handing them bars of soap and pouring buckets of clean water over them. I too did as I was bid and removed all my convict clothes before casting them down into the Fleet. Then the ladder was pulled up, the home-made trap shut over it, a rug covered the trapdoor and a wardrobe was moved on top of it all. If any investigating gaolers were to search this cellar later on they would find nothing untoward. I joined the others then and stepped into one of the tubs to wash myself also. We all smelt and looked disgusting so the scene of me in a bath with four naked women was not as stimulating as you might imagine. I was too busy scrubbing shit off my skin to really enjoy the moment.

'Don't get comfortable,' said the housekeeper as she handed

towels to the first women out of the tubs. 'Once the gaolers notice you all gone they may find the passage. Unlikely, but it don't mean nothing anyway if you ain't here.'

'We need clothes, don't we?!' Meg demanded. 'You can't sling us out into the night like this.' As she said that a box was produced full of dresses and ladies under-things. These was handed out to Sessina and the others.

'The Rum said it was to be all women,' the housekeeper smirked as she eyed me up and down. 'So you have a choice, my pretty one. You can leave here in the clothes of my dead grandfather or you can put on one of them frocks. Either way, the street entrance is up them stairs.' I covered myself in the towel and stepped out of the tub. 'So congratulations ladies and gentleman,' she then grinned as she took the coin-purse what Sessina had brought with her. 'You're all free to go your separate ways. Be dears and shut the door on the way out, why don't you?'

As I stepped out onto Old Seacoal Lane, dressed in the ill-fitting clothes of someone's dead grandfather, I could hear the faint but too familiar sound of the St Sepulchre bells chiming four times. That was when the glory of being outside of the prison walls really struck home and I wanted to bend over and kiss the wet cobbles. We was still far too close to the prison however, and Sessina and the others all planned to head southwards down the Old Kent Road without delay. They asked me whether I wished to come with them.

'We could use a man in our party, Dawkins,' said Sessina, whose plan was to make for Dover and get passage abroad. 'To look out for our interests.'

'Yeah, why not?' said Meg. 'Our little band might need a bawd if we're to earn our keep as we travel.'

'You ladies need nothing of the sort,' I told them before I made to head off in the other direction. 'You're all more than capable of looking after yourselves.'

I bid them all goodbye and good luck, and dashed off in a different direction, hoping that those smelly women all travelling as one might lead any pursuers off in a different direction to mine. As I ran off towards Fleet Street, I thought I heard the voice of young Alice wish me good luck in return.

Getting free of Newgate had been enough of an ordeal but – as the hapless Jack Sheppard had discovered – keeping free of it was an even tougher challenge. I spent much of the next hour scurrying around most frantic in an effort to stay away from the main lights of the thoroughfare. This vicinity was close to several police stations and I was sure that their carriages would be galloping around in all directions as soon as the alarm from Newgate was raised. So I kept moving along the shadows and hidden passages to avoid recapture, staying out of sight whenever I heard hurried footsteps in a nearby street in case it should be a peeler on patrol. I was so conflicted as to what my next step should be that I had not advanced far enough away and instead kept moving in circles. But revenge dominated my thoughts. Billy Slade had visited me in prison less than nine hours before to boast of his victory over me. So I was desperate to get to that brothel where he lived so I could make a surprise appearance, kill him, grab Lily and flee London. How hard could all that be?

But the morning was dark, I was tired and the clothes I wore was so soiled that it was unlikely that I should be able to pick a pocket to pay for a cab fare anytime soon. But if I travelled on foot I would lose more precious hours. What I needed to do was find a friendly place to change into something less conspicuous and to borrow money. I would have to find someone who was sympathetic to my plight but who I also knew I could trust. I considered going to the Three Cripples and waking up Barney but I was unsure what I would find there. My old gang was all Slade men now and if I were seen then word of my escape might reach him before I did. No, I needed the aid of a friend unconnected to the underworld and also one what lived nearby. And it was then, on the very moment when I reached that conclusion, that a little boy told me what to do next. He must have been about eleven years of age and was strolling past the place where Fleet Street meets Fetter Lane, clutching a big stack of broadsides and calling out for custom. It must have been not even five o'clock by then and this boy was the very model of the early bird. By the confident and full-throated way he was calling out the headline of the broadside itself I guessed that he must have been a news-vendor's son, but it was his three word cry what grabbed my attention. Monday morning was, dare we forget, gallows day and it was clear that this industrious young cove had an intention of beating the competition when it came to selling these one-sheet documents to those heading towards Newgate for a good spot. And today was to be a busy day, as his vocal advertisements was making clear. It was the morning when the Artful Dodger – the notorious killer of Anthony Rylance – was going to drop for the deed and so attendance was expected to be high. But it was the headline, as I poked my head around the corner of a narrow alley across the way, what provided me with inspiration as to how to proceed.

'Dodger to Twist!' the boy shouted like it was the most obvious suggestion. 'Dodger to Twist!'

I crept out of the alleyway where I had been hiding and I began to cross the road to where the boy stood. Night would not be lifting for some hours and, as I got close, I saw the boy jump at the sight of me. I stopped in my tracks and tried to strike as inconspicuous a pose as possible but I could see in his face that I must have appeared most terrifying. He stopped in his patter and took a step back. This, after all, was a boy what made his living shouting about murderers in the early hours of the morning so I guessed that he must have had a fertile imagination when it came to strange-looking men appearing from out of the shadows.

'And a good morning to you, my dear,' I smiled, using the sort of language what I felt would be most effective at putting a child at ease. 'Is that a newspaper you've got there, I wonder? I should very much like to procure a copy of the *Morning Chronicle* if you have one.'

The boy still eyed me with deep suspicion and his nose crinkled in disgust. It seemed as though that quick wash I had taken had not rid me of the raw smell of sewage. But the boy did not run. This was his job after all and he was standing in full view of a major thoroughfare where carriages was passing, so he had no reason to be scared. He shook his head and held up the broadside so I could read it for myself.

'*Chronicle* won't be printed for hours,' he said as if I were a fool to ask. 'My father makes these. It's about the Artful Dodger of Seven Dials. That's him what's going to twist later today. If you go to Gallows Corner now you should get yourself a good spot. It'll be heaving with people soon enough so I wouldn't tarry. One penny if you want the broadside as a remembrance of the fine occasion.'

I refused the offer of such a glorious souvenir and told him that I was a *Chronicle* reader what was most anxious to get myself a copy as soon as the ink was dry. 'Any idea where the offices might be?' I asked him. 'I expect you must know something like that being a Fleet Street boy and all.' The boy shook his head and told me he had no idea where the newspaper offices was but agreed that it must be hereabout. He then told me that if I wanted to read one of last week's editions for gratis then he knew where they threw the unsold copies. It was in a dustcart off an alley further towards the Strand if I wanted one. I thanked the boy and I felt his curious eyes follow me as I darted straight off in that direction.

I found myself somehow disappointed, when I at last found a whole heap of unwanted newspapers just where the boy had directed me, not to find more headlines about the famous Dodger of the Dials emblazoned across their various front pages. It's amazing how fast one gets accustomed to fame. Instead, the *Chronicle* seemed preoccupied with whatever Queen Victoria and her German husband was up to that week and I considered, as I flipped through its pages, that its middle-class readers must be a very dull bunch if they would rather hear about their daily doings than mine. However it was not for any news story that I had tracked down this particular organ but for something much more important. Oliver Twist had told me that he would often spend all night above the offices of the *Morning Chronicle* and so this was where I was headed in the hope that he would be there. And, sure enough, I soon found that very address written in very fine print on the inside cover.

Number 332, the Strand. It was, as both myself and the broadside boy had suspected, very close to where I then was. In no time I found myself at the corner of Wellington Street looking up at the tall building with its many windows, behind any of which Twist could be sleeping. Furthermore, because the area was very busy with carts, vehicles and pedestrians even at this early hour, there was no chance that I could lurk about unnoticed for long. The place was a news office though, and there was already a number of well-dressed and important-looking coves arriving at the front door and unlocking it for work. Also, behind a number of the uncurtained windows above there seemed to be candlelight and so I reasoned that this was a place where people worked throughout the night. It may have been a reckless act for a man what has just escaped Newgate Prison, but I made up my mind to march straight over to the offices of that newspaper and knock. A small and rectangular gold plate declared *The Morning Chronicle* outside and so I rapped on the thick door hard. It was then opened by a short, hunched little man who I had seen admitting the last person to enter. Now he had placed a little chain over the door and was poking his face through the gap in a quizzical manner.

'How do you do there?' I said and gave a short bow as I had no hat to remove, 'I'm looking for Oliver Twist.'

'Never heard of him,' said the old man and he went to shut the door on me.

'Wait!' I said and put my hand in the way to stop him. 'Not Twist. Brownlow! I'm after Oliver Brownlow.'

'And what business might you have with Mr Brownlow, sir?' asked the old boy as he looked me over with a disapproving sniff. I took him to be some sort of doorman what had been employed to keep undesirable callers away from the men of letters within and he was doing a decent job of it.

'He won't thank you for turning me away, my old geezer,' I said with some urgency. 'It's about a story he's interested in. So if he's up there then give him my message sharpish, will you?'

'What's your name then, *sir*?'

I was prepared for this.

'My name is Blake,' I told him. 'William Blake.' The old man chuckled.

'Is that right?' he said with an amused shake of the head. 'Well, you'll have to make an appointment I'm afraid, Mr Blake, as Mr Brownlow already has a meeting scheduled with a certain John Milton after breakfast.' He smiled at his own wit and began to shut the door again. 'Good day to you, sir.' I shoved my foot into the gap preventing its closure.

'I'm William Blake,' I insisted in a harder voice. 'And I have important information concerning "Jerusalem"! Be sure to tell him that. Jerusalem and all its dark satanic mills!'

The old boy looked up at me then and his face altered. I would have thought that journalists might be used to having people pass secret information to them and it was clear that this door cove had begun to suspect that he might get into trouble if my cryptic words were not delivered. He nodded then and told me to wait outside while he went up to see Mr Brownlow.

'I'm not staying here,' I told him. I knew that if I was made to wait too long a policeman could be fetched and I did not trust Oliver that much. 'Tell Mr Twis— *Brownlow*, that if he wishes to speak to William Blake then I shall be over in that there direction.' I pointed northwards up Wellington Street and away from the river. 'By that theatre, see. If he's longer than five minutes then I'm going so tell him not to dither.'

The posters outside the Theatre Royal Lyceum all advertised its current production, *Babes in the Wood*, a Christmas pantomime. There was still the last of the evening's inebriated street-walkers bumping around the columns of the theatre's locked doors but none of these paid me any mind due to how I still smelt like I had been crawling through a sewer earlier that night. Some hackney carriages had reared up by a nearby trough for their horses to drink and there was some tramps sleeping under the theatre arches for me to blend in amongst. I slumped down behind the furthest column with the intention of feigning sleep but as I shut my eyes I realised that it would be easy for me to drop into slumber for real. The events of the last few hours – and of the last few weeks – had been so exhausting that my body pleaded with me to let it just lie

there until daybreak and forget all else. But Lily needed rescuing –
among others – and I was not safe on the streets so I gave myself a
slap in the face and kept waiting for Twist. I rolled my head over so
I could see who was approaching from the Strand. There was some
still-lit gas lamps along this stretch of street but these was starting
to dim as daylight crept closer. In a short time I saw the silhouette
of a man walking with purpose up the street. I could not make
out his features in the dark but something about the rigidness of
his gait and the straightness of his hat told me that this was Twist.
As he neared the theatre I saw him look about for the person who
had summoned him but I was crouched behind the column and
only the top of my head poked around it, covered by shadows.
The Lyceum prostitutes was of course much more interested in
this affluent gent than they had been in me but he gave them all a
curt shake of the head as he walked on.

He passed by the theatre columns, avoiding the black mass
of homeless bodies what was slumped all around, and I sensed a
wariness in his manner as he slowed before reaching where I was. I
moved around my column so I was now behind him, close enough
to reach out and touch his shoulder if I wanted to go for the full
melodrama of the scene.

'Mr Blake!' he called out in strong voice. 'It is Mr Brownlow.
You wished to see me, sir.'

At that, I stepped out into the street so I was now standing just
behind his back. I cleared my throat and spoke the same words I
had uttered nine years ago when the two of us had first ever met.

'Hullo, my covey,' I whispered. 'What's the row?'

Twist spun around and I saw the plain shock on his face. He
looked even more frightened than I had reckoned on and he lifted
up his arm and pointed at me. Because it was still so dark I did not
realise what he was holding at first, but when I saw the flash of

silver it was my turn to jump. There was a pistol just inches from my nose.

'Stand back,' he ordered, and I staggered away from him. 'A step closer and I'll shoot you dead.' Some of the watching prostitutes screamed in fright to see the weapon and ran off in various directions while the vagrants in the shadows all woke themselves to hear what the shouting was about. 'You won't kill me like you did Anthony!'

'Oliver!' I pleaded. 'Don't fire. I'm not here to hurt you and I didn't kill Anthony. I thought you believed me.' He blinked then and I could see him straining to see me in the darkness. Then recognition seemed to dawn.

'Dodger?' he spluttered, his voice all astonishment. 'How are you here?'

'Checked myself out of Newgate about an hour ago,' I replied. 'Didn't care for their hospitality much. The food was horrible for one thing.'

'I thought you were from Mills and come to assassinate me,' he exclaimed with the gun still pointed. 'I imagined you to be this Billy Slade character you told me about.'

'Well, I ain't,' I replied and indicated the gun. 'I'm just your old pal, the Artful. But I have come to warn you about Slade, in truth. You're right to think yourself in danger, he knows your name from the visitors' book in Newgate. He don't know who you are yet but a man like that has ways and means of finding out.'

Oliver's mouth was open as he heard that. 'And you broke out of Newgate Prison,' he gaped, 'just to warn me?'

'Yeah, if you like,' I replied as if my own self-preservation had never once crossed my mind. 'So do me a favour and point that elsewhere, eh, poorhouse? I've been through too much tonight to get shot by you.' Oliver pointed the pistol away but kept staring at me as if I were a ghost and, on reflection, I suppose that explanation might have seemed more plausible to him. When he spoke there was a clear uncertainty in his tone.

'I was praying for your soul not ten minutes before,' Oliver went on as if he thought that that meant something. 'I had risen early because I wanted to get to Newgate in time to see you hang.'

'Oh, charming.'

'No, I don't mean I was *happy* to see you hang. I mean, I wanted to be there for you considering I had failed to secure your release in time. I wanted to be a friendly face in the crowd.'

Just then the cab driver who was tending to his horse across the way at last plucked up the courage to call over.

'Are you all right, sir?' he said from a safe distance. 'Shall I fetch the police?'

'No, thank you,' replied Oliver, his startled eyes not leaving mine. 'It's quite all right. This man isn't here to harm me, it's just a misunderstanding.'

'I was speaking to the other gentleman.'

Oliver then noticed that his pistol was still exposed and that from an outsider's view it would appear as though he was the threat, not me. As he placed it back beneath his coat I considered what an enormous amount of trust I was placing in him. Now that I was an escaped convict there was sure to be a large reward for my recapture and Oliver had a gun on him. He was a flat, meaning he was a man of principles, and there was nothing more dangerous than that. I realised that this would be my last chance to run for it but I held fast regardless. I decided instead that I would just brazen this out.

'Thank you, coachman,' I called back. 'But all is well. We're just two old school pals with plenty of catching up to do.'

Oliver then grabbed me by the arm and we both stepped away

from the gaslight. 'You frightened the life out of me, Jack,' he said. 'What is going on?'

'Listen, Twist,' I said wanting to get straight to the point of the matter, 'did you mean what you said to me in my cell the other night?'

'About thinking you innocent? Yes, I do. I've made even more investigations since then and I've no doubt that Detective Superintendent Mills arranged for Anthony's death and that of Constable Wingham. Those crimes are linked and I think I could convince a court if I could just . . .'

'I meant what you said about Nancy?' I interrupted. 'About how you still wished you could have helped her?' Oliver hesitated for a moment but then nodded his head. 'And would you help someone else in the same situation now, if you could?'

'Of course I would,' he replied. 'I wouldn't hesitate.'

Through my tiredness, I prepared myself for what I had to ask him next. Oliver occupied a different world to me now and I knew that he would be unwilling to involve himself in underworld activities after having worked so hard to distance himself from that background. Genteel people like him talk a lot about what they intend to do for the poor but it was rare for one to plunge their hands into the same filth as us.

'There is another woman then,' I began, speaking fast, 'of about the same age what Nancy was when she died. Lily her name is. She's of the same profession too – or at least she was. And I think she's in great peril now. Weeping Billy Slade has her over at a brothel in Hammersmith and I'm sure that he means to do her as much harm as what Bill Sikes ever did to our Nance. Now if you really want to help me, Twist, you need to lend me some money to pay for that carriage so I can go straight over there and save her from his violent hands. I ain't got time for police visits, they take too long and peelers only ever arrive after blood has spilt. You can go and report the crime if you care to, I know you're one for a peach and I ain't going to stop you. But this is criminal business and if I'm too late to save her life then I shall settle Slade another way. He's a man I don't mind swinging for.'

'Hold on!' interrupted Twist. But when he spoke next it was in clear and calm voice what contrasted with my own frantic babbling.

'Are you saying this woman is in danger now? At this very moment?'

I nodded.

'Then I have money for the ride and a pistol in my pocket. Take me to wherever you think she is.'

I was overcome with relief to hear him offer his services like that and I went to thank with an embrace. But as I did so I must have staggered because the next thing I knew he had caught me in his arms.

'For pity's sake, Dodger, you look like you're going to die and you smell foul. What have you been doing?'

'Twist, I don't think you'd believe me if I told you.'

'You need to be taken inside before we do anything. You need rest.'

'No! I need to get Slade before he learns I'm free from prison. You don't understand, Twist, the surprise of the thing is to my advantage.'

'You are about to collapse, man. You're no good to anyone like this. Let me take you to my lodging to get you washed and changed properly. It's not far from here and I have some coffee and some food also. Don't tell me you're not hungry.'

I was not just hungry, I was ravenous. And yes, I was desperate to get to Lily and help her but the evening's exertions had caught

JAMES BENMORE • 304

up with me and I would be useless to her if I did not attend to myself first.

'In all truth, Twist,' I said as I placed my hand on his shoulder to steady myself, 'I could murder a bacon sandwich if you got one.'

Chapter 22

Streaky Well-Cured Bacon

*I am invited into Oliver's lodgings and encouraged
to consider myself at home*

'Sausages and bacon,' said Oliver once he had both sizzling in his frying pan for me. 'What does their smell remind you of?'

I had been rattled when Oliver had told the coachman his address, as it turned out that he lived in the very same stretch of houses near Hungerford Stairs where I had broken into just a few weeks before. Oliver said that this was not a coincidence as many young journalists took lodgings near Embankment as the rooms was affordable for bachelors and it was close enough to Fleet Street where all the action was. He also added that when he had first returned to London to embark upon this writing career of his, he and Anthony had wanted to live close to one another for companionship's sake. As he spoke about his fondness for this dead childhood friend I could hear how much pain and anger he felt at his sudden death and I heard my own feelings about Mouse echoed.

Oliver had sat me down on a small and comfortable armchair while he spoke to me from the kitchen and it gave me a chance to look about. This apartment was just three doors down from the one where I had discovered Anthony's murdered body but this abode was less austere than the other, more lived in. They both shared a fondness for having more books than their bookshelves could hold though and beside my chair, on the floor, was a tall stack of poetry.

This similarity brought back to me the image of the bloody crack I had seen in poor Rylance's head as he slumped over his desk and I had told Oliver that I would like my meat served not too rare if possible. He at last came out of the little kitchen carrying a full breakfast of meat, eggs and a bun, and a cup of coffee in his other hand. I took these from him, set the plate down on my lap and began feasting.

'Fagin,' said Oliver as I gobbled down the bacon and reached for the coffee he had placed on a small table beside me.

'What about him?' I asked after taking a big slurp and returning to attack the sausages.

'That's what the smell reminds me of,' he explained. 'Fagin's kitchen. When you first took me to meet him he was cooking breakfast over a stove and held a sausage at the end of his fork as he welcomed me in. I thought he looked like the very devil at the time and ever since the smell has conjured him for me.'

'He enjoyed his sausages all right,' I agreed as I chewed on these and closed my eyes with the raw pleasure of food. Hours earlier I had turned away my last meal from the turnkeys as I felt no appetite for it. This meal, however, was restoring me to life.

'I know,' Oliver nodded, 'which was peculiar considering that he was a Hebrew.' I tore the bun in half and started dipping it into the egg yolk. 'But then he wasn't what you would call "a good Jew", was he? Of course you knew him much better than I.'

I was too busy concentrating on my plate to want to respond to any of these observations about my late teacher's religious habits or lack thereof. Instead, I just finished devouring the food and once that was done, I licked the knife, the fork and the plate clean of any fat. I suppose Oliver must have considered me a very uncouth individual as he watched me display all the social graces of an undomesticated dog but I was so hungry that I did not care much for whatever he might be thinking. Once I was finished I lay the plate down onto the table and got up again.

'Right then,' I said as I stood. 'Let's go and get Lily.'

'You need to change first,' Oliver replied. 'I have some water heating in a pot and a bathtub through that door. Once washed you can borrow a suit from me. We look to be the same size near enough and they will fit you a lot better than these old clothes seem to.'

'Ain't got time for that,' I told him.

'Jack, you look like an escaped convict and, frankly, you smell very conspicuous. Do you want to be recaptured within the hour? If not, then go to the bathroom and undress while I fetch the water.'

The soap what Oliver Twist handed me as I sat in his bathtub was of a much gentler and more fashionable sort than the rough blocks I had been given in that cellar in Old Seacoal Lane and, before long, I was sharing the aroma of an English garden in springtime. Oliver spoke to me from the other room as I soaked and rid myself of the Fleet.

'I must ask, Jack,' he said as I heard him searching through his wardrobe, 'what you intend to do once we have recovered this Lily of yours?'

'I'm leaving London with her,' I replied without a beat, 'and I ain't returning.'

'I thought you might say that,' he sighed. 'I must ask you not to.'

'What else can I do, Twist?' I shouted through to him. 'I ain't going back to Newgate and if I loiter in this city long enough then they'll catch me. I'll head to the continent. New life, new name.'

'But what about proving your innocence?' he said and he brought me in some towels and left them on a chest beside the tub.

'And getting justice for Anthony? You're a key part of proving that Mills is guilty.'

'We both know that's never going to happen,' I told him as he left the room, and I got out of the bath. 'Nobody believes the burglar. My only chance of survival is clearing off out of it, so don't you try and stop me.' I wrapped the towels around me and again I could not help but notice the quality of his luxury possessions. It seemed as though our Oliver liked the finer things in life as much as I did and, even though he acquired them in a more legal way then I ever would, it was something else we had in common.

'I'm helping you with some degree of personal risk, Jack,' Oliver called through as I dried myself. 'And I'm doing it for a reason. I need to mount a case against Detective Mills and Slade – two highly dangerous men – and I'm currently gathering enough evidence to present to the right policeman before either can intervene and kill me. I'm very close to having all I need but someone has to verify my claims. You're not an ideal witness but your story supports mine and that will help your Inspector Bracken take me seriously.'

'You want me to talk to Bracken?' I exclaimed as I stepped back into the living room, wrapped in the towels. 'He'd sooner see me hang than anyone.'

'Not if it means toppling Mills, he wouldn't,' Oliver insisted. 'Earlier today I discovered that Bracken and Mills are rivals in career advancement. If Mills were to fall then Bracken's own prospects would elevate fast. He could become commissioner, perhaps, with no one to challenge him. So he'll want to believe us as long as there is enough there for him to act upon.'

I was still not happy about placing my life in the hands of a man what had lied to me about my own mother being dead, and so I shook my head at him.

'I can hide you somewhere until it's time to go to trial,' Oliver continued. 'By then it will be too late for the state to execute you as the truth will be out. You might be gaoled for burglary but your life would be spared. Jack, these are my terms. It's what I want in return for helping you to rescue this Lily woman.'

He stood there with a tailor's hanger in his left hand. The suit hanging from it was dull grey and not unlike the one he himself had on. I wondered if he had a wardrobe full of clothes all of the same colour. He held it out for me to take but there was a sense that in doing so I would be agreeing to this foolish business of cooperating with a policeman what I knew hated me. But then it was true that Oliver's assistance was proving invaluable and I was unsure if I would be able to rescue Lily without it. If ever there were an opposite of making a deal with the devil then this was it.

'I'll think about it,' I said as I reached for the hanger and took the suit from him. 'But if I get the slightest sniff that my life is in danger then I'll be off like a gunshot, Twist, I tell you that.'

'That's all I can ask,' he said as I begun to put on the clothes. 'Oh, and one other thing?' I asked him what as I started buttoning his shirt and marvelled at how well it fitted me. The whole suit was a beautiful piece of tailoring but was far less flashy than I was accustomed to. 'Please stop calling me Twist. I haven't used that name since I was a child.'

'Fair enough, Brownlow,' I replied hitting both syllables heavy enough to accentuate the gentility of the name. I was sure that the name Twist must have aggravated him as it would have acted as a reminder of the humble origins he had tried so hard to distance himself from.

'Not that either,' he replied as I continued dressing myself in this outfit what was starting to make me look like his brother. 'I would prefer it if you just called me Oliver.'

Daylight had still not broken over the city as the curricle what Oliver was driving raced around the walls of St James's Park heading west. This vehicle was a two-wheeled high-flyer, sleek and beautiful, and it was pulled by a single strong horse. It did not belong to Oliver however – we had stolen it from a nearby stable.

'We have *borrowed* this, Jack,' he corrected me once we was out onto the long stretch of the King's Road. 'And we'll return it as soon as our business is done. We'll also pay for the damage you just did to that stable door.'

The sporty and fashionable vehicle belonged to a neighbour of Oliver's and it was him what had at first suggested that we take it on account of how it was sure to move faster than any hackney carriage we might hail at this hour. But he had wanted to waste more time by knocking on the door of this neighbour to ask his kind permission and I worried that this would slow us down if said neighbour proved difficult. So instead, I grabbed Oliver's walking cane from out of his hand and showed him what else it was good for. I took one strong swing and it smashed into the weakest looking plank of wood on the stable which woke the horse inside up. His cane, much like the ones my gang and I used to parade around in, had a silver tip only this was one was shaped like a T. Its protrusion was not quite as effective as my beak-cane was at peeling off the damaged plank but it did the job and I had soon crawled into the stable to unbolt it from within and smash away at any other obstructions. Oliver pretended to look scandalised by the efficient and speedy way in which all this was achieved but I could tell I had impressed him. He had always found my artfulness to be brilliant no matter what he might tell you to the contrary.

In turn, I was impressed with how hard Oliver was riding this curricle and we both began bumping up and down in our seat as the horse gathered pace. As we bounced, Oliver was full of questions about what the scene we was heading towards.

'So this brothel has an outhouse at the bottom of the garden?' he said with his hands gripped on the reins and his eyes fixed upon the road. 'Which is where Slade beats his victims. How do you know about it?'

'He took me there once to show me the violence he'd done to some others,' I replied and Oliver's lip curled in distaste. 'I was disgusted by it too, Twist – I mean Oliver. Slade mocked me for not having the stomach for such damage like he had. He called me unblooded, which was true at the time. But if he's hurt Lily – or little Scratcher as he might have done – then that won't stay true for long.'

'Why?' asked Oliver as he negotiated Sloane Square and managed to pass some carthorses what was slowing us down, 'What will you do then?'

'I'll kill him.'

'Jack, don't,' Oliver pleaded with me. 'Not now. Not when we're so close to proving you innocent of one murder.'

'The courts of this country have proven themselves my enemy more than once, Oliver. So there's only one form of justice for me, and it's an eye for an eye.'

'You sound like Bill Sikes,' Oliver said with some contempt in his voice. 'Billy Slade murdered my friend too, remember. Or arranged for someone else to do it. And I don't want him dead, I want him brought to trial because that is the way of a decent society.'

'If they charge him for murder then he'll be sentenced to hang like I was. So there ain't much separating the way of your decent society and my way, is there? So what's the bleeding difference?'

'The difference, Jack,' Oliver replied, 'is that nobody will hang you.'

Soon I was directing Oliver through the streets of Hammersmith towards the house of Molly Gay. Oliver did not seem that shocked to learn of the existence of a high-class bawdy house in an affluent district as I thought he might have been and I wondered if he were in fact more familiar with this place then he was letting on. A monied and genteel cove like him was, after all, just the sort of clientele that this brothel catered for. As we turned into the street we was after Oliver looked out for a convenient place to tie up his horse where the curricle would not be noticed but I doubted that it – or us in our smart suits – would look too inconspicuous outside this establishment at such a queer hour. Still we left it just a few doors down from Molly Gay's, close and concealed enough for us to get back to in a hurry.

'Should we go to the front door and knock?' Oliver asked as we approached Molly Gay's. 'Or would you rather make straight for this outhouse where you think she is held?'

'The outhouse,' I said as we came to the front garden and positioned ourselves behind the high part of the front wall so I could inspect the house unseen over the evergreen shrubbery. 'If she's still in there and unharmed then I'd prefer to just steal her away than risk confrontation.'

None of the windows of that house had much light shining behind them and it was still dark enough to creep into the front garden and work our way through the shrubbery and around to the side of the house. I asked Oliver if he was up for some sneaking about.

'For your information,' Oliver whispered as I pointed out to him what the most hidden path to follow would be. 'I've burgled a house before.' I gave him a look of genuine surprise. 'It was with Sikes in Chertsey.'

'Then you should be even better at this than I had hoped,' I said as I pulled him by the arm and we made towards the front gate.

'Unlikely,' he whispered just before we darted into the front garden. 'I got caught, remember?'

Despite Oliver's uninspiring record as a cracksman, the two of us was across the large front garden, sticking to the shadows of bushes as we went. We then headed down the side of the path with silent ease and crept into the back. All these houses had deep gardens what dropped down towards the Thames and I wondered if Slade had chosen this location as the place where he would torture his enemies on account of how easy it would be to dump the bodies into the river after a fatality. The entire garden was surrounded by a high fence though and as we moved halfway down it, I pulled Oliver into a bush so we I could show him the outhouse where the Turpins had been tortured what sat shadowed among some overhanging tree branches. From this angle, the windowless brick building looked as bland and as characterless as evil things often do.

'Someone is coming out of the house,' said Oliver then and I turned to see that he was right. From the parlour entrance of Molly Gay's, a man had emerged with a tray of food. We edged further down into the garden so we could watch without him spotting us and I hoped that it would be the man himself so I could pounce out on him from the darkness. 'Is it Slade?' Oliver whispered but the moment I saw this stooped and thin figure shut the door after himself, I knew that this could only be one person.

'This is Morris Bolter,' I whispered to Oliver as I watched Slade's underling turn and walk in our direction all slow and careful so as not to drop his tray. 'He's a worm with limbs.' The advantage of darkness was just starting to desert us and the morning light would reveal our movements if he were to walk up to us too quick. So before he got close, we scudded around to the space behind the outhouse so we could hide there unseen from him or from any of the windows up at the main house.

'This person works for Slade?' whispered Oliver as Bolter was still coming down the garden path and through the low hanging branches around. 'He looks familiar.' Only then did I remember the day Bolter came to visit me in Soho with a newspaper under his arm.

'You've met him,' I whispered before Bolter got too close to us. 'He told me so.'

'Really? I don't recognise the name.'

'He comes from the same part of the country as you. Mudfog. He boasted that the two of you once had an altercation and he gave you a hiding.'

'I've been in few fights in my life, Jack, but I've won them all,' Oliver replied with steely confidence. 'This Mr Bolter is a liar as well as an imposter.'

I was about to ask what he meant by that but Bolter was nearby now and I wanted to peer around the walls of the outhouse so I could get a better sense of what he was doing. He was whistling a little tune as he walked towards this hidden building and I could now see that his silver tray had one bowl and one mug on it while a bunch of jingling keys was attached to his belt. He must be taking breakfast to someone who was locked in the outhouse, I realised, and I was glad to see it because it suggested that Lily was still alive at least. I then heard Morris place his tray down on the ground by the corner of the building on the opposite wall to us. Oliver and myself crept around to get closer to him and I saw the bowl of what looked gruel and water. We heard him address the person inside.

'Gerrup, sniveller!' he was saying as he opened the door and bent down to collect the tray. 'Yer've had yer punishment, now here's a treat!'

He entered the outhouse but I dashed in behind him before he had a chance to shut the door. As I stepped into the dim light of that musty and ill-lit room, Bolter spun around and dropped the tray in shock. The gruel and water clattered to the ground and he made to shout but I prevented this by punching him in his objectionable face good and hard. His head jerked backwards but he had enough fight in him to strike me with the tray which his left hand still had hold of. This did not hurt much however, and I grabbed him by the coat lapels and forced him further inside and away from the light of the door.

'HELP!' he at last called out as I manhandled him away so he could not be heard from the main house and told him to shush. 'Help us, someone! It's the Artful Dodger! It's Jack perishing Dawk—'

Then there was a pistol click from behind and I could tell by the look on Bolter's face that my friend with the gun had stepped through the door after me.

'Keep quiet, Noah!' I heard Oliver command in a low voice as he shut the door behind him, making the room much darker. 'Or whatever you're now calling yourself.'

Bolter looked most astonished to be addressed by this name and he blinked at Oliver's weapon in the dim candlelight. I darted over to him and removed some matchsticks I could feel in his pocket while he sneered at us. There was just three flickering candles about the place and most of that horrible dungeon was still in shadows.

'I don't know no one by the name of Noah,' he said as his chin raised in defiance, 'yer've mistaken me for another, sir.'

'You're Noah Claypole,' Oliver continued as I lit the nearest lamp to get a better look around, 'and I would recognise you anywhere. We worked together in Sowerberry's funeral home in Mudfog when I was a boy. You made the mistake of making disparaging remarks about my mother if I recall and I made you pay for it. Do not test me again, Noah, I have not become less sensitive with age.'

'*Twist!*' Bolter hissed the word like it was poison to him. Then he looked to me as my eyes scanned the large and cluttered outhouse to see who else was in here. 'What's this, Dodger? You and Twist, is it? And after what he done to dear old Fagin, eh? Yer a disgrace.'

'I ain't the one working for a police informant, Morris,' I shot back regardless of what Oliver was calling him. 'Billy Slade serves the peelers. Or rather one peeler in particular. But then why am I telling you? I'd wager you know all about it.'

'Lies!' Bolter protested. 'Slade's an honest crim.'

Oliver walked over to him, muttered something about contradictions in terms, and grabbed him by the arm. I went back to searching the room what was full of nasty-looking gardening implements to see who was here.

'Lily!' I called over to the darker half of the outhouse where the Turpins had been tied up. 'Are you in here? It's me, Jack, come to rescue you.' Then I heard something metal clatter to the floor from off a workbench. Somebody was crawling out from their hiding place and had knocked over a box of horseshoes. 'Who is that?' I asked as I stepped towards where the noise had come from. The voice what responded was tiny but straining to sound brave.

'It's me, Dodge,' I heard a boy say as he poked his head out into the light. 'Paul.'

'Scratch!' I called out and ran straight over to him. 'Are you hurt? What have they been doing to you?'

'Let's get out of here, Dodger,' he said. 'I've had enough.' I threw my arms around and gave him a big embrace as I told him that this was exactly what I was about to do. His body stiffened and he showed little emotion. He was behaving in such a tougher manner to the little boy what had burst into tears before the crack in Kent just six months before. 'It's all right, my young covey,' I promised him, regardless of his grown-up posturing. 'You're safe now.'

'What is that child doing in this place, Noah?' Oliver demanded behind me, all fury. 'What have you done to him and, for pity's sake, why?'

'We was never gonna kill him or nothing,' the squirming Bolter said as I continued to hold Scratcher tight. Scratcher resisted my affections for a second but I could tell he had been through some ordeal. 'We was just keeping him here for punishment, like. Serves him right for running away an' all. Mr Slade was going to put him to work once he'd learned his lesson.'

'To Hell with all of you people,' Oliver said in a raw voice. 'That's what Sikes and Fagin wanted to do with me.'

I then drew away from Scratcher so I could ask him some questions and, as the candlelight allowed me a better view, I was shocked to see his face. There was two big purple bruises on either cheek.

'Who done this?' I cried out in anger. 'Was it Slade?' Scratcher nodded.

Oliver, with his pistol still pointed at Morris Bolter, came over so he could see what I was talking about. His reaction to Scratcher's face was even more outraged than my own and, as I stroked Scratcher's cheeks and promised him that I would see that Slade pay for hurting one of my best boys, I heard him cross back to where Morris stood. Then there was the sound of a sharp punch and someone stumbled to the floor and cried out in pain. I did not need to look behind me to know who had proved victorious in the long-awaited Twist versus Claypole rematch.

'What'd I do?' Morris moaned from the floor. 'I never laid a finger on the boy!'

'You've locked him up in an outhouse like a dog,' Oliver charged him with. 'Just knowing about his maltreatment is enough for me to have you arrested, Noah.'

Oliver then proceeded to explain to his fellow funeral boy that he was now going to fetch some peelers, as well as other journalists, this very morning and that, if Morris had any sense, he would tell them everything he might know about the dark dealings between Weeping Billy and any corrupt policemen of the Metropolitan Police Service. Bolter began protesting his innocence in an unconvincing voice but, as he babbled, I had my own things what I wanted to say to Scratcher.

'I'm sorry they done this to you, Scratch,' I said as he looked at me with much older eyes than when I had last seen him, 'and that Slade was ever able to track you down in the first place. I thought I had taken you somewhere safe. But I need to know where Lily is. She was brought here with you, right? What have they done with her?'

'She's up in the big house,' he answered with no expression. 'He keeps her in the attic.'

'The attic?'

'Yeah. He locked her up there. She tried to stop him from hitting me,' his voice paused and I heard the child again, 'and I ain't seen her since.'

I turned back to the fallen Bolter and stood beside Oliver. We both looked down on him as he wiped some blood from his face.

'What's this attic, Morris?' I asked him. 'Is he forcing her to work for him again or what?' Bolter said nothing and even when

Oliver's pistol was pointed at his damaged nose he still stared us down.

'Yer can punch a man, Twist,' he snarled. 'I'll give yer that much. But yer ain't a shooter, I see it in yer eyes.'

'Perhaps not,' said Oliver as he lowered the weapon. 'But I am the pressing charges sort so don't get too comfortable. And here's another question. Why are you Morris Bolter now? People don't change their names unless they're hiding from something?'

'Dunno what yer on about,' he snorted.

'If I were to tell the police that I knew your real name, your town of origin and your previous employer, what would we discover? What crime is Noah Claypole wanted for?'

Bolter went to speak again but nothing came out. Then he sank further down onto that dusty floor and his eyes flicked to me. 'Don't let him tell on me, Dodger,' he whimpered in a voice what was close to begging. 'I know yer hate a peacher.'

I was disgusted by the sorry manner what he was so quick to adopt when beaten. His eyes was now pleading and pitiful and struck a sharp contrast with the strength and endurance what I had just spied in Scratcher's.

'Oliver won't be telling no peelers about how he knows you, Morris,' I said and I sensed the respectable Brownlow turn to me in displeasure. 'He'll keep whatever secrets you're hiding.' Before Oliver could inform me that, as a professional journalist, he had no intention of keeping any of Bolter's secrets, I added the caveat. 'But that is only if you've got something worth peaching to us. About Slade and Detective Mills.'

I glanced at Oliver and I saw that the idea appealed to him. 'An anonymous source,' he agreed and looked back to Bolter. 'Very well, *Morris*. If you have some decisive testimony to give me which will link Mills to the criminal underworld then I shall never call you by your given name again. But it'll need to be good, so if you continue to insist that you know nothing then the police will hear all about where Noah Claypole has ended up.'

Bolter let out a little groan and then rolled over onto his knees. He was a born sneak and it was only a matter of time before he began peaching on Slade.

'I knows about this Mills, yeah,' he admitted after a long cough. 'He's a Detective Super-something from Hampstead way.'

'What about him?' Oliver said.

'He's the master,' Morris confirmed. 'Slade's the dog. Only nobody around here knows it save for me.' Oliver asked him how he knew all this. 'I ain't deaf, dumb and blind,' he shrugged. 'I learn lots through holes in the wall.' I recalled then that I had heard a noise behind those walls in Slade's pub on that occasion when I had been engaged to break into the Rylance home. That noise, I was now sure, was Morris Bolter eavesdropping. 'I knows the deals and I knows the dates. I know that Slade hired Dodger here to go into that home and made it so that a body would be there to greet him. I knows lots of interesting stuff.'

'Then we're going to my office in the *Chronicle* where I shall write them all down.' Oliver was still holding his pistol in a threatening manner as he smiled. 'If you can prove that any of this "interesting stuff" is true then we have a deal, you and I.'

'We're here to rescue Lily!' I reminded Oliver in sudden agitation. 'Or have you forgotten? I'm going to this attic up there to get her.' I turned to Bolter. 'Has he hurt her?' I demanded.

'He was in a vicious mood when he got back from visiting yer in prison,' Bolter shrugged. 'Went straight up there and locked himself in with her. That woulda been an uncomfortable few hours, I should think.'

'Right, that's it, I'm killing him!' I announced then and reached over to Oliver. 'Give me that pistol. I'm going up there to shoot the bastard.' But he refused to hand it over.

'You didn't murder Anthony Rylance, Jack,' he told me. 'And I certainly won't help you to kill Slade.'

'But the whole of London reckons I've got blood on my hands already, Oliver,' I shouted, no longer caring if we was heard from the main house. 'If they catch me again I'll hang, so doing in a man like Slade, who deserves it more than most, can't cost me more.'

'It can cost you your innocence and that's a heavy enough price.'

'Slade ain't up there anyway,' said Bolter who was making a shaky attempt to stand back up again. 'He left the place hours ago.' Oliver and myself both turned to him as he rubbed his bruises and steadied himself against the wall.

'In the middle of the night?' asked Oliver. 'Why?'

'Dunno,' Bolter answered, 'the master whistled, I s'pose.'

'Yeah, well, there'll still be plenty of those red hats though,' I said as I kept my hand held out for the gun. 'Give me the barker, Oliver. I just want to wave it about if I need to.'

Oliver hesitated but I knew he would agree. He could not come with me to get Lily as he had promised because he now had Morris to keep an eye on and Scratcher to look after.

'I'm taking these two back to the curricle, Jack. We'll wait for you to come out with Lily there, but don't be too long about it. Here, take the gun then.'

I snatched it from him and forced Morris to show me which key on that big chain of his opened the garret room where Lily was being held. Before I left, Oliver had more that he wanted to say to me.

'I never thought you were as bad as some of the others, Jack,' he said as he grabbed the miserable Bolter by the arm and gripped tight so he could not run off. 'I knew you were a thief, a liar and a terrible influence on other boys. But I have never considered you to be as black as somebody like Bill Sikes.' He looked down to the barker I was holding before we went our separate ways. 'Don't prove me wrong.'

Chapter 23

Execution Monday

Relating the events surrounding my second visit to
the house of Molly Gay

On that first occasion on which I had approached the front door of this house of ill-repute, I had been led up the rose-garden path by Slade himself as if I were a favoured customer. My impression of the place then was that it was a veritable haven of luxury and sin. Now, months later, when winter had deadened the garden, I considered it to be a very different place. I gripped Oliver's pistol tight as I crept up the porch towards the Goblin Victoria knocker what was again frowning out at me from the door. As before, the crimson curtains was drawn tight and so I could not see who was inside, but the house was still quiet so I was sure that all the prostitutes and their callers would all be in a deep sleep after a long Sunday night. I took the bunch of keys what I had snatched from Morris Bolter and slipped the correct one into the lock. The door opened but there was these two gold chains preventing my entrance. But a skilled burglar, such as myself, had no trouble squeezing a hand through the crack and releasing them from within. Soon I was into that hallway and I shut the door behind me as silent as could be.

Even if it were true that Billy Slade was not at home that did not mean that I should be too careless on my way up to the garret, however. There was still sure to be several of these red-hatted Slade men what he kept about his places of business and Bolter had told me that there was at least six staying in this house that morning. But as I looked around that hallway I got no sense that anyone was stirring. The place was in a mess, with empty, upturned spirit glasses rolling about on hall tables, fresh stains upon the new rugs and a large pair of men's trousers what had been discarded on the floor. There was plenty of men's coats upon the racks though and I counted two red bowlers hanging on the hatstands. I heard no voices or footsteps but there was the ticking of the grandfather clock what I was surprised to see was now past seven o'clock. My execution had been due for eight and I wondered if the news had left the prison yet that the star attraction was going to disappoint his adoring public. The realisation that there was still just time enough for me to be recaptured was a sobering one. London could still claim its Monday hanging after all and so I stiffened my resolve to stay quiet and I proceeded to tiptoe onwards.

The only other sound I could hear was that of some heavy male snoring and when I reached the open door of that close drawing room – the one where Tom and I had been invited in to drink with Slade and where we had heard the half-naked harpist – I was able to peep in and see who the snorers was. There was two men in that room, one of them was sat in an armchair with his back to me but I could see his red bowler on the floor beside him and two extinguished cigar butts in an ashtray. The other man was laid out on the long settee with his red hat over his face, an empty bottle of brandy in one hand and the other around one of several sleeping whores what was draped on the furniture. There was some lacy underwear thrown over the harp and the man on the settee was fully dressed from the waist up but bare-legged below. I gathered that the trousers in the hallway was his. It must have been a very debauched night for this handful of Slade boys and girls and the scene supported Bolter's assertion that the master of the house was not present. I cast my eyes around the women to see if any was Lily but none even resembled her so I continued onwards through the house.

The other doors along the hallway was all shut but, as I approached the staircase, I could hear the murmur of voices from behind the one what led into the kitchen parlour. Bolter had informed me that in there was a handful of more alert Slade men playing cribbage and I knew that if any occupants of the place were to hear me creeping around then it would be these ones. I braced myself for a confrontation as I passed the shut kitchen door but the thick red carpet served me well and my movements was not heard. I made it onto the staircase without being detected and I made even less noise as I continued upwards.

The whole place was still dark as every curtain was drawn and there was the strong smell of tobacco and rich perfume throughout. I reached the next floor up and I saw another door unlocked and ajar. Although I had been told that Slade had Lily locked in the garrett room in the top of the house, I thought it worth poking my head through there to inspect if she was within. I inched the door open in as soundless a way as I could and peeked inside. There, under the thick blankets of a wooden four-poster bed, was a large form and it took some squinting before I guessed from the shape that it must be Molly Gay, the official proprietress of this upmarket den. There was also a number of kinchins both sleeping under the sheets there with her and around the room on mattresses. These was the children what had been presented to myself and Tom on our first visit and whose presence here had angered me so much then. Now I just felt ashamed of myself for ever having entered into business with the devil who really ran this wicked place. The sight of these innocents just confirmed to me that there was few men in this city what wanted murdering as much as Billy Slade did. I shut the door on the roomful of kinchins and continued upwards knowing that I could not leave Oliver waiting outside in the curricle for long.

As I made it to the top floor of the building, treading over more items of clothing what was strewn about on this much rougher carpet, I tried to guess which of these many doors would lead up into the garrett room. I then noticed a discreet door what was half the height of all the others and on the far wall. I was sure that that this would be the one what led up to the garret. I slipped Bolter's key into the lock though and it fitted and turned with ease. Inside was a low box room but one what had a wooden step ladder inside. I crouched in and saw that this indeed led upwards. I climbed the steps and released the metal clasps what was locking the entrance.

'Lily!' I called out as I shoved the door over and climbed up. 'Are you here?'

This garret had some light hanging from the beams but it was still darker than the other rooms in the house and I needed to blink for a few seconds while forms took shape around. As I pulled my body further up into this high-beamed attic, I saw an empty bed and a tiny dormer window with bars across it out of which escape would have been impossible. At first glance this dark little place appeared to be empty. It was only when I turned my head up to the sloping roof that I discovered where she was.

I saw her shadows first, all three of them rocking against the light of the lanterns. And then I spotted her, dangling up high, her black shoes swaying beneath her familiar green dress, her neck lurched over to the side of the rope. The noose had been tied around the highest rafter and a broken chair had been kicked away beneath.

It seemed that London had not been denied its Monday hanging after all.

I cried out her name and then slipped down some steps of the ladder back at the horror of it, almost dropping Oliver's gun. But then I gripped it even tighter and forced myself up again so I could see better what had happened to her. She looked dead all right and her neck seemed as crooked and as grotesque as any I had ever seen at a public hanging. I could not tell at first whether or not Lily had done this to herself in despair or whether Slade had strung her up but for me it did not matter. Either way, he was a dead man the next time I saw him.

The agony I felt at seeing her hanging there like that was so sharp that it took me some moments to stand to my full height in that garret and I could not even cry or speak. I crossed over to her and at last managed to whisper her name again as I felt for her dress and shook it to see if it would move. She was strung up high enough so I could not touch her face but I looked for her hands to feel how cold they was. I could not find them as they seemed to be tied behind her back and this, I realised with a coldness, meant that she had not killed herself. The roof had a number of other nooses hanging from the rafters and I knew that this garret room, like the outhouse, was a place of execution.

My eyes became blurry with tears as I looked up to her face what was hanging down towards me. Her eyes was shut and I wiped my own on her emerald dress and then I found voice at last. All I could think to whisper in that moment was that I loved her.

'Yeah?' came a voice from above. 'You've a funny way of showing it.'

I snapped my head up towards her in surprise and saw her blinking down at me as her neck straightened. I would have cried out in joy at such a miracle but I instead I was hit in the face by a wooden stick being swung out from behind her back.

'Ow!' I staggered backwards against the wall and felt the pain sear through my cheek and up to my temple. It was no soft blow and I dropped the pistol. My hands stopped my fall by grabbing the mattress of the bed and I looked up to where Lily was now swinging. She still had that stick in her hand, what I now realised was a leg from that broken chair, and her body was bent over and struggling with the rope what was tied around her waist. This rope had been hidden by the folds in her dress and I saw that it was the one what was tied to the rafter. The rope around her neck was tied to nothing.

'What did you do that for, Lil?' I complained, clutching my hurt face as she dipped forward like a circus performer and tried to free herself from her own knot. 'I've come up here to rescue you, you ungrateful cow.'

She jerked her head over to me as I spoke and her expression changed from one of wild attack to sheer wonder as she pulled at the knot around her waist. 'Jack!' she squealed as she did so. 'You're alive!' Then she crashed down onto the floorboards, face first.

'As are you!' I cried out in sheer relief as I crossed over to help her up. 'I thought you'd been hanged.'

'I thought *you'd* been hanged,' she replied, as she'd thought that I was just another Slade trick. 'You was set to die this morning, my love?'

'Morning ain't over yet,' I replied as I reached her and went to help her. 'I still might be at this rate.'

She got to her knees and looked at me with astonishment on her face. Then a smile broke out and she reached forward for an embrace.

'I can't believe it,' she said, becoming all emotional. 'I thought you was done for. Sorry, love, I didn't mean to hit you. I thought you was Billy Slade come back.' She apologised more by kissing the spot on my face where the chair leg had hit. 'I've been hanging like that for the past hour waiting for him and I was going to make my lucky while he was down on the floor.' Despite the joy with which she was now greeting me I could see the exhaustion in her face and knew that she had passed a hell of a night in Molly Gay's garret. 'What are you doing here?' she asked.

'As I say,' I said after kissing her back. 'I've come to rescue you, you silly mare.'

'Well, as you can see,' she yanked at the loose rope from around her neck and we both got to our feet, 'I don't much require rescuing.' She reached down for her wooden stick then but I was so overcome with love for the girl that I had to pull her close again. I had just spent a fortnight in prison so having a woman in my arms again was producing a powerful sensation within me.

'When I saw you dangling there,' I told her, once I broke off to give her lips a rest, 'I was going to kill Slade for it. And I still will if he's hurt you, Lily!'

'No, Jack,' she said, as we continued embracing. Her face was nuzzled into my shoulder as I stroked her back and felt her tears on my neck. 'You can't kill him.' I was about to respond by saying that Billy Slade was a man undeserving of our pity but she lifted her head up so I could see her wet and angry face again. 'Cos I'm going to do for the rotten pig before you!'

'That's the spirit!' I cheered as I brushed the loose tendrils of her hair behind her ears. It was then that Lily started to crack and I realised that she was not joking. It was clear that whatever horrors I had been through that morning, it was nothing compared to what Lily had endured and her whole self began to surrender as her arms dropped. Her chest was breathing hard though and whole attitude was like I had never seen it before. In truth, I was most taken aback by how fierce she seemed when she talked about Slade and I did not have to ask if she had been suffering at his hands. 'Let's just get out of here,' I said in the hope that this would snap her back into action, 'I've a friend outside in a curricle who is waiting to speed us away.' I let her go and went to collect the fallen pistol. I was glad that it had not fired when it fell but I was worried that we had made enough noise without it.

'A friend?' asked Lily as she wiped her eyes. 'Who's that then?'

'Oliver Twist,' I answered, trying to avoid her searching gaze. 'You might have heard me mention him on occasion.' There was a pause as I went over to the hatch in the floor I had just crawled up through and I could hear Lily repeating the name behind me as if trying to recall it.

'Isn't he the peaching boy?' she said as I peered down to see if anyone was listening in below. 'Oliver. The one what you're forever ranting about after you've had too many gins. The one you're always saying that you would batter to bits if you ever met him again? That Oliver?'

'That's the fella,' I said feeling a bit embarrassed about my recent shift in allegiances. I waved her over to follow me. 'We've made it up, you know. Bygones and that.'

'How nice,' she remarked with a hint of irony as she took my hand and let me lead her downwards into the space below. 'And he drives a curricle, you say? Sounds quite the dandy.'

I was about to explain that the vehicle did not belong to him so she shouldn't be too impressed when a woman's voice was heard from behind that short door what led back out into the landing. 'Mr Slade?' she called through, 'are you all right up there, lover?'

It sounded like Molly Gay was awake and had come to investigate all the noise we must have made. The sounds of children padding about was also heard as one of them went to silence a crying baby. I turned back to Lily and it looked like she was already steeling herself for a fight, but I had my hands on this side of the door so Molly could not burst through.

'The Lennox girl giving you aggravation, is she?' Molly persisted on the other side. 'Just tell me to mind me own business and I'll scuttle off back to bed.'

'It's all right, love,' I called out in as close a mimicry of Billy Slade's northern accent as I could manage. 'We're good here, thanks.' Lily looked at me in alarm but I think I made a good job of it. 'Go to back to bed, woman!'

Outside went quiet then and I placed my ear against the door to hear if she were leaving. Lily came over to join me and I took her by the hand while we waited to hear whether the ruse had worked. We paused for as long as we dared and then I whispered that I thought the path must be clear. This Molly Gay would no doubt be used to all sorts of bizarre noises coming from rooms in this house. So she would not be lingering out in that hallway now, I hoped as I opened the door at last, and we would be able to pass down the staircases and to the front door in as unobserved a way as I had come up them. However, as soon as I dipped my head underneath the low doorway, I saw that Molly Gay was still standing there. When she saw me coming through with a gun in one hand and the other holding Lily's, she let loose a wild scream. I pointed my pistol right at her and told her to shut her fat mouth up.

'Bernard!' she cried out, even louder. 'I have a husband in that room and he'll kill you if you hurt me.' Then she turned towards the door behind her and banged on it. '*Bernard!* Leave the strumpet alone and get out here! I want defending!'

The door on the opposite side of the landing opened, a naked man appeared, took one look at me and then slammed the door shut again. It seemed that Bernard would not be giving us any trouble. His wife, however, had an enormous set of lungs on her and was happy to use them regardless of the pistol pointed at her.

'*INTRUDER!*' she hollered out for the rest of the house to hear. Molly Gay then began backing down the stairs and created a blockage what we could not pass. By the time she had reached the floor below she had become even more hysterical.

'Where are the men in this house?' she cried. 'Gerrup here!'

From further down in the house I could hear the sudden rush of footsteps. As we turned onto the next set of stairs we saw several naked bodies appearing out of every door and they all panicked at the sight of us. In her rush, Molly Gay tripped and fell at the bottom of this flight and landed straight down on her face. Prostitutes scurried out from Molly's room and headed downwards, and I heard them push past some men what was coming up the stairs. The men in their red bowler hats was here to confront us and, by the time Lily and myself had reached the bottom of these stairs, the first of these Slade men had made it up to this part of the house. I turned and pointed my pistol at the three of them and told them to let us pass.

'That woman,' said one of the red bowlers pointing to Lily, 'is the property of William Slade. You put her back where you found her.'

'But Mr Dawkins here,' returned Lily as I continued brandishing my gun at them, 'is my property. And if I tell him to shoot you, he will.' These boys exchanged glances on hearing my name. I was the man what had killed Anthony Rylance, after all.

'Step aside, gentleman,' I said, indicating that they should just come up the stairs so that we could pass. 'Or catch a shot.'

None of them had the steel to rush me and instead they just did as bid. Then Lily and myself – still holding hands – edged past them and rushed down to the landing below what led to the front door. There, two more red-hatted Slade men was stood blocking our path – our final obstacle. They was the pair what I had seen earlier asleep in the drawing room and the big one had still not had a chance to put his trousers back on. Lily and I was in such a hurry that I did not recognise either until the trouserless one, who from the waist down was just wearing old and yellowing underwear, called out my name. It was only then that I noticed that it was Georgie Bluchers.

'Dodger?' he gawped as we both stared at one another in amazement. 'Haven't they hanged you yet?'

Just at that moment the grandfather clock in the hallway chimed eight.

'Damn it, Georgie,' I replied. 'I knew there was somewhere I was supposed to be.' I looked from him to the man on his right. This, I was also surprised to see, was the Chickenstalker – another of my old Diallers. 'More to the purpose, boys,' I asked, 'is what you two are doing with those stupid red hats on? You look like a right pair of clowns.'

Behind us, I could sense that the other Slade men was creeping down the stairs to this floor. It would not be long before somebody summoned the courage to make a run at me.

'We ain't your Diallers no more,' sneered the Chickenstalker. He was the man whose nose I had thrown the pewter pot at on that occasion in the Three Cripples taproom and had taken a sour attitude to me ever since. 'We're Slade men. He pays us twice what we earned under you.' Then he reached for his belt and pulled out a sharp-looking blade what he had tucked under it. 'You was always just a mouth, Dodger. Nothing else.'

Lily and myself was moving down the length of this corridor slow, knowing that the men behind was closing in. My gun was pointed at the Chickenstalker but I would be able to turn and shoot those behind if I had to. But whoever I shot, the others would be able to jump on me afterwards so it was just a question of who had the nerve to lunge for me.

'Slade is a thief-taker,' I said loud for every crook in the place to hear. 'He works for the police, see. He set up my murder and he'd done it before. To one of you red hats!' Disbelieving laughter came from one of the Slade men up the stairs. But, as I continued talking, another told him to shush. 'Tanner his name was,' I shouted, knowing that it was over for me the moment the trigger was pulled. 'He swung for killing a policeman. Slade made that happen, an' all. That's the man you're working for now, Stalker.'

'The police got him to kill a police?' he jeered, turning the knife in his hand. 'More mouth!' Then he flashed me a sick grin and when he spoke next it was for the benefit of those what was coming up on me from behind. 'I know this Jack Dawkins of old,' he announced. 'It's all posturing with this one. Ain't that so, Georgie?'

Georgie's answer was short and succinct. He punched the Chickenstalker in the side of the face. Stalker crashed hard against the wall, dropping his knife, and the men behind me called out foul.

'Don't be daft, Stalks,' he said as he turned and opened the front door. 'The Dodger's back!' Then he waved Lily and myself through and we dashed past, thanking him as we did so.

'We can't leave Scratcher,' Lily exclaimed once the three of us was out into the front rose garden and Georgie was shutting the door behind us. 'Let's get him. He's in the outhouse round the back.'

'Not no more he ain't,' I assured her and pulled her up the garden path towards the front gate. 'He's with Oliver Twist. Come on, I'll show you.'

Daylight had at last broken over London as we ran through

the garden gate and out into that genteel Hammersmith street. I pointed further down the opposite side of the lane where our curricle was waiting for us. In the driver's seat was Morris Bolter holding the reins while Oliver Brownlow was sat next to him giving him orders. Scratcher alerted them to the fact that the three of us was running towards their one-horsed vehicle and Oliver seemed unhappy by the presence of Georgie Bluchers, a big man in a red hat he had not expected, who was not wearing trousers.

'This curricle will not carry six,' he complained as the three of us jumped on to the back of the carriage and held onto the part what was just designed for one footman. 'We'll topple under the weight.' But then the remaining red hats all poured out into the street behind us and by now some of them was carrying firearms. So Oliver nudged at Morris to crack the whip hard and the horse began galloping off in the other direction carrying a load far heavier than it was used to. One of the Slade men fired at us with his barker but we was too far away for it to do any damage and it just had the effect of spurring our steed on even faster. Georgie then removed his red bowler hat from off of his head and chucked it into the air. It landed on the cobbles of that pleasant tree-lined street and he whooped at our pursuers.

'Thank Mr Slade for his employment,' he shouted at them just before we turned out of the street and galloped away. 'But red ain't my colour.'

Chapter 24

Strange Reflections

A race is on between the authorities and the underworld to see which can catch me first

The lightweight body of the curricle almost overturned twice by the time we had passed Kensington Canal Lock and whenever our horse made a sharp turn the three of us what was clinging on to the back was almost tossed away like unwelcome insects. It was when we reached Little Chelsea that Oliver decided he had tolerated these driving conditions for long enough. He must have told Morris Bolter to draw up in a discreet courtyard by a water pump so we could refresh ourselves and the over-relied-upon horse could drink from the trough. Then he came around the back to reclaim his pistol, introduce himself to Lily and ask me who the man in the underwear was.

'It's Ollie Poorhouse!' Georgie exclaimed. I had already told him about my reunion with Oliver during the ride and he jumped down onto the pavement and took his first proper look at the adult Oliver. 'C'mere, you daft sod!'

It seemed that Georgie had not been carrying about with him the same animosity that I had for the pale-faced orphan what I had brought home to our den all those years ago and he pulled Oliver towards him and crushed him within his warm embrace. Oliver looked most uncomfortable by this extravagant display of emotion from such a rough character in a state of half-dress and I was unsure if he even remembered who Georgie was. Then Georgie released Oliver from his grip and turned his attention to little Scratcher and he seemed just as thrilled to see the boy. Whether or not jolly Georgie had known that Lily and Scratcher was being held on those premises against their will, and had both suffered physical abuse from the hands of his former employer, was an issue I would raise at a later date. To be fair to him, he had just helped us escape and his celebratory outpourings was going some way to lift what might have otherwise been a sombre mood and so I decided not to press the matter just yet.

'Oliver Brownlow,' I then announced, remembering to use his preferred name, 'allow me to introduce my lady friend, Miss Lillian Lennox.'

Lily had also alighted from the back of the curricle and had grown most pale from the rough ride we had just experienced as well as – I would imagine – from the ordeal what she had suffered through that night. But as soon as she noticed Oliver standing there, dressed all smart with nice shiny buttons and a gold pocket watch chain visible from his waistcoat, her face grew much brighter and she gave him a gentle curtsey.

'Very pleasant to meet you, Mr Brownlow,' she said as she offered him her hand and he took it without hesitation. 'I hope we shall come to know one another better, you and I,' she added after he had kissed it. Nothing brings out the charming, gentle side of a life-hardened prostitute quite like finding herself in the presence of a young man what smells of money. In turn, Oliver smiled back at her like he had never in his life seen a woman before.

'Right, that's enough of that,' I said, keen to break up the tender meeting before Oliver began finding her a bit too appealing for his own good, 'we've matters to attend to.'

'Quite right,' nodded Oliver and he at last moved his eyes away from Lily before I had to tell him to find his own fancy woman. 'I need to get Morris back to the office of the *Morning Chronicle* so I can get down every detail he knows of the plot between Slade and Detective Mills. Including anything that will help to clear your name, Dodger.'

'Just leave my name right out of it, eh, Poorhouse?' Georgie winked and punched him in the arm. 'Don't forget, we know where you live now!' he laughed. Oliver winced and bent his knees so he was eye-level with Scratcher.

'This child should be returned to his mother,' Oliver said and placed a comforting arm over the boy's shoulder. 'That should be our first priority. After all,' he looked up at Lily and spoke in a gentle manner, 'is not a child's safety more precious than anything?'

'So true, Mr Brownlow,' sighed Lily in an accent much posher than her own. 'So very true.'

'Call me Oliver, please,' he smiled back at her. I was starting to get good and sick of Mr Wonderful here. I clapped my hands to snap them both out of it.

'It's decided then,' I said in a firm voice. 'Georgie'll take young Scratcher back to his home in Bethnal Green where I'm sure his mother is worried silly about him.' I spoke fast, so that Scratcher did not have time to mention that it was me what had snatched him away from the maternal bosom in the first place. 'Meanwhile, Lily and myself need hiding before word of my escape gets out and I'm spotted by a conscientious peeler. Not to mention the army of other Slade men what will be hunting for us already.'

'I'll get Scratcher home safe,' said Georgie as he took the boy's hand. 'If someone else pays for the omnibus fare.' Oliver reached into his coat for his purse, while muttering a remark about how they might not let him on a bus looking like that. 'But, Dodger,' Georgie said ignoring him, 'you've got to tell us how you escaped first!' His face was as wide with dog-like expectation. 'And, most of all, where is Mouse hiding?'

I looked back at them all and was at a sudden loss as to how to respond to that. I realised that news of Mouse's death had not travelled far beyond the environs of Newgate and that it was probable that it was only Oliver among this company who knew about his fatal fall from the prison walls. Lily, Georgie, Scratcher – and even Morris – all had their heads turned towards me to hear what had happened to my convicted partner, although it was only Georgie who seemed to assume that the news would be good. But the cold truth was that Mouse Flynn had died during a failed escape attempt of my devising. Had I not persuaded him to try and liberate himself in that way then he would have still been alive when the Rum Mort arranged for the more successful gaol break two nights later and would have crawled with me to freedom. These facts was impossible to deny and the thought of them made my eyes sting in shame. I decided then that I would not dishonour the memory of Mouse by softening the account of his tragic end and nor would I be evasive about my own role in it. I stood there in that obscure courtyard in Little Chelsea and confessed to the whole truth and nothing but. Nobody said much back to me.

As far as the good people of London was concerned I had been dead for over an hour when the curricle at last returned to the street where Oliver lived. By then, if events had proceeded as the judge had intended them to, the small coffin what was meant for me should have been nailed shut and placed in the ground with me in it. I flattered myself that many of the spectators what went along to my hanging would have cheered in support when they was informed about my sensational escape from Newgate. But you never knew with some people – there was a chance that most would have felt cheated out of a spectacle and booed in disappointment.

But in the humble vicinity of Hungerford Stairs, where poor Anthony Rylance had met his end just a few doors down from Oliver's home, I was not such a celebrity. The early risers here did not react to seeing me riding on the back of that small vehicle with any recognition or surprise at all. I was holding hands with Lily as we trundled along and she rested her head onto my shoulder and I had my other arm around her. Since we had been travelling she had become much more withdrawn but had shown me some bruises underneath her clothes what had not been there when I last saw her. My anger at Slade for his mistreatment of my love was matched only by her own. Lily flinched and her skin coloured redder whenever his name was mentioned.

'My landlady is accustomed to me resting at home during the daytime,' Oliver explained after he had returned the curricle to its nearby stable and left a short message of apology for its owner. 'I'm well known for working in the office through the night so it won't seem strange to her if she hears that someone is in the bedroom during light hours.'

Oliver was keen to get Morris Bolter back to his office so he could get his full testament about Slade's dealings with a high-ranking peeler down onto paper. He was unsure as to how much of Bolter's story would be useful in presenting his case to a safe policeman, such as Inspector Bracken, as Morris himself would have his identity veiled. But he also knew that if the story were thought to be sound then it would be the beginning of the end for Mills, as a career-minded cove like Bracken would have all the details to prove the rest for himself.

Bolter himself was already starting to look as though he regretted agreeing to act the Judas but he had been seen by the other Slade men fleeing the brothel with us so there was no turning back for him now.

'It's very well yer hiding these two, Twist,' he moaned after Oliver had unlocked the doors to his lodgings so that Lily and myself could rest there. 'But where'm I to be hid, eh? My life's in forfeit now I'm helping yer in this. Yer'll be the death of me!'

The four of us entered into Oliver's home again and I noticed more the smell of the rooms now – what earlier had been covered by the bacon and the terrible stench what I had dragged in with me from the Fleet. There was a warm aroma of paper, ink, leather and house-plants. I saw into the study what was almost the same as the one his friend Anthony had been killed in, but Oliver's abode was much more cluttered with stationery and expensive pieces of furniture and other items. I had to remind myself that we was now almost-friends before I slipped any shiny objects into my pocket.

'There are people I trust at the *Morning Chronicle*, Mr Bolter,' said Oliver as he gathered some things he needed from his desk in that study and came out again. 'Who I want to be present when I hear your story.'

I plonked myself down in the same well-cushioned chair from earlier and told Lily she should make herself comfortable too. She stood rooted to her spot though and her eyes was fixed upon a small sprig of mistletoe what was stuck up over Oliver's door to the kitchen and had not yet been removed. I wondered who he had been kissing under it.

'I thought yer said yer wouldn't name me, Twist!' Bolter spat in alarm as he shifted his way around the room, keeping tight against the corners as if he thought the walls would keep him safe. 'Anonymous! That's what yer promised! If I go to prison over this I shall end up suffering a nasty accident in the cells, Lor' help me!'

'As soon as you have told us all we need then you can be on

your way. But not before. Then you can travel to another city and change your name again, if you want to. And we can both hope our paths never again cross.'

'D'you think Mills suspects you're investigating him, Oliver?' I asked as I helped myself to two of the red apples from his fruit bowl since he wasn't going to offer me them himself. I tossed the first over to Lily's catching hands and I crunched into the second. 'He could have sniffed you by now like he did Anthony,' I said once I had wiped the juice away from my lips.

'Impossible to know,' said Oliver as he buttoned his coat again. Then he pulled out the small silver pistol from his pocket and went through to the bedroom with it. 'But he'll certainly be on the alert as soon as he hears about this morning's adventures so there's no use hesitating further. Our best chance to stop him is to move fast which is why the two of us,' he pointed at Bolter, 'must go to the *Chronicle* directly. You two can remain in my home until things are safe.' He appeared to be making his bed for us and I was most grateful for it. I was keen to fall asleep with Lily in my arms once more and as he came out of the room carrying a blanket I stood up in readiness to be invited through. 'Miss Lennox,' Oliver said, not looking at me, 'you must be exhausted after your traumatic experiences. Please feel free to sleep in my bedroom for as long as you wish.' Then he turned to me. 'Jack, this blanket is for you. You may sleep on the settee.' I did not hide my disappointment from him and wondered if he even understood the nature of the relationship between Lily and myself.

'Why, that's very decent of you, Oliver,' I began in a small voice. 'But – the thing is – I've been in a prison for the past fortnight if you follow my meaning.' I glanced at Lily and then back at him and then gave a broad wink just so he did not miss the subtlety of what I was suggesting.

'You are not married,' Oliver observed in a firm voice. 'And my landlady would be quick to evict me if she detected the slightest whiff of impropriety. So respect my hospitality and confine yourselves to separate rooms, if you please.' He gave a curt nod to convey that this was his final word upon the matter and I was about to protest further when Lily spoke first.

'A big bed of my own would be lovely, Oliver,' she said and I noticed how drained she now looked. 'I could sleep until next year.' It was clear that she would not have been in the mood for love-making even if it were permissible and so I took the blanket from him while trying to avoiding the dirty grin Morris Bolter was giving us all from his corner.

'The settee will do well enough then,' I said as I laid it out. 'Thanks again.'

Oliver then showed Lily into his bedroom and as she passed him she looked most unsteady on her feet. Her recent ordeal at the hands of Billy Slade seemed to be catching up with her and she did not say a word to any of us as she closed the door behind her.

'Now then, Mr Bolter,' said Brownlow as he crossed over to where our former friend was, 'let me take you to Wellington Street. Our work is just beginning.' He turned back to me before leading Bolter out of the building by the arm. 'There is still some food in the cupboards for whenever Miss Lennox rises, Jack. I don't know how long I shall be but, needless to say, I won't tell any policemen that I have seen you until things are a good deal less hot.' He cast a threatening glance towards Bolter. 'And neither will my old Sowerberry associate if he expects me to keep my end of the bargain.' Before he led Morris out through the door he said one last thing. 'I'll need your evidence at a later date though, Jack. So be here when I get back, eh?'

It occurred to me then that Oliver was about to leave myself and

Lily, two people who he knew full well was of the criminal kind, alone in his lodgings. It was a large amount of trust to put in us and I thought it very sweet of him. It was as if he was under the impression that I, at heart, was a good person like himself. It was a misconception I found most flattering.

'I'll look after the place, Oliver,' I said with a playful little salute. 'You can trust me.'

Oliver smiled back, thanked me and closed the door after himself. Then, as soon as it had shut, I crossed straight over to the window of this top-floor residence – careful to tread light so as not to disturb the delicate landlady in the apartment below – and I peered down onto the street. I was waiting for Oliver and Morris to emerge from the front door as I needed to be sure that they had disappeared altogether before I gathered some things, woke Lily and made our dash for the continent.

'Lily!' I called out as I saw the two Mudfog boys at last step out onto the pavement and Oliver raised his cane to try and attract the attention of a hackney cab. 'We're off in a second!'

No sound came from the bedroom what she had just one minute ago entered and I kept my hands pressed on the thin panes and continued watching. It seemed to be taking Oliver an age to attract the attention of a cabman and both he and Bolter shivered and buttoned up their coats in the January cold. My own breath was misting up the glass as I wondered how long I could dare to stay here after they had gone. Every bone within me was jumping to get out of London before I was recaptured. I did not doubt any more that Oliver meant me well but there was still a chance that my whereabouts would be detected if he trusted the wrong person and spoke about seeing me. I had no way of knowing who worked for Mills and I could not risk being recaptured before my innocence was proved. I could feel the rope tighten around my neck as I thought on it.

I watched Oliver lose patience with the passing traffic and whistle for a cab and at last one came trotting over to collect them. 'Lily?' I said again as they climbed inside. 'Are you ready to go? We can't stay here, my love.' Again no answer from behind the shut door and once I had watched the carriage containing Oliver disappear around the street corner, I went over to the bedroom and looked inside. She was asleep in that bed and I could see that it would be cruel to wake her from what must be much-needed slumber. So I shut the door again and went back to the settee where my blanket was. I should have been falling off just as quick considering how little sleep I had enjoyed in the past week, let alone the past day. But my mind was too restless for that and I continued fretting over whether or not I should just bolt while I still had the chance. I did not want to let Oliver down and I still wanted my revenge on Billy Slade. But I had not forgotten that even the legendary Jack Sheppard had been caught one too many times. Remaining in this city was a folly, of that I was certain.

My thoughts was not peaceful in such lonely moments. They kept leading me back to Newgate, to Mouse, to the Rum Mort – in short, to all manner of upsetting scenes and incidents from my recent history. Unable to settle, I got up again and paced the room, trying to change my mind's direction. Instead I began thinking about my obligations to Oliver and whether I even had any. Would his case really be damaged if I were not around to give evidence against Slade? I decided then that the best way to use this dead hour while Lily was resting was to go through to Oliver's small study and get my evidence down in writing too. That way, even if I were not in London when a trial took place, my account could still be read out to a judge – for whatever that was worth. I went straight through to that little study and as I entered I jumped with a sharp shock. Out of the corner of my eye I saw another man dressed just like Oliver Brownlow there in the room with me. It was a second before I realised that the person what had startled me so was my own reflection from the glass of one of his many bookcases. Oliver had mentioned that we resembled brothers when I had put on his suit earlier and I could now see what he meant. We had the same build and bore ourselves in a similar manner. Also, although I was darker-skinned and -haired, we shared some features in our faces what could have marked us out as blood. I peered closer at myself though and, in the dim light of that glass, saw that for all that we could never be mistaken for twins. I would always make for a rougher image.

Oliver's study was far less tidy than any other room in his crib and I guessed that he must spend most of his time in here when home. The desk was too big for the room and there was all manner of papers scattered all over it. A small picture frame was among the clutter with a sketch of a young woman in and I picked it up to admire how pretty she was. There was also some Christmas cards on the windowsill and I looked at one with a robin redbreast pictured on the front. Once I had finished rifling through his more personal possessions I started flicking through his professional papers. There was a small mahogany letter rack and in that was a stack of leaves all of which had the same words printed along the top. FROM THE PEN OF OLIVER BROWNLOW. There was also a rubber stamp in a rack compartment and I pressed it into some ink and tested it against an envelope. THE MORNING CHRONICLE it printed. I supposed these items was impressive if you cared for that sort of thing but they would be worthless to any self-respecting pawnbroker and so I soon lost interest in them.

I took one of the sheets of paper and decided that I would

write my true account of what had happened on the night when Anthony Rylance had died and leave it for Oliver to find upon his return. I had already written my version of events once before in prison but that had been for Billy Slade to read and was composed before I had become aware of his full villainy. This new document would be for the benefit of the courts of England – for whatever that was worth – and Slade was now the subject of my story and no longer the recipient. As I pulled out the leather chair – what I was impressed to find was on little wheels – I decided not to write one word of a lie. So I picked up a quill, dipped it into an inkwell and began to confess to the burglary just as I had done before Judge Aylesbury, only this time with the added information that Billy Slade had hired me to enter the building and that I had seen Aylesbury himself in a brothel in Hammersmith what Slade owned. I also intended to add what I had since been told by another convict in Newgate – that the man what had been hanged for killing Constable Wingham prior to that had also worked for Slade and that his case had been presided over by Aylsebury too. It was a spidery web of connections and not one what was easy to believe, but if it were any use to Oliver in obtaining justice for his friend, then it was worth jotting down. But the quill produced inky scratches what made the writing hard and I did not find it easy to know where to begin. I managed to compose less than three sentences before I rested the quill down again and my head dropped at last. The curtains of this room was drawn with just a small chink of light falling through but, despite it being morning now, it felt late. Sleep was overcoming me and I found myself resting my crossed arms onto the desk to use as a pillow. I could hear some dogs barking in a courtyard nearby and it took me some moments to recall that these must be the same bull terriers what I had almost been savaged by on the evening of my arrest. The only other sound in that room was the quiet ticking of a small clock on a mantel behind me and, once I grew used to the monotony of it and the outside barks, I soon drifted off without any more resistance.

I did not know for how long I had been asleep on that desk – it could have been three minutes or three hours for all I could tell – but the moment my eyes snapped open I just knew that something was wrong. Although I had not shifted from my slumped position and all I could hear was that continuous ticking from that unseen clock, I felt as wild animals must do when they sense the approach of a predatory creature. It was hard to identify the exact thing what had alerted me to it but I could sense that Lily and myself was no longer alone in that apartment and that an intruder had entered through the front door of these lodgings. It was not Oliver returned, of that I was certain, as whoever was out there in that main room was being far too furtive. I wondered if it was Oliver's nosey landlady who had become suspicious about the unusual goings-on up here, but I doubted such a flat could be so quiet. I then imagined, with a slight panic, that perhaps it was Lily herself and that she was fixing to abandon me while I slept. I was almost ready to get up and go after her when I lifted just my eyes to the half-drawn window in front of me. There, between the crack in the curtains, I saw the faint reflection of the light what came in through the door behind me. A tall man's silhouette was moving into this room and I could see that the ghostly vision was trying hard not to wake me. I was in as vulnerable a position as Anthony Rylance had been when he was killed at a similar desk and it seemed as though history was set to repeat itself. As I watched that reflection in the window I saw the man grow closer and his arm raise. He was holding something long, sharp and metal.

I kicked out the chair on wheels back towards the man and I

grabbed the first missile that my hands could reach – the ink pot on the desk. I then spun around and threw it straight at his head. The ink pot struck him square on the nose and the shock of it stopped him in his tracks as black liquid exploded all over his face. He was not slow to recover and he lunged at me with his knife. I had already picked up the next handy object on that desk though and I ran towards him for a follow up punch and landed it before he could strike. This knocked my assailant back two steps and I grabbed the arm with the knife and tried to force it off him. I was now face-to-face with him and as we wrestled for the weapon, he looked as astonished as you can look when one cheek is splashed with ink and the other has the words THE MORNING CHRONICLE stamped on it.

'Dawkins?' cried Billy Slade in outrage as our eyes and arms locked in struggle. 'What in hot hell?'

I could have replied to this with some dry and cutting retort but I instead decided that a more clever riposte would be just to knee him hard between the legs. He bent over and moaned but his grip held and he would not drop the knife. He seemed surprised to see me which, in turn, was a surprise for me, considering that he was the one what had crept up on me with a deadly blade.

'You're supposed to be dead by now!' he grunted as I kept my hands over his on the knife handle and I fought hard to stop him from using it on me. 'You annoying little bastard!'

'I *am* dead, Billy,' I said as we continued to fight each other into a stalemate. 'This is my ghost come back to haunt you.'

Then I butted him in the head with the only other weapon I could find which was, unfortunately, my own head. Like most butts there was a strong chance it did more damage to me than to him and I regretted it at once. Slade called out in pain but he did not release the knife and we staggered into the centre of the room.

'Why are you here, of all places?' he demanded as if I still worked for him. 'Where is Brownlow?'

'Oh, I see it now!' I snarled, as I tried tripping his legs with my feet. 'It ain't even me you've come to kill. I'm offended, Slade!' Our feet became entangled but there was a chance that I would be the one to fall if I were not careful. My hands was still over his though as I held down his arms and I remembered that here I had an advantage. I made my hand a claw and I dug into his smaller glove where his severed nubs would be. I had hoped to exploit this weak spot of his and sure enough he dropped the knife. But his legs tripped me as it fell and I crashed backwards against the wall.

'Don't be!' Slade said as he reached down to collect the dropped knife. 'I'll need to gut someone anyway or it'll be a wasted trip.'

I charged him before he could grab the handle and we both smashed backwards into that glass-fronted bookcase where I had seen my own reflection. This made an almighty noise and the glass smashed as the whole case rocked. When I pulled Slade back again I could tell that the assaulted piece of furniture, what was already overloaded with Oliver's books, was threatening to lurch forward in this small room. So I decided to help it along and I let go of Slade and pulled the whole thing towards him. The books poured out onto the ground making a thunderous noise and the tall case itself hit the top of the opposite wall. This formed a sort of barrier between Slade and myself with me on the side of the room where the door was. I dashed out of the study into the main room of the apartment and I almost called out for Lily. But then I remembered that he might not know she was here and so I decided not to give her away if she was hiding in there. Of course, I would never abandon her and so by the time he emerged from the study with the blade back in his good hand I had already obtained my own weapon. This was a brass poker what was resting by the fireplace and seemed to have a decent reach on it. I took that and readied myself to swing at him should he charge me with the knife. He just flashed me a foxy grin as if he thought me the fattest chicken in the coop.

'You should have stayed in Newgate, Dodger,' he taunted. 'Because a quick drop would have been a lot kinder than what I'm going to do now. I'll make ribbons out of you.'

The blanketed settee was now between us and we stalked around it slow, both of us waiting to see which way the other would go. My innards was hammering hard now that I was confronted with him again. Here was a man I had been wanting to kill for many reasons but now all I could think about was how to stop him from killing me.

'Detective Mills gets you at it, eh, Slade?' I said as I brandished the poker at him. 'Was it you what killed Anthony Rylance, then?' We was edging closer together by inches and I could tell he was preparing to make a strike. 'Because I'd wager it was. And Constable Wingham too? The master keeps his dog busy.' Soon it would be time for one of us to make a lunge at the other and the game would be over in seconds.

'I haven't got any masters, Dodger,' he returned as he moved around the settee. 'I have a client who pays very well.'

'Ever worry that one day he might pay someone else?' I asked as I prepared myself for a strike. 'To come calling for you?' Slade laughed.

'He'd have to pay a heavy fee to convince someone to try and kill me, Dodger.' He was starting to enjoy himself now. It was as if he already thought he had won and was now just relishing the play of it. 'There would be severe consequences for those that failed.'

'I'd give it a try for a bent farthing.'

'No, you wouldn't,' he jeered as he drew closer. 'I keep saying it, Dodge. You're not the killing kind.'

'He might not be,' said Lily from elsewhere in the room. 'But I bloody am.'

We both turned our heads around sharp to see her standing in the doorway of the bedroom. She had Oliver's pistol pointed right at Slade.

'Lily!' Slade gasped as he saw her. 'How are you here?' Then he turned back to me. 'You stole her from me again, Dawkins? Will you never bloody learn?'

'He didn't *steal* me, bastard!' Lily shouted, her face fierce as the gun trembled. 'I ain't your possession and I never was!'

Slade chuckled which was bold considering he was staring down the barrel of a gun with a woman of high emotion at the other end of it. He began walking towards her then and spoke as if they was just lovers having a tiff.

'Petal,' he said with his arms out but the knife still in his fist. 'Don't be like this, eh? I get angry sometimes and I know I shouldn't. I definitely shouldn't. I've hurt you in the past, yes, and I may well hurt you again. But it's only on account of how much I love you, see? And you love me too, eh? That's why you'd never pull that trig—'

Lily pulled the trigger.

Slade jumped – as did I – before we both realised that no shot had been fired. Oliver's gun, it now appeared, was unloaded and may have been all along. Lily dropped it in horror while Slade recovered from the shock of an attempted assassination from someone who he seemed to think he had mastery over. When he spoke next his voice was quiet but never more menacing.

'You disgusting little pipe-hole,' he said. 'You nasty little whore.' Then he ran towards her with his knife raised high only to find his path blocked by my good self. I darted into his way before he could reach her and I landed a hard strike into his stomach with the edge of the brass poker. He dropped in front of me and I grabbed a small ugly vase from off a nearby shelf and brought it straight down onto his head. This shattered and black dust began to scatter all about from within.

'That's for Anthony Rylance,' I said, as Slade raised his hands to cradle his head. I looked at the cracked vase and saw that it had come from a crematorium. 'And from him, I think.'

I was about to tell Lily to run for it but Slade was not bested so easy and he dealt me a sharp uppercut just as I was saying her name. His fist hit under my chin, causing me to bite my own tongue as I was between her two Ls, and I was shocked by the pain it caused. This did not stop me from kicking him in the face though and, before he could reach the knife, I pounced on him so that Lily was free to take the deadliest weapon in the room for herself. She picked it up and turned back to us.

'Stop struggling, Slade,' I said with a lisp, as I at last got him lying face down on Oliver's rug with his arms locked behind his back. I had beaten him into submission, having received far fewer blows than he had, even with my cut tongue. 'Or Lily's gonna stab you!' He lay underneath me and I had my foot on his back. He was writhing like a savage and if I released him by any degree he would be up again. 'Ain't that right, Lil?'

As I held him down, Lily walked over to us and spoke in a voice I had never heard her use before. It was cold but there was a shake to it.

'Not *or*, Jack,' she said, and I looked up to where she was standing as Slade remained trapped beneath me. 'I *am* going to kill him. And you're going to hold him down while I do it.'

For all my talk to Oliver of wanting to settle Slade with his life, I was still stunned to hear Lily say such a thing. Now that the chance was here I had lost all appetite for blood but I could see as I looked into her eyes that she had more violence in her than I did. Slade meanwhile, seeing that his life was in mortal danger, began kicking out at me even harder and he used his now free arm to try and punch me off. I was then in the difficult position of having to keep him restrained with one arm while trying to talk some sense into her.

'You can't kill him like this, Lily,' I told her. 'It's a barbarism.'

'We need to do this now while he's down,' she said as he screamed. 'You hold his neck back while I do the rest.'

'Don't you cut me, you bitch!' Slade yelled as his skin turned red with the sudden terror. 'Don't you do it!' I could not help but feel as though this raw language was not going to cool things down very much and I told him to shut his trap as I kept holding him down. Lily stayed staring at him with sheer hatred in her eyes but something rooted her to the spot.

'Slade's a killer, Lily,' I said, seeing that she was losing her nerve already. 'But you ain't. If you do this, if you make a murderer of yourself, you'll be bound for the noose like I was. And – speaking as someone what has just spent the worst weeks of his life in a condemned cell – I wouldn't wish that on a dog.'

'We'll do it,' she answered. 'Then run.'

'But we'd still be murderers, Lily,' I told her, recalling those what had sat beside me on the condemned pew. 'And there's no running from that.'

She stopped then and her whole body slumped in defeat. She threw the knife onto the settee and flopped down beside it. 'So what do we do with him, then?' she asked, close to tears. 'You can't sit on him like that forever!'

There was a few moments' silence from all three of us as I puzzled over it. Then a shaking and timid female voice called out from behind the front door.

'Mr Brownlow?' said a woman what I took to be the landlady who lived below. I would imagine that the racket we had just made must have terrified the very ears off her. 'Are you all right in there, sir? What in heaven's name is all that crashing?' Lily and I looked at one another, unsure of how to respond. The she nodded at me to indicate that she would be doing the talking.

'Mr Brownlow isn't in at the moment, dear,' she called out. 'We're . . . *friends of his!*'

'Friends?' shrieked the now hysterical voice.

'Yeah, if you like,' Lily shrugged. Silence from behind the door. There was a chance that the respectable woman had been turned to stone with the shock.

'My husband has gone to a fetch a policeman,' she announced at last. 'They won't be long.'

Slade cursed from his position underneath me. 'Let me up, Dawkins,' he pleaded. 'That way we can all escape out the back window. It's in no one's interest for us to be here now, is it?'

I considered this and then shook my head at the lunacy of what I was about to shout through to the woman beyond the door.

'Get them to hurry up, then,' I told her with some urgency. 'My lady friend and I have just caught a burglar in the act. And we don't want him getting away now, do we?' Slade almost choked as he heard that. Footsteps from behind the door was heard scurrying away down the steps and into the street. I sighed and glanced at Lily. 'I never thought I'd hear myself say anything like that,' I remarked.

'Perhaps it was the suit talking,' she replied.

Chapter 25

The Morning Chronicle

*Seven months after the events of the previous chapter, I am at
last at my liberty*

'Somebody important has come,' announced Turnkey McColl
after he and another guard had unlocked the door to my cell on that
stuffy July morning in 1848, 'to take you away from us, God bless
his kind soul.' McColl winked at me as he handed over some boot
polish and a suit of clothes what I had got laundered in readiness
for this, the day of my release.

'Don't go pretending like you won't miss me, Barry,' I grinned as
I got dressed in front of them and my two cellmates who had risen
from their beds to bid me farewell. 'I can see the tears glistening in
your eyes already, you hopeless bugger.'

Barry McColl and his colleague both scoffed but I had my
suspicions that they was indeed a bit sorry that I was leaving
Horsemonger Lane Gaol that morning as I had brought a lot of
excitement into that prison with me. I had been in their custody
ever since the trial what had followed my re-arrest in Oliver
Brownlow's apartment and I felt like the biggest celebrity the place
had ever entertained. On the day I was first brought here, after I
had been cleared of murder but not of house-breaking, the streets
leading up to the gates was lined with a great many spectators. The
population of London had enjoyed reading of my exploits in the
newspapers – of how I had been condemned to die for a crime I had

never done, escaped from the walls of Newgate and apprehended the real killer myself – and I must have been even more adored by the poorer class than Jack Sheppard had once been. When the police van in which I had been transported from the court at last made it to the prison gates of Horsemonger Lane the crowd had grown thick and I could hear them stamping their feet and chanting my name over and over from within. As I emerged from out the back of the van and into the daylight, with my hands still manacled, and escorted by two guards, a huge roar went up from all around. Men and women was looking down from all the surrounding windows and people was pointing at me and whispering into their children's ears. Someone shouted 'Dodger!' louder than the others and I spun around to acknowledge him and held my chained hands into the air in triumph. A bigger cheer went up from all about as the peelers tried to force me into the prison and away from my excitable admirers. The whole street then began chanting my moniker, over and over, and I could still hear them by the time I was in my new cell.

'I will miss the many coins I made from you,' Turnkey McColl laughed as I tied the laces of my now polished shoes. He pointed to my cellmates. 'I doubt anybody is going to pay to draw their ugly faces, I'm sorry to say!' The two other prisoners made out like they was much offended but it was all in good fun. The guards in this prison was as genial a bunch as you could expect men with keys to be and I preferred them to those miserable sods what had watched over me in Newgate.

I said my goodbyes to my cellmates – telling the pair of them that if they needed gainful employment once they too was set free then they should look for me in the Dials where I might have some jobs for them – and I let Barry and his friend escort me through the prison to a dusty old office where I would sign the release register.

'You should count yourself as very privileged, Mr Dawkins,' the turnkey said as he opened the door of the office and I was surprised to see the figure of a tall policeman standing with his back to us at the window, 'to have a Detective Superintendent want to escort you beyond the gates himself.'

The peeler turned his mutton-chopped cheeks towards me and then his whole body followed as if he was a queen's guard who had been at last relieved from standing stone still for hours and was about to start marching towards me. It was Wilfred Bracken, fresh from his recent promotion.

'Dark Satanic Bracken,' I muttered as he raised his chin and glared at me. Then I addressed him direct. 'I see you've done alright for yourself then, Wilf. Come to thank me for making room at the top, I suppose? That's alright, it was my pleasure.'

Bracken's face crunched. 'It is Oliver Brownlow who I credit with my predecessor's exposure and downfall, Dawkins,' he declared in his colourless voice. 'As ever, your involvement in that unpleasant business that took place in the winter strikes me as highly questionable.' His voice then dropped a note. 'Why is it,' he asked and pointed his middle finger at me, 'that whenever something happens in this city that is deeply embarrassing for the Metropolitan Police, *you* are there in the soup? You were somehow involved with that disastrous Evershed affair and now here you are in the middle of this mess like an unwelcome but irremovable fly. It's always a dark day for the force whenever you are released from imprisonment, Dawkins, and I doubt today will be any different.'

'And that's why you've come here then, is it?' I asked him with as much insolence as I could muster – and I can muster quite a bit when the mood takes me. 'To warn me off a life of crime? Much like that time when we first met and you told me to stay out of your city, remember? When you told me my mother had been hung.'

I stared at him then, knowing that this would land hard as there was no way he could pretend not to understand what I was talking about. Instead, he looked over to Turnkey McColl and asked him to leave us. 'I have matters to discuss with the prisoner Dawkins before he is released into the wild once more. I'll see to it that he leave the premises safely.'

Once we was alone Bracken pulled up a seat and told me to sit. As I plonked myself down in the leather desk chair he leaned on the side of the office desk and loomed over me. His manner now was that of a disappointed parent.

'On the day you escaped from prison,' he began as I looked up to his nostril hairs what seemed to match his mutton chops in all their grey bristliness, 'I was woken early. Holborn was my division before this promotion and when the messenger informed me that four female convicts and one male had escaped from Newgate I knew full well who was responsible. And, with that in mind, I was not surprised when I learnt the identity of the sole male escapee.'

'So you knew all about the Rum Mort then,' I said and wondered how much he liked being the accused for once. 'You knew that my mother was alive and unhanged and you told me otherwise. You're a bit questionable yourself, ain't you Bracken?'

'I've known of your mother for many years, young man, from before you were even born. Her name has often been spoken of as one of the most dangerous, untamed and villainous creatures in the rookeries and the day I arrested her was one of the most satisfying of my career.' He sniffed then and I got a sense that he was attempting to alter his tone into one of kindness. The attitude didn't suit him. 'I took a particular interest in your half-brother after Kat Dawkins had been sent to Newgate and I helped elevate him enough so he could become a policeman. I'm proud to have taken the son of a notorious criminal and shown him the straighter path as it proves that the same could be done for other children of the slums given enough attention. But when I discovered that you had returned to England I did not flatter myself that a similar trick could be performed. And so instead I lied about your mother's fate to keep you away from her. She had never really been condemned to death but I had hoped that if you thought that there was nothing left of your old life here in London, with Fagin, Sikes and your mother all gone, then perhaps there was a chance that you would be less likely to return to your nefarious ways. I considered it a noble untruth and I still do.'

'Yeah, well, if there's one thing I've leant over the years it's that you peelers are full of "noble untruths" when you want to be,' I returned. 'To the point where an innocent man — that's me in case you hadn't noticed — was almost hanged over them. A right dangerous lot of untamed, villainous creatures you've proven yourselves to be.'

Bracken jerked towards me then and his meaty finger was prodding me hard in the chest. 'Don't you judge the rest of us by Mills' standards, Dawkins,' he snarled and I began to worry that I had gone a bit too far. I was very much at his mercy within the confines of this prison office and I doubt that Turnkey McColl would be able to protect me from such a high-ranking officer even if he wanted to. 'Mills and his small collection of accomplices have been stripped of their uniforms and have already faced justice. Do not forget that I,' he then prodded at his own chest as if this next bit was the most frustrating part of all for him, 'even acted as a character witness for you after Brownlow convinced me that you were innocent of his friend's murder. Not an easy thing to do, believe me, and had I not done so I doubt you would not have been given such a short sentence for the burglary that you *did* commit. So you have been more than paid back by the Metropolitan Police for any inconvenience you may have suffered at the hands of rogue officers.'

'Inconvenience?' I coughed in disbelief. 'Is that what you're calling that disgraceful travesty of justice? I'm an honest Englishmen I am, what now dreams of a rope tightening around his neck every time he shuts his eyes. I've suffered from emotional distress over all this the like of which you can't imagine. I expect financial compensation and plenty of it an' all. As soon as I'm out of here I'm going straight to my solicitors and we're going to build a case against you, your precious force and even old Bobbie Peel himself. I want justice,' I tapped my own finger against the desk to stress my seriousness, 'the sort of justice what'll buy me a nice house in the countryside.'

With one swift movement, the Detective Superintendent got up off his desk reached down and forced me upwards. Then he pulled my face close to his so I could see his true fury up close.

'An honest Englishmen?' he seethed as my feet left the floor and my eyes was level with his. 'Dawkins, I doubt if a month passes before you are in the hands of the law once more. I wish it weren't so. I wish I could just deposit you on the pavement outside and never expect to hear your name uttered again but that is not how it goes for your kind. So before you get carried away with the penny press declaring you the new Jack Sheppard, remember that men like that – such grubby heroes that the London rabble enjoy in their wrong-headed way – they always meet the hangman in the end, no matter how many times they evade him beforehand.' Then he released me from his grip and I dropped down to my own height. 'Heed my advice, Mr Dawkins,' he warned me then in a calmer manner. 'When you walk out of here, keep walking. Don't look back and don't come back. I certainly won't be defending you ever again.'

I stepped away from him and straightened my suit what he had ruffled so with his manhandling. 'The *London rabble*,' I said after I finished making myself look presentable again, 'are out there now waiting for me to make my exit from this place as free as the day on what I was first born. So if you're done delivering your sermon I think its time you let me go out and face my adoring public, eh? I've got a whole life out there I need to be getting on with.'

My adoring public, however, must have been given the wrong date for my release as there was hardly a soul out there when I stepped through the prison gates and into the summer light. Those cheering masses what had been so pleased to support me on my arrival to this prison had long since dispersed and there was only one person waiting for me to emerge onto those Borough streets now. She was wearing a very fetching green dress and was stood across the road outside Chivery's tobacconist. She looked just as lovely as she had when I had first spied her across another road and standing outside the Theatre Royal Haymarket.

'Her Majesty's Pleasure has made you thin, Jack,' Lily said after we had finished our long reunion kiss, I had taken her hand in mine and we begun walking through Southwark. 'My pleasure will be to fatten you up again.' She had visited me often during my months behind bars and had read out extracts from various newspapers to me what contained details of the downfall of Mills, Judge Aylesbury and various others what was involved with the now notorious Billy Slade. She seemed to enjoy this new celebrity of mine and the dark stain of her association with Slade had long since left her. The bruises what she had received at Slade's hands had healed and she had no murderer's mark to conceal.

'So,' I had to ask her by the time we reached the bank of the Thames, 'did you see him off?' The river was busy with vessels, many of which was sailing to and from different parts of the empire. 'Billy Slade, I mean.'

'No,' she replied while staring out at them. 'But many did.'

'I bet Tom Skinner went along,' I said and raised my face up to the sun. It was a pleasant morning and I was keen to get some colour onto my brow after so many months inside. 'That would be just like her.'

'Oh, yeah,' nodded Lily, 'she even bought one of them wooden toys of his likeness. You know, the ones what Dick the Dollman makes. I think Tom collects them or something.'

'Well,' I sniffed as I took her hand again and we strolled back to our new lodgings, 'I just hope that Slade's gallows doll was uglier than mine.'

The anonymous testimony of Morris Bolter had just been the start of a number of journalistic breakthroughs made by the most intrepid young reporter *The Morning Chronicle* had ever employed. Oliver Brownlow had even presented his evidence to Bracken as soon as he learnt that Slade had tried to break into his home with the intention of murdering him and had been overpowered by my good self. This was the start of a short series of events what ended with my acquittal of the Rylance murder and Slade's conviction for it. I might have lost my taste for Slade's blood once I had him under my power but the British Legal System is not so merciful and he was sentenced to death by hanging with little delay. I have often imagined that he might have spent his final nights alive in that nasty little cell what I had been thrown into with Mouse and Old Edwards and what Fagin had occupied years before. But either way, Billy Slade was now just like those others – one of the many ghosts of Newgate.

However, although Oliver had come to talk to me in prison during the period that his newspaper was covering the whole unfortunate business, I had not seen him since March and was unsure if I ever would again. It was not until a month after I had been liberated from Horsemonger Lane Gaol that Lily and I received an unexpected visitor to our new crib.

The red and white slices of bacon had just begun to sizzle on the pan next to the sausages when Lily dashed into our kitchen to tell me that we had a caller. I was most put out by the intrusion as I only had rashers enough for two and had not been expecting any visitors this morning.

'It's not one of those kinchins from Low Arches again, is it?' I sniffed and pointed to a clothes lines full of handkerchiefs what ran across the far end of the kitchen. 'Because I haven't pawned that lot yet?'

'It's a gentleman,' she said with mischief on her lips. 'Have a guess.'

'Is he handsome?' I asked as I went back to turning the fat sausages. I could see that whoever it was had made a strong impression on her alright. 'Is he all fine tailorings and a show off with the diction?'

'That's the fella!'

'Better send him up then.'

Oliver had visited me a number of times in the early months of my imprisonment in Horsemonger Lane so he could interview me for his newspaper and keep me informed about what was happening in the trial of Mills. But I had not seen him since March when he had told me about how Mills was to be imprisoned somewhere up north and I had not expected our paths to ever cross again. So I was surprised that he had tracked me down to this new crib as I had left a fictitious forwarding address with the prison register and had not told anyone outside of the criminal world where I now lived. I had been following his progress as a reporter though and was glad to see that he had been making a name for himself in the newspaper game. His articles had very much helped to cast me as the victim in the whole affair and for this service I had never really thanked him. I wondered if he had come here to collect some sort of reward.

As I waited for Lily to fetch him up the stairs and into the kitchen, I crossed over to one of the drawers on the big wooden dresser, dipping under the line full of fogles, and grabbed a third plate from a pile of crockery. Then I dipped under the clothes line again as I crossed back, and I began sharing the breakfast out between three.

'I'm happy to see you again, Miss Lennox,' I heard Oliver say as they came up the stairs. 'We hardly got to know one another during our brief meeting last winter.' He was still hitting every 'h' and 't' as though his middle-class life depended upon it. 'I recall how frantic Jack was about your well-being on the night of his escape.'

'I know, he's a sweet boy, ain't he just.'

'But should I call you Mrs Dawkins?' he said as if he had somehow offended her. 'I see that the two of you are sharing lodgings.'

'Oh no, Oliver, it's still Miss Lennox,' she said as she reached the landing and showed him what door the kitchen was behind. 'He ain't made an honest woman of me yet. And call me Lily. We're all very friendly here.'

She opened the kitchen door and was ushering him through, but had not removed herself out of the way enough so he could enter without having to brush by her. She gave him the smile of her former profession as she did so and I could see that her forward attitude was making him most uncomfortable as he stepped past her and into the now steamy room. He then looked around, at her and at me, at the fogles hanging from the line and at the pig meat at the end of my fork.

'Sausages and bacon,' he muttered with a distracted air. 'Every time.'

'Welcome, covey,' I said in my most ingratiating manner. 'Charmed to see you, my boy. There's some breakfast going if you're hungry for it and some coffee on the boil. Sit yourself down while I open a window.'

Oliver thanked me and took a seat around the table as Lily and I began fussing around him. He apologised for appearing here unannounced and I told him our door was always open to old school friends. I handed him his mug and plate.

'I wanted to see you, Jack,' he explained once we all began eating, 'and so I paid a visit to the Three Cripples public house last night. They really ought to change the name of that establishment.'

'I'll have a word with the landlord if you'd like,' I suggested. 'I carry a lot of influence down there. Who gave you my address, if you don't mind me asking?'

'George Bluchers,' Oliver answered with a sigh. 'I was pleased to see him actually, even though he does insist on calling me Ollie Poorhouse. Some of your other associates who didn't recognise me weren't being very helpful. Tell me, why do all your friends wear matching hats now? Every one of them had a green bowler on.'

I kept on cutting up my food, careful not to meet his eye. 'That just means they're part of my community, Oliver,' I explained with a shrug. 'The Dawkins men I call them. It's just a bit a fun among some of the lads, you know. Don't you worry about it.'

'Well, there was one person in particular – a short woman who was dressed like the others – and she became quite hostile when I asked after you.'

'Don't you worry about her, Oliver,' Lily smiled and she reached over to pat his hand. 'She's all bark.' Lily had not taken her eyes off him since he had entered and was as observant as I when it came to things worth having. 'That's a nice gold chain you've got dangling out of your top pocket there, Oliver. You want to tuck that away in case some dirty pickpocket runs off with it.'

Oliver did indeed have an interesting gold chain exposed and he reached for it with the same embarrassment that a man might display on being told that his trousers was not done up right. I had been quick to notice the chain myself when he had walked in the room and I could see from this and other tell-tale signs that he was earning more now than he was before I went to prison. I asked him what it was before he could tuck it away again.

'It's a locket,' he explained and took it out then to show me. "With a picture of my wife in it. I like lockets.'

'How nice,' Lily said, as he put it away again. 'You wasn't married last time we met. She's a lucky lady.'

'There is a Mrs Brownlow now, yes, I'm delighted to say,' Oliver said and he looked away from Lily as if he thought it wrong to mention his new wife while talking to her. 'We got married in February. The ceremony was in a small church in the country where my mother is buried.'

'It's a pity,' I said after taking a slurp from my own coffee 'that I was in gaol then. Lily and I could have come and joined you otherwise.' I winked at her. 'You love a good wedding, don't you, girl?' Lily nodded and she too smiled again at Oliver who said nothing. Instead he just looked even more awkward and some seconds passed before Lily and myself both burst into fits. 'I'm only having a joke, Oliver,' I said and slapped him on the arm in fun. 'Don't fret, we'd never show you up like that!'

'Picture it?' Lily giggled. 'Us turning up to a nice wedding like his, with all his family wondering who we was?'

'And him,' I thumbed at Oliver, 'having to introduce us to the bride? Oh, that is droll, I must say.'

We both chuckled some more while Oliver just sat there looking mortified.

After some more merry banter had passed between us, we at last finished our plates and Lily excused herself. 'I'd better check on baby Robin,' she said and she went over to a shelf in the kitchen to pick up his wooden toy.

'You have a child?' Oliver said, looking confused. 'I didn't know.'

'He's not ours,' I explained, 'he belonged to a friend of mine.' Oliver looked troubled by the phrasing so I made it clear. 'I don't mean I *stole* him, Oliver. Give me some credit.'

'Robin is the orphan of Mouse and Agnes Flynn,' Lily explained and held up the little wooden toy. 'This is Mouse,' she rattled his gallows doll. 'We keep him around as a reminder.'

'And you two are raising him as your own, then?' Oliver seemed impressed for the first time since he had been here. 'Is that what you meant by community, Jack?'

'Yeah, it is, I suppose,' I said and pointed with my greasy knife at the wooden likeness of my fallen friend. 'I was his top sawyer.'

'And what does that mean?'

'It means a lot.'

Once Lily had left us, and the door was shut, Oliver and myself could talk with greater ease. I sat back in my chair and waited for him to come to the point of his visit.

'Jack,' he began in an awkward manner. 'I wanted to talk about what you said to me that time when I came to visit you in Newgate.'

'Not again,' I protested, failing to repress a yawn. 'Slade has been hanged now, Oliver. It's over. What more talking is there still to be done on the matter?'

'Not that,' he replied. 'I mean, the things you said about me. About how you feel I was indirectly responsible for the destruction of your criminal family.'

'Oh,' I said and felt a shadow pass over me. 'That.'

'I've thought about Nancy and Fagin a lot since that night,' he continued. 'And I wanted to come here to tell that you that I can see that there is a strong chance that they would both still be alive if you had never taken me home with you all those years ago. And I'm sorrier for that than you can know.'

I did not know how to answer him at first. In truth, I had spent a good deal of time blaming him for the death of those loved ones and I had often wished I had never met the boy. But that was before he went to such lengths to help clear my name for Anthony Rylance's murder, so I could no longer hold onto those sentiments now no matter how hard I tried.

'Look here, Oliver,' I said and leaned closer, patting him on the hand. My voice was almost a whisper as I hated saying this sort of thing. 'Don't go giving yourself a hard time over it. Bill Sikes killed Nancy and the state killed Fagin. But you was an aid to me in my most desperate hour and you saved me from the noose. I won't be forgetting it any time soon and I'm in your debt now.'

'Thank you, Jack,' he replied and I heard him breathe out as he spoke. 'I appreciate you saying that.' Another silence fell between us and this one was broken by the sound of Lily singing a sweet lullaby from the other room.

'So if you ever want something stolen,' I offered as I got up to boil another kettle, 'don't hesitate to ask.'

Later, when I walked him down the steps of this house and back onto the streets of Seven Dials, I realised that we had talked about many people during his visit save for one. The person who he had worked hard to prove that I was innocent of killing was one of his few friends and it was only as we was about to shake hands and part company that he at last brought him up.

'I miss Anthony terribly,' he said out of nowhere. 'I had wanted him to be best man at my wedding and I felt the lack of him on the day.'

'I know what you mean,' I said, meaning it. 'Mouse Flynn's loss was a deep cut for me too.'

I realised then what the real reason for Oliver's visit was. He had come here because he was in grief still over the loss of his friend, and was looking to make a new one. That was why he had tracked me down to these new lodgings even if he himself did not know it.

'Well, I had best be getting back to Wellington Street,' he said after we had said our goodbyes. 'There's always something new to write about.' He turned and walking away and had only walked a short distance before I whistled for him to stop. I let something dangle from my hand as he turned back to me.

'Don't forget the wife,' I grinned as he marched straight back and snatched his gold locket out of my hand with a tut.

Once I had shut the door on him I wondered if our paths would ever cross again. We had always occupied different worlds – even before he became genteel – and I doubted he would be inviting me to his gentlemen's club to play billiards any time soon. But this was a city of coincidences so who could ever tell?

When I returned upstairs I went into the bedroom where Lily was rocking little Robin Flynn to sleep in her arms. They looked a proper picture and I took off my shoes before crossing over so that the creaky floorboards would not wake him. The wooden doll of Robin's late father was resting there on the bed and I picked it up and sat beside her.

'He's better than gold,' Lily said, as she stared down at the sleeping Flynn, 'and the image of his mother. Are we keeping him?'

I stroked the hair on this one-year-old's head and wondered if that was such a good idea. In prison, during my lowest hour, I had questioned whether or not this Robin Flynn would not be better off without me in his life, getting him into trouble, teaching him dangerous tricks. I looked at the gallows doll in my hands, what was supposed to resemble Mouse, and wondered whether he would want me to keep his son to raise as my own or whether he would prefer it if I found him another place to grow up, away from my bad influence.

'It's like I kept telling his father, Lily,' I said at last before placing down the Mouse doll and taking his baby from out of her arms and into mine. 'It'll be the genteel life for this little bugger. All will be just rosy.'

ACKNOWLEDGEMENTS

Much of this novel was written in libraries and in particular I would like to acknowledge the reading rooms of the British Library which continue to be a tremendous writing space as well as providing a treasure trove of research material for the historical novelist.

Sincere thanks to everyone at Heron Books but especially to my patient editor Jon Watt for his invaluable notes and advice throughout the various stages of the writing process. His support was enormous.

I also very much want to thank my parents and the rest of my family for their ceaseless love and encouragement. I'm more grateful for that than I will ever be able to articulate.

Lastly, and as before, special thanks are reserved for Charles Dickens. In the incorrigible Jack Dawkins he created a character who has captured my imagination more than any other and I don't doubt that his work will continue to inspire countless other storytellers for centuries to come.